Meet Me
on the
Riviera

Fliss Chester

ORION

First published in Great Britain in 2019 by Orion Books,
an imprint of The Orion Publishing Group Ltd
Carmelite House, 50 Victoria Embankment,
London EC4Y 0DZ

An Hachette UK company

1 3 5 7 9 10 8 6 4 2

A CIP catalogue record for this book is
available from the British Library.

ISBN 978 1 4091 7867 5

Typeset by Born Group

Printed and bound in Great Britain by Clays Ltd, St Ives plc

MIX
Paper from
responsible sources
FSC® C104740

www.orionbooks.co.uk

'As soon as you set foot on a yacht you belong to some man, not to yourself...'

Coco Chanel

1

'And . . . flip!'

Jenna Jenkins tossed the perfectly cooked pancake in the pan, just as she heard the sound of the front door of their house closing. *Their* house. She and her deliciously (her mind was concentrating on the pancakes, obviously) handsome boyfriend Angus Linklater had finally moved into their very own house together. *Angus* . . . she watched the butter froth around the side of the pancake as she thought of him . . . he of the wondrous six-foot-four physique of nicely toned muscle, he of the sandy-coloured schoolboy hair and Atlantic-blue eyes, he of the striking (and let's face it, quite sexy) white welt of a scar down his left cheek, a stark reminder of the time he fought off Triad gang members to save his boss's — and his own — life. Like a pancake smothered in Nutella, there was no doubting he was yummy.

To say their courtship to date had been somewhat of a rollercoaster, however, would be fair — compared to the normal Tinder date or office romance it had weathered more storms than a smugglers' cove. *It's not every guy,* Jenna thought to herself as she moved the sizzling pancake around the pan, *who can smash his way into closed mountain restaurants to save us from a deadly blizzard one moment, and rescue me from Interpol the next*. And then, just a few months ago, one night while they sipped martinis in the City, he had asked her to move in with him. And no, not in with him *and* his parents in their huge house in Barnes, where he'd been staying since he moved back from Singapore last year, no, he wanted them to get their own place. She'd relished the property hunt – should they go for original Victorian details in Battersea or stark minimalism in Canary Wharf? In the end they found a rundown little gem of a house, going cheap for a quick sale, in a road just behind Waterloo Station and Angus had spent most of his trust fund buying it . . . *trust fund*, Jenna gave a little snort, still finding it amusing that she was living with someone she would have laughingly called a 'trustafarian' back in her university days. Still, since she was about as close to having a deposit to buy her own place as Kim Kardashian was to winning the Nobel Prize for, well, anything, she had leapt at the chance of living with the man she loved – even if it did mean trying to cook pancakes on an old gas stove tonight and helping him peel faded wallpaper off the walls most weekends. She had to help out where she could, as at the moment, her purse was as empty as a Saharan well and she felt terrible that Angus was paying for almost everything.

'Halloo,' Angus called out as he closed the front door and dropped his bag down in the hallway. He followed the smell of cooking batter to the kitchen where he found Jenna shimmying to some eighties track while tossing a pancake over the ancient stove top. The temptation Angus felt to surprise her by wrapping his arms around her from behind was tempered only by the thought of cleaning a messy pancake splodge off the ceiling. Instead he called out again and caught her attention.

'Oh, hi, sweetie!' She beamed at him as she deftly flipped the pancake again. 'Quite good at this, aren't I?'

'If I say "surprisingly so" will I get half rations?' Angus kissed her neck hello.

'Half? Quarter if you're lucky! Did you even realise we'd totally missed pancake day? I had no idea until Sally mentioned it. So I whizzed off to that new Little Waitrose by Blackfriars Bridge and got all the bits and pieces — so, *voilà*! Pancake à la Jenna.'

Angus laughed and tried to ignore the mess. Flour dusted everything, while egg shells that had missed the bin glistened under the kitchen's single bulb that dangled on an old cord from the slightly flaking ceiling.

'So I was thinking,' Jenna continued, 'what we should give up, you know, for Lent?'

'Or at least what's left of it?'

'Yes, well, two weeks is still something. We can practise and be better for next year.'

'Afraid I've never really been one for getting into that whole *hallelujah* Easter stuff.'

'Well, me neither, except we used to a get a Cadbury's Creme Egg at church on Easter Sunday from the vicar.'

'The true meaning of Easter?'

'If there was a religion,' Jenna playfully batted back at him, 'that really did derive its true meaning from gooey-centred treats, then sign me up and baptise me in the name of chocolate Jesus!'

'Every knee would bow . . . under the weight of obesity . . .'

'Ha.' Jenna slid the pancake onto the waiting plate. She carefully poured another ladleful of raw batter into the pan and swirled it around. Angus wandered into the hallway to kick off his shoes. He'd been working hard recently, aware that his trust fund had significantly dwindled — although tying it up in London property, especially a doer-upper, was probably no bad thing — but he had lost his rather large safety net, and it made him more hungry to succeed, more intent on making his own way in the world. He undid the top couple of buttons on his shirt as he went back into the kitchen.

'I was thinking about giving something up though,' Jenna carried on, as he slipped his arms around her waist and rested his chin on her shoulder.

'Oh yes?'

'I mean, it's quite good to challenge oneself.'

'If you say white wine, rosé wine or even red wine, I'll really wonder if this is a challenge or if you're expecting a miracle to happen.'

'Oh shush.' Jenna pulled herself away from Angus and got ready to flip the pancake. 'No, I was thinking of something much, much harder.' She paused while she nudged the edges of the pancake away from the pan with a spatula before giving it a quick flip. 'Ta da!'

'Very impressive.' Angus moved towards the fridge and got himself a beer, plus, as if to emphasise his point, he refilled Jenna's glass of wine from the nicely chilled bottle of white in the fridge.

'It will affect you too, Gus.'

'Oh God, you're not thinking of giving up sex are you?'

'No, you idiot! Though I wish I had thought of that to tease you with! No, I've decided.' She paused for dramatic effect. 'I'm giving up Waitrose.'

'Wow. That is possibly . . .' Angus took a long swig of his beer. 'The most middle-class thing I've ever heard.'

Jenna shuffled the pancake around in the pan for a bit. 'I know. But no less hard for it. I mean, I really, *really* like Waitrose.'

Angus laughed and kissed Jenna on the cheek. 'Fine. But I bet the *essential* pecorino and the organic quinoa will get the better of you. You'll be back in your happy place way before Easter — bet?'

'Bet.' At that Jenna shook Angus's outstretched hand and he chuckled again as they laid cutlery and plates out on the rickety picnic trestle that served as a kitchen table for the time being. Jenna cut a lemon into wedges, found the sugar and grated some cheese. It was happy, easy evenings like this that made all those weathered storms seem like a distant memory and Angus prayed it would be as plain sailing as this for ever more.

2

'You're what?'

'Twelve weeks gone, sweetie. Just had the scan!'

'Shit!'

''Scuse your Anglo-Saxon . . .'

'Oh God, yes, sorry — I mean, oh congratulations!' Jenna flung her arms around Sally, who forgave her friend for her initial outburst. She'd been waiting in the bar for Jenna to turn up and had been nursing the sparkling water in front of her for about fifteen minutes as she pondered how to tell her best friend. In the end, as per usual with Sally, she had just gone in blunt and fast.

'I've been feeling like death — morning sickness sucks.'

'Oh, you poor thing. God I feel old. My best friend is having a baby . . .' Jenna took a swig of the large white wine she'd got herself at the bar and then indicated the glass. 'I thought it was odd that you hadn't got a bottle on the go.'

'I know, sorry, JJ. I really have lost all taste for it, plus being pregnant and swigging back the Sauvignon is frowned upon these days.' Sally raised her eyebrows at her friend, who snorted into her wine.

'But I mean, you know you're old, don't you, when your friend says she's pregnant and it's all "well done you, yay" rather than "are you going to keep it?"'

'Well, of course we're going to bloody keep it,' Sally laughed at Jenna who rolled her eyes at her wilfully misunderstanding friend. Sally became serious. 'Hugo's terribly excited, though terribly terrified all at the same time. And I can't blame him as I'm terrified too. I mean — a baby!'

'God, yes. I struggle to keep plants alive.' Jenna pondered the seriousness of the situation. 'But you were trying?'

'Yes, but we didn't think it would happen this quickly. You never do, do you? There was a bit of a "fuck . . . I'm pregnant" moment.'

'I think it's the fucking that gets you pregnant, Sals . . .'

Sally rolled her eyes at her friend but carried on telling her about her plans for a nursery ('the box room will have to do, I can't possibly give up my dressing room'), reeling off their posh family names ('Horatio for a boy, we think') and how Hugo was already planning on putting the baby down for his old school.

A baby. That will change everything. Jenna felt bad even thinking it, but selfishly she wished her friend had kept her legs crossed just a little bit longer. Just until they could have had a few more devil-may-care adventures, just a few more nights on the toot. Or, at least, until she caught up and started trying for a baby too . . .

'Sweetie?' Sally's voice jogged her back to reality. 'You are happy for me − us − aren't you?'

'Oh, Sals, yes, yes, of course I am.' Jenna reached out and took Sally's hand in hers. 'So, so happy. I just . . .'

'I know, I know.' Sally put her other hand on top of her friend's. 'But you and Angus will get there, I'm sure. I mean, look at you two now! How long's it been since France last year? Eight, nine months? And you're living together and doing up your little house?'

'*His* house, technically.' Jenna looked down into her glass and frowned.

'*Tush.* Get one of these on your finger,' Sally pulled back from Jenna and waved her left hand with its sizeable diamond on it at her, 'and then it'll be yours too.'

'That's just the problem, Sals. One thing at a time, and we've only just moved in together . . .'

'Nonsense, sweetie. I had Hugo on his knee within weeks of us buying our first flat. It's simple, just leave lots of lovely adverts in those Sunday supplements, you know, the ones for De Beers and Cartier, lying around the flat — especially next to the loo, men love reading on the loo — and he'll propose in no time. Honest to God, worked like a dream on Hugo.'

Sally chinked their empty glasses before realising how silly that looked. 'Look, I'll get you another glass of bitch diesel — and a boring old tonic for me — and you can tell me all about how your new job is going.'

As Jenna swigged back the wine she told Sally all about her latest role. She'd managed to talk her way into organising little pop-up exhibitions in a temporary gallery just behind the Tate Modern — at least, that's how she'd described it to her parents. In fact, it was slightly more precarious — the 'gallery' was an empty retail unit and she knew the landlord would have her out in a trice as soon as a proper tenant came along. And the exhibitions . . . well, suffice to say there wouldn't be any new artistic movement named after her. Her lack of career success upset her. But not being able to support herself independently upset her more. Working in the art world had always been her passion and she'd never been overly fussed about 'making it big' or 'reaching her earning potential' as long as she was fulfilled in her job, working with amazing art and artists, and paying the rent. The only problem at the moment was that she was basically unemployable in the real art world. She'd been unceremoniously fired last year from Roach & Hartley, the very reputable gallery in Mayfair she'd worked in for years — she still winced when she recalled the day the rare and expensive limited edition Picasso prints had been stolen on her watch. She'd do anything to get that job back — and bumping into a forgiving Clive Hartley last year in France almost gave her hope that she could, but the memory of Martin Roach, spittle flying as he told her to basically 'eff off' in the aftermath of the robbery, was enough to remind her that she could never show her face there again. So, she had thought inside, outside and all around the box and found another way of working in the industry she loved. The only downside was that if you totted up all the hours she spent there, she was basically on less than minimum wage, and if it hadn't been for Angus stumping up for the house all on his own, well, she'd probably be homeless as well as practically jobless.

'The problem is, Sals, well, Angus pays for *everything*.' Jenna wasn't quite slurring, but the third large glass of wine had definitely loosened up any inhibitions she might have had about talking about Angus and their finances to her best friend.

'And why is that a problem per se, sweetie?'

'Well, y'know. That . . .' Jenna tried to nod and wink at the same time and the effect was more comedic than informative '. . . fight we had, last year. Well, it was all about me not wanting to take his money or be supported by him, and here we are now, Situation Stepford.'

'Didn't Angus promise you it was only until you get back on your feet? Then you can start paying for a few things?'

'*Pft*. Like when will that happen? I earn about thruppence an hour and can barely afford to treat him every now and again, let alone spoil him rotten when it comes to his birthday.'

'Oh of course. When is it?'

'Not until September, but I so want to make it special — everyone else seems to be jetting off and surprising their boyfriends with mystery weekends away or trips to swanky hotels. I'd just like to be able to afford to treat him to more than a homemade cake and a birthday blow job.'

'Knowing Angus, honey, he'd be more than happy with both, or either, of those things.'

9

'But mostly the latter . . .'

Sally grimaced, then stuck her tongue out at her friend. Jenna laughed but couldn't shake how unsettled she was starting to feel. She wanted desperately to be able to repay Angus and show him that she could spoil him too. She felt like she was letting him down, being as poor as she was.

'You could try something different?' Sally interrupted Jenna's thoughts and carried on her theorising. 'I mean, I know your passion is for art and all that, but it doesn't seem to be paying that well, honey. Maybe it's time for a rethink. Finance? You could be a super PA to someone in the City and earn a fortune.'

'I can't think of anything worse – bowing and scraping to some City fat cat who just wants to look at my arse as I lean over the filing cabinet.'

'It's not the eighties any more.' Sally rolled her eyes at her friend. 'And you know what I mean. Better paid jobs do exist.'

'I'll have a think. Maybe Bertie can help out again.'

At the mention of her name, Sally bristled. There was a long-held mutual distrust and frenemy situation going on between Sally and Bertie, known to the world of *Tatler*'s 'Bystander' and the *Daily Mail* online as Roberta Mason-Hoare, and to her close friends as Bertie. And to her even closer friends – mostly of the hot, rich, male persuasion – as Dirty Bertie. She had been to university with Jenna and Sally and had once dated Sally's husband Hugo before winning their friend Max's affections. If Sally had grown up and settled down, then Bertie had *glowed up* and settled for nothing but the best, and Jenna had a begrudging affection for the party-loving, paparazzi-attracting, clean-eating super 'It' girl. For every snobbish thing she said, and catty comment she made, there was usually a party invitation to be had and a tabloid column's worth of gossip to be chewed over – Bertie was Jenna's window into the world of the super-rich and she loved twitching her curtains every now and again. It was Bertie who had helped Jenna get a job in France after she'd been fired for the Picasso debacle last year, but that had ended with Jenna being arrested, albeit briefly . . . Sally reminded Jenna of this fact.

'God, yes.' Jenna paused, then admitted, 'But she does *know* people.'

'Hmm. But the people she knows tend to land you in a lot of trouble.'

3

Angus's phone glowed blue and he noticed the screen brighten from the corner of his eye as he tried to concentrate on the plans on his desk. It was hard enough trying to focus on the black lines, etched like mini railways across the thin tracing paper, without knowing that his phone was probably being illuminated by his favourite distraction. He pulled it over and unlocked it as he stretched out his back, aching as it had been from being bent over both drawing board and desk all morning.

Loose Change Lottery – you are a WINNER!! No cash prize – just cheese and pickle sarnies outside your office in half an hour? xJx

He grinned. The Loose Change Lottery was what Jenna called her weekly splurge on him. Sometimes, when she'd saved enough cash, she could afford to take them both out for noodles or a curry — but most weeks she made sure she made him something, wangled them invitations to a private view in one of her friends' galleries or brought him lunch into work — something to show him that she appreciated him. And he loved her for it.

Winner, winner, cheese and pickle dinner. See you out front at 1 xx

He texted back and slid the phone over to the other side of the desk. But the damage had already been done, and instead of concentrating on his technical drawings of a rather beautiful new villa being designed for a secretive celeb on the Côte d'Azur — Angus was entrusted by his firm to see the project through from start to finish — he refreshed the screen on his large Mac and brought up the internet browser. A few clicks later and he'd found exactly what he was looking for, and the next thirty minutes passed all too quickly as he browsed websites absorbing all the information he could about cut, clarity, colour and, most importantly, carats.

'Lame, I know, sorry, but afraid *el crédito cardo* was the real winner of my particular financial giveaway this month — honestly, this interest malarkey doesn't half eat into your disposable income.'

'I would offer to help you out, but before you . . .' at this Angus raised his sandwich in self-defence as a piece of cheese almost got flicked at him, 'chastise me with the Cheddar, I'm pretty much skint too.'

'You know I couldn't possibly accept anything else from you, Gus.' Jenna took a bite of her own sandwich and leant into her boyfriend, giving him a friendly nudge with her shoulder as they sat on a bench in Postman's Park. This tiny corner of London was a hidden gem. More often than not, when Jenna had time, she'd leave her little pop-up exhibition (this time with the door firmly locked — she'd learnt her lesson last year), and walk over the wobbly Millennium Bridge to the City of London. Here in the heart of the financial district, side by side with the besuited bankers, Angus worked as an architect. Jenna loved spotting him on the pavement among the pin-stripes, his shirtsleeves rolled up to reveal his toned forearms, his chinos or smart jeans so much more sexy than a badly fitting suit. And they'd then mooch over to Postman's Park and sit among the tiled plaques that celebrated the bravery of the common man — some of them heart-wrenching as they described acts of astounding bravery and self-sacrifice made to save the lives of others. Between matchstick factory fires and runaway horses the Victorian era seemed a pretty dangerous place. Today, though, they hadn't much time to stop and stare and Jenna carried on their conversation.

'So what's this snazzy villa going to be like?'

'You know, standard A-list stuff — cinema room, pool complex, helipad — the usual.'

'Ha, the usual. Love it. Who's it for?'

'Oh JJ, you know I'd love to tell you, but . . .'

'Even me?'

'Confidentiality clause. Honestly, if I even give them a whiff that I've broken it, then it's a hundred grand off my pension pot.'

'Pension pot? What is this of which you speak?' Jenna smiled knowingly at her boyfriend and he biffed her gently on the arm. 'Just a hint?'

Angus sighed. 'Fine. Well he already has a huge yacht, currently on its way from Miami to Monaco and I wouldn't be surprised if he pays for most of this commission in bitcoin — he's some sort of tech wizard.'

'Ooh, intriguing. Sounds like he might be one of those nerdy Silicon Valley types rather than a celeb?'

'No more clues!' Angus took a massive bite of his sandwich, which helped to shut him up.

She broke the brief silence with a complete non-sequitur as soon as she had swallowed her own mouthful. 'I still can't believe Sally's having a baby.' She'd told Angus the news when she'd got home the night before.

'More to the point, I can't believe Hugo is.'

'Yes, I suppose. Maybe that's the odd thing — he still acts like a massive child himself most of the time.' Jenna sighed. 'Even so, I suppose they're at the right point in their lives for it.'

Angus didn't really reply, but then he was chewing the end crust of his sandwich. He nodded at her in agreement. The moment passed, and after a few more minutes they got up from the park bench and tidied their Tupperware away into Jenna's bag. A second later, when a panicked Jenna had just seen what the time was, they hurried away from the park and back towards their respective desks.

'Netflix and chill later?' Angus asked her as they kissed goodbye near his office.

Jenna nodded and smiled up at him, but as she waved goodbye she wondered how far Netflix and chill was from Netflix and children . . . and how close were they to getting to that point in their lives?

4

A few weeks later, Jenna gripped Angus's hand as they stood at the top of the steps that led to the front door of what could only be described as a mansion in London's fashionable Holland Park. Angus had pressed the button on the sleek stainless-steel intercom, which seemed at odds with the Victorian portico they were standing underneath and the wide stained-glass-panelled front door. Okay, so mansion was perhaps over stating it. Italianate villa, perhaps. The house's facade was beautifully symmetrical with two wide bay windows, one either side of the front door. The steps that led up to the door were made of stone and were wide and shallow, flanked each side by incredibly modern lead planters, each with a lollipop-style box tree in them — lending the whole entrance area a feel of magazine-quality chic.

'I see Bertie took no time in glamming up this place.' Angus nodded at the lead-grey planters and impeccably topiaried box trees, each one wired with twinkling lights.

'Well, she never was one to shy away from prettying up her front entrance.' Jenna giggled and squeezed Angus's hand tighter just as the front door was opened by a butler.

'Good evening, sir, madam.'

Angus managed to compose himself first and, still holding Jenna's hand, he introduced them both to the doorman.

'Of course, sir, do come in. Ms Mason-Hoare and Maximilian Finch Esquire will receive you on the terrace.'

'A butler?' Jenna's incredulous whisper to her boyfriend was luckily lost in the cavernous, vaulted hallway. Modern art — daring, bright, garish almost — hung either side of the passage, its style at odds with the period coving and below-dado panelling. The butler (Jenna couldn't stop staring at him, in his full white-tie outfit) led them through the hallway, past large double doors on either side, each one leading into one of the huge front reception rooms, then past the sweep of the staircase, its carpeted stairs curving softly up to the first-floor landing of the house. The passageway finally ended at a glazed door, which led on to the garden terrace and there Jenna and Angus were met by a soft evening breeze, imbued with fragrance from a dozen flickering Jo Malone candles.

'She might as well be burning fifty-pound notes!' Jenna whispered to Angus.

'Not just citronella, then?'

'God no. Every mozzie in London will be here, if only to get a whiff of how gorgeous this garden smells!'

A few other guests mingled in and out of groups, laughing and chatting as a waiter patiently refilled glasses of champagne. Another member of staff, an older woman who looked to Jenna to be an old family retainer or house-keeper, followed the wine waiter around with a silver tray of exquisite little canapés. Jenna noticed the women — all bar none stick thin and wearing something so much more fashionable than her — flick away the offer of food with a wave of their manicured hands, while their menfolk happily took their share instead. Jenna looked down at her own chewed fingernails as she scooped a smoked salmon blini off a tray. *Ha! I'm shabby to their chic*, she thought to herself.

'Darlings! Come here and embrace *moi*!' Bertie called out to them from the far end of the terrace. She was in a floor-length floral dress, its gentle femininity contrasting with Bertie's rock-hard and toned figure. Jenna, in her skinny jeans and floaty top, wondered if she really should have notched the clothing stakes up a gear tonight. Bertie had expressly said casual on the invitation, but of course casual to Bertie was red-carpet glam to your average woman. Jenna gave herself a mental kick — she should have remembered that. 'So glad you could both come. Mwah, mwah. It's been yonks!' Bertie air-kissed her friends.

'The place looks wonderful, Bertie.' Jenna genuinely was in awe of what a stunning home Bertie and her fiancé Max had managed to make.

'Yah, so you haven't been here since the decorators left, have you? Naughty, I'm sure I've invited you to countless *soirées*. The most wonderful thing, you see, is that for a *recluse* like me I barely need to leave the house now — everyone just simply comes *chez nous!*'

'Bertie, don't tell me you don't love a party. Weren't you in the 'Sidebar of Shame' just the other day leaving Annabel's or something?' The reference to the *Daily Mail*'s online celebrity-spotting column wasn't lost on Bertie and she smiled graciously as Jenna took a glass of champagne from the tray that was wafted in front of her and, unlike the waifs further along the terrace, tucked into a few more of the smoked salmon canapés.

'Oh, it's so infra dig, you know though, sweetie, this "going out" business. So last season. It's all about being *à la domestique*, you know? Plus, massive bonus, outfit change whenever you fancy it. Heels not working with the mid-calf pencil skirt? No prob, your shoe room is moments away. Air too clammy for silk shirt? Maid will iron you another one, pronto. It's just so much more, how can I put it, *civilised*.'

'I guess as long as you have a house mahoosive enough to fit the whole of London in . . .'

'Oh God, yah. I know. Plus it's Instagram gold — I've grown my followers, by like, half a mil since we bought this place.'

'Wow.' Jenna was actually quite impressed. Bertie, however, had been distracted by the arrival of another designer-clad guest and air-kissed her friends again as she floated off.

'Classic Bertie.' Angus grinned at Jenna once she was out of earshot.

'At least with Bertie you never get bored. I *do* like her, honestly, it's just . . .'

'. . . "and the maid irons another one, pronto" . . .' Angus paraphrased. Jenna winced.

'I've never liked that word anyway.'

'What? Ironed?'

'No, silly.' Though Jenna did pause to brush out a few creases in her floaty top. She had given it a quick once over before they left, obviously not bothering to iron the back as she assumed, even in this unseasonably warm spring weather, she could get away with keeping her cardigan on all night. 'The word "pronto" — it's like "chop chop".'

'Another one of Bertie's favourite phrases if I remember rightly.'

Jenna raised her eyebrows. 'Maximilian Finch Esquire better watch out then.'

'Speak of the devil, hi, mate.' Angus stuck his hand out to Max and the two men brought themselves into a hug. Max then leant down and kissed Jenna on each cheek, his aftershave once more conjuring up all sorts of emotions and memories. Jenna had suffered years of unrequited love for Max — until Angus had come along and she'd realised what real love was — but occasionally something would momentarily transport her back to those years of lusting, wanting and waiting. Luckily, another tray of excellent canapés came along and brought Jenna back to the here and very tasty now.

The old friends chatted and Max filled them in on the interior designer and the work they'd had done on

19

the place. Or at least the work Bertie had commissioned, proving Jenna right in her own little theory that Max had had almost zilch to do with the redesign of the interiors. Still, by looks of the dark circles that prematurely aged his boyishly blue eyes, he was working late and hard enough to pay for it all. She thought back to Bertie's thirtieth and the surprise proposal Max had thrown into the speeches. He'd mentioned they were looking to buy a house back then, and Bertie had gone on about it last year too, but to be here now, in the reality of the fact that her friends, really some of her very best friends, were living in about ten million pounds' worth of London real estate was a bit of an eye-opener. Jenna reckoned she could have bought her dream house in some West Sussex village for just the price of their stamp duty bill.

Jenna let the boys catch up — Angus refused to let slip to Max about who had commissioned the chi-chi villa he was designing on the Riviera — but Max listened intently at the tech spec that was going into the place. Jenna's eye wandered to the other guests and once again was amazed at how Bertie found the room in her glamorous little black book for 'normies' like her and Angus. She also noted that Sally and Hugo were absent, maybe not making the cut this time, or perhaps Sally was finding all the socialising a bit too much now baby brain and tiredness were kicking in.

Jenna turned her ear back to the guys chatting and picked up on a few things. Various sound systems and speaker set-ups — all very dull, she thought, but then it did get her thinking about what on earth she was going to get Angus for his birthday. Her chat with Sally a few weeks ago came back to her and she remembered that Bertie might be just the person to quiz over job possibilities. So, giving a quick smile to Angus and a nod to a passing waiter to refill her glass, Jenna went off in search of Bertie and hopefully a little gold mine too.

'You know Monty Blake-Howard don't you, darling?' Bertie reintroduced Jenna to the handsome, if slightly podgy, aristo who somehow had managed to resurrect his family's failing estate into a multi-million-pound business. His hair was blond and tightly curled, which reminded Jenna of a teddy bear she used to have. All in all, he struck her as being the sort of man who was more interested in nursie's puddings than boardroom punch-ups — more currant buns than current affairs. 'And the Honourable Emma, his wife.'

'Hi, hello, howjado.' Jenna gabbled out all her greetings at once, cringing as she realised what an arse she must sound. Thankfully, Bertie ignored her.

'Monty and Ems are going to Monaco this summer to launch Ems' fabulous fashion line out there and we're just chatting yachts.'

'Oh right. Wonderful. When you have a mo, can I chat to you about something.'

'Of course, doll, but first,' Bertie put a taloned hand on Jenna's shoulder, and like a mouse under an eagle's claw, Jenna froze, 'do listen to Monty's story.'

'Just to fill you in, sorry, I've forgotten your name already?'

'Jenna.'

'Gemma, excellent. Had a rather lovely Labrador called Gemma when we were growing up.'

Jenna stayed quiet, too embarrassed to correct him, and too aware of Bertie's vice-like grip on her shoulder.

Monty carried on. 'Anyway, I was telling the ladies here about the time we were moored just off Sardinia and were invited aboard a much bigger boat, huge one, stupendous. Had its own helipad and everything. Can't tell you who it was, awfully private, you know, these rich folk . . .'

Jenna raised her eyebrows but no one seemed to notice.

'We were invited for an afternoon party — you know the sort, Bertie, music on, speakers thumping. Beautiful girls all swimming and then getting a few more cocktails inside them and stripping down to their birthday suits. We were just enjoying the view, ow!' Jenna smiled as she saw the Hon Emma whack her husband on the arm, but let him carry on, obviously enjoying the story too. 'Anyway, massive chopper came in to land on the pad and the down thrust or whatever it's called blew all the bikini tops off the deck.'

'Not to mention the olive out of my dirty martini,' added Emma.

'Gosh.'

'Amaze, isn't it. I can't wait to go there this summer.' Bertie tightened her talons into Jenna's shoulder.

'I thought you didn't like going out?'

'That's the point, JJ sweetie, once one has one's own yacht you can basically do *à la domestique* again, but it's more *à la yacht* — everyone just parties on their own boats. There's this wonderful privacy, you see. No public spaces, no *hoi polloi*.'

No reality, thought Jenna. 'I wish I had enough money just to party, let alone on my own yacht.'

'I do forget what it's like to be poor sometimes, or even just to be one of the mere *haves* rather than the *have-yachts*,' Bertie mused absent-mindedly, obviously totally unaware of how that came across. Jenna decided not to take offence and as Monty and the Hon Emma chatted to another aristo, she cornered Bertie and asked if she knew about any jobs going.

'Hmm. I must admit, you did do a superb job organising my birthday last year. In fact, dolls, I was wondering if you'd like to help with my wedding?'

Jenna gulped, wondering if she'd just accidentally fallen down the mad rabbit hole of party planning for Bertie again. The image of the thirty-foot-high inflatable gold elephant that Bertie had insisted on, and which dominated the terrace of the château, still haunted her dreams — and her Instagram feed. 'I was thinking it could be in Monte Carlo, channelling the Grace Kelly vibe with a hint of super-fun Eurotrash? Good plan, yah?'

'Wow, *yah*.'

'*Hello!* magazine would love that. We'd def get coverage.'

So much for privacy then, Jenna thought to herself.

Emma Blake-Howard seemed to float ethereally back over to them and blinked a couple of times, then looked at them lazily and louchely, through thick dark eyelashes. Her hair was raven dark and her skin pale, which made Jenna think of her as being a sort of exceedingly fashionable Snow White.

'Gorge party Berts,' Emma drawled, 'Damned if I can find anyone to help me out in Monte Carlo this summer.'

'Ems darling, there must be heaps of events organisers out in Monaco. The place must be swimming in them.' Bertie tried her best through her Botox to look concerned for her friend.

'I organise events . . .' Jenna spoke the words before her brain had a chance to caution her, '. . . sort of.' Her voice trailed off as she wondered if she was about to go from the Bertie frying pan into the Blake-Howard fire.

'Darling — weren't you just saying you needed a job for the summer?' Bertie seized on the idea and poked Jenna in the back with a shard-like nail, which she took as a cue to stand up straighter and move forward just a little.

'Yes. Definitely — I mean, I'd have to chat to Angus, but if it meant earning some more cash and basically doing what I do now — then, um — sign me up.'

'And if you worked on their lovely yacht you'd be in situ to help me plan our nuptials, darling, it works brilliantly!'

Uh oh, thought Jenna, *that's frying pan and fire all in one*.

'Monty!' Emma called her husband over. 'Daaarling, we're sorted.'

'Oh well, I mean, I need to check with my boyfriend—'

Bertie hissed in Jenna's ear, 'You're an independent woman, Jenna Jenkins, and you don't need a man's permission to do anything, let alone something as *menial* as a job.'

'No, but, I mean, well I'd like to run it past him.' Jenna felt herself withering under Bertie's glittering gaze, and she twitched as her friend's talons once more latched onto her shoulder. 'Fine.' Jenna acquiesced and Bertie finally released her grip.

'Jenna, be a dear and comms me in a few weeks and we can orgs.' With that the Honourable Emma Blake-Howard drifted away again and Bertie slipped off too, to go and chat to some other friends.

Her mind full of new possibilities, Jenna headed back over to where Angus and Max were chuckling about something, making sure to scoop up another couple of canapés on her way.

5

As they made their way back from Waterloo Station that night Jenna paused in front of the window of the fancy cake shop at the end of their road. Even if she wasn't tempted by the sugary treats within, she loved peering in through the panes of glass in the Georgian bow-fronted window, the whole place reminding her of a Dickensian sweet shop. The customers and staff had all gone for the day and the lights were low, softly illuminating the heavily iced cakes and tray bakes.

Angus squeezed her hand to hurry her along.

'Just looking,' she told him, letting her eye linger on some prettily decorated cupcakes. 'It's not like I need any more to eat tonight.'

'Yeah, I knew you liked canapés, but . . .' Angus received a biff to his arm.

'That was a, um, snaccident. I didn't mean to eat them all. But they were so delicious . . . the truffle bit on the mushroomy sauce, oh my word, I mean, I was in food heaven.' Jenna clasped her hands to her chest remembering how amazing the canapés had been. Angus grinned at her and Jenna knew he'd just been teasing. His face was glowing from the warm lights of the cake shop and Jenna couldn't resist reaching up to stroke his scarred cheek, and in doing so brought his face down to hers for a kiss.

'Now this is a late-night treat I could get on board with,' Angus murmured into her ear, before kissing her neck.

'This,' Jenna kissed him again, 'has always been' another kiss 'my favourite way to burn off calories.'

Tempting though it was to carry on kissing each other, they realised that the shop's CCTV might catch it all on tape, and although Jenna wouldn't begrudge the owner his £250 for *You've Been Framed*, she didn't want to risk becoming an overnight viral sensation either. Clasping Angus's hand in hers they carried on down the street, and around the corner to their own front door. As Angus placed the key in the lock Jenna slipped her hand around his waist.

'Whoa, wait till we get inside, JJ.'

'I just feel a bit naughty — a bit wild!' Jenna let Angus's waist go and cocked her head on one side as she tried to work herself out. 'Maybe it's hanging out with louche aristos — but I want to do the central London equivalent of running naked through the topiary or having sex in the duke's library while everyone else drinks sherry in the drawing room.'

'Feeling frisky over the Fauntleroys?' Angus unlocked the last catch and opened their front door. As soon as they were safely in the dark little hallway, with the outside world closed off he took her face in both his hands and leaned down to kiss her. 'You are crazy and mad and totally bonkers, but I love you.' Angus's eyes never left hers as he spoke. Before she could answer he kissed her again and their bodies pressed closer as his hands slipped down from her face to her shoulders and her back, pulling her into him. Jenna was rather gratified at how her own little personal fantasies had so quickly led to real-life pleasure and she closed her eyes and pretended that the dark little hallway was actually a book-lined library and Angus was a battle-weary soldier just back from the front line, dressed in a tux with Brylcreemed hair . . . Okay, maybe not that last bit, but as he kissed her and held her close she felt so turned on that when he took her by the hand and led her to their bedroom, she practically fell up the stairs in anticipation.

Jenna rested her head on Angus's chest and played with the hairs that peppered the skin across his torso. A mix of moonlight and streetlight illuminated their naked bodies as they lay among the tangle of duvet and quilt. Telling him about the done deal of the Blake-Howard's job offer had been skitting across her mind since the party, but her overdraft, credit-card bill and total lack of any sort of career had been doing more of a military tattoo, so she thought now was as good a time as any to ask his thoughts on it.

'Gus . . .'

'Hmm?' He sounded sleepy, as if he'd already dozed off, which after that display of dexterity and stamina was probably allowed.

'I've had a job offer.' Jenna was taking a leaf out of Sally's news-giving book. Blunt and to the point. Angus stirred and raised his head to meet her eyes.

'Oh yes? That's good news. Which gallery?'

'Ah, so, it's not in a gallery as such.'

'Right . . .' Angus pushed himself upright and gently punched the pillow behind him so he could lean back against it. Jenna did the same and girded herself for 'the chat'.

'So you know how I've been asking around for something, and well, I would very much like to have a bit more spare cash to chip in with the bills here and . . . and . . . you know, buy you something nice for your birthday.'

'You don't have to worry about that, JJ.'

'Yes, but I do, I do want to.' Jenna was getting into her stride now, although she was slightly sent off kilter every time she glanced down at her boyfriend's naked chest. She couldn't resist running her hand over the soft hairs again and only continued when Angus prompted her to continue. 'So, at Bertie's tonight . . . well, Monty and Emma Blake-Howard have offered me a sort of party planning job with them.'

'Oh, great. Whereabouts in London is their house? I assume it's one of those classic Eaton Square jobs. Very nice.'

'Um, it's not in London. And it's not based at a house.'

Angus looked quizzically at her.

'It's in France, well, Monaco. Monte Carlo harbour, to be exact. On their yacht, I think'

'Right. Wow. That's . . . well that's interesting.'

'I haven't spoken to them properly about it yet, but do you think I should go for it?' Jenna sat more upright and stared at him, her eyes flicking across his face searching for a clue as to what he was thinking.

'Okay, so here's the thing.' Jenna wasn't expecting what Angus had to say next — and was equally as surprised as she just had been when he'd done that rather amazing thing with a feather. 'I've been offered a few months' work abroad too.'

Jenna was flabbergasted. 'Oh. When were you going tell me?'

'I haven't accepted it. I wanted to talk it over with you — see what you thought, maybe even see if you want to join me . . .'

'Where is it?' Jenna anticipated his reply and rather hoped this luxury villa in the south of France he was working on might be the answer. 'Fra—'

'Hong Kong.' He said the words as she was suggesting the slightly closer-to-home option. They both fell quiet as the news sunk in. Angus was the first to break the silence. 'It would only be for a month or two. A last job for Pei Ling before she retires.'

Jenna recognised the name. How could she not? Pei Ling was the senior partner at Stafford Ling, the firm Angus had worked for in Singapore when he and his team had been ambushed and attacked by a local gang. He'd fought back and in so doing saved Ms Ling's life but for his trouble he'd got the long white scar that coursed down his left cheek. Jenna reached over and placed the palm of her hand over it. She looked into his eyes, wondering what her reaction should be, wondering if he really wanted her to go with him. Two months in Hong Kong would be a fabulous holiday – but that's all it would be, and holidays were the very opposite of how one could earn an extra bean or two. She couldn't justify letting Angus pay for everything here in London, *and* look after her in Hong Kong at the same time. It just wasn't fair on him.

As she was mulling this over, Angus reached up and put his hand over hers and moved her palm across his lips and kissed it. 'Penny for your thoughts?' He pulled her in close and she lay, her head once again on his chest, his hairs tickling her nose as she gathered some semblance of a thought together.

'I think, well, I think I'll have to say no to coming with you. But I do think you should go. We could Airbnb this place and I'll earn some decent cash in France and then once you're done in HK you can meet me there. On the Riviera. Wouldn't that be better than us spunking cash on me being let loose, with no job or anything to occupy me in Honkers except a rapidly expanding noodle habit – and waist line to match, probably – and my only career goal being to find the cheapest, but best, fake Chanel handbag in the side streets or from some dodgy out-of-town retailer?'

'It's almost like you know exactly where you'd start looking . . .'

'Well, exactly – so it wouldn't take me long and then the noodle habit would take over and then you'd have to roll me back to the British Embassy for repatriation via crane and shipping container.'

Angus chuckled. 'Hmm, when you put it like that . . .'

Jenna raised herself up on an elbow and looked at him. 'Oh fine, don't try and convince me!'

Angus leaned in towards her and gave her a lingering kiss. 'I know you too well, Jenna Jenkins. Once your mind is made up, well, it would be like squeezing bird's nest soup from a stone. So what is your job then?'

'No idea yet. Emma was talking about starting a fashion company — or in her case, *faarshun cumpnee* — did you notice all the floaty dresses at Bertie's party tonight?'

'Er, not really.'

'Well, that's her thing. I think she wants them shown off in grand style and I mean, when you're married into a family with their own super yacht, then how much more style can you wish for?'

'I hope they're paying you well.'

'Cash in hand, I think. I shall become a temporary tax exile!'

'In true Monaco fashion! Still, I do hope they'll pay you properly. It'll be hard work pandering to those pampered, precious, princesses twenty-four seven. I can't think of anything worse.'

'Well, I can't think of anything worse than slipping into a diabetic coma from eating too many Hello Kitty candy sweets as I sit alone in a hotel room while my boyfriend achieves his career dreams, so there.' She smiled.

'*Touché*,' said Angus as he pulled Jenna into a bear hug and kissed her wherever he could until they fell into an easy repeat of the lovemaking from just a few minutes ago.

Angus stroked Jenna's hair until he felt, rather than heard, her breathing alter slightly, telling him that she was asleep. He hadn't wanted to sound like a wimp when they were chatting just now, but he'd really wanted her to come to Hong Kong with him. She could never understand how he really didn't mind paying for her, and although he didn't have as much ready cash any more, he was sure he could have funded her noodle habit and treated her to a handbag or two. Anything to have her reassuring presence, her positivity, her bounciness, by his side as he faced his demons once again about going back to the Far East. He had to remind himself that last year, when he and Jenna had temporarily broken up and he'd accepted the offer of work for Pei Ling again, it had all turned out fine — better than fine. But he couldn't shake the feeling that the Triads might have unfinished business with him. Jenna pulled the covers up in her sleep and turned over, mumbling a 'love you, sweetie,' to him. He released his arm from under her and pulled the quilt over himself too.

'Love you too, Jenks.'

6

The aeroplane landed at Nice airport with a few bumps and the usual chorus of slight inhalations and then relieved exhalations. The cabin crew were the first to un-click their seat belts and the rest of the passengers followed suit. At this point, Jenna had realised that she'd managed to use the wrong seat belt (as the seat next to her had been empty — bliss), which explained why it had been quite a struggle to stretch one across her tummy. *I haven't even been on the carbs*, she'd thought to herself as she'd loosened the strap as much as she could. Now landed, and gratefully released from the super-tight belt, Jenna waited until the twangy voice announced over the tannoy that mobile phones could be turned on and she quickly flicked it back off flight-safe mode and sent a little text back home to Angus. *Arrived safely — let's hope Nice is nice!*

The last few weeks had seen the pair of them rushing around, prioritising DIY and decorating jobs in the house that they'd only really just moved into, but Angus had appreciated Jenna's idea of renting it out while they were both away for a bit and as soon as it was registered on Airbnb potential guests had been emailing them. It seemed London in the spring was a honey pot for buzzing tourists and their house, and its position right next to the river and Waterloo was obviously a sweet spot, even in its slightly dilapidated state. What wasn't so sweet was Sally's initial reaction when Jenna had phoned her to ask her the huge favour of managing it for them.

'What — like change the sheets and stuff?'

'No, Sals, not that — just making sure it's clean when the cleaners say it is. No one can spot a greasy cooker ring at twenty paces like you can.'

'And my hospital corners *are* legendary, I suppose . . . but honestly, darling, this is hardly fair!'

'I know, it's a big ask, but it's just for a couple of months.' Jenna hated having to beg.

'Months, years . . . whatever! What's not fair, sweetie, is that you get to jet off on some *jolly* while muggins here sweats it out — literally — here all summer. I need you to mop my brow and have pretend gin with me while I grow more fat and ungainly!'

Jenna knew her friend well — and realised that once this level of exaggeration had started she was home and dry.

'Pretty please, Sals. Promise when I'm home I'll come and help you with the babies, or scrub your bathroom or, or . . . how about some horribly expensive designer baby clothes from Monaco and a massive slab of Milka chocolate from duty free?'

'Make it a giant Toblerone and you're on.'

'Oh thank you, thank you, you're a star! And since you only work a few minutes away, well, hopefully you could just pop across in a lunch break? The pub across the road will keep the spare key and show the guests in, so really it's just to oversee things while we're, well, overseas.'

'You're lucky this bean is not yet a watermelon, though I do seem to have expanded hugely in the last couple of weeks.'

'Ooh, what size is baby Portman? Surely not in the melon stakes yet?'

'Size of a baked potato — though I am now one spud that a jacket won't fit on any more!'

*

So, with Sally on board to act as 'estate manager', Jenna had busied herself preparing for life on the high seas. She'd popped over to the Blake-Howards' flat — if you could call a four-bedroom lateral mansion conversion in Belgravia something as mundane as a 'flat' — to chat to Emma about what exactly she'd be doing for them and the conversation had been like something from a reality TV show, or as Jenna narrated it to herself in her head (in a sort of out-of-body-experience-way), like the transcript from a *Hello!* article. It went something like this: *On entering the glamorous home of our hostess, the Honourable Emma Georgina Foxthorpe Blake-Howard, two things become apparent — how very elegant she is, and how very stylish her life is. In conversation she is as ethereal as she looks, with words wafting out of her like the diaphanous folds of her new fashion collection, to be launched this summer in Monaco and the Côte d'Azur with the help of Jenna Jenkins, party planner to the rich and famous. Jenna's parties will catapult the Honourable Emma into the couture stratosphere, and if we may borrow the cosmonautical metaphor one more time, we think the stars will truly be out to greet her.*

In reality, the conversation had been more along of lines of Emma asking Jenna *who* exactly was in her little black book and when Jenna admitted that she not only didn't have a little black book, but if she did it would basically top out at their mutual friend Bertie, well, the flight to Nice was almost cancelled and Jenna would have been back to square one. Luckily, Jenna brought the conversation round to what she had done to help Bertie with her thirtieth birthday party last year (the *Hello!* magazine narration at this point had gone into overdrive and Jenna was experiencing an internal voiceover along the lines of: *Mutual friend and society connection Roberta Mason-Hoare is a great fan of Ms Jenkins' work, citing her as the brain behind the orchestrated release of thirty peace doves, the firework diorama and thirty-foot-tall inflatable gold elephant at her own exquisite and exclusive special birthday party last year.*).

'Well,' purred Emma, 'Bertie says you did a marvellous job and I hear you organise little "pop-up" exhibitions now?' Her voice was both languorous and staccato — the word 'marvellous' had been drawled over three whole seconds, while 'pop-up' was almost machine-gun fired out to her.

'Yes. They're really on trend, you know? I did enjoy working in the more traditional gallery, but faster, shorter more dynamic exhibitions are definitely the future, I think.' Jenna hoped she was saying the right sort of thing. The long pause Emma gave her before answering had her feeling as awkward as a nun at an Ann Summers party.

Finally, she broke the silence. 'I get it. I like it. Short little parties. Leave on a high. That sort of thing?'

'Yes, exactly. Like my mum always says, leave the party when you're having the most fun, as it only goes downhill from there.'

'That's what I just said.'

'Yes. Quite.' Jenna was almost preparing to take holy orders and join Mother Superior behind the sofa when Emma laughed and joshed Jenna on the arm, which wasn't pleasant, as her fist, though gentle, was all knuckle and adorned with so many gems that one or two quite dug into Jenna's skin. Still, she was pleased the awkwardness was over and the rest of the conversation revolved around diary planning and launch dates. Finally, they came to logistics and it was because of Emma's insistence that she wanted as many new customers wearing her new couture range by July, in time for the annual Red Cross Ball in Monte Carlo, where anyone who was anyone would be, that Jenna now found herself disembarking at Nice off the early morning flight ready to head into Monaco and start her new job.

7

Bertie flicked the pages of the glossy magazine with her perfectly manicured nails. She paused and skim read a feature on how one of the Bulgari heiresses had created a riad in Morocco and doubted for a moment her decision to spend so much money on a yacht. But riads weren't sexy like yachts were sexy. And yachts could take you all over the place — or at least the captain could take it places and you could just jump on board, whether it was Saint-Tropez or Timbuktu. Okay, probably not Timbuktu. But the point was, yachts were sexy. Better than sexy — they were statements, they were something else . . . they were superstars.

'Ms Mason-Hoare?' The young, cheap-skirted secretary tried to emulate her client's natural confidence and swagger, but Bertie put her in her place by a mere raise of a perfectly plucked eyebrow. 'Mr Thorncombe is ready for you in the conference room.'

'About time too,' Bertie said, standing up from the plush sofa in the waiting room of her wealth manager's office and smoothing out the creases from her satin Moschino trousers. 'I have no idea why I was kept waiting for so long.'

'Sorry, ma'am,' the poor underling stuttered and Bertie tried not to break her ice-maiden facade and smile at the slip up she'd no doubt scared her into. She may be a princess at times, but referring to her as if she were the Queen . . . well, one *is* amused.

'Richard,' Bertie stuck her hand out and greeted her financial advisor.

'Roberta, do come in, I'm so sorry for the delay, I just wanted to get all your files in front of me before we begin our chat.'

'And no doubt not hurry back from a rather good lunch?' Bertie was taking no prisoners today.

'Ah, ha ha. You know me too well, my dear. Now, let me see, what can I do for you?'

As they sat there, in the conference room of his little set of rather swanky offices in Mayfair, the spring sunshine glinting off the wide mahogany table, Bertie outlined her idea to buy and refurbish a super yacht.

'The figures we're talking about here . . . we're into the tens of millions of pounds, plus yearly running costs,' he said, rather pathetically Bertie thought, but she knew enough of how fund management worked to realise that every penny she withdrew and spent on fibre glass hulls and faux fur pillows, was going to be earning him less commission on her investment funds.

'Yes. Millions and millions. But I'll still have a million or so left, so don't worry — you'll still get to dine out at Petrus rather than Pret, oh I don't know, once a year!'

Bertie left the meeting with her usual sense of smugness, assured in the knowledge that the cash was there and ready for when her broker found her the perfect boat. *Well done, Daddy*, she thought, *you and Einstein were right, compound interest really is the eighth wonder of the world*. Startling the secretary as she left, she scooped up the glossy magazine from the coffee table in the little waiting area and ripped out the page about the Bulgari riad. Those cushions were lush. Let the mood-boarding begin.

8

Jenna had never seen anything like it. The harbour in Monaco was crammed with yachts of all sizes, the largest of which were nearer the sea wall, dominating the horizon from where she stood, facing the water from the harbour-side. She'd arrived on the transit bus from the airport, which had taken her about forty minutes from Nice airport. She'd followed a trickle of well-dressed travellers from her plane and found the kiosk in the arrivals lounge where you could buy a bus ticket into Monte Carlo. At the airport bus stop she had double-checked that she was at the right spot — perhaps this was a private transfer for a special party or something? But no, Emma Blake-Howard's words came back to her, 'in Monaco, even billionaires take the bus, darling' and indeed, her fellow travellers at Bus Stop 2 were some of the poshest bus passengers she'd ever seen. One lady leant against the raised handle of her Louis Vuitton suitcase, her emerald-green silk blouse and bright white jeans set off by a large pearl necklace and emerald rings on her fingers. *Who travels in white jeans? The stress of it,* thought Jenna. A gentleman next to her had a pronounced stomach, his tailored shirt stretched across it; his blazer hadn't a hope in hell of doing up. He puffed on a fat cigar and the smoke had wafted over to Jenna, who didn't mind as the tobacco smell reminded her of college balls and excitable young men, thinking themselves so much older and more important than they were.

The bus ride itself had been uneventful, but the views as the bus had travelled along the A8 from Nice into Monte Carlo were breath-taking. Glimpses of aquamarine sea through rocky valleys teased her and just as suddenly as they appeared, they disappeared, the rocky hillsides rising up again, while tunnel after tunnel punctuated the sunlight. At first, the outskirts of Nice seemed a little industrial and quite down at heel — and Jenna was astonished that such low-grade, high-rise housing could exist alongside the rich of the Riviera. Clothes hung from makeshift lines and graffiti scarred the dirty walls. *Staff have to live somewhere*, she'd mused. But then in a flash she was through another tunnel and caught a glimpse of the sea again. She could see why this area was called the Côte d'Azur — for the jewel-like blue glimmered in the sunshine and reflected the sunlight back into the cloudless sky.

Jenna noticed the landscape change as the road came closer to the coast itself. Hillside houses clinging onto each precious precipice were replaced by seaside villas, their terraces all facing the water. With no fanfare or border control they drove into Monaco and the houses became more densely terraced, each one vying for hillside space. Occasionally, Jenna spotted a glistening pool, then the sea again, and then there was the AS Monaco football stadium and Jenna knew she was getting close. Before long the residential houses turned into more commercial, French Imperial-style buildings with shops and restaurants dominating their ground floors and the road narrowed as the bus drove downwards towards sea level and the centre of Monte Carlo.

Jenna had got off where Emma had told her to, at Place d'Armes, and found her way down to the harbour. Dragging her large suitcase behind her, she'd navigated through the narrow streets and busy locals until she'd spied her first boat. And wow — just wow. Jenna looked at them there in the harbour sitting idle and empty, each one worth hundreds of thousands — millions — of pounds, bobbing up and down in the gentle waters of Port Hercule.

She couldn't imagine that other famous Hercule — Poirot — thinking much of what his beloved Monte Carlo had become, his perfectly groomed moustache would wilt at the sight of such brash wealth.

The Blake-Howards had choppered in earlier and Jenna had memorised the name of their boat, the *Wavy Sloanes* — a play on good old Davy Jones and his locker — and knew that it was moored alongside the Quai des État-Unis — the far side of the marina. She couldn't help but gawp at the sterns of the boats that were butted up against the harbour — some with red-carpeted walkways extended out, with twee little doormats with the name of the boat on them neatly placed under where they teasingly hovered above the quayside. And she chuckled at a few of the names of the yachts too — *NautiBoy* suggested a playboy (or at least someone who thought he was) as an owner, whereas *Aquaholic* perhaps belonged to someone a bit more jovial or maybe obsessed by the sea? It took her a little while to work out the relevance of a large vessel being called *Hedgehog* — until she remembered that hedge-fund managers took up quite a high proportion of the yacht owners round here — and she supposed the more 'hog-like' they were the bigger the yacht they could afford.

Next to the more traditionally named *Ocean Dream*, she found the Blake-Howard's addition to the fun and games. A metal, balustrade-edged gang plank was sticking out, but it was raised above the quayside by a couple of feet — making it impossible for Jenna to leap up onto it, let alone drag her old suitcase and handbag with her.

'Halloo!' she called out, feeling incredibly self-conscious. But her voice must have been lost to the background noise, of which there was quite a lot, and she felt drowned out, not by the mass of water around her, but by the frenetic noise of the town behind her — the revving of supercar engines, the clanking of chains as construction work happened behind the Avenue J. F. Kennedy, the beeping of reversing lorries and constant thrum of a lunch party on board somewhere, already in full swing. She called out again but then noticed the little keypad at the end of the walkway. *How bloody swish is that!* Jenna left her suitcase on the pavement and leaned up towards the buzzer. She got the idea that Monte Carlo wasn't like London and you could turn your back on your belongings for a minute or two before you need worry about a little scamp making off with them. There was a button on the silver unit that looked like an intercom and Jenna pressed it and waited for the buzz. *Buzzzzz.* After a second or two a deep Australian voice answered her and she introduced herself.

'Jenna Jenkins — I'm the new, er, PA or party organiser or whatever.' *Why could she never sound confident and nonchalant?*

'G'day, Jenna — permission to come on board. You might want to stand back though if you don't want a plank in the face.' The line crackled and Jenna jumped back as the walkway made a jolt forward and then started to lower itself down towards the quayside. Wondering if it could take her weight, not to mention that of her suitcase, she tentatively put a foot onto the immaculate red carpet that lined the ramp.

'Wait!' The Australian voice boomed out at her, this time not from the silver intercom, but from the deck just above her. 'Shoes off.'

'Oh right, sorry, of course.' Jenna stepped back and accidentally fell over her suitcase. 'Whoaaaa. Bugger.'

'Yeah . . . when you're finished wrestling with life down there, come on up.'

'Rightio!' Jenna tried to cheerfully call back as she extricated herself from the pull-out handle of her case, which was currently acting as rather an effective stirrup. 'Jenna rides again,' she whispered to herself and finally managed to get free from her luggage, remove her shoes (luckily just slip-on plimsolls anyway), shove them in her capacious handbag and attempt the walkway again.

'You can leave your case by the companion way, one of the boys will come and get it for you. *Ed!*' he yelled the name out across the deck and Jenna made the decision to leave the case right where it was, half on and half off the ramp or companion way or whatever it was called. Straightening her T-shirt and giving her hair a quick flick she boarded a super yacht for the very first time.

9

The *Wavy Sloanes* was a yacht and a half. A yacht and a lot, even. There must have been some very put-upon peasants around the ancestral Blake-Howard home, thought Jenna, to afford their lord and masters this level of luxury. James Avery, the blue-eyed Australian captain, had greeted Jenna on the main deck as she stepped aboard and told her that 'Mister and missus' were out to lunch.

'Mister and missus?'

'You know, your new bosses.'

'Emma and Monty, you mean?'

'Shh. It's policy that we never say their names out loud.'

Jenna looked around her. Now on board the yacht she felt like she was in one of the most exclusively private spaces she'd ever been in. The deck was plush and luxe, but it was also sheltered and discreet, even the noise of Monte Carlo was muffled by the soft furnishings and glazing.

She leaned into Captain Avery and whispered, 'Why?'

Expecting an explanation, not a guffaw, Jenna was a bit taken aback when the captain laughed so heartily that he even took off his neat, white captain's hat and wiped his brow. She noticed that his blond hair was slightly fluffy and thinning, but nevertheless it suited him and she noticed for the first time how tanned he was as he swept his hair back and placed his cap back on.

'Oh, girly. You have so much to learn about life on board. Let's start with the basics, shall we?'

'Please.' Jenna was feeling all sorts of confusions — was she laughably silly or doing something wrong? Or in this man's confidence already? Or just some 'girly' who, like he just said, had a lot to learn . . .

'So, we refer to our employers, the owners, as mister and missus as it's just what's done. We all know who we mean, but it's discreet and any eavesdroppers, be they near or far,' at that he nodded into the corners of the rooms and Jenna realised he was indicating the possibility of electronic listening devices, 'can keep guessing.'

'Oh, I see.' Jenna sagely eyed up the cabin they were in with all its plush furnishings and mentally tried to calculate just how many places someone could place a bug. Then she had to stifle a giggle as she realised that anyone listening in on the Blake-Howards would take away no greater secret than how Nanny managed to get the Marmite on the boiled egg soldiers so perfectly and what to do if Dodo the pug was feeling a bit peaky. 'Are many yachts bugged?'

'More than you'd think.' Captain Avery pulled a pad of paper out of his back pocket and scrawled a quick note before flashing the pad in front of Jenna. It said: *Scan 4 bugs due in 2 weeks. Schtum till then.*

'Schtum — get it.' Jenna saluted Captain Avery, who rolled his eyes at her mock-military stance.

'And, most importantly. You work for mister and missus, but all of you, them included, answer to me. Anything to do with this boat gets run past me. I am the law.'

'Oh.' Jenna was a little taken aback at the fervour of his insistence in his place in the hierarchy and made a mental note to check with missus — Emma — when she got back from lunch. If Jenna was going to have to run every party favour, pretty fairy light or cocktail combo past him, this was going to make her job so much more difficult.

'Who else is on board?' By now Captain Avery had led her from the main deck down the stairs to the lower deck.

The corridor was luxurious — all gold-plated handles and wooden door surrounds sitting neatly into magnolia walls and cream carpeted floors. Their bare feet barely made a sound as they padded along the corridor towards the front of the boat. Cabin doors punctuated the hallway walls and finally Captain Avery opened one up, revealing, to Jenna's surprise, her suitcase. How it had got there in the time it had taken Jenna and Avery to have a quick chat she had no idea. Perhaps bugs weren't the only secrets on board, maybe hidden passages played a part too?

'So this is me?' Jenna realised Captain Avery would have no truck with someone expounding theories on sub-aquatic hidden tunnels so kept her surprise at the speediness of her suitcase delivery to herself.

'This is you. Settle in, and I'll meet you back up on board deck to go through the rest of the house rules.'

'Yes, sir.' Jenna almost clicked her heels in a military style, but thought better of it and instead gave his departing back a weak wave. She was more exhausted than she'd given herself credit for and plumped herself down on the single bed that was nestled up against the wall.

The cabin was small, but perfectly formed, as they say, and although her suitcase took up most of the free floor space she reckoned that once it was housed under the bunk (probably via brute force) she'd be able to swing the proverbial cat. The room comprised a small single bed, which took up the whole length of the room. Shelves above it framed a round porthole, which Jenna could just about see out of if she stood on the bed. The porthole was just above sea level and she had the amazingly glamorous — *not* — view of the neighbouring boat's giant foam fender. The opposite end of the cabin from the corridor door was a little louvred door that led into a tiny shower room with a loo and basin. It was small, but clean and a damn sight more luxurious than some hotels she'd stayed in. The only other point of interest in the room was a smallish cupboard, which Jenna opened out of pure curiosity. Folded up on one of the shelf cubbies next to the hanging rail were five pristine white polo shirts. Jenna picked one up and shook it out. It was a really good quality one and embroidered in gold thread over the left breast was the name of the boat. A mere microsecond passed before Jenna realised that this was no chance find — this was, in fact, her new uniform.

Face splashed, polo shirt collar turned up, and loo made use of, Jenna headed back up to find Captain Avery and continue her tour of the Blake-Howard's yacht. Luckily, super though it was, it wasn't hard to navigate around and she found her way back up to the main deck and the luxurious seating area remarkably easily. Another liveried member of crew nodded to her and smiled as she emerged, before scurrying past her down another set of steps to the very bowels of the ship. Perhaps he had been her suitcase sherpa? Ed, was it? 'Thank you!' she called after him, her voice disappearing down the stairs behind her.

'Jenna!' Avery barked her name and waved her over to where he was sitting on a plump-cushioned sofa. The rear of the main deck was open to the elements and was given over to comfy seating and sunloungers and Avery in his seaman's whites looked every inch the blue-eyed charmer of a captain as he sat, legs splayed, on the cushioned wicker chair. 'Glad to see you found your uniform — we'll let missus decide if you have to wear it all the time. Sit down.' Jenna complied and wished she had the temerity to interrupt the captain to pour herself a glass of water from the ice-cold jug on the coffee table in front of her as he began his monologue of dos and do nots. 'As staff, but not exactly crew, I assume you'll report straight to mister and missus, but as I said before, everything gets run past me. That includes guests — both party and personal — and any online orders. I will not accept mysterious packages onto this boat and everything must have a reason. The *Wavy Sloanes* might have a terrible name but it's a clean ship and I intend to keep it that way. Eyes will not be blindly turned to drugs, prostitutes and gambling without a licence.'

Jenna took his pause as a chance to grab a glass of water. She was parched. And it wasn't just the heat causing her to boil. Captain Avery was starting to get quite annoying with his domineering approach and laying down of the law. 'I think it's quite funny, actually.'

'There's nothing funny about breaking maritime and Monégasque law.'

'No, not the sex and drugs and rock and roll, the name of the boat. I mean Mon— sorry, mister, is *such* a Sloane Ranger, it's hilarious.'

'A what?'

'You know, a Sloane Ranger. A Sloane. Spiritual home Sloane Square in London. A posho, a nob, that sort of thing.' She could sense she was losing the thin-at-the-start patience of the captain, who looked pointedly down at his wrist to his very large, overtly masculine watch.

'I really don't have time for this.' And at that he quickly ran through a few more boat basics, emphasised again that he was in charge of everyone, and then left her, to her huge relief, to await the return of Emma and Monty.

'Oh, he's a terror that captain of ours,' Emma flopped down next to Jenna on the sofas and held her hand over her stomach as if to emphasise how much she'd had for lunch. If Jenna was a betting sort of woman she would have guessed that Emma's version of a 'large lunch' was one more lettuce leaf than usual and — shock — perhaps a nibble of a breadstick. 'And Jenna, sweetie, please don't feel like you have to wear that ghastly polo shirt. I don't know who left them for you in your room, but as my personal PA I'd far rather you wore something more stylish.'

'Thanks, Emma — oh, sorry.'

'What for?'

'Using your name. Captain Avery said I must only address you as missus for security reasons.'

Emma burst out laughing. When she'd recovered herself she raised her voice and announced to the world, 'The Honourable Emma Blake-Howard here of Blake Manor, Oxfordshire. Owner of this yacht the *Wavy Sloanes* and I very much don't care who knows!'

It was Jenna's turn to giggle a bit and she added her own postscript to the announcement, 'Jenna Jenkins here of 39 Whittlesey Street, London and I'd like anyone listening to know I'm about to take off my shirt!'

'Oh, good girl, that will get the Ruskie spies excited.'

'I better go and divest in private though — I suppose Monte Carlo is just a tad too classy for me to get my kit off on day one.'

Jenna was surprised at how easy it was to get on with Emma. She was far from being the drawling aristo she'd had that semi-awkward interview with in London; here in Monaco she was definitely more fun and laid-back. Jenna left her new boss absorbed in her mobile phone and trotted back down the steps to her staff quarters to get changed. Grumpy captain aside, she could very much see herself having a rather good time on this yacht over the next couple of months — she'd be working, of course, but how hard could a bit of light PAing be? And once Angus came out to meet her here on the Riviera then she thought her summer was going to be, if not perfect, then pretty bloody good.

10

'Maxie, baby, I just don't see what's so important that you have to stay late for?' Bertie whined down the phone at her fiancé. While he was at work she was lying on a chaise longue in the drawing room of their Holland Park villa, swiping a nail file back and forwards across her fingertips while cradling her mobile phone between her ear and her shoulder.

'Berts, you know what it's like here. We're days away from signing this deal, unless it all falls through, which it will do if I bugger off home now and watch TV with you rather than the markets with my team.'

'But I'm bored, Maxie.'

Max recognised the tone. It was the wheedling start that usually ended in her getting exactly what she wanted. But she had to realise that while her money was all inherited, his was earned — and sometimes that meant staying at his desk, trying to motivate his team as they worked into the early hours compiling reports, figures, bids and counter offers for what always seemed to be the next big deal — the one he could 'retire' on. Max had been fast-tracked through his company and was doing well — really well — and although he wanted to be rich, he also got a buzz from the work — the late nights and adrenalin rushes. And he liked what it bought him . . . he rested his head on his shoulder, clamping his desk phone to his ear as he humoured Bertie telling him all about her day.

If he was going to be distracted from work, he might as well make the most of it, he thought, and swiped across his phone screen while he 'ahhed' and 'oohhed' over

Bertie's little stories. An interesting notification popped up on his home screen. Isabella Glaston-Smythe had sent him a message. Isabella. Izzy. The nubile young chalet girl from last year's ski holiday. Izzy, who had helped cater for Bertie's birthday party last summer and got caught shagging the nefarious Jonty Palmer-Johnston. Hadn't she been sent to the most convent-style woman-only Oxbridge college by her father after failing to prove to him that she could basically shag her way to the top? Or 'network', as she'd put it. Max hadn't been much interested in her after he'd got together with Bertie, but with the simultaneous demands for more attention and for him to earn more money coming from his betrothed, Max was rather nostalgic for the fun, quick shag Izzy had been back in the Alps. She had been as impressed with his largesse as with his, well, his *largesse*, and had never demanded he earn more money, or be more fun, or achieve more so quickly. He swiped open the message and grinned to himself. A few more late nights 'at the office' might be on the cards, whether Bertie liked it or not.

Bertie tapped her phone and ended the call to her fiancé. *How dull*, she thought to herself. Why couldn't he finish one of those deals he went on about the whole time and make some decent moolah? Perhaps he needed more encouragement, more of a push? She texted him a quick if slightly paraphrased inspirational thought her new yoga instructor had told her as she'd been practising her hip openers this afternoon — *push yourself a little harder every day, darling one* — and was only slightly miffed when she just received a 'k' back. Well, if he was going to insist on this sordid working thing, she would just have to get on and plan their wedding and her summer on the Riviera without him. She shuddered at the thought of really being without him. She knew he wasn't perfect, but he completed her like no one else could. If only he could be as rich as Monty BH. Damn Emma snagging him at that bloody ball a few years ago . . . Still, Bertie reassured herself that bedtime with Monty would be about as exciting as hot milk and Horlicks, more comfy Labrador than cunnilingus, and Max had so much more va-va-voom . . . it just frustrated her that he couldn't, or wouldn't push himself, for his sake as much as hers.

She dropped her nail file on the floor, the cleaner would be in early doors tomorrow and tidy it away for her, and rose up off the chaise longue. Wrapping her wafting dressing gown around her she left the room and headed upstairs, deciding to work out what in her wardrobe would be chic enough for her summer on the Riviera.

11

'How's it going, JJ? No, don't tell me, I actually don't want to know!' Sally's phone call had roused Jenna off her sunbed during the all-important siesta hour, which Emma and Monty believed to be a highly civilised way of breaking up the day on board their boat.

'Oh, Sals, it's amazing . . . we were invited onto another yacht the other day, some friend of Monty's, and each guest was given, check this, a Chanel bikini.'

'What?'

'I know — designer covers for designer boobs is what Emma called it, pointing out all the, well the augmentations, that were on board with us.'

'Oh, don't talk to me about boobs — mine are huge!'

'You'd go down a storm here then, sweetie!' Jenna felt a bit silly as she realised she'd just winked down the phone line.

'Somehow I think the enormous tummy would be somewhat of a negative . . .'

Jenna took a deep breath. She knew her friend's pregnancy was, of course, the most important thing in her life, but she wished she could maybe *not* mention it, just occasionally. She changed tack, away from boobs and tums.

'I think Angus is enjoying Hong Kong. Though he only mentions the work side of things. I'm not sure he's going out much or seeing many people besides the other staff.'

'Do you wish you'd gone too?'

'Part of me does, of course. I miss him terribly. I wish he was here, on the Riviera with me. And you, lovely, I wish you were here too.' *With no bump.* The rather snide thought caught Jenna by surprise. She was obviously being affected by this pregnancy thing a little more than even she thought.

'I wish I was too, sweetie, but we have so much to do and your bloody Airbnb tenants are being a right pain. While you're swanning around I've been fishing clogged hair out of swan-neck pipes — it's disgusting.'

'I'm so sorry, Sals. Honestly — mega-big Toblerone for you when I get home.'

'And that designer baby gear you mentioned, please!'

'Yes, yes . . . I've got to earn something first, so I better trot on. Emma's such a cool boss, but even I need to show up to work occasionally.'

'Back to the coalface . . . Bah, don't make me feel sorry for you, sweetie!'

'Mwah, bye, Sals, love you!'

Jenna disconnected the call and placed her phone down on the sunbed next to her. She really did wish she had her best friend out here — Sally would love the people-watching, the two of them could snigger to their hearts' content commenting on the flash Harries and primped and preened princesses here in Monaco. But with every mention of her sore boobs and growing belly, Jenna was reminded that very soon her best friend would become all-consumed with nappy rash and feeding schedules and have no time for girly drinks and suppers out. And what was worse, having spent a decade or so doing so much together there was now going to be such a massive part of Sally's life that she just wasn't going to be able to understand.

'I have got a Chanel bikini, though,' she muttered to herself as she picked up her towel and headed out of the sun and back to work.

'So.' Emma had switched into post-siesta business mode, which basically meant she reclined slightly less on her sunlounger and had replaced her copy of *Tatler* with a small, Smythson notebook, complete with its own gilt metal twist pencil. 'Let's get down to business.'

Jenna was getting used to Emma's style of working now. Her daily PA duties always started off in the same way. After an early-ish breakfast, Emma and sometimes Monty would spend time with their small children — taking them out in the tender for a whizz along the coast, or up into the town for ice creams and treats. Then by mid-morning, when the kids were napping or back with the nanny, the boat would motor out to sea so Monty and his assorted day guests (business associates, Jenna guessed as they occasionally dropped their aitches, while their knives, were at times, held like pens) could play on the jet skis and sea bobs, which were small, hand-held units that propelled the swimmer through the water at exhilarating speeds. Then long discussions about money markets and horse breeding would take place over Mediterranean-style lunches of lobster ravioli, bruschetta and ice-cold rosé. While this was all going on Emma would treat Jenna like a paid companion or trusted lady's maid — they'd spend hours in one of the guest cabins which had been taken over by dresses and tailor's dummies and Emma would ask her advice on where to pin fabric in such a way, or ask her to hold her pins while she made slight adjustments to the chiffon and silk. To say that Jenna had been surprised that Emma actually *made* her own designs was an understatement. But the more she got to know the slightly erratic, totally eccentric Emma, the more she liked her. She had used the term BoBo so much that Jenna one afternoon had to ask her what it meant.

'Bourgeois Bohemian, darling. BoBo. You know — something that the middle classes go bonkers for, although it's sort of down-at-heel and folksy. Like that wonderful circus chap everyone loves in the Cotswolds or one of the nicer festivals.'

'That's hilarious.'

'It's why it's just the perfect name for this collection . . . imagine some Claudia or Tori from Clapham swanning around the school run in one of these, or teaming one with wellies if they venture outside SW11 — so BoBo.' And so between them they'd picked out which dresses would be best to showcase the BoBo vibe at Emma's launch party and then over various light lunches and afternoon chats they'd worked out what canapés would be served, how the boat should be decorated if at all and what champagne would be best to serve to the guests. Never having worked in fashion, Jenna had no idea how much work went into just designing a few dresses, but she was enjoying it. So, along with organising various flights for Emma and Monty's friends, and chartering helicopter transfers and liaising with the yacht's crew about restaurant bookings and the like (Avery, it seemed, could get bookings at even the most exclusive restaurants), she had passed a happy few weeks so far with the Blake-Howards, their family and guests.

This afternoon though, as the late spring sunshine shone down on the sun deck — the topmost deck of the yacht and the one that Emma liked to use, claiming it helped her 'blue sky thinking' — Jenna suggested a few final decorating ideas for the fashion launch party, and of course the pair of them discussed where the models who would be showcasing Emma's designs would be 'walking'.

'Do you want a proper catwalk? Or more of an exhibition — like beautiful, fashionable works of art placed strategically around the boat?'

'Oooh, I don't know. What do you think?'

'Well, if they're on little pedestals they'd look so statuesque and of course then you'd have more room for your guests mingling if you don't have to have a catwalk.'

'But the dresses do flow so beautifully on the runway — you can't take away my *Britain's Next Top Model*, moment.' Emma lowered her large sunglasses and winked at Jenna who smiled back at her. Honestly, planning this fashion launch party was so much more fun than she'd first thought it might be. Since Emma had taken her on, and very much under her wing, Jenna had happily existed in the Blake-Howard bubble and she'd got used to her little cabin too, especially now her suitcase was squeezed under her bed and her limited, but she hoped chic enough, clothing was unpacked. She'd popped a little picture of Angus up by her bunk and the pair had been texting as much as time zones and work schedules allowed. Although perhaps the term 'work schedule' applied more to Angus than Jenna. Emma and Monty were genial hosts — bosses — and, except for the slightly cramped cabin, Jenna was never made to feel like an underling or servant. In fact, as she'd said to Sally earlier, she was even invited out with them to other yachts — something she never thought would happen.

And now, as Emma and Jenna lay basking in the Côte d'Azur sun, they discussed the final piece of the party puzzle: the guest list.

'Can you note this down, Jenna sweetie, I'm going to have a brain dump.'

'Ready when you are, Ems. Shoot.' Jenna sat up into a cross-legged position and pulled her slightly less glamorous notebook out from under her sunlounger and got ready to make some notes with her not-so-golden pencil.

'So, in port at the moment there's obvs Sir Philip Green. Now — good or bad? Who knows. But he still has clout so I suppose we should invite him since *Lionheart*, his yacht — it's that ghastly one that looks like a massive Nike trainer — is literally a one-pound coin's throw away.' She chuckled to herself over her BHS joke and kept going.

'Bertie will be flying in, so add her and Max. Then of course there's the Von Arkles, the Christous and their cousins in shipping, the Antonis, the Rollikoffs and the Popacokkovs.'

'Oh — I know that name.'

'Yes. Old banking friend of Bertie's father, I think.'

'Um, might be wise to skip him as we had a little run in with him last year in Val d'Argent.' Jenna filled Emma in on how Bertie had had a quick fling with the Russian oligarch to make Max jealous, while Poppa, as they called him, had also allowed his heavies to beat up their old friend Hugo. 'I think his hospitality was more closed fists than open-armed, if you see what I mean . . .?'

'Oh, terrible of him. Poor Bertie. Poor Hugo. Scrap him. It's like Nanny always says: if you don't give them firm boundaries then they play up like toddlers. Popacokkov is NFI'd.'

'Right you are.'

'So, then there's the Beckhams, ooh, and have you heard of TG Wilkinson?'

'No. Should I?'

'Oh, only if you read *Time* magazine as avidly as Monty does. He's some tech billionaire who's flying in tomorrow, I think. He owns a massive yacht and is super keen on eco stuff and philanthropy now, apparently. He invented that terrible app, you know, Clickbait. The one where you double tap if you like the look of someone — or you can just search for them or something — and every link on Google that's about them comes up. And not even the easy-to-find ones. Terribly stalkerish. It's all a bit beyond me, these dating apps. I don't know why everyone can't use *the season* like Monty and I did. I mean, there's no romance in swiping right when you could be swigging Pimm's, stomping divots or swinging rackets at each other.'

Jenna snorted a little laugh. 'Okay, so TG Wilkinson. Will he be interested in fashion, though?'

'I don't care, sweetie, but *I'm* interested in his investment if he wants to back my next collection!'

With a stonker of a family pile, this rather swanky yacht and a stableful of race horses, not to mention Monty obviously running some sort of business, Jenna wasn't sure quite why The Honourable Emma needed any more investment but she nodded and added him onto the list, which by the end of their meeting, had grown to about forty of the most influential people currently in the port of Monaco. Emma suggested they celebrate with a sundowner or two before seeing what chef had prepared for supper.

12

'How's it going?'

'It's brilliant, Gus, I'm still loving it here. Hang on.' Jenna clasped her mobile to her chest as she dashed up from her cabin on the lower deck to get a better signal. 'Hello? Still there?'

'Yes, still here.'

'I wish you were here, you'd love it.'

'Would I? Isn't it just a lot of very expensive margarine tubs floating around in dirty diesel harbour water?'

'Ha! Stop it. If you could see this boat, even just from a design point of view, it's glorious. Anyway, how's work going?'

'Sod work, tell me more about the filthy rich and dirty rotten scoundrels of the Riviera.'

'Oh I've heard some amazing stories, you wouldn't believe them.'

'Try me,'

'So grumpy old Captain Avery — you know I told you about him being the boss round here? Really, I mean, you'd think owning your own super yacht would give you some sort of authority, but no. Anyway, Avery said he once captained a yacht that was chartered to someone very famous for a week.'

'Ooh anyone we know?'

'Like you and your confidentiality clauses, he kept schtum.'

'How dull of us. Carry on . . .'

'Well, this rapper decided to have a party — with like no notice whatsoever — two hundred and fifty guests or so.'

'Anyone we'd know?'

'He couldn't say, but celebs — mostly music ones, and rock stars. Anyway, Captain Avery, who I know from my first chat with him is really anti-drugs, well, he got called over by one of the stewies on the boat.'

'The who?'

'The stewardess — apparently the boat was massive so had a much larger crew than this one. Anyway, she found loads of coke, like *loads*, in the day heads — you know, the loos, so she called Avery in and he basically got the vacuum cleaner and sucked it all up!'

'God, I wonder how much that would have all cost.'

'I know. But here's the funny bit. So later on, this party is raging and someone breaks a glass on the dance floor. As it's all shoes off on these boats he had to get one of the stewies to clear the area and vacuum up all the glass pretty quickly before someone cut themselves. But she didn't know how to work the Hoover and instead of sucking she pressed blowback or something and this dance floor, who were still raving out to the DJ, were covered in this white powder!'

'Fuck, really?'

'Really! Funny thing was, not one of them complained. They thought it was the host being really generous with his coke.'

Jenna heard Angus laugh at the other end of the line and the sound of his voice made her miss him more than ever. 'I can't wait until you can come out here, Gus.'

'I know, JJ. I miss you too. And I bet you're looking sexier and sexier with your Côte d'Azur tan . . .'

'. . .And French bread tummy. Yeah right.'

'I know you're still gorgeous.'

'I miss you.' A tear formed in the corner of Jenna's eye — moments ago it would have been from laughing so much, but now she just missed Angus and wished he was here with her, in this paradise by the sea.

As they finished their call she looked out over the water and wiped another tear away. Her attention was caught by the largest yacht she'd ever seen slowly slip into the other side of the marina. Although there were quite a few boats between the *Wavy Sloanes* and this aquatic juggernaut, it towered over most of them and blocked the view that she'd been enjoying over the water towards the vast sea behind the harbour wall. The sleek lines and glistening metallic paint finish of the yacht were the only things to stop her from thinking some cross-channel ferry had just pulled up, and she watched as the crew expertly guided it into its mooring, getting it into its spot to the nearest inch. She saw its name — *Clickbait* — written in metre-high letters across its bow. She remembered the conversation she'd had with Emma and the article she'd found in Monty's *Time* magazine, which he'd left open in the main saloon, and realised that in Port Hercule, as in life, the tech billionaire had arrived.

13

Jenna looked over the main deck of the yacht. Flickering tea lights (battery powered, Captain Avery had an aversion to real flames) edged the wooden deck, while white and silver helium balloons were tied in little bunches and floated up above the balustrades of each deck. Trellises of white flowers and pale green foliage arched over the entrances to the yacht, firstly over the walkway that stretched out enticingly onto the quayside, covered tonight in green baize with a green welcome mat marked with swirly writing saying 'BoBo', and then over every little run of steps that led between decks. The whole effect was one of etherealness, a sort of *Midsummer's Night Dream* scene, where one might expect fairies and elves to appear at any moment. This being a super yacht in Monaco, though, and not a woodland grove in Elizabethan England, the fairies were instead elegant models, each dressed in one of The Honourable Emma's dresses. And they were as beautiful, captivating, dreamy and otherworldly as anything from the fairy realm could ever be. Especially compared to Jenna, who had been donated one of last season's dresses – although the sample size 8 had come up a little tight, so Emma, in a moment of practical tailoring, had sewn in a back panel to allow Jenna to breathe for the night at least, if not sit down, bend over, turn to her left or right or walk at more than a snail's pace. If the models in the BoBo gowns were fairies, she felt much more like Bottom the ass, or at least as if *her* bottom was the size of an ass.

Still, here she was, wearing a couture gown (well, it *was* hand-tailored for her by the designer) surrounded by this simply sublime setting (this was definitely worth signing up to Instagram for), and she had pulled off this wow of a party in just under a month since arriving. The hardest part had been the guest list. The fashion launch happened to coincide with another party planned on the massive yacht *Quicksilver*, owned by a secretive industrialist from the States. Well, secretive up to a point – he had just invited two hundred of Monaco's A-list, including Prince Albert, to a soirée where he intended to show off his come-of-age daughter, fresh from Switzerland and versed now in all things etiquette, including dropping her natural southern American accent.

'I suppose I shouldn't grumble,' grumbled Emma as she and Jenna had bemoaned the lack of RSVPs a few days before their launch party. 'I mean, he is at least recreating a deb-style event and I have mine to thank for first attracting Monty's eye.'

'I thought you said you'd met during the season – swinging rackets at each other or something.'

'And my deb ball was the pinnacle of that season. What an evening.' She'd sighed and looked up to the clear blue sky as the two women caught a few rays up on the sun deck. 'Until Cheska vomited in the faux-Ming vase and the Dorchester claimed Bertie had been caught *in flagrante* in the loo with a Spencer-Churchill.'

'Ha. *Of course*, Bertie was a deb . . .' Jenna rolled her eyes. 'But I didn't think deb balls happened any more anyway?'

'Oh, there's the International Debutant Ball and the Queen Charlotte's but they're all for ghastly upstarts with more money than class. No, we had a private affair – just some chums from the best families and old school friends. Not a foreign industrialist in sight!'

Jenna was still intrigued as to what Bertie had been doing in the loo at the Dorchester and wondered if Max knew much about her dodgy debbing past.

Emma carried on. 'Still, if old Mr Quicksilver over there wants to hog society for his night of showing off Miss Albuquerque — well, who am I to argue?'

In the end, *Quicksilver*'s plans were sent to the bottom of the sea when the wealthy industrialist had discovered his daughter on the front page of the *National Enquirer*, the *Daily Mail* and *Paris Match*, caught by the paparazzi giving a blow job to one of his wrinkly, sundried-tomato-coloured friends.

'His loss is our gain,' Emma had congratulated Jenna when the news had broken and suddenly they had a lot more positive RSVPs. 'Seems like Miss Albuquerque was more of a quick swallower than a quicksilver.'

Jenna had giggled, but did feel just a little bit sorry for the non-debutant daughter. Mostly as there must be some screw loose for her to feel the need to service one of her father's leathery old friends like that.

'It is odd though,' mused Emma. 'Switzerland should have at least taught her to "shield the sausage", if not, then old Mr Quicksilver should really get his francs back.'

So, the guest list had come together and the evening of the fashion launch was upon them. Monty, to his credit, had pulled his weight too and shown quite some skill as a seamstress, helping his wife put the last few stitches on the dresses — although he was more pincushion than couturier. And when the glamorous denizens of Port Hercule started to arrive Emma and Monty were dazzling together, networking the yacht decks as the DJ worked the music decks and introducing friends and potential clients to each other. Jenna oversaw the caterers and organised the models. The catwalk would begin at 10 p.m. and last approximately twenty minutes — such a short period of time, thought Jenna, compared to the days of planning and hours of partying. Captain Avery was in charge of taking the yacht out of the harbour so the back drop would be the beautiful twinkling lights of Beulieu-Sur-Mer and Villefranche rather than the fenders and crews of the neighbouring yachts — plus, with the boat out at sea they had a captive audience for the fashion show. Jenna was starting to learn these little techniques the super-rich used to control you — including the super-strong cocktails handed round when they first came in. What had Emma said? *Get them drunk enough and far enough away from any other temptations and they're yours . . . you're in control then, sweetie.*

Jenna was just edging past a tray of caviar-topped canapés when she was caught off guard by the screeching of her name.

'Jenna! Dolls!'

It was Bertie, who was dressed in neck-to-floor sequins, which would seem overpowering except that there was very little cloth actually on her body. The 'dress' was really only a couple of strips that fell from her shoulders over her breasts and met up at the waistband, exposing almost all of her cleavage and stomach right down to her tummy button. The straps were even thinner down her back, showing off her toned arms and sharp shoulder blades. The skirt was just a couple of panels, split to the thigh, so that Bertie appeared to be constantly walking through a beaded curtain.

'Bertie, wow! Hi.'

'Mwah, sweetie, mwah.' Bertie air-kissed her friend and stood back to look at her. 'Squeezed yourself in to something passable, well done you.'

Jenna knew that this was about as close to a compliment she would ever get from all-round socialite and bark-worse-than-bite Bertie. 'How was your journey, Bertie?'

'Well, Max let me down last minute as he had something boring, *like work*, to do.' She spat out the words with the distaste she felt they deserved. 'But luckily the darling Fitzalan Carters were coming here anyway so I jumped on their PJ and we wheels downed at Nice and got the helicopter transfer over here. I'm *proppo-exhausto*. I was up until the early hours last night with my wedding dressmaker who just could not get her head round the fact that I want tailoring like Meghan, with Kate's lace, but obviously much more contemporary than both of them. We really had to have it out over the pattern books.'

Jenna was used to Bertie jabbering on about herself and used the time to make contact with the models in the corridor and motion to her watch telling them to get a wriggle on.

'All sounds amazing, Berts, but afraid I really have to help out Emma now.'

'Oh God, yah. You're *working*. I totally forgot. But of course, why else would someone like you be here.' Even for Bertie that hit slightly below the Versace belt.

'Right.' Jenna decided to let it slide. 'So I better skedaddle. Models need me!'

'Probs to balance out about three of them.' Bertie guffawed into her champagne coupe glass and Jenna pushed past her. Enough was enough. But a scene maker she was not.

TG Wilkinson watched the little tableau in front of him. He'd accepted the invitation from The Honourable Emma Blake-Howard as he was new to the Monaco scene, and quite frankly flattered to be asked to join the British aristocracy within moments of sailing into port. He wasn't going to kid himself that it was because of his personality or knowledge of ladies' clothing. No, as one of Silicon Valley's brightest stars, he knew he was accepted here as long as his Black Amex card was. And with his personal fortune — thanks to Clickbait the app — soaring into the hundreds of millions of dollars, it was no surprise that his fame was on the rise too. He watched as the pouty, annoying — but to give her credit, stunningly beautiful — girl belittled and bullied the other one. He analysed the alpha nature of the louder girl, her dominating words, hand gestures and stance. He also analysed the other girl. The one who accepted the verbal arrows and let them rebound off her as if she was wearing plate armour. She interested him, as anyone did who had that ability to stay so grounded, so down to earth, in this chaotic, head-turning world of the super-rich, and the super bitch. And she was beautiful too, her golden hair tousled in the wind, her eyes bright and her figure temptingly hidden in the flowing skirts of the dress. He kept his eye on the worker bee as she detached herself from the queen and made her way towards the cabin full of diaphanously dressed models, thinking to himself how much nicer her rounded bottom looked in that flowing dress compared to the emaciated hips and jutting elbows of the professional girls.

14

'Go, go, go!' Jenna shout-whispered to the lead model on the catwalk — gesturing for the second and third girls to start their walk too. The runway was on the main deck, with the girls starting to walk from the starboard side of the boat to the port side, sashaying through a cleared path among the guests, floral arrangements, waitresses and furniture. They looked stunning — like beautiful human gazelles or racehorses. Hours of preening and primping had gone towards a look that was so natural, it looked as if no effort had gone into it at all. Glowing skin, loosely plaited hair with curling tendrils, flat leather sandals and perfectly rosy cheeks epitomised the BoBo look — the dresses were floaty and the swirls of silk and chiffon caught in the evening breeze that drifted across the water and over the decks of the yacht. The guests stopped their conversations and quietly sipped their champagne as they looked on at the bucolic spectacle walking among them.

Jenna was concentrating on getting the models who had finished their first round of the deck back into the changing-room cabin for a quick dress change, but she heard the boat's built-in sound system carry Emma Blake-Howard's voice across the party as she talked about the dresses and her inspiration for the collection. *Sod being born with a silver spoon in her mouth*, thought Jenna, *Emma had been blessed with something much more useful: a salesperson's silver tongue.* Her soft, upper-class accent cajoled and tempted the assorted guests and Jenna realised that the little Smythson notebook would soon be out, taking orders and noting down potential investors. Jenna couldn't help but feel just a little part of the success. But her own inner glow-bug was quickly extinguished when a familiar voice — upper class, yes; soothing, no — squawked in her ear.

'Jenna!'

'God. Bertie. What?' Jenna sounded irritated, more than she really felt, but rather than feel bad about snapping, Jenna realised that Bertie wouldn't have even noticed . . . probably.

'Question.' The It girl raised a finger. She had not only *not* noticed Jenna's tone, she was also completely ignoring quite how busy her friend was, with her headset buzzing in her ear and a model leaning on her elbow to steady herself as she dropped her dress to her ankles, stepped out of it and slipped a new one over her head. 'Do you think Max would like it if I had my lips done. I know it's more the rage to go natural, and I mean these dresses and these gorgeous girls here tonight — oh hi, Kiki,' she broke off to wave at a semi-naked model before carrying on, 'are all in that sort of vibe, but really I do feel like my upper lip is a bit thin.'

'Bertie. I really don't have time to talk about this at the moment.'

'You're right, important things first — will you take a picture of me here, under this soft light, for my Insta?'

'No!'

'Why not?'

'Well, I'm kinda busy.' Jenna gestured to the chaos in the cabin around her while also holding a mirror up for a model to check her lipstick and ushering another one — possibly Kiki — out of the cabin in order to walk the runway at the same time as Emma's matching dialogue.

'Busy, *schmizzy*.' Bertie harrumphed and walked away, with considerably less swagger than usual as she'd been forced to leave her staggeringly high heels on the quayside, alongside those of the other guests.

When the last model had done her final outfit change and Jenna had yanked the call-centre style headset off her aching head, she emerged from the cabin and looked out to see if there was anything else she should be doing. She excused herself past a couple of snogging guests — who were making use of the romantic flowers and lighting — and made a beeline through the crowd to Emma.

'Dolls, not so busy now?' Bertie caught her by the arm and Jenna felt the bony fingers and sharp nails dig into her skin.

'Still busy, Berts. What is it now?'

'Photo time. Sans Max you see, so I need someone to help.'

'Fine. Where do you want to pose?'

'So — my aim in this shot is to make my followers think I've bought a boat. Owner chic. So . . .' Bertie revealed from behind her something that looked very much like Captain Avery's hat.

'Oh Bertie. No. Uh-uh. Put that back, he'll go spare.'

'Tosh, it's just for a minute or two. Now bring those tea-light things and that lamp and we'll find the bridge and I'll pose there, or . . . no, no . . . on the top deck. Perfect. Dominating society. Great.'

Jenna let Bertie talk to herself as she dutifully followed her up to the top deck and helped her pose in such a way that her hair flowed out caught by the breeze, her dress slipped open to reveal her thigh and the light hit her made-up face to perfectly highlight the professional contouring. A few snaps later and Jenna thought she was done. A few more snaps, with Bertie in slightly different poses — one with the captain's hat on, one with the hat covering her bare chest, one with the hat thrown up in the air which gave Jenna the willies as she expected a very grumpy Captain Avery to find them out at any minute — and then she really was done.

'God, it's so artificial, all this posing.' Jenna handed Bertie's phone back to her.

'I don't see what's wrong with it, chick. It's only the modern version of those funny little round-robin letters our parents used to send out at Christmas. I mean, Instagram is basically the same as my mum writing "Bertie did really well in her exams and thoroughly enjoyed the gymkhana" instead of "Bertie failed Latin even though she shagged the teacher and then got shitfaced at Pony Club".'

'Did you?'

'Don't be foul. But you know what I mean.'

Jenna wasn't entirely sure if Bertie really had just slipped up and given away a few Dirty Bertie secrets, but she took her leave while Bertie was busy uploading her best photo and carried on her mission to find Emma and see if she could do anything for her.

Jenna wished she hadn't asked when, in the nicest possible way, Emma suggested that she might want to chase up the long list of enquiries that had emerged during the fashion show and before the boat re-entered Port Hercule and their quarry could escape.

The task, it seemed, was not a straightforward one, though one at least that did have its merits as Jenna had the perfect excuse to go up to some of the more impossibly glamorous on board and introduce herself. This would usually be something that would send her into paroxysms of fear — the embarrassment of having to hand round plates of nibbles at her parents' drinks parties when she was a gawky teen magnified a hundredfold — but there was something of a buzz about the night, and Jenna felt alive to it, emboldened by the fact that she had more-or-less single-handedly organised this entire, successful affair.

She took Emma's notebook and felt the power that it gave her. Finding the fashion set was easy enough, those who had placed an interest in featuring the dresses in photo shoots or buying in the range for their boutiques. Those ladies were the epitome of style, quietly confident, in trouser suits with barely there camisoles underneath or palazzo pants and high-collared, crisp white shirts. They were rich, yes, but they were businesswomen and creatives and Jenna enjoyed asking them their thoughts on the collection and scheduling in meetings with them, here on the yacht over the next few days before they flew back to Paris, London and Milan. Then there were the investors — a more secretive bunch who came with entourages and advisors — albeit advisors in the guise of teenage daughters and just-over-teenage girlfriends. These were the Monaco set — those with tax-friendly residency and permanent moorings on neighbouring yachts. The dark glasses on their security guards gave them away, but Emma's notebook was Jenna's calling card, and she was let into the presence of the big dogs and able to set up meetings too. Some of them were friendlier than others and her buoyant sense of self-confidence and general well-being was only threatened once when one of the Russians reminded her of the ice-cold shoulder she and her friends had received from Popacokkov. She shuddered and carried on down the quickly scrawled list of potential 'friends of the brand'. TG Wilkinson was the last of the wannabe investors and Jenna began to scope out the decks looking for someone who could fit the description Emma had hurriedly given her, which was 'hot, thirty-something, rich, Indian-ish, did I say hot? He's so hot'.

Jenna spied him, and as fate would have it, he was chatting to Bertie. For a woman apparently very much in love with her fiancé (and with the astonishingly blinging Cartier engagement ring to prove it), she was doing a very good job of making TG feel incredibly welcome — if someone could welcome another person through sheer cleavage alone.

'Jenna!' Bertie's voice was no less squawky than before, but Jenna didn't mind it so much now. Getting access to these high rollers wasn't always a given and to find one looking so casual and relaxed — and Jenna had to admit, really quite hot — was a relief. She walked towards them both and couldn't help but meet the billionaire's eyes. They were deep chocolate brown, the same colour as his hair, and his skin was the colour of the sauce on top of a crème caramel. He wore a white linen shirt which was unbuttoned to reveal a few wisps of dark chest hair, and as he got up to greet her, Jenna noticed how it was barely tucked into his fashionably distressed jeans. Jenna had never felt eye contact like it — she was almost mesmerised by its intensity. It was only the particular pitch of Bertie's voice that broke the spell, and brought Jenna back to the reality of who she was, where she was and, more importantly, that there was someone else in her life whose eyes were the only ones for her.

'Dolls! Finally finished your tawdry little day job?'

'Hi, Bertie. And hello, you must be Mr Wilkinson?'

'Hey,' the billionaire spoke. 'Call me TG.' He held out a hand to her and she took it while trying to think of something to say to both introduce herself and undo the harm from probably the first of many 'Bertie barbs' she was about to receive. She made a mental note to try and remember them, so she could moan about them to Sally sometime.

'I'm Jenna Jenkins, Emma's assistant, and I'd love to chat to you about the interest you showed in the collection tonight. If that's OK with you, Bertie? Not too tawdry?'

'Oh, dolls, I mean — talk *moolah* if you must. I'm sure TG won't mind if little old me listens in.' She wiggled her sit bones into the soft cushion of the sofa they were on, making herself very much at home.

'Actually, Roberta,' the accent was warmly American, or Canadian perhaps, Jenna couldn't quite work it out, but wherever he was from, she was in awe at the way he could dismiss Bertie so easily. 'Do you mind if Miss Jenkins here and I have a little one-on-one time?'

Jenna had never in her whole life seen Bertie rendered speechless. Or indeed see anyone stick up to her — or dismiss her — as easily as this brave man had just done. Friends they might be, frenemies at times even — and sometimes, for her sins, they could be classed as close — but at whatever stage their friendship was at, Jenna was relishing this dressing down. She smiled. *And to think I thought fashion shows were all about dressing up*, she thought. Bertie forced out a thin smile and then excused herself, but Jenna could see the clench of the jaw that lay behind the smile and felt the drag of her manicured nails across her bare shoulder as her rival for TG's attentions left the deck.

'So, how can I help you, Miss Jenkins? Or is it Mrs?'

'It's Miss, just, I mean, still . . . Oh whatever, it's Jenna. I mean, please do just call me Jenna.'

'Cool, hey, Jenna, come sit down, you look beat.'

Jenna gave him a quick smile and sat down next to him, though not as welcomingly close as Bertie had just been sitting. She may have momentarily forgotten her one true love as soon as she gazed into those mahogany eyes, but Jenna wasn't going to let this get anything other than professional.

'I am, actually. It's been, well, it's been quite a day.' Remembering her mission, and seeing the lights of Port Hercule come closer into view, she cracked on with business. 'Thank you for coming tonight and for showing an interest in Emma's work. As you can see she is a designer with a huge future in front of her and with her background in fashion design at Central Saint Martins and her incredible passion for the fabrics she uses and her—'

'Hey, slow down. Is this the PR bit?'

'Um, yes, sorry, I was just, you know, filling you in.' Jenna realised her double entendre was left hanging in the air and she hoped that it wasn't quite such an ambiguous phrase in the States.

'Let me fill you in.' His answer did nothing to help her work out the answer to that one — delivered as it was with a totally straight face, yet perhaps with a twinkle in his eye. 'I'm interested in the collection, yes, but I don't give a rat's ass for design schools and fabrics. Schedule me in for a private meeting with Emma — say, Monday?'

'Of course,' Jenna quickly checked her scrawled notes on when other potential investors and fashion buyers wanted to come in and see Emma and found a time slot. 'Three o'clock?'

'Cool.'

'Cool.' Jenna was slightly bamboozled by this man. He'd been open and friendly, but also weirdly closed and abrupt. She couldn't put her finger on it.

'Hey,' he said as she noted down his appointment time. 'Nice to meet you, Jenna Jenkins. I'm sure I'll see you again. Very soon.' At that he stood up and, although not as tall as Angus, he towered over her as she sat on the deck's sofa. He reached down and Jenna took his hand to shake it, but instead he pulled her up and in so doing, pulled her in close to him. She was off balance and felt herself fall forward towards him and only managed to steady herself by placing her free hand against his chest. *Of course*, she thought, it had to be against the bare skin, *I couldn't have found the normal shirty bit*. But there, for that moment, she felt the beat of his heart under her palm. She held it there for a moment more then, quickly rebalancing herself, stood firm on the deck. Thank God for the shoes-off rule — any footwear other than climbing cleats would have had her toppling over altogether.

'See you around.' He lowered his head and brushed his cheek against hers in a casual goodbye kiss.

And then he was gone and Jenna was left standing there, the hand that had felt his heart beating beneath his bare skin resting on her own chest, feeling her own heart beat — beat, beat, beat — until she finally calmed herself enough to find Emma, her notebook now filled with as many appointments as they could wish for, and her head filled with an equal amount of unanswered questions.

15

Hong Kong — hot, clammy, frenetic, dynamic. Angus didn't exactly love it — its similarity to Singapore and the memories that city held for him meant he could never truly feel comfortable there — but he loved its energy and its sense of purpose. Everyone was doing something — whether it was hawking goods on the corners of the roads, cheap stalls full of plastic toys, rain ponchos and street food, or smart businessmen in fitted grey suits, desks loaded with files, taking their air-conditioned offices for granted.

And he was hard at work, too. Pei Ling had been so grateful to him for coming over — *a safe pair of hands*, she'd called him — and he wondered if that related to his skill as an architect, or if she had been alluding to that night years ago when he had saved her during that gang attack when they both worked in Singapore, a near-fatal case of mistaken identity. He returned his attention to the large screen of his computer. Her project this time was a pro-bono one — a school for the orphans of victims of gang warfare — a cause that had perhaps become a little too close to Pei Ling's heart in recent years. A few hours passed in happy concentration, the clicking of the mouse becoming plans, ideas, connecting up and forming a building that would one day house the city's most vulnerable children. Angus loved the idea that his skills could help people.

Feeling an ache creep across his back, he stretched up away from the screen and reached his arms up and over his head in a massive yawn. It was gone 7 p.m. — time to go back to his hotel, though without Jenna here with him he had little appetite to venture out past the hotel bar or local noodle place. He'd spent a few happy nights out with associates from the firm but, more often than not, the conversation always seemed to return to that night and the fight; he felt their eyes trace the length of the scar on his cheek, weaving its way as it did from ear to mouth. He'd shaved off the beard he had grown to disguise it, as Jenna had given him the confidence to own up to the fact that this was just how he looked now, and it made him miss her even more. If she was here, he'd show her the sights and introduce her to Pei Ling and the other colleagues he'd made friends with out here so far, and last summer when he helped Pei Ling with what he had thought then would be 'one last job'. He had to hand it to the old girl, she was still working at a relentless pace when most people her age were flicking through the Saga cruise catalogue and comparing garden centre cafés. *Still*, he thought, *time for this much younger architect to call it a night*. He picked up his light jacket from the back of his chair and left the office, calling out a goodbye to the other late workers, heads buried in plans and hands hovering over keyboards like his had just been.

The downside to the Stafford Ling offices was that you had to leave them fully to get anywhere — it wasn't in an air-conditioned mall or part of a long line of buildings connected by an enclosed passageway. He got down to the street and felt the wall of humidity hit him as he left the lobby of the building. His jacket stayed over his arm; putting it on seemed madness in this sweaty climate. But the heat warmed him up and loosened the aching muscles in his neck and shoulders. He walked out towards his hotel, pausing to eye up a street stall boasting bags by Channel, Mucci and Michael Cors. He chuckled at how Jenna had claimed her only Hong Kong pastime would have been tracking down the best fake handbag she could find and he wondered again if those umpteen 'innocent' girly chats she had over bottles of wine with Sally and co were actually just fronts and in fact they talked like a gang of fraudsters, swapping tips on where to find the best fakes, lacing their chat with the language of the street, justifying their illegal shopping any way they could . . .

'Ow.' A wasp or something had stung him in the neck. Angus rubbed it, but the pain, instead of subsiding throbbed and grew and Angus felt himself falling to the pavement, the grubby concrete the last thing he could remember before blacking out entirely.

Angus woke up feeling like he'd been coshed on the back of the head and his first instinct was to check for an injury, but as he tried to raise his arms he realised his wrists were tied behind his back. He jerked them around a bit, thoughts running through his mind — *Where am I? Why am I tied up?* He tried to calm down and look around the room in which he was kept prisoner. It was dark, but his eyes were getting used to it, and his thumping head was grateful that it didn't have to cope with blinding lights as well as whatever it was that had knocked him out. He remembered a sting, a wasp . . . an injection? He wanted to scratch his neck — the frustration of not being able to move his arms took over him again and he rocked the small wooden chair he was tied to backwards and forwards in his attempts to free himself. He was about to try and stand up and smash the chair away when a door opened and the lights blazed on.

'Mr Linklater.'

The voice was well spoken, but obviously belonged to a Hong Kong local. He couldn't see who it was, though, as not only had his eyes not acclimatised to their bright new surroundings but Angus was facing away from where the voice was coming from. He tried to turn himself and the chair around but found it harder than he imagined — his legs were tied together loosely, but effectively — he could stretch them no more than a small stride before the rough rope scratched through his chinos. If he couldn't face his oppressor then he'd have to gain more clues from what he could see — and hear.

'There is no point you trying to escape.' The voice was closer now and Angus's fear was rising. What on earth was going on? 'For one, I have many, many associates here with me . . .' the word reminded Angus of his more benign work colleagues, but he knew this guy's 'associates' would be more handy with a gun than a protractor. 'And also, I am about to untie you so we can have a civilised conversation. I warn you, though,' the voice was right up close to Angus's ear now, 'try anything and you will be scarred worse than you already are.'

The scar. It must all link back. Angus took his mind back to that brawl. The restaurant had been raided by a gang believing that his firm was in the pay of a rival — designing and building on the wrong patch of land. The ambush had lasted less than fifteen minutes probably, but he'd been badly hurt trying to save Pei Ling . . . and he'd lashed out in fear too. His only weapon had been a chair leg, but his adversary had had a knife . . . He felt the bonds around his wrists loosen and he shook out his hands as they were released. There was a part of him tempted, in a James Bond type way, to karate chop the lackey now loosening his leg bonds, but there was a much greater part of him who realised that would be a very, very unwise idea. He was close to freaking out altogether, but something told him that staying calm was probably his only safe ticket out of here.

'Please, Mr Linklater, come and join me at my desk.' Angus stood up and turned around and in so doing realised that his chair had been facing the far wall of what was actually a large room — a basement office — although only seeing the one wall he'd not taken in the length of the space. The walls were covered in movie posters — both local Chinese ones and Hollywood classics. Sideboards held photo frames and *objets d'art* — ornate vases, ginger jars and jade lion bookends. Behind him sat The Voice — it had become capitalised now in his mind in lieu of a proper name — and he could now see that the well-spoken man was as equally well dressed. His adversary was wearing a grey woollen suit, which suggested a life spent in air-conditioned rooms, hair slicked back and a face that looked far too benign to have just been threatening him with violence. It was almost cherubic in its roundness. 'Please. Sit.' It was a command, not an offer.

'Who are you?' Angus was scared, but he needed answers.

'The important thing, Mr Linklater, is who you are.'

'I think you must have made some sort of mistake, sir, I'm just an architect.' *This was the problem last time*, he thought, the attackers at the restaurant had thought the architectural firm was corrupt and in someone's pockets — striking deals over land that wasn't theirs. Pei Ling had reassured him from her hospital bed after the attack that she would never have had anything to do with the Triads. And he believed her.

'I have made no mistake. You are exactly who I think you are. The murderer of my nephew — Ho-Yin.'

'Murderer?' Angus could barely get the word out. His throat was dry and he felt a cold dread come over his body.

'Your firm worked for the Emerald Dragons, our rivals in Singapore.'

'No, no . . . you're wrong . . .' Out of nowhere Angus felt a firm hand on his shoulder, shutting him up faster than a slap on the face.

'Your firm was working for the Emerald Dragons,' The Voice, repeated. 'And during your time working for your overmasters, you killed my nephew. You.' He raised his hand and pointed accusingly at Angus. Angus really thought that this was it and prepared himself for the single gunshot to the head, or the garrotting wire to quickly close in around his throat. The Voice lowered his accusatory finger and continued. 'I'm a fair man and I work in the old-fashioned way. An eye for an eye.'

Angus froze in his seat. This was it, surely.

'A loved one, for a loved one.'

The respite was brief. His life wasn't in question, but whose was?

'I don't understand?' Angus had nothing left to lose. If his brains hadn't been blown out yet, he might as well use the time to get some answers. 'I didn't kill anyone. Not that night, not ever. I don't even know your nephew.'

'He was the one who gave you that scar and who you in turn, beat until his face was barely recognisable, his life as vanquished as his features, his mother — my sister — not even able to identify her boy.'

'No, no . . .' Angus's voice was as strangled as it might have been had the garrotting taken place. 'I was only defending myself. I left him alive . . . I . . . I . . .' he struggled for the words. His mind full of snatched memories of the night. His blood from his glass-hewn face gash mixing with that of his attacker. Admittedly, he'd lost it and lashed out in rage, but . . . could he really have killed that guy?

'His mother still weeps every night. And you, you are happy with your beautiful girlfriend.' The Voice turned the computer screen in front of him around and showed Angus a picture of Jenna. If that wasn't bad enough, it was a picture of Jenna leaning over the deck of a yacht — it couldn't have been more than a few days old. And that's when he realised. They — the gang — were there, in Monte Carlo.

'She will die and you will suffer the same heartbreak as my sister suffers.' The Voice turned his computer screen back round and looked down nonchalantly at his finger-nails, picking a bit of grit out of one as Angus let out a roar of anger and frustration.

'No. *No*. She has nothing to do with this. Please, please don't hurt her. I beg you.'

'Did my nephew beg you for his life? Did *you* spare *him*?'

'I didn't kill him.' Angus's head fell into his hands, the frustration getting too much, tears of anger and anguish building up behind his eyes, the pain of them filling his head. He looked up and implored The Voice one more time. 'Please, please. I'll do anything. She's innocent — she's got nothing to do with this.' *I'm innocent too*, he thought to himself, but knew he was beyond being able to convince The Voice of that. He took a deep breath and tried to state his case as clearly and reasonably as he could. 'She isn't part of this world. Your nephew was. He ambushed us in that restaurant, he was part of your gang. It's not a fair swap. Kill me, take everything I own, but please, I beg you again, don't hurt Jenna.'

The Voice laughed and turned the computer screen around again to show Angus something.

'Look! Ha ha. I have just won on the, how do you say, "gee-gees".'

All Angus could see was a screen with a never-ending list of numbers and what must be odds — a private betting site, perhaps. Whatever it was, it took The Voice's focus temporarily off him and he relaxed just a fraction — but he was unsure if this was The Voice ending the conversation or if he still had a chance to bargain over Jenna's life.

'Five million US dollars.' The Voice looked up from his screen, breaking the momentary silence.

'Sorry?'

'This win, it has made me happy, Mr Linklater, and I am now in a forgiving mood. So I say this, I will spare her life for five million US dollars.'

Angus was broken — he knew he couldn't find that much money but what else could he say? To negotiate down would risk the whole new deal — money, not Jenna's precious life — being wiped off the table. But where would he find that sort of cash?

'The deal is on the table, Mr Linklater, and the clock is ticking. You get me five million US dollars by, hmm, let's see . . .' he paused and considered his fingernails for a while, before picking what Angus assumed was just an arbitrary date. 'Midsummer. You English love your *Midsomer Murders*, ha ha. John Nettles — very funny. Money by then and your girlfriend is safe. You insult me again, and she dies. Contact the police, and she dies. Fail to meet the deadline, and — yes you are right in your nodding head — she dies. You will probably die, too. Tick tock, Mr Linklater, tick tock.'

At that, The Voice got up abruptly from his desk — his grey suit, so smart, so tailored, so businesslike . . . well, Angus thought, a business deal had just been struck by this psychopath. As his tormentor left the room via one of the doors behind his desk, Angus felt himself being roughly pulled to his feet by the guard behind him. He was frogmarched out of another door where another gang member shoved a cloth bag over Angus's head. The pain he then felt was blinding — a real cosh to the back of the head this time — and his nightmare was over for now.

16

The next day, over breakfast on the *Wavy Sloanes* — as usual, the fresh fruit platters and pastries were arranged on the table up on the sun deck — Emma answered a few of Jenna's burning questions from the night before. Yes, TG was Canadian, well, half Canadian and half Indian, and yes he was super, super-rich.

'I mean, crazy rich. Like blow us out of the water, and use that water to merely fill his pond, rich.'

'Wow.'

'You know I told you he invented that awful app? Clickbait? Well turns out it's awfully clever and he sold a minority share for something ridiculous like half a billion US dollars to Facebook or the government or something. There was some algorithm he'd invented that meant it was far beyond just a dating, swiping, perv-on-girls app. Then of course he invested in bitcoin and other crypto currencies and I mean his wealth just soared. He'll be an excellent investor — cash in, hands off. Just how I like them.'

'Well, he's due in at three o'clock on Monday — oh, and he specifically asked for a private meeting.'

Emma lowered her sunglasses down the bridge of her nose and with all the subtlety of a pantomime cow deliberately rolled her eyes towards where her husband was sitting at the end of the table. 'Darling, it should be you having a private one-on-one with him. I'm spoken for.'

'As am I!' Jenna's little outburst was almost to remind *herself* that her one true love was merely not present, rather than non-existent. 'Plus, I'm sure it's purely so you can talk giant figures in private.'

Reminding herself about Angus — even if it was in the context of the slightly mysterious, but undeniably sexy TG — made Jenna miss him so keenly, she had the urge to go and find a few minutes to herself and try to FaceTime him or at least send a little message. It being 10 a.m. in France meant it was only 4 p.m. in Hong Kong — surely time for a little sexy afternoon chat with his girlfriend? She pressed 'call' on her phone and listened as the ring tone tried to decide what country it was in. After a few very strange beep-like things she heard the familiar voice of her beloved.

'Hello, Gus!'

'Jenna — are you okay?'

'Um. Yes. Fine, why?' There was a pause and Jenna wondered if this perhaps hadn't been such a great time to call after all. She never usually had to fill a silence with Angus but he was quiet so she carried on talking. 'Just thought I'd see how you are — I miss you.'

'I miss you too, Jenks.'

'You sound, I don't know, unwell. Are you okay?'

'Terrible headache. Must be the humidity out here getting to me.' As he spoke, Jenna thought about how perfect the sea breezes made the temperature out here on the Riviera — her hair had barely frizzed once — and she wished she could make Angus feel better. Maybe she should have gone to Hong Kong with him? She hated the thought of him being so uncomfortable while she lapped up the luxury on the yacht.

'Do look after yourself, darling. I've got heaps for us to do when you get here — plus I've just met someone so rich he makes Monty BH look like a pauper. And the best thing was, he managed to even shut Bertie up — I've never seen her gawp like a trout before, which is kind of apt as she's off to get lip fillers so she might look like one too, soon.'

'Steady on . . .'

'If you'd seen how rude she was to me, you'd be much less "judgy", oh darling one.'

'I'm sure.' He paused a little bit. 'Tell me though, you are okay, aren't you? Nothing odd going on?'

'No. Why on earth do you ask?'

'No reason. Just take care of yourself, JJ. Got to go — Ms Ling needs to see me. Speak later, though.'

'Love you.'

'Love you.'

Angus made sure the call was properly disconnected before slipping his phone into his back pocket. He'd woken up that morning by the kitchen doors of his hotel. The morning porter had almost tripped over him, and thinking he was just another drunk Westerner, had left him there, but not without turning on the radio really loud in the washing-up room and sloshing a bucket of water all over him. Angus hadn't been in much of a mood to complain, his head felt like it'd been split open and the pain raced through his brain from ear to ear as he staggered round to the front of the hotel. A rather disdainful look from the doorman was the only welcome he got and he had to prove he was a hotel guest by delving into his wallet — luckily still on him — to find his electronic room key before they'd let him in further than the lobby. The doorman had leant down and picked up a plain business card that had fluttered to the ground as Angus had tugged at the room key to get it out of his wallet. As the doorman passed it over to Angus he noticed there was nothing on it, save a golden sun and a neatly handwritten phone number. A reminder of his midsummer deadline and his contact, no doubt, for the five million US dollars that he'd have to hand over to save Jenna's, and probably his own, life.

By 9 a.m. he was showered and had gulped down three paracetamol, but was feeling no better as flashbacks of the previous night's conversation filled his head. Jenna would die unless he could find five million dollars. The Voice had made that abundantly clear. He also felt ashamed of himself — that one lapse in his self-control all those years ago had killed a man. But had he? He could have sworn he had left him groaning but very much alive on the bar's floor as he and Pei Ling had made their escape out of the kitchen fire escape. But The Voice didn't seem like the sort of man to listen to his defence and he'd made his mind up, rightly or wrongly, that Angus had been responsible for his nephew's death. Angus had considered his options as he walked the short journey to the Stafford Ling offices. By mid afternoon he'd decided and as he had explained to Ms Ling when he resigned from her project, he felt he had no choice but to quit now and head back to Europe. He had to be there to protect Jenna, and do what he could to raise the money. So when Jenna had phoned him, just two minutes after he'd left Pei Ling's office he'd been caught by surprise — the sound of her voice, so upbeat, so cheery — he was worried at first that something had happened but no, she was fine. The Voice was at least keeping to his end of the bargain and Angus had until 21 June — just two weeks — to find the ransom. He pocketed his phone and looked at his desk. Not much to tidy up from only a few weeks of work. He logged out of his machine for the last time, grabbed his coat and left.

'Love you.' Jenna wished she could chat all morning but as she hung over the main deck, her phone clamped to her ear she'd spied something — someone — on the quayside.

Angus said his goodbyes and Jenna kissed him lots down the phone line and then disconnected the call, placing the phone safely into the back pocket of her jeans. She looked down at the harbour again but he was gone. She was sure she'd seen TG Wilkinson walking towards her boat — well, the Blake-Howard's boat — but it was starting to feel like a rather luxurious home-from-home for her now. Jenna peered over the balustrade again and had just decided to give up and go to find Emma and no doubt something to do when she felt a hand on her shoulder. She turned and her eyes were once again consumed by the mesmerising dark chocolate of those of TG Wilkinson.

'Oh! Hell . . . I mean, hello.' Jenna blurted out — wondering if she looked and sounded as much of an idiot as she felt.

'Hey, Jenna.' If he did think she was a complete numpty, TG was giving nothing away.

'I'm so sorry, you've caught me a bit on the hoof. I thought you were scheduled in to see Emma on Monday?'

'Happens it's not Emma I'm here to see.'

'Oh, right. Well I'm not sure where Monty or Captain Avery are—'

'Jenna.' His tone confirmed Jenna's tiny bit of suspicion that he was actually here to see *her*.

'Oh. Um. What can I do for you?' She felt, rather than saw, him move a bit closer towards her and she subconsciously took a little step back, but was caged by the varnished wood of the balustrade. TG laughed, not a scary 'I have you now' laugh, but a warm, innocent chuckle.

'Jenna.' He stopped laughing but a smile stayed on his face as he spoke. 'I want to make you an offer. Come and work for me. Your party last night was sensational — you handled everyone so well. It was a pleasure to watch you work.'

'Thank you, I . . .' Jenna was totally lost for words. His compliments were making her feel amazing — in fact, what with her career recently being about as successful as a waterproof teabag, hearing such positive praise was quite mind-addling. She pressed her lips together in thought and tried to think of something professional to reply — something that a successful career person would say.

'If you came to work on my yacht *Clickbait*, I'd offer you a proper guest cabin, the work would be light but hopefully fun — just your average PA stuff, a few parties — and the pay would be, well, good.'

'Wow. I mean, thank you Mr Wilkin—' his slight frown made her change tack, 'I mean, TG. I'm flattered, really I am, but I'd feel terrible leaving Emma and Monty in the lurch when really it was them doing *me* the favour.' Jenna told TG about how she'd needed to earn some extra cash and how her friend Bertie had come up with the idea and introduced her to Emma Blake-Howard. TG listened but Jenna, who knew full well her mouth was running away with her and she was helpless at stopping it, perceived him to have slightly switched off. Although she knew she was doing the honourable thing (*bloody noblesse oblige – should be called jobless oblige*), she couldn't help but think she'd just turned down the opportunity of the century.

'Hey, no worries. Look, I've gotta split. See you on Monday.'

His retreating figure caused a little flutter in Jenna and she was about to call out after him, to say . . . what? She didn't know. Perhaps just to make the moment of being headhunted, the pleasure in being praised, the joy of realising that you can be recognised for a job well done, last a bit longer. But before she could mention anything she heard her name being called from the sun deck and Jenna knew — even though it was a Saturday — that break time was over and the post-party debrief, plus plans for more meetings, was all she would have time to think about for the rest of the weekend.

17

The next day was Sunday, and as Jenna had earned a bit of time off she caught the bus down to Larvotto Beach in the morning. This stretch of stones and sand was to the east of Monte Carlo and Emma had recommended it as a swimming spot, especially as they had no plans to take the *Wavy Sloanes* out for a while and no one would ever consider the harbour a nice place for a dip. And Emma had been right, as the shallows near the beach, with piers and swimming platforms, were much more pleasant to swim in than the deep-watered bays or open sea that the yacht sometimes moored up in.

Jenna had taken a towel and her new Chanel bikini and thought she'd recce the place for when, eventually, Angus could join her down here. She thought about her little staff cabin on the *Wavy Sloanes*, and then rather naughtily remembered TG's offer of a proper guest cabin on *Clickbait*. If she worked somewhere with better accommodation, then surely when Angus finally got back from Hong Kong he could stay on board too? Although, to be fair, the Blake-Howards were so accommodating no doubt they would let him stay — and maybe upgrade her room for the weekend?

She pondered these things as she braced herself for the chill of the seawater, and kept wondering as she tried to do a few strokes while keeping her hair dry. Kids played in the shallows near her and there weren't any breakers as such, just a gentle swell every time a jet ski got a little close. After her swim, she found the municipal changing rooms — their peeling walls and drab lighting something of an anachronism compared to the luxury of the facilities on the *Wavy Sloanes* — and then decided to have a little light lunch all by herself — bliss — in one of the restaurants that lined the sea front. As she walked along she paused by each one, and scanned the menus. Some — even with their beachcomber-style decor and rushed-off-their-feet waiters — were the same price as white-tablecloth places she'd been to once or twice in London. But then they were serving truffled lobster and caviar-topped salads. Luckily there were a few cheaper ones with simpler food that she reckoned she could justify with her first pay packet. Perhaps somewhere along here could be where she treated Angus to a birthday lunch — maybe they could come back after the summer?

She chose a restaurant and found herself a table in the shade. With so much sand underfoot, she kicked off her white plimsolls and scrunched her toes into it, then looked down at the menu wondering what would be beneficial to the waistline. A waiter whirled past with an enormous pizza going to another table, and waistline be damned, the thought of a quattro stagioni with extra olives had made up Jenna's mind for her. Once she'd ordered and confirmed to the waiter that yes, the *grande* pizza was just for her, and no, no one was coming to join her, she rested her chin in her hands and looked out over the buzz of the other diners, past the sand of the beach and out to sea. Massive yachts were moored out there and jet skis zipped around them. The aquamarine-blue sea glinted and shone in the sunlight — if she could bottle that colour, this feeling of freedom, the smell of the sea, the hormones rocketing around from the beautiful, long-limbed teenagers lunching with their well-to-do parents — well, she'd make a bloody fortune selling it on a cold February day in London. Monaco, she mused, was a playground for the rich — and boy, what a playground. Boats, bikes, cars, casinos, restaurants, shopping . . . It was all about pleasure. There was nothing to fear here either — there was no street crime, or dodgy-looking blokes on corners — nothing to ruffle the feathers (or fur coats) of the super-rich as they went about their day in a wonderfully guilt-free way.

Her pizza arrived and once more she had to insist to the waiter that she was dining solo so he could clear the other place setting away. Just as she was tucking in (honestly, so worth the calories) her phone buzzed on the table.

Max is here. Come and play.

The lack of niceties was Bertie to a tee. That self-belief that the person reading the message would be so desperate to join you that a little thing like 'hello you' or 'xxx' at the end wasn't needed. Still, although proving Bertie right wasn't one of Jenna's favourite pastimes, she was coming to the end of her this-is-nice-being-alone tolerance and did quite fancy seeing what kind of mischief Bertie was getting up to. Plus, every evening Emma and Monty had invited her to join them as they ate and she really felt very lucky to have done so, but now all the major conversational topics had been covered (and for the Blake-Howards these were, in no particular order, where you went to school, where you live in London, where you live in the country — this is not an either/or situation — who you employ to look after your children and where you ride/shoot/hunt) Jenna thought it might be good to find some of her own fun. She quickly typed back a little message — *Sure thing, where and when?* — and had to swallow a little laugh when the answer came through.

Nikki Beach. Now, sweetie.

Of course. Where else would Bertie have set up residence for the afternoon than at the very exclusive poolside bar at the top of the Fairmont Hotel.

I have a cabana.

The staccato texts were coming through now, and Jenna could imagine each one being tip-tapped out with Bertie's long, immaculately manicured nails.

Max has a surprise for you.

God, those words would have made Jenna tremble with excitement a couple of years ago. But since she'd met Angus — darling Angus — her long-held lust for Max had totally disappeared. Still, she was intrigued as to what this surprise could be. She tapped back a holding message and weighed up the pros and cons of going out with Bertie dressed like she was — slightly grubby white jeans and a baggy Breton-stripe T-shirt. Cons: not the usual Nikki Beach attire, or so she'd heard, but what the hell. She wiped the corners of her mouth with her napkin and checked her make-up in her compact mirror. Not great, but it would have to do — and, pros, the yacht wasn't so far away if she absolutely had to go back and change. She finished her pizza — yes, all by herself, thanks Mr Waiter — and paid her bill.

18

'Honestly, my friend is over there. Look she's waving at me.'

Jenna was struggling to convince the bouncer that for once in her life she really was meant to be the right side of the red velvet rope. Perhaps the plimsolls and baggy T-shirt hadn't been the best idea when trying to get into one of the most glamorous and exclusive pool bars in the world, situated as it was on the rooftop of the famous Fairmont Hotel. The hotel was right on the edge of the water and the views from the bar — and its pool — were fabulous. The sun was still high in the sky and party-goers were lounging in and out of the pool during a chill-out session by the DJ. Jenna had spotted Bertie in her private cabana — one of those four-poster bed type things with wafting white curtains. The bouncer followed Jenna's pointing finger and saw the woman in the gold lamé swimsuit with a mane of golden hair accept and sign for another bottle of Cristal champagne. He raised his eyebrows at Jenna as if to say, 'you honestly want me to believe that *you* know *her*' when Max came up behind him and vouched for her, with the help of a fifty-euro note. Once past the ropes, he enveloped Jenna in a big bear hug and then blew his usual raspberry on her neck as his endearing form of hello.

'Urg, gerrroff.' She playfully batted him away. 'Thanks, though. I thought old jobsworth back there wasn't going to let me in!'

'And suffer Bertie's wrath? I don't think he'd dare . . .' Max winked at her and Jenna laughed, relieved that even if he did notice her completely unglamorous clothes he hadn't called her out on them. He led her over to the cabana, passing white-mattressed sunloungers that butted up against the pool, glamorous denizens of Monaco and wealthy holidaymakers enjoying the atmosphere of the chilled-out DJ and her mix of tunes from the decks. Max made small talk as they navigated their way through the bronzed and toned sunbathers, and Jenna started to tell him about the party on the yacht and how much she was enjoying her job when she noticed that Bertie wasn't alone in the cabana. Jenna saw a hand reach over and pass the golden swimsuited goddess a glass of champagne and Jenna's heart quickened as she recognised the pale blond smattering of hairs and classic Omega watch on the wrist. She almost burst into a run when she realised that the mystery man hiding behind the purposefully discreet curtains of the cabana was . . . Angus!

'Gus!' Jenna whipped back the curtain and almost fell on her boyfriend, who wrapped his spare arm around her while flailing the other one around trying to find somewhere to put his glass down.

'JJ,' his voice was muffled by her hair in his face. Max helped Angus out with his glass and Jenna felt his strong arms wrap around her completely.

'Oh God, I've missed you, I've missed you.' She kissed his neck and pressed her face into his chest, relishing the feeling of his arms caressing her back.

'When you two have quite finished . . .' Bertie's voice brought Jenna back to reality (if you could call this bizarre set-up anything close to Jenna's usual reality) and, once she had untangled herself from her boyfriend, she accepted a glass of fizz from her friend.

'Surprised?' Angus looked earnestly at her.

'Yes!'

'You can thank *moi*,' Bertie chimed in. 'For it is I who organised this little *ménage à quatre*.'

'Really?' Jenna looked over to Bertie and back to Angus.

Bertie changed tack. 'Well, you know, this bit. The *denoue-ment*,' she waved her hand over the cabana, 'the surprise. I thought it would be more fun than the usual "I'm coming", "oh good, see you soon" blah blah type of thing. Yawn.'

'But how did you know Angus was coming over at all — if I didn't?' Jenna felt a little bit hurt that Angus hadn't even hinted that he was on his way over — she'd only spoken to him yesterday morning. 'You didn't say anything to me.' She released her grip on him slightly and took another sip from her glass of champagne, hoping no one could notice the slight shake in her hand.

'No.' Angus reached over and held Jenna's hand tightly as he explained. 'I got press-ganged into coming over here earlier. The guy who wants his villa done was shouting louder than usual at the chaps back in London so the whole project has been brought forward. So I had to leave HK pretty damn quick and fly over.'

'Why didn't you text me?' It wasn't that Jenna wasn't happy to have Angus here now, or that she didn't like surprises, but she did feel a little left out.

'It was honestly so last minute, JJ. I was out of the office and on a plane before I could think. Then I bumped into Max at Nice and he offered me a lift in the helicopter charter he had booked — hence why I'm here.'

Max chipped in. 'Afraid I let slip Angus's whereabouts to Bertie as we took off and she took it on herself to surprise you.'

Jenna didn't want to look miffed in front of her friends, and really, she wasn't, but there was something odd about the situation. Still, as she sipped her champagne she soon forgot any misgivings and settled into the cabana as if she was a regular.

The four friends caught up over more champagne — Jenna dreaded to think what Bertie's bar bill was going to be — and as the DJ's music grew louder and Jenna grew more weary — the hard work and adrenalin of the last few days, plus the extra excitement of seeing Angus today, and quite a few glasses of champagne, meant she suddenly felt incredibly tired.

'Where are you staying, Gus? I don't think, I mean, Captain Avery's very strict.'

'Don't worry, JJ, it's all sorted. Fancy a personalised tour of my suite?'

'Suite?'

'Comes with the territory.'

'What do you mean?'

'Well, the villa owner. He decided he needed his architect close by, so he's rented me a suite. Here. In the Fairmont.'

Jenna threw her arms around him again — tiredness replaced by more adrenalin — and once they'd bid goodnight to a very smug Bertie and chilled out Max, she happily took Angus's hand and followed him down into the hotel.

Angus was so relieved to see Jenna alive and well that his little lie was, he hoped, forgivable. This hotel suite wasn't being sponsored by his rich client — far from it, that had been a lie too and the project on the hill wasn't due to start for a week or two. He had enough to pay for this hotel suite, sure — and keep Jenna feeling happy and safe and as if nothing was wrong. But where on earth was he going to get five million dollars? Even at Nikki Beach he'd seen them. Or at least he thought he had. Every breeze-licked curtain revealed an assassin, every shadowy corner concealed a foe. All he could do was hope that they stuck to their word, and their deadline, and gave him the time to find the money. And in the meantime, he had Jenna now, in his arms, in his bed, her warm, soft body pressed up against his, their skin clinging together as they each found their own bliss between the sheets and then, once both completely satisfied, they lay there together, the sheets now as tangled as their legs as they wrapped each other up in their loving arms.

19

Jenna brushed her hands down her trousers to try to rid them of any lingering creases. She'd crept back onto the Blake-Howard's yacht at about 7 a.m., and although she got a few raised eyebrows from the crew who were already up and about, cleaning the deck and laying out breakfast, she'd been able to sneak down to her cabin without Emma or Monty, or even worse, the judgmental eye of Captain Avery, seeing her. Not that it should matter — she was a grown adult who as far as she was aware was an employee not a prisoner — but there was something deliciously naughty about creeping around having done, probably, the most glamorous 'walk of shame' ever through the early morning, just waking, streets of Monte Carlo. Where else would you see, as you yourself were still dressed in yesterday's clothes, a bell boy in full uniform walking three elegant saluki dogs, a Ferrari revving past, complete with bejewelled and sunglass-wearing passenger who was otherwise naked, and no fewer than forty boxes of fresh oysters being loaded onto a yacht in the harbour.

At least the way back to the port was downhill from the Fairmont and Jenna wasn't in too bad a state hangover-wise, as she and Angus had worked off their alcohol quite sufficiently. In fact, Jenna had pondered as she slipped her plimsolls off and scrambled up onto the walkway, which had been raised enough to deter most people trying to get on board, she should probably write an advice piece for the *Huffington Post* — or perhaps *Cosmopolitan* — on how proper, sweaty, passionate, elbow-grazingly great sex really was a hangover buster. She hadn't felt this fantastic for ages. She'd had a quick shower and found some slightly crumpled khaki Capri pants in her cabin (*I really must send some bits and bobs off to the laundry*, she thought, but she still couldn't quite get her head round the fact that there was someone specifically paid to wash her knick-knocks) and a white shirt and now she stood, up on the sun deck of the *Wavy Sloanes*, gazing back up towards the Fairmont — her heart sending out little messages of love to her boyfriend, who she hoped was still lying sexily naked in the tangle of sheets left over from their lovemaking.

Lunchtime came and went and Jenna was doing a masterful job of keeping Emma up to date on who was next in her schedule, briefing her on their background (thank you, Linked-In) and arranging dresses on mannequins to appeal to who was in the meeting — be it couture styles for the magazine editors and photographers or more wearable creations for boutiques and investors. At about five minutes to three, Jenna, who was in the guest cabin which had been taken over by Emma as a temporary office-cum-dressmaker's studio, was told by one of the crew that 'some hot guy' was waiting on the main deck to see her. With a roll of her eyes, Jenna reprimanded the younger girl, but chuckled to herself. TG Wilkinson ready for his three o'clock meeting. Some of the dresses that had graced the catwalk only a couple of nights ago were looking slightly more crumpled now as they were tossed on the wide king-sized bed, so Jenna scooped them up and found a hanging space for them in the spacious wardrobe. Her meeting with TG on Saturday had played through her mind quite a bit and she glanced at herself in the mirror — just to check it was only her going to greet the potential investor, not any remnants of the kale-leaf salad stuck in her teeth — before heading down to the main deck to find him.

'Hey, Jenna!' He was waiting for her and thrust out his hand as she descended the narrow side staircase down to the deck.

'Hello! Welcome back to BoBo by Emma Blake-Howard.'

'There you go with the corporate spiel again.' He winked at her. 'Tell me something, Jenna, don't you wish you could just be you — say what you want to say, do what you want to do?'

Jenna was a bit taken aback — not just at the bluntness of the question and slight rudeness of it, but at the sheer breadth of it. How was she to answer that level of existentialism in a professional, breezy manner?

Luckily, TG chipped in again. 'Hey, just kidding. You're doing great.'

'Thank you . . . I think. Anyway, do come this way.' She led him up the staircase that she'd just walked down and up another one onto the upper deck. 'There's iced water and lemonade up on the sun deck with Emma, but can I fetch you anything else? Coffee? Tea?'

'Me . . .' TG finished off the old flirty saying and Jenna blushed. He carried on, 'No, you're fine. I'm sure I'll get everything I need from Emma. I'll see you after the meeting.'

Jenna nodded at him in some wonderment — he was still a total enigma to her — but if he went into business with Emma then at least the last few days of schmoozing and meetings could be classed as a success and she was sure Emma would give her a few days off to go and play with Angus. With this thought in mind she showed him up to where Emma was sitting and then retreated back to the main deck and the shade of an awning. She popped her phone out of her back pocket and responded to her messages, saving the one she saw from Angus until last. Her mum wanted an update and Sally had sent one too — *Feeling fat and hot and bored. Wish you were here, or even better wish I was there with you! News please!!* — Poor Sals, Jenna had hardly had time to update her properly on the fun she'd been having — and the fact that she finally felt like she'd found something she was not only good at, but also was quite fulfilling. Then she flicked onto Angus's message — *Can you escape for supper tonight? Little Italian up the hill . . . xxx* — she smiled at the message and slipped her phone back in her pocket as she considered her reply. Jenna may not have mastered many skills over her varied career, but 'looking busy when the boss walked by' was one of them, and she didn't want to be caught gawping at her phone screen by Emma if the meeting ended early.

Up on the sun deck Emma was having a very different meeting with the startlingly handsome TG Wilkinson than she had prepared for. Far from doing the major sales pitch about Indian FairTrade deals and financial forecasting, she had in fact spent the last ten minutes discussing Jenna with him. She hadn't really ever considered that her PA — and for quite some days now, she really had started to think of her as a friend — might be *headhunted* from her. Not by someone like TG Wilkinson anyway. It was a frightful bore, to be fair — Jenna had been such a dream with the organising of her launch party and fashion show and she was one of those few people who could mix with princes and paupers and be able to chat to both the same.

'There's no real contract, per se.' Emma answered one of TG's queries as he wrote a number on a piece of paper in front of her.

'Oh, I say.' Emma looked at the paper. And then at the zeros. If this billionaire wanted her PA so bad, then really he'd only need to ask *her*, not buy her. But those zeros would count as a wonderful cash injection for the brand . . . 'I mean, it's not what I thought this meeting was about, TG, but I would be very happy to accept this *investment* on behalf of Jenna, if perhaps we could think of it like that?'

'You can think of it any which way you like, your honourable ladyship.'

'Emma, please.' She was looking at the paper still and wondering if this counted as pimping. 'Of course I can only agree if Jenna is happy with the situation.'

'Leave that to me. I spoke to her before and I got the impression that her loyalty to you was the only thing holding her back.'

Emma was about to be a little miffed when he mentioned speaking to Jenna before about it, but at his insistence that her friend had been loyal . . . this man was a charmer.

'Well, if you think she's happy. I mean, I will miss her. Tell me again, you're not thinking of launching a fashion brand or anything, are you? Industrial espionage?'

Emma couldn't think why on earth this tech giant would be the slightest bit interested in fashion, but she had to do her due diligence.

TG laughed and Emma smiled back at him. 'Emma, you're a funny lady. I like it. But I like Jenna even more, so if you don't mind I'll go and offer her my proposal. And you can keep that little sum we agreed to yourself, if you like — as you say, it's my private investment in securing a glowing future for your company.'

Emma leaned over and shook his hand, the bangles on her wrist clattering as if to ring in the deal, and watched as he confidently left the table and hopped down the stairs to where Jenna was waiting on the main deck. She couldn't help but feel slightly uneasy, as if some whisper of the slave trade had just blown across her table, but she reassured herself that it was merely a business transaction — a settlement payment for break of contract, even just a verbal one, and an investment that could take BoBo stratospheric.

Si, signor, but only if you promise to do that thing to me again tonight . . . xxx

Jenna sent the flirty message back to her boyfriend and looked up from her phone. She quickly pocketed it and went about 'looking busy' again, sorting through some papers on the bench seat next to her, as TG Wilkinson ambled down the staircase towards her. Judging by the look on his face, the meeting had gone well. If *he* looked this happy then Emma must be cartwheeling across the deck! As Jenna raised herself off the seat, she was surprised that TG instead bounded over and sat down next to her.

'Come, sit down again,' He indicated the seat next to him and once again Jenna felt the power and intensity of his deep brown eyes.

'I really should go and see how Emma is—'

'Why do I get the feeling that you're always trying to avoid me?'

Jenna was mortified. Was she? And why was she? It had just taken all her willpower to even suggest leaving his presence — perhaps avoiding him should be exactly what she *should* be doing. She opened and closed her mouth a couple of times, trying once again to find something vaguely professional to say. Admitting to him — and to herself — that she found him intriguingly beguiling probably wasn't going to help matters.

'I'm not, I mean, I—'

TG burst out laughing and patted the seat next to him. 'Come on, sit here. I've got something I want to ask you.' Jenna paused and then sat down next to him. If she had antennae they would be vibrating like crazy right now. 'So, I've had a chat with Emma and we've agreed that she can let you go — if you think you'd like to come and work for me.'

'Work . . . for you?' Jenna was flabbergasted — and felt foolish knowing that she'd just been discussed and possibly bartered over behind her back.

'I know you said before that you owed her for the chance she gave you. Well, I've sorted that out.'

'But . . . I mean, I'm a bit confused to be honest.' And more than confused. She was a little hurt that Emma Blake-Howard wanted rid of her so easily.

'Look — I saw how you handled yourself with the models, your boss — even that wasp of a woman, your friend, Bertram or whatever she's called.'

'Bertie,' Jenna corrected him, but smiled. His words had mollified her — if he could see that a Nobel Peace Prize was the least that was deserved after dealing with Bertie — well, maybe he would be a good boss. 'What would you want me to do for you?'

'Same as here. Organise a couple of parties. Help me out with some admin.' His eyes were locked on hers and again she was captivated by their beautiful conker-like brown. Flecks of gold rimmed the irises — she hadn't noticed that before. 'I had to leave my last PA in Sacramento — she was too tied to her kids to spend a summer out here. So I need a bit of help just keeping up to date with my emails and that sort of thing.'

'I'll have a think.'

'Fifty thousand euros a year.'

'Bloody hell.' Jenna was taken aback by TG's instant offer. But before she could blink the dollar signs away from her eyes she realised something. 'I don't really want to be here all year, though — it's only a summer job.'

'Fine. Fifty thousand for the summer.'

'Wow.' Jenna did a mental check and worked out that that was roughly 100 serious shopping trips round Selfridges with still a bit left over to get Angus something for his birthday.

'Let me know by tomorrow. Here's my card.' He passed over a thick business card — blank except for a small, gold embossed TG and underneath that his mobile phone number. 'It's my private cell. I don't give this to everyone, you know.'

Jenna fingered the heavy card, looking down at the gold embossed letters and numbers. Then she braced herself to look into his eyes again. 'No need. I'll do it.'

'Great!' TG's demeanour changed — he was open and friendly again, a broad grin showing off his perfect white teeth. 'Come over to *Clickbait* tomorrow and we'll get you settled in.'

Jenna, slightly dumbfounded by her own sudden decisiveness, just nodded to him and smiled as he got up to leave.

'You won't regret this, Jenna. It's going to be out-of-the-park amazing.' He casually saluted a goodbye and left her sitting there. What was it her mother had once said? *If they say you won't regret it, you almost certainly will . . .*

20

If you mean the thing with the feather then YES. Supper's on me x

Jenna looked at Angus's reply as she slowly walked up the road towards Casino Square. The little Italian restaurant that Angus had suggested was a bit of a hike from the Blake-Howard's yacht and the harbour in general, but she felt like she needed the exercise. If this Italian restaurant had portion sizes the same as the one on Larvotto Beach, then she reckoned she could easily come out as round as a meatball and plump as a *pomodoro*. The walk also gave her the time to think over what she was going to tell Angus. Emma had been sweet about her leaving their employment after Jenna had found her up on the sun deck of the yacht following their separate meetings with TG.

'I really thought it might be better for you, sweetie,' Emma had said. 'He can pay you so much more than we can and I don't think it'll be half the work.'

'I said yes. But it is with your blessing, isn't it? I don't want to leave you in the lurch. He wants me to move over to his yacht tomorrow.'

'These types always get their way.' Emma had sounded rather sanguine.

Jenna had tried to lighten the mood. 'Well, he won't be getting *that* sort of way with me!'

Emma smiled at her but didn't comment and instead said, 'Think of it as a bursary.'

A bursary, a bursary . . . Jenna repeated the word over to herself as she walked around Casino Square passing the front of the Café de Paris on her way up to the Italian restaurant. She'd have to come back here one night with

Angus and do some serious people-watching. Angus, though . . . how would he feel about her working one-on-one with a handsome billionaire? Of course he could trust her, she'd just have to convince him of it.

'You're joking?'

'Nope.' Angus had just delivered a particularly interesting bombshell in reply to Jenna telling him her job news.

'TG Wilkinson is the tech spod who wants that fancy villa up in the hills?'

'So, in a way, we'll both be working for him.' Angus, although not over the moon at the prospect of his girlfriend cohabitating — or co-yachtitating in this case — with someone he knew to be incredibly rich and incredibly driven, was quite relieved at her news.

'It's great money.' Jenna had sounded like she was hell-bent on justifying her new job, and Angus took a moment for the reality of the situation to sink in. On the plus side, if it was anything like the specs for his villa, TG's yacht would have so much more protection on board than the Blake-Howards' one. There would be panic rooms and state-of-the-art security — plus good old-fashioned heavies, no doubt. The parties would be more discreet and harder for assassins to infiltrate — these were all positives — but of course the downside was that Jenna would be working for some get-what-he-wants, control-freak billionaire, with all that entails. If only he could tell her the truth, why he was okay with her going on board another man's yacht and working so closely with him. She would never forgive him though. He ran his hand down his cheek, feeling the white welt of the scar that was a constant reminder of the death he supposedly caused a few years ago. And now he was going to have to make pay back — and he was damned if he was going to sacrifice Jenna to their demands.

'I think it's a great opportunity,' he said, at least without lying this time. 'But maybe you could add a little condition onto your contract? That I'm allowed on board occasionally?' He winked at Jenna, who much to his pleasure reached out and held her hand against his cheek, his scar.

'Oh, as his architect extraordinaire, that is a given, Gus, don't you worry. Plus, you and me, we're a package. Speaking of packages . . . I told Emma not to wait up, so you can bet I'm ready to unwrap your Italian sausage later.'

Jenna's natural flirty behaviour and good humour worked wonders to ease the stress that had been building in Angus since he last saw her this morning. His logical mind knew she would be okay — the deadline wasn't for a while yet — but he had thought of her every moment during the day, even taking a pair of binoculars and standing at a view point overlooking Port Hercule, focusing on the *Wavy Sloanes* so he could check up on her.

The starter of oozing burrata cheese with truffle arrived and Angus watched as his beautiful girlfriend tucked in. It was one of the many things he loved about her — her love of good food and wine made her excellent company, whether it was at home on the sofa or here in Monte Carlo in a gutsily good restaurant. He vowed again not to let anyone hurt a hair on her head. He changed tack on the conversation.

'Looks like my project is slightly delayed in starting after that mad dash to get out here.'

'What a pain. Typical rich sod.' Jenna smiled and winked at Angus, who nodded in agreement as he chewed. 'Poor Pei Ling — I'm sure she would have appreciated you being out there longer in that case.' Jenna paused as she popped a ripe tomato into her mouth. 'I'm glad you're here, though.'

'And Bertie got to play the hero of the hour pretending she'd reunited us.'

'Ha.' She filled Gus in on some of the barbs Bertie had thrown in her direction while she'd been bored and Max-free hanging around on the Blake-Howards' yacht. 'It's one of the things TG said he was impressed by. How I handled her.'

'Well, as long as he's more interested in you handling her and not him handling you, I agree with him. You are amazing at dealing with her.'

'It's like I say to Sally,' she shrugged. 'Just occasionally you get a flicker of the old Bertie, the fun Bertie, our old mate. And I guess there's also a part of me that quite likes hanging around with her for the glamour — I mean, here I am in Monaco, working on a bloody super yacht, for God's sake!'

'And all I could offer you was sweaty Hong Kong.' *And a world of danger and lies besides*, thought Angus.

'You know I'd go anywhere with you — if I could work too.' Jenna pressed her hand into his and his heart welled up with love for his honest, innocent, genuine girlfriend.

Luckily for Jenna, the Fairmont was mostly downhill from the little Italian restaurant — as their meal had indeed been a feast and after the burrata with truffle, they'd shared bruschetta with deliciously ripe tomatoes, then linguine with lobster and garlic and finally an affogato dessert — the chilled espresso helping keep Jenna's eyelids open as her stomach did its best to send her to sleep to give it time to process all the fabulous food. She held Angus's hand as they wandered down through a small park and around the back of the Café de Paris, past the Buddha Bar with its glamorous female clients — and *their* 'clients' — sipping champagne and tossing their blow-dried locks. A party in one corner roared with appreciation as five bottles of Laurent-Perrier Rosé arrived at their table, each one topped with a sparkling mini firework. Jenna

remembered how Max had always referred to that champagne as LPR — he said the initials really stood for Liquid
Panty Remover — and in this case he might genuinely be
right. She wondered why Angus wasn't really watching. He
seemed more intent on staring into the darkness, behind
the stone balustrades, as if he was searching for something
she couldn't see.

'You okay, love?' she asked as his grip on her hand
tightened.

'Hmm? Oh yes, fine. Sorry.'

Stopping to let a mini convoy of Lamborghinis go past,
they crossed the road and were at the Fairmont just as
Jenna decided that Angus's hand was only the start of
where she wanted to touch. As the lift took them up to the
floor of his suite, she had untucked his linen shirt from
his jeans and was already running her hand up his taut
back, feeling his muscles react as she lightly scratched her
fingernails over his skin. By the time Angus unlocked the
door of his room, she had done her best to undo his belt
buckle and as soon as the door was kicked closed behind
them she had his shirt off over his head and her hands
running down his chest towards his waistline.

'Now, where was that sausage you promised me?' She
tried to sound sexy, but the word sausage just sounded
silly and she giggled to herself, but in so doing made
Angus even more aroused than he already had been and he
turned his attention onto her, which Jenna was not about
to complain about. Wordplay was fun, but foreplay was
so much better. She let Angus remove her silky top, and
relished the touch of his lips and fingers on her slightly
sunburnt skin. His hands pressed into her and she was
enveloped by his arms, wrapping her own around his
naked torso, once again using her nails to entice him and
stimulate him. In seconds her bra was undone and falling
to the floor and Angus released her slightly in order to

twirl her around. With her back to him now she reached her arms up to cradle his head to hers and let him wrap his arms around her, cupping her breasts and playing with her nipples as she nipped at his ear and arched her back so that she pushed herself more forcefully into his hands. He gradually moved downwards, slipping his hand into the waistline of her short skirt and without any hesitation she helped him rid herself of it so she was merely down to her knickers. Twirling back round she faced him and pulled him down onto the bed on top of her and let him slip down to her most private area, carefully removing her lacy briefs before kissing, nibbling and licking her into paroxysms of absolute delight.

21

In another room in the same hotel, Bertie was being treated to the same ministrations by her handsome fiancé. Unlike Jenna, who was absorbed with every lick, kiss, nibble and smooch, Bertie was looking up at her hand, judging her manicure as Max finished off pleasuring her.

'Oh, oh . . . yah, that's right. Uh-huh . . .' she made a few reassuring noises and clenched her thighs together, shaking out her beautifully pedicured foot to simulate her point of climax. Max emerged looking as pleased as punch with himself and Bertie gave him one of her rare smiles − the wrinkle tax was too severe to waste them on too many people.

'Thank you, darling, orgasmic as always,' she lied.

'Pleasure, Berts . . . God, I'm feeling horny now though. My turn?' He indicated his massive erection and started to move towards her for a blow job.

'Ew. No. Maxie. Not now. Get that thing out of my face.' She pushed him back and sat more upright in bed. It wasn't that she didn't want to give her fiancé the same pleasure as he'd just given her, or at least thought he had, but she had some important things to discuss with him.

'Now, Maxie, I'm so glad you're finally here. I say we check out tomorrow and go and stay with Ems and Monty. She's texted to say Jenna is leaving her to go and work for TG Wilkinson, of all people . . .'

'The Silicon Valley guy? Wow.' Max interrupted her and paid for it by having a toe nudged a little too close to his crown jewels for comfort.

'Yes. And I think we should really start looking at yachts to buy ourselves.'

'Bertie, darling, I know you've got the capital arranged, but I'm not sure it's a great idea.'

'Why not?' Surely Max — who should be aligned to her ideals in all ways — would agree they should have their own yacht?

'The running costs can be millions of pounds a year. I don't think, what with the mortgage payments too, that we can afford it, darling.'

This was not the right thing to say to Bertie, who pulled herself away from his hands that had been running up and down her perfectly smooth legs. She got out of the bed, walked in silence across to the bathroom and pulled one of the robes off the back of the door. Swinging it around herself she turned back to the bed and glared at her fiancé. Why wasn't he as ambitious as her? Why didn't he want it all, like she did?

'I don't understand you sometimes, *sweetie*.' She emphasised the final word. 'I feel like sometimes you say things just to hurt me.'

'Berts, don't be silly. Come here.'

'No. *Poor* people don't get blow jobs.' *Or me*, she thought, wondering how long she'd have to leave it before she could invite herself onto TG's yacht.

'For heaven's sake, Bertie, come here and talk to me. Look,' he pulled a pair of pyjama bottoms on to hide his still quite enormous erection. 'All covered up now. Little Max knows playtime is over.'

Even Bertie could see the effort Max had to make to cool himself off. She accepted his invitation back to the bed and they chatted a bit, culminating with the decision that Max should perhaps head back to London to put in some more hours at the office. But she was still annoyed at him. If he couldn't be the one to share her dreams, then should he even be sharing her bed? Or her life?

22

Another day, another walk of shame, thought Jenna to herself as she scrambled on board the *Wavy Sloanes* just before breakfast. Angus had held her close and kissed every inch of her goodbye — the old romantic. Though Jenna wasn't sure if that thing he'd done with his tongue would fall under Jane Austen's view of romance. There seemed to be a new sense of urgency, or intensity perhaps, to Angus's lovemaking at the moment. Jenna couldn't put her finger on it. Still, with the fizz of her orgasm still echoing inside her, she pulled herself up onto the walkway (think of the upper arm toning these early morning break-ins were allowing her!) and tiptoed across the main deck to the stairs down to her cabin.

Clicking the door shut behind her she pulled her suitcase out from where she'd shoved it under the bed and started to pack. She unhooked dresses from the wardrobe hangers and scooped up underwear from the cubby holes. She left the pile of branded white polo shirts, which apart from the top one, hadn't even been touched, let alone worn. Thinking a little souvenir wouldn't be too much of a naughty steal, she folded the one she'd worn momentarily on her first day into her case and concentrated again on clearing out the cupboard. Looking at what else hadn't been worn, Jenna realised that her hastily packed summer wardrobe of floaty skirts and formal wear hadn't really been touched; her life on board a super yacht, though glamorous, had been more white tee than white tie — not to mention, white jeans, white shirts and white linen trousers. There was no end to the amount of white clothing the

Riviera wore. In fact, Emma had told her that just down the coast in Saint-Tropez there was a shop that only sold white clothes. Incredible. And testament to the fact that the lady shoppers of the Côte d'Azur obviously would never have to handle a greasy fuel pump or peel a few beetroot. By about 9 a.m. she was packed and she lugged her case up the stairs and onto the deck. Knowing Emma and Monty would be on the sun deck eating breakfast she headed up there to say her goodbyes — with more than a few mixed emotions.

'We'll miss you, darling girl.' Emma jutted her chin out and raised her cheek expecting a kiss — as if she were receiving the children freshly bathed from Nanny.

'I'll miss you too, Emma.' Jenna meant it too — she'd grown fond of her ethereal, gilded, but masterfully business-minded boss.

'Do come back and say what ho — and do get me invited to any of your new shindigs! I'm really quite jealous. *Clickbait* is by far the biggest yacht in the harbour — you lucky thing.'

'Large or not, I'll be working, so I'm sure it'll be far less glamorous for me.'

'Working, eh?' Monty raised his eyes from the pink pages of the *Financial Times* and grinned at Jenna and then his wife, who grimaced at him.

'Yes, I mean, that's what TG has employed me for.' Jenna knew exactly what Monty was insinuating, but she sure as hell didn't want them to think she was baling for some sort of free ride or, even worse, cheating on Angus. 'I'm definitely working for him.' She added, to underline her point.

'Of course you will be, darling,' Emma reassured her and shot another glare at her husband, but it was deflected by the raised newspaper. 'Don't listen to Monty, he's just being a pickle. And don't worry about me, we've got Bertie and Max coming to stay for a few nights to make up for the fact that you're leaving us for such elevated company.' She winked at Jenna.

Jenna fiddled with her top a bit and then decided to take a seat at the table. TG hadn't told her when he was expecting her and she suddenly felt a bit at sea with the whole situation. She leaned over and picked up a lonely croissant and tore it apart, not bothering with any butter or jam. She paused before shoving a piece into her mouth.

'Emma?'

'Yes.'

'You don't think I'm being a total fool, do you? I mean, it is okay with you that I'm off?'

'TG compensated me very well for losing you.'

'What do you mean?' Jenna felt her hackles rising. She hated feeling like she might be a commodity to be bought or traded.

Whether Emma could sense this or not, she changed tack slightly. 'I mean he's invested heavily in BoBo, which is so marvellous of him, and in turn I said I wouldn't kick up a fuss if you decided to leave us. I am sorry to lose you, though. Though I am also rather grateful for his money. I can whizz off to India now and find a lovely fairtrade factory to upscale the production of the dresses. Oh, Monty!' She tapped his paper to get his attention. 'I've had a *fabulouso* idea. We should see if your friend Chandra will be at his place.'

'Palace, more like.'

'Yes — Udaipur was it? Or Jodhpur?'

'Sounds exotic,' Jenna marvelled at the international reach of Emma and Monty — *of course* they knew a maharajah in Rajasthan, who doesn't? *Well, me*, thought Jenna as she slowly chewed the croissant and pondered what Emma had said. Her hackles had lowered when Emma had described TG's payment as an 'investment'. Perhaps she was getting a bit egotistical, assuming she was worth bartering over. Perhaps, and this would be a career first, she actually had been headhunted for her talents — and if so, she better look professional and not be late for her first day at her new job. So, goodbyes were said, fond farewells uttered and Jenna blinked away a little tear as she hugged Emma a warm goodbye.

'Oh, please say bye to Captain Avery for me,' Jenna added just as she was leaving.

'Will do, though I'm sure you're not going to miss the grumpy old thing.' Emma winked at her. 'Oh but this is too funny — I have to tell you before you go. You know he was adamant about his mister and missus thing — because of bugs?' She made her fingers into quotation marks as she said 'bugs'. 'Well they didn't find anything — *quelle surprise* — but apparently our CCTV feed had been hacked, which is actually a little more serious.' She frowned as if only taking this on board for the first time.

'Who by?'

'He said it was some Chinese coding or something. I don't really understand the ins and outs.'

'Industrial espionage, maybe?' Jenna thought of the dresses all stored on the boat and the lavish launch party.

'Who knows. It's sorted now anyway and we've pulled up the virtual drawbridge! Anyway, off you trot, darling. You'll knock his socks off.' Jenna grinned at Emma's parting shot, but was out of earshot, luckily, when Monty added, under his breath, 'and his trousers.'

23

Even if Jenna had been unsure of which one TG's yacht was — and by now everyone in the harbour was eyeing up the eighty-metre-long Feadship — a Dutch brand, considered to be the best make of yachts in the world ('Ours is only a Heesen, sweetie,' Emma had said, as if it was something to be embarrassed about) — she would have had no trouble finding it as just as she was lugging her suitcase off the *Wavy Sloanes* a large, black Range Rover with tinted windows pulled up on the quayside next to her.

'Ms Jenkins?' the chauffeur asked, but the way he was already walking towards her suitcase told Jenna that he already knew the answer to that one.

'That's me!'

'Please, madam,' the chauffeur gestured to the car — its dark plush interior at odds with the sunshine outside. Jenna climbed in and waited slightly awkwardly as the chauffeur loaded her case. She suddenly didn't know what to do with her hands and scrabbled in her bag for her phone, but then put it back hurriedly in case she was told off for taking photos or something. *There was something almost obscene*, she thought to herself, *about the luxury of being driven a few hundred yards around a marina*. The chauffeur settled himself into his seat and started the engine. As they drove off the doors of the car automatically locked with a 'clunk' that was both reassuring and sort of menacing, and Jenna was encapsulated in the cool, air-conditioned space, closed off from the natural, beautiful light and warm breeze of the world outside.

If the *Wavy Sloanes* was a super yacht, then *Clickbait* was on another level. A mega yacht . . . a super-dooper-I'm-a-super-trooper yacht. The size, Jenna reckoned, of a small cross-channel ferry. The chauffeur drove her right along the harbour — even when it got so narrow that Jenna assumed it was pedestrian only — and as the Range Rover came to a stop she could see nothing of the harbour around her, just the vast exterior of this gleamingly, luxurious yacht rising out of the water before her. It was moored over the other side of Port Hercule from the Blake-Howards' boat because it would not have fitted into the bays next to the *Wavy Sloanes*. It needed to be on this peninsula of moorings, as it was closer in size to a warship than a sailing boat. She felt it loom up over her, almost oppressively. It looked so otherworldly, the metallic finish on the exterior reflected the world around her in a distorted way, and it only felt slightly humanised as she noticed crew were cleaning it, using safety harnesses and carabiner-linked ropes as pulleys to move themselves up and down the storeys of windows. It must be four or five decks high — plus whatever was below the waterline.

Jenna stood and looked up at the behemoth in front of her. Balancing herself with her hands on the small of her back, she arched her neck up and squinted into the bright blue sky trying to see the very top deck. Raising one of her hands to shield her eyes she got a shock when she saw someone leaning over from on high and wave down at her. Her instant impulse was to wave back, but as she did she was blinded again by the brightness of the sky. Was that TG? It must have been. Blinking as she was, it was a disembodied voice that yelled down at her to come on up — but the accent was unmistakable, its warm Canadian tones buffeted by the breeze that swept over the harbour.

The chauffeur brought her suitcase round to the back of the boat where a walkway was partially extended out to meet the quayside. Without either of them needing to buzz, the noise of hydraulic lifts accompanied the movement of the walkway automatically lowering itself down to the quayside. Out of habit Jenna removed her shoes and by the time she was wondering how she was going to carry both handbag, suitcase and shoes, she was rescued from the predicament by two utterly charming – and on instant appraisal, rather hunky – men in white shirts and shorts.

'Let us help you, missus.' The South African voice stopped her from picking anything up.

'Leave it to us, missus,' Tweedle-Dee added, this time the accent was English – London, probably. Jenna chastised herself for thinking of them like that, but they hadn't told her their names, and in this moment her mind was devoid of any better temporary name for them, so overwhelmed was she by the sheer size of the boat she had boarded.

'Thank you both, but honestly I'm not the missus – there's some mistake there!'

'Uh-ha,' The South African, or Tweedle-Dum as Jenna thought of him, managed to both acknowledge and ignore Jenna in one go.

'Still, follow us please, we'll show you on board and to your suite.' Dee took over.

Jenna dutifully followed them on board and tried not to gawp as she was led onto the part of the boat she now knew was called a beach club. In reality, it was a cascade of sand-coloured wooden steps, the full width of the back of the yacht, leading up to the main deck. If it was anything like the Blake-Howards' yacht, these steps would move to reveal storage for the tenders and jet skis, plus make an amazing 'beach' area for lounging around on when the yacht was anchored in a beautiful bay. As she climbed up the steps, the first of many surprises greeted her — at the top there was a swimming pool, which divided the top of the staircase and almost the whole of the main deck in two. Sitting at the top of the steps like this made it into an infinity pool — the view would be awesome, gazing out of the back of the yacht on a day trip out to sea. This, though, was nothing compared to the saloon cabin which led off the main deck. It was a glorious rounded room with vast sliding, curved-glass doors. Inside the pale wood theme continued, picked out with high-lights of copper and rose gold — a metal bookshelf held up-to-date magazines and hardback coffee table books, and copper-coloured light fittings illuminated paintings and architectural details in the room. Two huge, curved, cream-coloured leather sofas were obviously made to fit the shape of the rounded room, and they were tastefully covered in beautiful copper-coloured cushions, with hints of teal and rose pink. A clear glass coffee table sat in the middle of the saloon, and upon it was a copper pot used as a vase that was full of exquisite white peonies in full bloom. The walls that weren't made of glass were hung with paintings of old master-style landscapes and Jenna glanced at them, making a note that she must come back with her art dealer hat on and see if her suspicions about that haywain-looking picture were correct. There was a high chance that they were worthy of national collections. The whole effect of this rounded cabin, this state saloon was one of a constant sunset or sunrise, the pinks, coppers and teals reminding her of those last few moments before the golden orb sets behind the azure horizon.

Tweedle-Dee led her through to another room, this one a smaller reception area dominated by two striking things — a beautiful dark mahogany grand piano and the swirl of a polished-wood spiral staircase — but not the sort you'd find in a normal house, tightly wound like a DNA helix, no, this one was languorous and wide, the steps illuminated by frosted lights on each tread, the handrail a gleaming polished wood that invited anyone to follow it up to the deck above. Jenna did just that and found herself in a dark mirrored internal corridor, the flooring the finest parquet she'd ever seen, the lighting soft and sensual. Tweedle-Dee opened a door and Jenna knew that this was to be her new home. Again, her suitcase had managed to get there before her — *there really must be secret passages, stairwells and hidey-holes all around this boat*, she thought to herself, and she looked around the cabin in astonishment at its beauty and luxury. Cabin really wasn't the word for it. It even kicked Angus's suite at the Fairmont into touch. It was rounded, like the saloon below, and the beautiful sunset colours were picked out again against the dark wood of the parquet flooring and the creamy softness of the bed linen, sheepskin rugs on each side of the vast bed and the interior walls, which were touchably soft and subtly lit behind the skirting boards and cornicing. The bathroom was sublime too, cream marble and copper taps — the widest, deepest tub Jenna had ever seen seamlessly created out of the same marble that lined the walls and floor. With this much marble on board, how did this yacht not sink? Jenna didn't care how, she just loved that she was here and this was her home for the rest of the summer.

A soft voice interrupted her thoughts, 'Hey there, Jenna. Welcome on board.'

'Oh, TG, hi.' He was standing in the doorway of the bathroom and Jenna wondered if owning a boat meant you never had to knock. His dark brown eyes projected such warmth and friendliness towards her, though, that she instantly forgave him his little indiscretion and uncrossed her arms, which had involuntarily gone into a slightly protective stance.

'Like it?'

She opened and closed her mouth a couple of times, and waved her arms around before settling for a simple, 'Yes!'

TG chuckled. 'If you're anything like me, you might never want to leave. Hey, look, I'll let you get settled in then come and join me on the weather deck. If you have trouble finding it, Rob or Seb will show you the way. It's the one with the pool, so hey, why not put your swimmers on — I don't see why we can't have our first meeting poolside.'

Jenna could think of plenty of professional reasons why they shouldn't have their first business meeting poolside, but in the instant that the invitation was offered she could think of none of them. As he turned his back on her to leave — the muscles of it clearly showing through the tight, lightweight cotton shirt he was wearing — all the reasons poured back into her mind. *Bikini? With him? Now?* She rested her hand on the marble of the basin unit to steady herself — *where was a large martini when you needed one*, she wondered as she girded herself for her first day on board *Clickbait*.

24

In the end, her professionalism — and slight worry over 'baguette belly' — won out and Jenna settled for her more modest one-piece costume, hoping that its red and white candy stripes and sturdy shoulder straps would suggest nothing more than a demure, modest woman who could not be tempted away from her boyfriend by some billionaire on a yacht. She had standards you know. Yes — that's definitely the vibe the costume was giving off and although a tiny voice inside her head — in fact, not quite a voice, just a seditious whisper — hinted that maybe the black bikini might be more fun, she quickly covered up both body and mind in a floral kaftan and grabbed her notebook before leaving her cabin suite and heading back down to where she'd first seen the long infinity pool by the steps down to the beach club. She found the saloon again easily enough, and couldn't resist a little explore — surely TG needed time to get into his swimmers too? — and as his new PA she really should know her way around a little . . .

There was no sign of TG there anyway yet, and with her back to the saloon and pool area she followed the corridor past the spiral staircase and piano through to a light-filled dining room, the oval table gleaming in the sunshine that flowed in from the floor-to-ceiling windows. And wow, what a ceiling — it was dotted with micro lights, which Jenna could only imagine gave the impression of a twinkling starlit sky when the sun had set and the dinners had begun. Tracing her fingers along the upholstered linen walls she retreated back to the spiral staircase again and paused to look up at it, noticing how the swirl became like that of an ammonite, the inverted stair treads like the grooves of the fossil's shell, as it wound its way upwards. She could perhaps sneak up there later when she was 'finding her room again' and see what − or who − lay up there. For now, though, she thought she better head out to the pool and begin her new job.

TG, all caramel-skin and toned muscle, was powering through the water as she neared the pool. Finding a place on one of the super-comfy-looking sunloungers to leave her belongings, she gingerly started to divest herself of her kaftan. Placing it carefully over her notebook, in case of splashes, she turned round to face the pool and saw TG, rising magnificently out of the water. After his head breached the surface, the water cascaded over his chest and dripped off his arms as he raised his hands up to his face to wipe the water away and smooth back his jet-black hair. Beads of water ran down his washboard abs, and Jenna couldn't help but wonder how an IT geek got so fit. Her legs betrayed her as her knees went a little weak at the sight of his V-shaped waistline, the muscles pointing towards his swim shorts in a really quite fascinating way. At least *fascinating* was the word Jenna wanted to use, to excuse the fact that she was staring quite so much at the definition around his trunks. In order to stop her knees from giving way altogether she stepped down into the pool, using each large, shallow step to get accustomed to the coolness of the water. It was only 11 a.m. but the sun was already high in the sky and the day was scorching. She couldn't really blame TG for wanting to cool off in the pool, could she?

'Drink?'

'Bit early for a G&T, even for me,' said Jenna − thinking back to her wish ten minutes earlier for something even stronger. TG smiled at her and then flicked a hand at one of the crew.

'I'm having my usual,' he said to Jenna and then turned to face one of the Tweedles. 'The blue algae and ginger thing please.' He looked over at Jenna who sort of half nodded — she thought the sound of blue algae was enough to render something utterly disgusting, and wondered if a martini really was off the cards . . .

TG made small talk as they rested against the edge of the pool until the drinks arrived, looking resplendently blue with a frothy top. They were served to them by a beautiful girl in a cream-coloured body-con dress, which Jenna noticed perfectly matched the sofas and walls of the yacht. *Designed to blend in, I guess*, she thought as she accepted the drink from a burnished copper tray. A reassuring thought crossed her mind — style like this, such perfect design — this had not the whiff of bachelor, no, this surely could only be the hand of a female designer, meaning TG already had a girlfriend and he really did only want her as a PA or — she toyed with the idea as she sneaked a look at his perfect torso again — he could be gay? She took a tentative sip from the sci-fi-looking drink and was pleasantly surprised that it tasted quite nice. With its white latte-like foam on top — and lurid algae blue colour — it did look more like a Smurf. Jenna was about to point this out when TG spoke to her.

'There are a few things I'd like to run past you.' He had finished his Smurf latte already and without him even needing to beckon her over, the beautiful stewardess appeared and took his empty glass. Jenna quickly finished off the rest of hers, trying not to gag as the ginger didn't quite mask the seaweed-like taste of the algae. Barfing blue into this pool would not get things off to a good start.

'Fire away,' she said, trying to disguise a burp as a cough.

'So, predominantly I want you to help me organise some parties — I take it you have plenty of experience there?'

'You mean, organising them? Yes, totally.' Jenna hoped TG didn't notice her cross her fingers behind her back and under the water. 'I'm not much of a party animal any more, really.' That was sort of true. To be fair it was at least three months since she'd last danced on a night-club bar, fuelled by sambuca shots and prosecco. Or was it two? Anyway, Jenna hoped that her new boss thought her more at home with an organiser's headset than a hedonist's hangover.

'Great. I mean I was so impressed at how you handled things at the Blake-Howard BoBo launch. And I was thinking — you know quite a few of the locals round here now — and although I want to remain sort of reclusive,' he winked at her, 'I better get to know the neighbours.'

'The English village equivalent of showing your face down the local pub.'

'Yeah . . . I mean, it's only polite, right?'

'Oh, it's terribly important. Some former girl-band member moved into the village next door to my parents and refused to even let the church warden in through her gates, even though he was only delivering the parish mag. She had to sell up pretty quickly and move on when the Parish Council refused planning for their indoor pool . . .'

'I literally have no idea what you're talking about, but yes. That sort of thing. I'll leave it all up to you.'

'Great.' Jenna said, hoping she sounded much more confident than she felt. She also almost ruined everything by butting in about hillside neighbours too, but remembered just in time that Angus was still technically under a huge confidentiality clause and shouldn't have told her about TG's villa.

'And then there's my daily schedule,' TG carried on, 'which hopefully this summer will involve breakfast, swimming, lunch, jet ski, cocktails, dynamic conversation with interesting people, dinner and bed.'

'Sounds desperately busy. I can see why you need a PA . . .' Jenna couldn't though, and hoped that Canadians were better at interpreting sarcasm than their American cousins. Luckily, TG seemed to have caught on.

'Well, between all of that hard work — and hey, it takes a lot of dedication to get this body,' he raised himself up and out of the pool and Jenna got an eyeful of the markedly toned abs and that cute V-shaped muscly bit again, 'there will be some business that I need to attend to. I'm going to give you a new phone so you can receive my emails on it and basically go through them and deal with the junk. It's quietened down now the major deals have been done — hey, you know what I do, right?'

'Sort of . . .' *Honestly, no*, thought Jenna to herself. But she was wary, even with what was seeming like the world's easiest induction day (so far there'd been no 'here's the tea and coffee station, don't steal my oat milk from the fridge' chat of the usual office), of admitting that she had only the slightest idea of what her new boss actually did. 'IT?' she ventured, feeling the urge to cling to the side of the pool for its support.

TG laughed at her. 'Kinda. I created an app — the coding for which has now been sold in part to various other organisations. My lawyers in the US have handled everything so far and this is my free time. I kid you not, I haven't had a day off since I started at CalTech.'

'No frat parties?'

'Well, of course, they're kinda forced on you, though. But I stuck to my screen most of the time, had to prove to Mom and Dad that being a doctor or professor wasn't the only way to be a success.'

'Are your parents, um, from Canada originally?' Jenna had been curious about the origins of TG's deliciously caramel-coloured skin (she really should stop looking at his toned chest) and dark chocolate eyes.

'Dad is. Born and bred Vancouver. Canucks till he dies kinda guy. Mom's Indian, though. They're both academics.'

'They must be so proud of you.'

'Yeah, I guess. More so now that I'm actually doing something worthy.'

'What do you mean?'

'Clickbait wasn't my first app I coded and designed, but it was the one that took off. Unlike some of the other straight-off-campus millionaires, I didn't get rich quick so I had my scroll and mortar board moment.'

'Which your parents loved?'

'Exactly. And I came up with loads more apps before Clickbait. PlasticPanorama, for example, you can use it to complain about plastic found on your local beach and river. Once enough complaints get logged in one location a letter is automatically generated to the local governor or state department to call their attention to it.'

'That sounds brilliant – just what the world needs right now.' Jenna pushed herself away from the poolside a bit and floated her arms around, enjoying the conversation.

'Know how much that app made me?' TG paused for effect. 'Zero dollars. Turns out big business isn't interested in recycling, whatever their PRs say.'

'Shit. But that was a great idea. Can I download it?'

'And make me another twenty-five cents, why not!' TG laughed. 'Anyway, now I can do all the eco stuff I want to do and fund the causes I want to fund. Take this boat, for example . . .'

'It's beautiful.'

'It's a death wish for the planet, even though it's the first super yacht to have a hybrid engine – so it's about thirty per cent more efficient than most. And I love that about it. But I have to offset the other seventy per cent somehow.' He smiled to himself before carrying on. 'Which is kinda why you're here too. I've started foundations and philanthropic societies and I need your help organising what the hell I'm actually doing — and working out how we can make this floating eco-nightmare pay for itself, not in cash, but in carbon footprint.'

'Wow, yes, I mean — that's such an amazing thing to think about. You're not your average billionaire, are you, TG?' Jenna wondered if she'd gone too far, been too over familiar already, but TG just smiled at her.

'How's your room, by the way? You do like it, don't you?' His eyes had turned on the dark-brown smoulder again and Jenna realised this guy definitely wasn't gay — was he a player, though? Was all that eco chat just some line he pulled out to impress the *laydeez*? She pulled her swimming costume straps higher up her shoulders just to be sure.

'It's amazing, TG — it's just, so — I don't know how to describe it. So sumptuous. Who designed it? Your . . . partner?'

His eyes levelled on hers and held them there. 'Nope. Hey — look, I bought the boat, said to my broker to get it done up. As far as I know his girlfriend did it.'

'Well, whoever it was, she did a marvellous job.'

'Speaking of jobs, I guess we better stop swimming around and get on with some work.'

'Gosh, yes of course. Thanks, by the way.'

'What for?'

'Giving me this opportunity. I thought it would just be a way to make some pennies, but if we can actually do some good for the world, well, that's pretty cool.'

TG nodded at her and smiled. And as Jenna swam the few strokes back towards the steps she had the uncertain feeling that she was still being watched. But, as she stepped up and out of the pool, another stewardess was on hand with a fluffy white towel and when she looked back at TG he was wrapped up in one too, his slim triangular waistline emphasised by the thick fluffiness of the towel around it. He was looking down at his phone, and Jenna felt just a tinge of disappointment that he hadn't been looking at her.

So, thought Jenna about ten minutes later, as she unpacked her suitcase into the huge built-in wardrobe in her room, *TG wants his corsage and curtsey moment here as a deb in Monte Carlo*. She smiled to herself, thinking of how if someone had told her a couple of months ago *she* would be the one to metaphorically hold a billionaire by the hand and show *him* the ropes of how to party with the filthy rich — well, men in white coats might be called. She took a deep breath as she hung up the last piece of her clothing in the wardrobe and closed the mirrored door. She looked at herself. Did she look like a billionaire's PA? No, not really. Did she know loads of famous people here in Monaco? No, not really. Did she have any idea of what the super-rich liked doing in their spare time? Again, no, not really. But did she know how to organise a bash, have fun, fly by the seat of her pants and generally fake it till she makes it? Hell, yeah. And she had one secret weapon in this flashy world of the super-rich: her old friend Bertie. She picked up her phone and brought up her contact details.

'Here goes nothing,' she whispered to herself as she hit dial.

25

'Five million dollars,' Angus whispered the amount to himself as he stood on the steps of the casino. 'Here goes nothing,' he tried to sound cheerful as the security guard nodded him through. He couldn't quite believe what he was trying to do — take on perhaps the most famous casino in the world, save those of the Vegas strip. The Monte Carlo casino on Casino Square — it didn't get more casino than that. The foyer was dark compared to the brilliant sunlight outside, but his eyes soon became accustomed to it and he took in the liver-coloured marble columns, set off by grey-and-sand-coloured surrounds. Stone staircases covered in blood-red carpet runners led up to the first floor, but he ignored them for now, heading towards the *caisse* — the place he could transform his relatively meagre amount of euros into chips, and from there to the gaming tables. His ability with cards wasn't all that great: he'd lost his shirt plenty of times over poker with his friends and he thought his luck with blackjack might be similar. Besides, the frustration of knowing that it was your decision to stick or twist was too much stress to add to the already highly charged pressure he found himself under.

Heading instead to the roulette tables he thought he'd stake it all on pure chance — then, apart from placing the bets themselves, he couldn't be responsible for which nook the ball landed in once the wheel was spun. The roulette was situated in a room to the side of the casino, and being only mid-afternoon there were few fellow players. In fact, far from being the romanticised temple to winning that it was portrayed as in films and on TV — there wasn't a tux or glass of champagne in sight — it felt almost sordid, as if it was just him and a few other losers — huh, losers — desperate to play, to gamble, even when the sun was still shining outside. Later, the place would be full of the glitz and glamour as you'd expect — the glint of sequins and crystal glasses replacing the hum of the vacuum cleaner, the dust motes gliding through sunbeams and the chatter of tourists on a guided trip, cooing at the marble bas reliefs and *trompe l'oeil* friezes along the gilded ceiling of the main atrium.

The Salle Medecin — with its soaring murals and gilded mirrors set off by a huge crystal chandelier — had opened a few minutes earlier for afternoon play. Angus had little choice at which table to place his bets — it being not exactly peak time there was only one open and manned by a croupier. Angus nodded at him and raised his eyebrows in greeting and was rewarded with a curt 'Monsieur.' He was the only one about to play — the only other punters in here were quietly concentrating on their hands of cards. Angus felt the chips in his pockets and built up the courage to start betting.

'Monsieur, your bets please.'

How do they always know you are English? Angus thought to himself as he withdrew his hand from his pocket and brought with it a chip.

'Minimum bet is five euro, sir,' the croupier added, which further hassled Angus a bit. Turning over the chip he had brought out of his pocket between his fingers he saw the croupier's face change. One hundred euros. Angus felt giddy with the weight of the decision hanging over him, but he placed the chip down on his lucky number — no wait, Jenna's birthday, the twelfth — he moved the chip to number twelve, one of the red numbers. All or nothing. The croupier raised an eyebrow at Angus and he almost imperceptibly nodded back. The wheel spun and then the ball — the pill — was pushed around after it.

'No more bets please,' the croupier said in English to an audience of just Angus and a hanger-on from the tourist party. The pill spun around the wooden wheel, faster than Angus could keep an eye on, until it gradually slowed and began the heart-wrenching descent into one of the pockets. Bounce, bounce, bounce − it hopped through reds and blacks, indiscriminate in its movement. The click, click, click of the wheel's mechanism was slowing and the pill found its final resting place. Twelve! Angus couldn't believe his luck and thumped his fist down on the green baize. A yelp of surprise came from the tourist behind him and Angus stood back from the table, needing to steady himself in his amazement. *I can do this* . . . in that moment he genuinely thought he could win his way to Jenna's rescue. The croupier obviously was not impressed at having his pristine baize thumped so hard and, so it seemed to Angus anyway, begrudgingly pushed over chips to the value of €3,500. The odds were high − 35 to 1 − but he'd beaten them once. Let's do it again. High on the thrill of winning, Angus placed €100 chips on several more numbers − Jenna's birth month, 2; his own birthdate, 15, 9; − that should do. If just one of them came up, he'd be quids in. The croupier spun the wheel again then set the pill off. Angus clenched his fingers into his palms and then crossed his arms waiting for the pill to stop. Bounce, bounce, bounce − the final few seconds as the wheel clicked to a stop. It was nowhere near 2 or 15 or 9. It was nestled in pocket 28 and Angus trembled slightly as the croupier pulled his chips away from him. The next few spins were much the same, with Angus reducing his odds, betting on just red or just black, or going for even numbers only. He clawed back a few hundred euros once or twice but by 4 p.m. he had to admit that like many schmucks who had gone before him, the house had won. He left with his shirt, yes, but barely enough money converted from chips back into euros for a few extra drinks tonight, and not enough, not by a long shot, to get him out of his current problem. He blinked back into the sunshine and nodded an adieu to the door security. They must see it every day — the losers leaving having played and been played.

He turned right and headed back to his hotel past the Café de Paris and wondered where the hell he was going to turn next, when a poster on a tabac stand revolved to reveal a lipstick advert. Angus stopped as something had caught his eye. Not the particular shade of Chanel rouge that the revolving advert suggested would make any woman alluring, but the poster just before it. He waited as an advertisement for a French magazine and then a popular French movie had had their turn before what he was looking for came to the front again. A seminar on coding and bitcoin mining. Bitcoin. The cryptocurrency so often now in the papers and the one that made million-aires overnight of investors and those able to mine for it. Angus turned away from the advert and with a glimmer more hope in his heart followed the path downhill to his hotel where he thought a worthwhile few hours on his laptop might be spent learning about this elusive and lucrative currency.

26

'Dolls, hi. Just the *persona-defo-grata* I wanted to chat to. How was the romantic reunion with the old boy by the way? Did you go *tout de suite* to the posh suite after leaving us?'

'Well, it was rather romantic yes . . . he did this thing where he—'

'Oh God — no! TMI, shush shush. Anyway, I was wondering if you could help me.'

'That's actually why *I* was phoning *you*, Berts.'

'Cool — tit for tat then. *Moi*, with the best tits, first.' Before Jenna could say another word, Bertie continued, 'So Max and I are obviously thinking about the wedding, but — and this is far too boring really — Max insists on actually going back to London for most of the summer and *working*.' Jenna could hear the distaste her friend had for that last word. 'So would you be a complete honey and help me organise a few things?'

Jenna had never experienced the whole 'life flashing before your eyes' thing — not even when she and Angus had been genuinely near death on the side of an exposed mountain, injured and cold, with a blizzard raging around them. But now, memories of last summer, of working at Château Montmorency as both winery PA and party planner for Bertie's thirtieth did indeed flash up as if she were reliving them all. The 6 a.m. phone calls, the countless boxes of props that arrived *ad hoc* throughout the summer, the changes of theme umpteen times . . . the thirty-foot-high gold inflatable elephant . . .

'Jenna? Haaallooo?'

'Yes, I'm here.' She took a deep breath. 'Actually, I'm quite busy, Bertie. New job and all that.'

'Rubbish. You did say you'd help back in London. And we all know you're just there because that billionaire has his eye on you.'

'That's not true!' Jenna hissed down the phone at Bertie. 'TG has so much he needs me to do — which is why I was phoning you!'

'Well, word is, he's on the prowl for a Mrs TG so, whatevs.' There was an awkward pause as both girls took stock of the conversation. Bertie broke the silence first. 'Put it this way — come out with me for an evening and we'll scope out the Hotel Metropole — ballroom size, glitziness and general ambience — and I will make sure that darling Angus won't hear any of those ghastly rumours from me.'

'Rumours? There's nothing to rumour! It's just not true, Bertie!'

'I mean — I know it's hard to believe — I can hardly compute the info myself, Jens — a hot billionaire and you? Pull the other one!' Her cackling laugh at the end of the line almost made Jenna end the call, but in a fantastic feat of self-control she took another deep breath and finally said what she had been wanting to at the start of the conversation.

'My turn for a favour now. As part of my *job*,' she emphasised the word, 'TG wants me to throw him a little housewarming party — or boat warming, I guess. And although I've picked up a few contacts from Emma, could you help me identify the other key players around here?'

'Time for the "tat", I suppose. Metropole, seven o'clock. Mutual benefits, doll.'

'Fine. I'll ask TG if I can have the night off.'

'Thought you were just *working* nine to five?'

'It's a bit more woolly than that . . .' Jenna thought of the swimming pool meeting, the amazing suite and, despite trying awfully hard not to, his taut and toned abs. 'And you say it's just a rumour, huh?'

Feeling a little foolish, Jenna agreed to the meet up and then quickly pinged another message off to Angus. If she was going on shore leave — and meeting Bertie — she'd need her safety net of a boyfriend with her.

Having Jenna on board had just exponentially raised TG's enjoyment of Monaco to a factor of . . . hell, he needed to stop thinking in algorithms and work out how to win over his new employee. He had to admit, he was spellbound by her — more than he'd ever been by anyone before. Making his millions in his thirties had given him a certain appreciation of how easily he could pick up women — beautiful, striking, willing, biddable women — but with every fake nail, hair extension and amazing rack came another credit-card request, expectation of gifts and the chink, chink, chink of the pick axe into his personal gold mine. But Jenna seemed different. She seemed comfortable in these lush surroundings, sure, but she sure as hell wasn't taking them for granted — there was no haughty demeanour about her, and she was reassuringly pleasant to the staff. His instincts when he'd first met her had been right — and he liked the way she seemed intent on working, even though he had barely described enough tasks to keep her going past eleven o'clock each morning. But he could make up things for her to do and pay her well for doing them — he knew how to control the situation and he got the feeling he needed to make her feel like she was earning his money rather than taking it.

Seeing her leave his boat at the end of that first day together irked him. Still, he could use the new 'work' cell he'd given her to track exactly where she was, that was something. She'd be off to see her perfectly nice boyfriend and hang out with her own friends. He supposed a few invitations to those guys wouldn't go amiss — get them all on board, keep them close. Somehow he'd have to convince her that life on board *Clickbait* was a hundred times better than life on shore. That life with him was a thousand times better than life with her boyfriend — and sleeping with him would be, well, his bank balance's worth of zeros better than anything she'd ever experienced before.

27

Angus threw his phone down on the bed of his hotel suite having just sent off a quick reply to Jenna. Yes, of course he'd go and meet her — help her — with Bertie. He tucked in his shirt. If they were going to the bar of the Hotel Metropole then he better posh up his act. He was just turning to head into the bathroom for a final check when he noticed his phone light up again. He reached over onto the bed and picked it up. Number withheld.

'Hello?'

'The time is ticking, Mr Linklater. And we do not yet have the money.'

The Voice. And the message was clear. Angus felt his knees give way beneath him and he sat down heavily on the bed, hanging his head between his knees, desperate to get much-needed blood to his brain.

'She will be dead by the end of next week if you don't pay me the money. This, how shall I put it, hesitation? It is worrying. You like to live dangerously, perhaps, and let us go right to the wire, as they say?'

'No . . . I—'

'Maybe you are planning to tell the cops after all? Don't be tempted, Mr Linklater, they will not help you with their Inspector Clouseau little magnifying glasses. Who do you think supplies their drugs for them?' The Voice laughed, and for the first time in his life Angus realised what it felt like to really hate someone.

'I still have time.' His voice came out thin and raspy.

'Tick tock, Mr Linklater, tick tock.' Click. The line went dead.

How was he going to get five million dollars by the end of next week? He'd just spent the last hour or two slavishly trawling websites finding out about server farms and share schemes that would enable him to cash in on bitcoin. He felt like he'd been getting somewhere until one helpful article not only pointed out that bitcoin values were falling due to the rise in other cryptocurrencies, but that mining for it — the only way of 'making' it other than using real currencies to buy it — could take thousands of pounds, and worst of all, thousands of hours. The terrible truth was he just *didn't* have time. He let the phone drop to the plush carpet of the floor and sat like that for a while, his head in his hands, his mind trawling over what possibilities he had left. Sadly, it wasn't very many.

28

'So I was thinking, drinkies maybe in here,' Bertie waved her manicured hand towards the Salon des Princes, a room so gorgeously opulent with its marble chequerboard floor, hand-painted doors and chandelier so large that Bertie's huge solitaire diamond glinted like a disco ball as it reflected the light off it. 'I mean, what was I thinking — the bar is so dark.' Bertie gave a little *pfft* to herself, then moved on, trailing Jenna in her wake. 'Then through to the ballroom for the wedding breakfast for say, four hundred of our nearest and dearest?'

'Wow. Just an intimate little wedding then.'

'How many did Sally and Hugo have at theirs in the end?'

It amused Jenna to think that with all her wealth and connections, Bertie was still concerned with the traditional one-upmanship she had with Sally.

'Only about sixty, I think.'

'Well, mine needs to be ten times bigger and better so I guess I need to widen the circle a little more.'

'Sometimes less is more though.'

Bertie glared at Jenna, whose hand, holding a flute of rather lovely champagne, started to involuntarily shake under the pressure.

'Maybe. Maybe.' *Phew*, thought Jenna as Bertie turned her gimlet eyes onto the decor of the room instead. Quite apart from anything, Jenna didn't think she had it in her to organise a party for six hundred people, even with the excellent events team at the Metropole as backup. Bertie started talking to her again, this time she was a little less effusive and slightly less confident.

'I mean, we're looking into booking the cathedral. It's so perfect for my Princess Grace theme, you see. And the lovely man at the *mairie*'s office thought I'd be able to wangle a special dispensation, you know, because of who I am.'

Jenna wanted to answer back; *and who are you?* Really though — who was this woman who used to be her old friend at university? Who had been fun and quite laid-back and more into horses than Hermès . . .

'But then any sexy yacht captain could also do the deed,' Bertie continued, 'and I do think that those rather fetching white uniforms might set off my dress perfectly.' Jenna took a sip and watched as the cogs turned inside Bertie's brain. 'Think of the Insta moment!'

Jenna nodded and wondered when Angus was going to come and rescue her.

'And then there's the benefits of being on a yacht, like a really big one. I don't think mine will be ready by then otherwise . . .'

'You've got a yacht?' Jenna almost spat out her champagne, but remembered how expensive it had been, and how for once Bertie hadn't offered to pay so managed to keep it in. She was, needless to say, pretty shocked.

'Oh, yah. I mean, Max is being a bit down about it, but it's in the hands of the brokers now and this lovely chap I know is trying to find the perfect one for me.' She held up her hand and started counting off fingers. 'Sleeps at least eight, on-deck swimming pool, spa area and, of course, all the toys.'

'Bertie — how, I mean . . .' Jenna just wanted to know when her friend had got so rich. She knew she was wealthy but buying an eight-berth super yacht was crazy money.

Bertie waved away Jenna's almost question with a bejewelled hand and then started waving for real as Angus walked into the ballroom.

'Live every day like it's your last, eh!' shouted Jenna a few hours later from the carousel as she clung on to the decorated horse on which she was sitting. Angus's heart missed a beat and he was tempted to tell her right there and then that they needed to escape, they needed new identities and they needed to be on the run for the rest of their lives but his voice was caught in the wind as he sat on the horse behind her, trying as hard not to fall off as to say something meaningful.

The evening, he'd thought, had started off in a far more civilised manner. He'd met Jenna and Bertie at the Metropole and they'd decided to have a few drinks on the terrace, a fantastic spot that looked over the rooftops of the ornate buildings on Casino Square. Seeing the dome of the casino had reminded him of his poor judgement in going there, and as he gripped Jenna's hand in his, listening to Bertie blither on about wedding plans, his mind was elsewhere. He had nine days now to find the money. Nine days to save Jenna's — and probably his — life.

As the second round of French martinis had appeared so did Emma and Monty Blake-Howard, no doubt invited by Bertie so she could pick their brains about wedding fashion. In fact, the conversation had turned to yachts and as Jenna and the Blake-Howards had got more and more pissed on fancy cocktails (thank God he hadn't lost more cash at the casino), Angus noticed that Bertie had done her usual thing of barely letting a calorie pass her lips — alcohol included — and he wondered if she perhaps had the cash to bail him out. His idea had been quickly squashed by her braying tones informing the table of her plan.

'My broker says I'll have to wait until the boat show here in Monaco in September to really be able to find the right yacht for me.'

'Oh darling, how thrilling!' Emma had chinked her full glass against Bertie's, but was the only one of the two to take a sip. 'You'll outdo us all!'

'I don't mind telling you, darling, that it'll take up most of my pennies.'

'Oh, they are frightfully pricey, yes.'

Monty chipped in with some sound advice. 'You can charter it, though. You could make back some of the running costs just by letting other people use it. We got a bloody fortune this year during Cannes.'

'Ew. Hoi polloi? On my yacht? I don't think so.'

'Not even film stars and Hollywood producers?' Monty had queried.

'I mean, I suppose if Ryan Reynolds asked nicely . . .' Bertie had warmed to the idea.

'Aw, Berts, could we borrow it?'

Angus had listened, and chuckled along, as Jenna had teased Bertie about stowing on board, especially if Ryan and Blake chartered her yacht in the future. He was a little surprised, but not entirely disappointed, at how easily she was fitting in with this super-rich set, with barely an eye-roll in sight tonight. He'd always felt that she was slightly derisory of inherited wealth, even his, and he wondered if she was getting rather used to life on board super yachts already. He reminded himself that she was rather used to *life* in general and wondered if he could convince Bertie not to buy a yacht and help her friend out instead. Her next declaration had pretty much put the kibosh on that one though.

'Max is getting rather dull about the whole thing and says we shouldn't but I just think it's such fun. No, my mind is made up. I'm determined. Come September I will be down to my last couple of million, but also the owner of my own super yacht!'

'Can we help you name it, Berts?' Jenna had asked.

'You *can* change a name of a yacht, yes . . .' Bertie had replied and Angus thought that perhaps it had only just occurred to her. 'Maybe *Sun Queen* or *Empress of The Riviera*?' Bertie was clearly captivated with the idea of naming her own yacht, until Jenna added her own suggestion.

'I vote for Bertie McBertface!' Jenna had sloshed her martini glass a bit too enthusiastically and despite Bertie's withering looks, the rest of them had collapsed into giggles.

The drinks had turned into dinner, and while Bertie stuck to mineral water and picked at a rocket leaf salad, the others had tucked into steaks and wine and the drinks that kept coming, with Monty BH leading the charge to the bar each time. By the time their car came to pick them up to take them and Bertie back to the harbour, and air kisses had been exchanged, Angus realised Jenna had given him the slip. His heart leapt into his throat as he tried to find her, aware that lurking around any corner could be her assassin. He found her wrapped around a pole on a stage in a corner of the restaurant, they'd just been in, the glittery curtain behind her revealing real cabaret girls who looked slightly miffed by the amateur hogging their pole, wearing a comedy pair of Playboy bunny ears and singing Madonna songs to herself.

Angus had just about managed to untangle her from the pole (she told him off for being such a spoilsport), when she slipped out of his grasp again and ran outside where she made a beeline for a vintage fairground carousel. So that was how they ended the night, riding brightly coloured horses, their steeds' faces set into a grotesque grimace with red lips and flaring nostrils, their hard manes offering not much in the way of grip . . . and Jenna squealing into the wind about how much she loved life.

29

The next morning Jenna awoke in her luxurious cabin with a pounding headache and a mouth as dry as a flip-flop. The Egyptian cotton sheets were tangled around her as she lay, star-fished on the king-sized bed, one leg still in her skinny jeans and her top still on, too. She ran her tongue over her teeth — verdict: furry. This small action exhausted her and she lay still again, weighing up the pros and cons of going to find some painkillers, and some water. She wondered if her head might fall off if she moved. She very gingerly opened her eyes and saw that the blackout curtains were drawn over her windows. *Shit*, she thought, what time is it? Wasn't this technically her first proper day working for TG, and here she was, hungover and . . . yes, that was bile rising in her throat . . . God, how did she get back last night? And what time is it again? Oh God, oh God . . .

Jenna fell out of bed and crawled towards the en-suite bathroom, reaching the loo just in time to do one of those lovely 'technicolour yawns', as her father had called them when she was a child. And she felt pretty immature now, too. At least she was certain of one thing: she hadn't smuggled Angus on board.

A knock at the door was almost unnoticed until it became too insistent to ignore and Jenna raised herself up from the cold marble bathroom floor using the loo as support. She glanced in the mirror and noticed that her make-up from last night was still vaguely in place and therefore she probably looked better than if she'd taken it off properly — her skin underneath must surely be nothing perkier than a greenish hue.

'Hang on,' she called back, adding a 'sorry, thank you, please' just in case it was TG himself. She stumbled across the room to the cabin door, fumbled with the handle and slowly cracked it open an inch or two, hoping that the least anyone saw of her, the better.

'Morning, missus,' it was Tweedle-Dee, or Dum, she couldn't remember which one had which nickname.

''Snot missus,' she mumbled, embarrassed by the moniker.

'Brought you some 'erbal tea,' the kindly South African voice informed her and she heard the sound of a tray being put down outside the door. 'I'll leave it here, missus, and you can get it in your own time.'

'What time is it?'

'Just seven thirty, missus.' Jenna leaned heavily against the door frame, willing herself to open the door fully and bend down to pick up the tray. 'I'd recommend getting the tea down you,' the soothing voice advised her, 'it's my own special recipe.' Jenna looked up at him and saw him wink.

'Thank you,' she mouthed at him and then left the door ajar as she rushed back to the bathroom — there was no way anything was going down her while so much was still coming up — but she did at least thank the gods of jobs, or hangovers or whatever, that it was still only seven thirty.

Whatever the Tweedle had put in that tea, it had magical restorative effects. Angus swore by drinking so much water that you were forced to get up and pee in the night, then drink more water and so on . . . *Well, blow that*, thought Jenna, as she had a very long wee, *this stuff is dynamite*. She didn't want to know what it was, but her headache had eased and although she could still be described as being *very* hungover, she was no longer at Def Con 1 and by eight fifteen she was showered and dressed in something much more befitting a billionaire's PA than half a pair of dirty jeans (how had that lipstick got on there?) and a pair of bunny ears (she had not the *faintest* recollection of picking them up). If only Sally could see her now, triumphantly battling a hangover like a true pro!

By nine o'clock she was sitting in the shade of one of the upper decks — there was a generously large U-shape sofa that surrounded a coffee table on three sides; a couple of pouffes provided seating on the fourth side and the rest of this slightly smaller rear deck — it was on the very top of the yacht — was taken up with super-comfy sunloungers. Trying to concentrate on work — and not on her thankfully now receding hangover — Jenna was taking notes from TG, who had greeted her with such warmth and ease that she felt he mustn't have heard her coming back in — at whatever time that was — until he said, 'Every project needs to be researched and I feel like you've got the handle on researching parties — putting in those late hours . . .'

'Oh.'

'Hey — your free time is yours, none of my business.'

Jenna just stared at her notepad and hoped that no part of today would involve one of those Smurf smoothies.

'Just maybe don't sing the opening, middle — extended, personalised middle — and final verses of your country's national anthem quite so loudly at one forty-five in the morning . . .'

Jenna was mortified. 'Oh God, TG. I'm so sorry.'

TG laughed and was still chuckling to himself when Dee or Dum joined them and whispered something in his ear. 'Show him up,' TG answered the discreet query and turned his chocolate brown eyes back to Jenna and half smiled at her. 'Visitor for you.'

*

151

Angus stepped up to the deck where Jenna was looking exceptionally comfortable with her new boss. After last night's boozing — for which he was still reprimanding himself — he was bleary-eyed too and noticed Jenna had possibly the largest pair of sunglasses on that he'd ever seen. How had he let himself — or her — get that drunk? The danger to Jenna was never closer than it was now and instead of protecting her, he'd put her in even more peril. Still, as he saw her curled up, one leg tucked under her, a mess of notebooks, pens and mobile phones and tablets next to her, her hair swept back into a ponytail and her ludicrous-sized sunglasses on; well, it made him smile. She smiled back and memories of last night — when she'd fallen off that carousel horse for one — meant he broke into an even wider grin. Angus was careful not to forget that he was technically trespassing on Jenna's place of work — plus it was hard to ignore the growing anxiety and worry that dominated his every second — and his face fell back to its now more usual serious expression.

'TG, hi, I'm Angus — Jenna's boyfriend.' He thrust his hand out at his host, who took it warmly and shook it.

'Hey. Good to meet you, Angus. I've not had much time to hear good things, but I'm sure I will.'

Smooth git, thought Angus to himself as he saw TG sit down next to Jenna, while offering him one of the awkwardly small, slightly uncomfortable pouffes opposite them.

'I hope I'm not speaking out of turn, TG, but I thought I should introduce myself on another level too. I'm the architect in charge of overseeing your build project in Eze.'

'No way! This is serendipitous. Drink?' Angus nodded politely, but slowly, to TG's offer — his head was still pounding — the peeing trick his grandfather had taught him had helped with the hangover but the heat of the day was building, not to mention Angus's stress at the pressure he was under to quickly find five million dollars.

'Apart from stalking our boss, what are you doing here?' whispered Jenna as TG was busy summoning one his immaculately turned-out crew.

'This.' Angus reached into his back pocket and pulled out Jenna's credit card. 'You left it behind the bar at the Metropole last night.'

'Fuck.' Jenna took it from him and returned to her seat. Angus felt a bit miffed — no thank you kiss or even a hug hello. But he saw the look of consternation on Jenna's face as she fingered the card before slipping it back into her pocket.

'I paid off your tab.'

'Oh Gus. You didn't need to do that.' He knew his girl-friend hated being bought and paid for but if he couldn't bail her out to the tune of five million dollars, he could at least settle a bar bill for a few hundred euros. Then TG came back over just as Jenna was telling him off. 'You are naughty, Gus. If I've run up some stupid bar tab then I should pay for it, not you. I'll pay you back.'

'Couldn't help but overhear that,' the soft Canadian tone irritated Angus somewhat, its cadence too sing-song, too soft for someone with TG's power and money.

'Oh.' Jenna started to fill TG in, leaving Angus to silently analyse how he felt about the situation. He wasn't proud of it, but he had to admit that he didn't like this easy repartee between his girlfriend and her boss. He had no choice but to smile and nod, though, as Jenna made light of the situation to TG; but he smarted when TG leaned in close to Jenna to listen to her and with every one of the billionaire's laughs and smiles Angus grew more wary of how this working relationship could turn into something a little more informal — especially if every meeting was conducted in the lush surroundings of your very own super yacht.

Angus forced out another fake smile as he watched TG clap his hand on his knee in laughter as Jenna finished off the humorous embellishments about the night before, which had led to her creeping back on board in the small hours.

'Well, it seems you Brits know how to have fun.' TG brought a halt to the storytelling and Angus inferred from his tone that it was time he was gone — the third wheel, the gooseberry to his own girlfriend.

'Thanks so much for bringing back my card, Gus,' Jenna sounded sincere and Angus was relieved when she slid her glasses up into her hair and made proper eye contact with him. 'I will pay you back.'

'Oh, honestly, don't worry about it.' Angus instantly knew that had been the wrong thing to say to Jenna, who furrowed her brow, but he'd wanted to show off to the richer man. 'Well, I better let you get back to work.'

He hoped she would forgive him and realise that all he wanted to do in this world was look after her. As he shook hands with TG and turned to leave he saw that as they'd all stood up TG had placed his hand gently at the small of Jenna's back — a subtle gesture — but one that spoke a thousand heart-piercing words to Angus. Clenching his teeth he didn't even notice the architectural beauty of the swirling ammonite-esque spiral staircase that he followed to get to the lower deck where another immaculately uniformed crew member was on hand to politely but definitely see him off the boat.

TG sat back down and gestured Jenna to do the same. He wasn't sure if she'd noticed his hand gently hovering behind her back, barely touching her as they'd waved goodbye to her perfectly nice, but as far as he was concerned, unwanted boyfriend. Jeez, though — he was his architect. How could he use this situation to his advantage? Angus was fast becoming a broken cog in his smooth-running plan. And the next stage of that plan, now he had Jenna *physically* on board, meant getting her *emotionally* on board, too. He frowned as he thought. One of the things he liked about Jenna was her loyalty — the way she'd resisted his offer in favour of staying with the Blake-Howards — well, that meant he wasn't going to be able to lure her into bed with him while Angus was on the scene. So, just like with her ladyship, he was going to have to offer Angus some sort of incentive — be it money, girls or a career high — to get right out of Dodge.

'Jenna?' He liked the way she was sitting now, one leg cocked up under the other, her hair messily blowing in the light breeze, tendrils escaped from the ponytail held back from her face by her sunglasses and one odd pen tucked behind her ear

'Aha?'

'How would you like it if Angus came to stay with us, here on *Clickbait*?' He knew it was a gamble — it could lead to them having the time of their lives at his expense — but he had to have Angus nearby so he could work out what it would take to then make him leave, what his leverage could be.

'Really? Oh, TG, that would be . . . I mean, yes, wow. Yes.'

TG fixed his smile in place. Her genuine excitement over having her boyfriend on board too hit him harder than he had anticipated.

'Sure. Text him, tell him to check out of his hotel tomorrow morning and meet us here in time for lunch. Maybe then we can head out to sea for a bit of fun.' The look on her face was priceless — as if he'd just concluded his TED Talk on How To Be Amazing.

'Wow. Thank you.' He wasn't prepared for the tingle he felt when she leaned over and clasped his arm in gratitude.

It was bittersweet — he liked seeing her happy, but not because of this. 'Can I text him now?'

'In a bit.' He couldn't help himself, he wanted her to focus on him, on his generosity, a little while longer. 'There was a board meeting in Sacramento yesterday, the minutes were emailed over to me, could you read them and give me bullet points, by, say, eleven o'clock?'

Wondering how he had managed to play that whole scenario so badly, Angus gradually made his way back up the hill from Port Hercule to his hotel. The road — for pedestrians, at least — followed the curve of the natural rocky outcrop on which Monte Carlo was built, and you had to climb up towards the casino before dropping back to the coast to get to the Fairmont. A buzz in his back pocket made him reach for his phone and he fished it out quickly, hoping it was a text from Jenna. He stopped in his tracks and had to lean on the wide, stone-topped wall that edged the road and pavement and separated it from the sheer drop down to the harbour below. The message was from an unknown sender and all it said was *Tick tock*.

His phone skidded out of his hand and he just managed to grab it before it careered over the parapet into concrete oblivion below. Not that he wasn't tempted to throw the thing and its cursed message as far away from him — and Jenna — as he could. He instinctively looked down towards the harbour to where *Clickbait* was moored over the other side. He couldn't make out Jenna or TG or any of the immaculately dressed crew on board. Feeling altogether uneasy he slowly turned and carried on up the hill, a knot in his stomach growing as he felt as if all around him eyes were watching his progress, and down below there was a yacht where his presence hadn't been that welcome, and not just because he was disturbing their working day. TG fancied Jenna, he was sure of it.

Another buzz — the phone was still clenched in his hand. The urge to smash it to the ground was huge, but once again Angus knew that would achieve nothing. He willed his hand to unclench and forced his thumb to activate the screen. Jenna! The name on the text instantly soothed him and he leant against the wall this time, wanting to give every ounce of his concentration to her precious words.

TG has invited you to stay here!!! Isn't that amazing! Check out of the Fairmont tomorrow and come to Clickbait in time for lunch xxxxxxx

The relief that Angus felt was like a scrabbling climber finally finding a hold on a dangerous cliff-face — his ropes were still frayed, the abyss below still deep, his carabiners weak — but he had a hold. He texted back a string of kisses and a thumbs-up emoji and pocketed his phone. Perhaps he had TG all wrong, perhaps he wasn't after Jenna after all? And perhaps he might know how Angus could conjure up five million dollars in a matter of a few days, or sail away with them all on board to the safety of international waters . . .

30

'I think it's perfectly rotten of you, sweetie, to keep feeding me tit-bits of glamour and glitz.' Sally sounded grumpy down the phone the next morning but Jenna knew she didn't really mean it.

'Honestly, Sals, you should see this boat. Google it, I bet you can.'

'I'm sure I can, JJ, I just don't think I want to! I'm so jealous!'

Jenna snorted down the phone, then asked, 'How's you? And the bump?'

'Oh, we're fine, sweetie, bowling along. Actually, I look a bit like a bowling ball.'

'Proper bump forming?'

'Almost to rival Hugo's!'

Jenna sniggered at her friend's joke at the expense — and expanse — of her husband and his waistline. Pregnant she may be, but Sally still knew how to make Jenna laugh.

'So what's this TG like then?' Sally asked.

'Oh my God, he's great. And so easy to work for. He's quite laid-back but . . . oh, I don't know, there's something I can't quite put my finger on. Still, he's turned a blind eye so far to me helping Bertie out with her wedding organising . . .'

'Don't tell me, gold elephants and synchronised dove releases again?'

'Don't joke, Sals, she texted me earlier to ask if I could source antique paper and a calligrapher for the hand-written invitations. Luckily — and I say that with my teeth clenched — that text was at six fifteen this morning so it's not like it's eaten into my working day. Poor TG, though. I think he will be funding some of Bertie's wedding simply by subsidising her wedding planner! Oh, I almost forgot to tell you the best bit!'

'What? Bertie's gained three stone?'

'No, I wish, but no. TG's invited Angus on board!'

'God, you'll never get any work done, darling!'

'Well, you say that but — and you couldn't make this up — TG is the one who commissioned Angus's firm to build him that villa. So in a way, we'll both be working for him!'

'You jammy dodgers. Speaking of which — now I want one of those! Urg, cravings are the worst, I'm getting so fat . . .' And with that the conversation turned back to Sally and her ever-increasing bump.

Later that morning, Jenna was keeping watch for Angus to arrive. Half expecting to see the tinted-windowed Range Rover drop him off, she was a little surprised when she picked him out, walking along the quayside towards the yacht. As she leaned over the railing and waved at him she noticed how fit he was looking, what with his arm muscles flexed and abs looking noticeably taut under his polo shirt. Hovering at the top of the beach club steps she could barely wait for him to climb them, and met him halfway up, grabbed his face in her hands and kissed him full on the lips.

Remembering where she was, and that she was technically at work, she reluctantly pulled herself away and instead settled for grinning at him like a loon.

'Hello to you too.'

'I'm so thrilled you're here, Gus.' Jenna fizzed with excitement. This was perfect. Yes, she was still working, but TG had just been so amazingly generous and nice and said he liked to think of them as friends now, one big yacht family, and that Angus should come on board for a few days before he went up to the hills to work on his project so that TG could get to know him. Jenna had sensed Angus getting a bit low over the last few days – and not just because, like her, he might have been suffering from a stupendous hangover. She couldn't put her finger on it, but he seemed to have perked up immensely when she delivered TG's invitation to join them on board.

'Isn't this exciting, Gus?' She pulled him along by his hand and led him to the guest cabins and along the corridor to her own. Clicking open the handle she took him inside and felt a little rush of pleasure as he showed how impressed he was. 'Nice, isn't it?'

'Bloody amazing, Jenks.' Angus dumped his bag down on the floor and Jenna laughed as he did a sort of surveillance-style search of the room.

'You do make me laugh, Gus. But don't worry – one of the first things I did when I got here was do a thorough search for Russian or Chinese bugs or whatever.' She wafted her hand around the room.

'Really?' He sounded a lot more serious than she thought he would at her little joke.

'No, not really. But the yacht has been scanned. They all are, quite regularly, you know, so that business deals can't be spied on and stuff. Poor old Monty found the Chinese had hacked into their CCTV!'

'What?'

Jenna wondered why Angus was so upset on Monty's behalf.

'They sorted it out, though. And yeah, this one's clean. As I said, just been scanned.'

Angus seemed to relax again. Honestly, her poor old boyfriend did seem to be on edge these days – perhaps it was time to help him unwind? She checked her watch.

'Half an hour until lunch on the sun deck . . . fancy putting your large boat into my small harbour and seeing what tidal waves you can cause?'

After a gentle shoulder massage and a temptingly enticing striptease, Jenna had persuaded Angus to forget about whatever was stressing him out and 'up periscope'. As he reminded her again quite how good he was at pleasuring her she let out a little involuntary 'yelp' and wondered what rate of knots he was going at before she was lost to happy obliviousness.

The lunch table was piled high with fancy food as if someone had done a Supermarket Sweep around Fortnum & Mason and not spared the horses. Platters and trays of charcuterie sat alongside bowls of brightly coloured salads bejewelled with pomegranate seeds and fresh herbs, seafood was displayed in silver dishes full of crushed ice and wooden boards held slices of freshly made baguettes and sourdough loaves.

'Wow, TG,' Jenna exclaimed as she and Angus reached the top deck of the boat in time to meet their host — or boss — for lunch. 'Are we expecting someone? I didn't organise this.'

Jenna was impressed, sure, but she was also a little perplexed as TG had suggested she make it one of her morning tasks each day to plan lunch with the chef for herself and TG and any one else who was on board — and she didn't remember asking for a state banquet.

'I added a few embellishments,' admitted TG as he waved them over and indicated that both Jenna and Angus sit around the table in the cool shade of the canvas sail, which was elegantly stretched across the top of the deck for that purpose. He poured them glasses of chilled rosé from a beautifully curved bottle and put it back in the ice bucket, fresh droplets of condensation disappearing into the ice cubes.

'This is amazing.' Angus thanked his host and soon the three of them were deep in conversation, and Jenna was delighted to see her boyfriend and new boss getting on so well. Angus got straight into talking about the villa plans and while the two men talked about French planning law she took a moment to take stock of the situation. It was truly bonkers really. Yes, she had rich and successful friends back in London, but nothing in her life had prepared her for this level of luxury — especially not as part of a job. From the shelter of the sun deck it was hard to see what was going on down in the harbour below, and she heard rather than saw the buzz of activity around her. It didn't feel right somehow — all those workers scurrying about, and even the crew here on *Clickbait* scrubbing the decks, washing the windows and preparing more and more sumptuous courses, while she lounged around drinking wine. It pricked her conscience. But a little voice inside her head whispered *just enjoy it* and she caught herself thinking *WWBD? . . . What Would Bertie Do?* She knew full well the answer to that, as she turned on her most full wattage smile and her attention back to her lunch companions.

'Hey, it's like I always say. Don't waste your time and money on the cheap stuff.' TG was eulogising. The conversation must have moved on from planning permission. 'Pay once for something quality. I like quality. It's why I wanted you as my PA, Jenna.'

'Oh, well — yeah . . . you see you might have just proved yourself wrong there.' She glanced over to Angus, wondering if he would big her up in front of her boss or just laugh at her as really she *wasn't* the best PA in the world.

'No, I don't think I have.' TG's enigmatic answer seemed to close the conversation and the threesome clinked glasses and carried on talking about other things.

Jenna became lost in her own thoughts again as chat turned to the more technical aspects of architecture and she tried but failed to totally understand the conversation about cryptocurrency that went on over pudding, which was a platter of fresh peaches and gorgeously ripe melon.

'Have you tried it?' Angus asked TG.

'Of course, I set up a data farm to mine for bitcoin a few years ago, and I did well out of it. But now other currencies are taking over — altcoins — and the market for bitcoin is dropping. Are you mining?'

'Thinking of it.'

'Try NEM or Swiftcoin. Increasing your portfolio will limit any vulnerabilities — like with any shares.'

Jenna phased out again. Sometimes she forgot that Angus was actually quite savvy with his finances, having managed his trust-fund account until he'd bought their house. Gradually as the sun moved over behind the sailcloth she started to yawn and blink into the sunshine. Too much rosé and food — not to mention the little 'welcome on board' private party she'd just thrown Angus — had made her incredibly sleepy and despite her guilty conscience over all the other workers out there, she just wanted to lie back and soak up the afternoon rays.

Angus watched as Jenna slowly blinked and nodded off as the sun carried on its daily journey towards the west. He noticed as TG discreetly asked one of the stewards to alter the position of the canvas so that the strong rays, which were falling directly on a snoozing Jenna, were deflected again. Angus couldn't shake his gut feeling that he hadn't been welcome here, despite TG's best efforts to make him feel otherwise. Was his heightened state of anxiety, which had made the sex just before lunch so intensely good, making him see things that weren't there? He was sure though, as TG poured out more wine for them both and they discussed the villa plans in sketchier, more drunken detail, that TG's eyes as often as not, fell on the somnolent body of his beautiful girlfriend.

31

Angus leant over the balustrade and looked down to the black waters of Port Hercule below him. Several days had gone past since he'd come aboard this palace of a boat and he chastised himself for letting time get away with him. TG had had him working down in the office suite in the depths of the boat, carrying on with the plans for the villa that he'd started in London. His firm had sent a licence across for the appropriate software and the yacht was equipped with fancy large Macs — natch — so he could work on the plans just as before. When he wasn't working he was trying to think of a way they could escape the promised assassin. He'd downloaded the blueprints of the yacht and tried to see which entry point was the most vulnerable, where a killer might attempt to get past the crew. He was growing more and more fraught and hiding his fear from Jenna was getting harder and harder.

TG had asked the captain to take his yacht around the coast to Saint-Tropez for a night and finally he'd been able to release the tension in his shoulders, knowing that whoever was spying on them would have had no idea where along the coast they'd gone. But sitting in Senequier, the famous bar on the harbour front with its iconic red awnings, drinking Aperol spritz and listening to TG telling Jenna — as it was towards her that his chat was mostly directed — about his philanthropic ideals, well, even then he felt the foreboding buzz in his pocket. He'd snuck his phone out under the table and opened the message. He hoped TG, and most importantly Jenna, hadn't noticed the blood drain from his face as he looked down to see nothing except a photo of them all sitting there, the blood-red canopy of the bar a dead giveaway. Jenna had tried to seduce him that night, and she'd succeeded — he was just a man, after all — but later as she lay there in his arms, her warm skin pressing against his, he'd wept.

His phone — the phone that had just delivered him another one of the gangster's stark reminders — dangled between his forefinger and thumb. Dropping it overboard, though tempting, would solve nothing — it would just make it worse. Would dropping himself over the edge of this yacht help? Falling metres and metres into the cool waters of the harbour, cracking bones and ripping skin as he crashed against the hull, smacking his head on a fender, knocking himself out so that he drowned before he even knew what was happening . . . would that be an answer? No, probably not. They'd probably just kill her anyway.

'Hey,' the voice he least wanted to hear, save that of The Voice itself, disturbed his dark thoughts.

'Hey.'

'You look kinda stressed.'

Angus turned to see TG, his head and torso framed in the light from the vast glass windows of the main saloon. He looked almost saintly — his white linen shirt like that of a latter-day Jesus, but this one with a lot more money than Bethlehem's original.

'Can I help?'

Angus pulled himself away from the balustrade and stood square-on to his host, trying to ease the tension in his shoulders. 'I don't think so, no.'

'Girl trouble?'

Why would he leap to that conclusion? Angus thought it odd, but in a way, yes it was very much girl trouble. He let out an audible sigh and although he was loath to confide in this slick silicon billionaire, the weight of carrying around the secret was killing him, almost literally. He glanced at the dark waters below him one more time and then turned back to the seemingly ever-patient TG.

'Where's Jenna?'

'Curled up on the couch in the cinema room. *Pretty Woman*, I think.'

'She is, isn't she.'

'No, *Pretty Woman*, the film.'

'Oh. Look, TG . . . I—'

'Come, sit over here. There's obviously something troubling you. Believe it or not, before I got into tech I wanted to be a summer camp counsellor.'

Angus followed him over to the deck seating area and sat down opposite TG. 'Well, I feel like I'm far from being your average boy scout.'

'Why? What's happened?'

With a glance into the boat to check that Jenna was well and truly out of earshot, Angus told TG the whole story — from the origin of his scar to the recent threats against Jenna's life.

'Boy. That's fucked up,' TG said when Angus had finished.

'I know. And I'm losing it. I'm going to lose her. I just can't find the money.'

'How much was it again?'

'Five million dollars. I've tried everything. I almost lost the last pennies I had at the casino trying to win big. I've tried mining for bitcoin and I've asked my family for help — but it's not enough, I can't raise nearly enough.' Angus shuddered with a stifled sob as the emotions he'd tried to keep a hold on over the last few weeks gave out.

TG barely paused. 'I'll pay it.'

'What?' Angus was genuinely surprised. He raised his head from his hands and straightened up.

'I'll pay it.'

'But it's five million dollars.'

'Pocket change.'

If the man wasn't offering to save his girlfriend's life, Angus would have found that level of bravado frankly boorish, but he let it pass without comment. He was too shocked to comprehend TG's tone.

'TG.' Angus leaned across and clasped his host's hands in his. 'I don't know what to say. Thank you, oh God, thank you.'

TG leaned back away from Angus and his thanks. 'There's one condition, though.'

'What? Anything.' Angus couldn't think what TG could possibly want — free architectural drawings for life? Galley slave for a year? He'd do anything.

'You give me Jenna.'

'What?' Angus leaned back too and drew his arms across his chest defensively. 'I don't understand.'

'I press send on the bank transfer to your gangsters and you leave this boat and Jenna and promise never to make contact with her again.'

'No, I can't do that. I love her.'

'Sounds like she'll die if I don't pay this money.'

'You can't ask me to dump her. She loves me too. I'd break her heart.'

'And I'd mend it. Look.' TG made to stand up. 'Take it or leave it. I'll give you a few minutes to decide and I'll see you in my study.'

Angus watched him leave. Loathing, gratitude, shock, fear, relief, pain . . . his emotions clashed chaotically in the light of TG's offer. But it was the only offer on the table and the only one that secured Jenna's life. But what would life be like for him, without her? He would be a half person, a shadow, a shell of who he was — but she would be alive. Better for her to be alive and hating him, than for her to be dead and Angus hating himself. He let out a huge breath — his heart ached already for what he was about to do, but he knew it had to be done. He looked out at the glistening water one more time, breathed in — relishing these last few moments of . . . well, this certainly wasn't happiness, and it wasn't normality — but it was his last few moments as Jenna's boyfriend. He exhaled and then followed TG into the boat and found him in his study, ready to make his deal.

TG closed the door on the grief-racked Angus and walked back around his desk to where his computer screen showed the recently transferred funds. He'd noticed the quiver in Angus's hand as he'd handed over the embossed business card and they'd called the number. A series of offshore account numbers had been sent through and in a matter of minutes the money had been wired into a holding account, with TG's guarantee it would be author-ised to proceed once Angus had signed a binding contract. He switched screens to the on-board CCTV and zoomed in on the discreet camera in the cinema room. Jenna was still curled up on one of the vast La-Z-Boy armchairs, absent-mindedly delving into a huge bowl of popcorn as she watched the classic film. He then switched to the camera in Jenna's cabin and saw Angus open the door and stand looking around him for a brief while, before slowly getting his bag out from the wardrobe and starting to fill it. The camera wasn't able to swivel round fully and see what Angus was writing as he leant over the dressing table and scribbled a note, but he trusted the sincerity of the man that whatever he wrote wouldn't give the game away.

He felt sorry for Angus, of course he did. The guy had carried a huge responsibility around for weeks — years, if you counted his feelings over his scar. But this was business and he'd traded his commodity for money. He got the assurance that Jenna would live, and TG got the girl. He'd not left Angus totally high and dry though. He'd put in a couple of calls and told Angus to go up to the building site in Eze, where he'd ping him the address of a hotel he'd put him up in. He'd get his lawyer to draft a contract and get Angus to sign it while he was there. The poor guy could work on the villa plans, take his mind off the whole thing — and keep him at least a few miles away from Monaco until he vamoosed back to London.

32

Jenna mouthed the words along with Julia Roberts. 'And then she rescues him right back . . .' and wiped a tear from her eye. She could probably quote that entire film if someone asked her to — although she thought *Mastermind* would probably shy away from allowing it as her specialist subject. She imagined the contest — Jenna, neck and neck with Graham, a librarian from Swindon after the general knowledge round, smashing it over *Pretty Woman* 101 . . . 'For your first point: in which car does Vivian suggest it's easier for women to drive as they have "little feet"?' 'Lotus!' 'What colour dress does she wear to the polo?' 'Brown with white spots!' 'And finally, for the winning point, how does she describe escargot?' 'Slippery little suckers!' Winner!

She made the sound of an audience applauding en masse and raised her arms up in victory. In so doing though she accidentally knocked over the large bowl full of popcorn which one of the Tweedles had made for her. 'Damn.'

She started to clear it up when she heard voices outside the room. The cinema room was in the very bowels of the boat, next to the gym and engine room, so it was odd to be able to hear anything outside. The interruption reminded her that Angus had said he was going to come down and see her once he'd done a bit of work on the plans.

She decided to go and see what had become of him and once she'd scooped up most of the spilt popcorn she headed upstairs to their cabin. She felt bad leaving the room in a bit of a mess. She had started to assume that someone would just come and tidy up after her, which was not like her at all, but then someone always seemed to. Whenever she left a pile of notebooks and paperwork on a sunbed she'd always come back a few moments later to find it all perfectly piled up in the shade, or if she half-finished a drink and left it by the pool, within seconds the glass would be gone and either disappeared altogether or magically refilled with a fresh little paper coaster underneath it. She'd have to snap out of this luxe lifestyle when autumn came round and it was just her and Angus back in the little terrace house near Waterloo.

There was no sign of Angus on the way back to the cabin and when she gently rapped on the door before opening it there was no friendly hello from him. As soon as she closed the cabin door behind her, she sensed there was something wrong. Within a second she'd started to notice the missing mess: his clothes were no longer draped over the chair, his deodorant wasn't on the dressing table . . . but a piece of ragged paper was, torn from her work notebook and scrawled with Angus's writing. Jenna's heart broke as she read the words.

I'm sorry. I love you so much, but I can't stay with you. Please forgive me.

Not even a kiss at the end, or his name, or a reason . . . not even a bloody *reason*! Jenna snatched the note into her clenched fist and swung open the cabin door, not caring that it smacked and rebounded back with such force that it slammed behind her.

'Angus!' she shouted out as she ran, heading for the main deck with its wide steps down to the walkway and quayside. 'Gus!' Her voice was raw, she never shouted like this and it hurt as the ache of tears made her throat seem to swell and constrict. 'Gus!' her voice barely scratched the sound waves as she ran out of volume and fell to her knees as she got to the bottom of the steps and saw the quayside empty, with no sign of Angus anywhere near it.

TG watched her as she got up off her knees and steadied herself on the handrail of the walkway. She picked up speed as she ran down it, the narrow walkway bouncing with the pressure from her feet. She ran along the harbour away from *Clickbait*, her sobs carrying over the light sea breeze with the gentle slap of her bare feet on the stone. He wanted to go after her, but he knew she needed to see for herself that her boyfriend was gone — long gone — and not coming back. As they had agreed. He should be on his way to Eze now, the blacked-out Range Rover hastily called and making an even hastier retreat up to the hills. A few minutes later he saw her walking back towards him and his boat. One of her hands wiped the tears from her face, while he saw in the other — clenched in her fist — a small piece of notepaper. He turned to go back into the boat. Let her grieve tonight and then he'd be there tomorrow to start picking up the pieces.

Jenna slowly walked back up the narrow walkway onto the boat. She felt like someone had just turned on one of the mighty propellers at the stern and thrust her heart through its rotating blades. Her life was over. Angus had left her. Why? She wiped another tear from her cheek as she stumbled over the end of the walkway and almost tripped up the steps that led up onto the deck. The first real sobs came as she walked through the grand main saloon to the beautiful spiral staircase. Her sight blurred from tears, she felt rather than saw her way along the corridor to her cabin. Her cabin. Not their cabin. Not any more. What had she done that was so terrible? Why had he left her? She racked her brains for a reason. There had been no drunken fight this time, no disagreement or shitty few months of slow-burning resentments or frustrations. He'd been distracted since he'd arrived in Monaco, that's for sure, but never shirty with her. In fact, they'd been amazing together recently — not even just recently. Ever since they'd got back from Montmorency last year they'd been like two peas in a pod — or two halves of the same pair of compasses, as Angus had rather practically, but sort of romantically, put it. She sat down on the bed and then slowly lay down, pulling her legs up and curling into the foetal position where she stayed until the crying abated enough for her to finally fall asleep.

33

'He's left me. He just went.' Jenna wept down the phone to Sally the next morning.

'Oh, my poor darling. I don't know what to say.'

Jenna gasped for air through the sobs and blew a few more snot bubbles before being able to continue talking to her best friend.

'There's nothing you can say . . .' Jenna burst into tears again.

'I wish I was there to give you a big hug, darling, I really do. I don't know what else to say to you, my love. I just don't understand it. One moment your life is so glamorous—'

'Ha. There's nothing glamorous about a broken bloody heart,' Jenna sniffled as she wiped her eyes and nose with her sleeve.

'Okay, sweetie, let's change tack.' Sally paused to let the most recent round of sobs quieten down. 'Right, think of it this way — you're on board a super yacht with a — and yes, I've Google-stalked him — very handsome billionaire who seems to have given you the easiest PA job in the world. If you could get over Angus anywhere, surely that's the spot.'

'S'pose so,' Jenna snivelled and wiped her eyes again, but then her bottom lip quivered and her nose fizzed and the tears flowed again as the words caught in her throat. 'But . . . I thought he loved me. He said he did a million times. And I love him. I don't want to have to get over him! Oh, Sals . . . I can't bear it!'

The phone call went on like this for a while — raw upset giving way to analysis as the two friends picked apart Angus's actions over the last few weeks.

'I can see it doesn't really make sense,' Sally pondered. 'I mean, he spent almost all his inheritance buying a house for you two to share. Plus, you seemed to be having fun and, you know, the sex, you haven't complained so I assume that was okay.'

'Really was, I've the carpet burn to prove it!'

'TMI, sweetie,' Sally paused as Jenna started to sniffle again. 'Oh, and don't cry, oh please don't cry . . . So . . . what was it then?'

Between more sniffles Jenna told her friend the one thing that had been on her mind. 'He has been a little distracted recently. Sort of jumpy. I don't know, though . . . why would that translate into dumping me?'

'Sweetie, we will never understand the less fair sex.'

'Cos they really are *not* fair. This whole shit-show is so not fair.'

'Quite. And remember: he's only a man. They're not famous for their multi-tasking. Maybe, if work is worrying him, he's had to get his head down and doesn't need the distraction?'

'Charming. And no. I don't buy that. He's been busy for months and even in Hong Kong we were calling and texting.'

'Has he texted at all?'

Jenna let out a snort. 'No. And he hasn't read any of mine either — I can see that much. He's completely ghosting me.'

'Well . . . if he carries on like this, sweetie, I don't care how friendly we are with him. If he ghosts you, then he's bloody dead to me!'

Jenna did feel an ounce or two better after speaking to Sally and she had been right about something — Jenna needed a hug from a friend and the nearest thing she had to that here in Monaco was Bertie, and her lovely ex-boss,

Emma. The thought of Bertie being able to gloat about how happy she and Max were was almost enough to put her off, but at least Bertie wasn't pregnant and was too obsessed with planning her own wedding to really turn the knife in Jenna's heart.

Once she'd washed her face about forty times and tried to trowel on a bit of make-up to hide the redness around her eyes, Jenna gingerly opened the door of her cabin — unsure if she was ready at the moment to face anyone. She both feared and desperately wished that she would suddenly come face to face with Angus, but all signs pointed to him being long gone. She met no one — luckily — as she escaped the boat and headed along the harbour wall to the *Wavy Sloanes* where Bertie was staying with the Blake-Howards to 'get her sea legs' before going yacht-hunting herself. Unsure of whether to buzz herself in with the code she knew would bring the boat's walkway to surface level (easy to remember — it was 0001, or Dodo the pug's IQ, as Emma had once joked) or ring the buzzer, she was hovering on the quayside when Bertie herself sashayed along the pathway, looking for all the world like she was walking in a Milan fashion show. She was in head-to-toe Hermès — the massive H as a belt buckle the main visual clue — and had one of the brand's much-lusted-over Birkin bags dangling from the crook of her elbow.

'Dolls! *Mucho bueno* to see you, sweet cheeks!'

'Hi, Berts.'

'You sound in the doldrums, sweets.' Bertie was close enough now to see Jenna's face, the blotchiness from crying poorly covered in even her thickest foundation and largest sunglasses. Bertie lowered her own Gucci shades and peered down her perfectly modified nose at her old friend. 'Gawd, dolls — what's happened? Has PoundLand finally gone under? Primark run out of your size? What could possibly be so wrong?'

Bertie's barbs bounced straight off Jenna today. It was as if the pain of losing Angus stopped her from feeling anything else.

'Angus has dumped me.' Jenna still couldn't believe the words as she said them and followed them with a gulping kind of snort that started her tears again.

Bertie pushed her sunglasses back up her nose again and stood watching Jenna as her shoulders heaved up and down. Finally, she reached out her hand and gingerly patted Jenna on the shoulder.

'Um. There, there.' She managed the slightest of platitudes.

'Sorry, I didn't mean to start crying again, I'm just so . . .'

'So ugly crying right now?'

'Oh, Bertie, can't you be nice for one second?' Jenna pulled her sunglasses off and squinted through the morning sunshine and her salty tears.

'I'm, like, totally not wrong, though. Still . . . come on board, we can have a debrief.'

With no other option — she had barely another friend in however-many-hundred miles — Jenna placidly followed Bertie onto the Blake-Howards' yacht once the walkway had been lowered to allow them in. She hoped Emma might be on board — she would at least be slightly more sympathetic.

And she was. Plus, after an hour or two of overanalysing everything Angus had said, done, thought and probably dreamt, they had a luscious lunch made by the new chef Monty and Emma were testing out.

'Best way to cure a broken heart,' Emma had reassured her, after giving her another hug in sympathy of her plight.

'Ems, for gawd's sake don't feed her.' Bertie had chimed in, as she had waved her own place setting away and instead just laid out a few brightly coloured vitamin pills and ordered some obscure filtered mineral water from the kitchen.

'Bertie . . .' Emma sent a warning glare over to her friend before continuing, 'And what on earth are you doing?'

'High-vit, low-cal, aqua-max diet, sweetie.'

Emma and Jenna both rolled their eyes and Jenna allowed herself to smile for the first time since she'd discovered Angus's note.

'I don't know about you, Jenna dear, but I'd far rather indulge in this crab linguine . . .'

'It might not cure a broken heart, but it certainly isn't *not* helping,' Jenna agreed.

'Honestly — I cannot believe you two, carb-loading midweek. It's unconscionable. I do have a couture wedding dress to fit into in a matter of weeks, you know, and the world will be watching.'

'Really?'

'The world?'

Jenna and Emma raised their eyebrows — something they both knew their friend could never do due to the amount of Botox in her forehead.

'Um, yes. I mean, it won't be televised, although I have got some charming cameramen straight off the movie lot at Pinewood to come and do the "vid".' She raised her fingers up and quoted the last word, just in case the others thought she was using the term non-ironically.

'Bertie, dear, I think the last thing Jenna here needs to talk about is your celebrity wedding.'

'No, it's okay.' Jenna sighed and nodded a thanks over to Emma. 'It's so far from my own reality . . .'

Bertie reached a slender hand across the table and placed it on top of one of Jenna's. 'Bless you, dolls, you do say the sweetest things.'

'Right . . .' Jenna paused and wondered when it was deemed polite to remove her hand from under Bertie's talons. 'I mean, I know I'm meant to be helping you, Bertie, with the organising and all, but I might need some time off.'

Bertie snatched her hand back and looked affronted. 'You cannot.'

Even Emma looked shocked at Bertie's reaction and Jenna started to quiver slightly.

'I need you.'

'You need me?' Jenna didn't know whether to be flattered or downright scared.

'Yes. Who else will do the donkey work? I need you. You cannot leave me now, Jenna, not so close to the big day — the *grand jour*, as it were. Max is insisting on *working*,' again, the word was almost spat out, 'and he'd be useless anyway, so I need you to do all the hard work.'

'But you're not even paying me, and I do have another job.'

'Pay you? How tawdry! We're friends. I shouldn't have to *pay* you. You should want to do it.'

'TG might get annoyed if I spend all my time helping you and not him. And Berts, I'm really fucking heartbroken right now and planning your wedding to *Max*,' she emphasised his name to try to remind Bertie of their shared history, 'well, it's a bit shitty.'

Bertie just stared at her. 'But what am I going to do? Who's going to corral the rent-a-choir? And confirm the dove handler?'

'You could pay someone?'

'But I want you to do it.'

'Why?'

Jenna and Emma both looked over to Bertie, wondering what her answer would be. Why did it have to be Jenna?

'Because you're my maid of honour.'

Jenna almost spat her rosé out onto the remnants of her linguine. Emma dropped her fork with a clatter into her wide-rimmed pasta bowl.

'Since when?'

'Well, in my mind, since forever. Didn't I tell you?'

'No, Bertie, you did not tell me. Or *ask* me even. I mean, I'm flattered, but . . .'

'But what? But nothing. As maid of honour you have to help me out.'

'I haven't got a dress.'

'Good thing we're lunching with the bridesmaid dress couturier then, isn't it?' Bertie toned her rattiness down and continued in a much more soothing voice. 'Emma, darling, tailor one for yourself too. You can be my other bridesmaid.'

Emma looked as shocked as Jenna. This was certainly a lunchtime chat neither of them had expected when a bleary-eyed Jenna had first turned up. But, if she had boarded the *Wavy Sloanes* with nothing more than a broken heart she left clasping a dress bag containing a couple of Emma's BoBo dresses ('Just the look I was going for anyway, dolls!'), a maid of honour gift of a discarded pair of Gina designer shoes ('Wear them sparingly, chicks, they might not take all your weight') and Bertie's second-hand, last season Birkin handbag ('Don't you dare eBay it').

'I guess when life gives you lemons . . .' Jenna said as she tried to balance all the bags and the shoe box.

'You pop them in your G&T?' Emma was still trying to boost Jenna's mood.

'Or just squeeze them in people's eyes,' Bertie said matter of factly as she waved her new maid of honour off the boat.

Maybe it was the fact she knew Jenna was off to that amazing yacht, maybe it was the brand-new Range Rover that picked her up — pulling up just at the right moment as she was waved off the *Wavy Sloanes* — but Bertie really couldn't muster too much sympathy for Jenna. *Oh boo hoo*, Angus had left her. Well, the pair of them had been so insufferably lovey-dovey it had probably just burnt out. And, stupid girl, she was in the lap of luxury and complaining about a broken heart! Who needed a heart when you could have anything in the world! Play her cards right and that girl could be married to a billionaire before she knew it. *Jealous much* . . . Bertie allowed herself a little sigh. How bloody typical that stupid, fat Jenna should land a billionaire and Bertie had allowed herself to fall for Max — middle-rung Max. She shook her head, trying to dislodge the feelings of jealousy. Still. If you can't beat 'em, join 'em. She'd made Jenna her dogsbody of a maid of honour; she could make her her best friend too. And if she ended up bedding her best friend's man . . . *Oh fuck it*, even Bertie couldn't quite go through with the idea of sleeping with TG; Max might be middle rung in the wealth stakes, but he was pretty bloody alpha otherwise and she knew she'd regret it if they broke up. Still, Max needed to be told to keep his game up. She dialled his number.

'Maxie, darling,' she purred down the phone. 'You'll never guess what. Angus has dumped Jenna . . .' she filled her fiancé in on the morning's news and ended the call with a not-so-subtle warning. 'At least that's her side of the story. Sly minx might have just bagged herself a billionaire. Maybe I should too?'

She disconnected the call. That should keep him on his toes.

34

The next few days passed slowly, but then days tend to do that when they're punctuated every few minutes by the urgent and uncontrollable need to check your phone. No messages, though. Not from Angus, anyway. There were plenty from Bertie, reminding Jenna of her maid-of-honour responsibilities, and quite a few from Sally, who was on one hand trying very hard to be caring and sympathetic, but on the other was spitting feathers that Jenna had agreed to be maid of honour to her least favourite frenemy. And through it all TG was very forgiving of the woman he'd employed and who was turning out to be perhaps the worst PA ever. He sent her on little missions, realising that the joint benefits of physical exercise (walking anywhere in Monaco's heat and up Monaco's hills was quite an exertion) and focus on a task (truffle-flavoured saucisson was proving incredibly hard to get) would keep her mind off overanalysing Angus's desertion. He even tolerated the amount of time she spent researching wedding things for Bertie — finding a fanfare trumpeter and florist able to fill a cathedral with flowers may have seriously eaten into his working day, but they also distracted Jenna enough to keep the tears at bay for hours at a time.

'Time we went for a spin,' TG said one morning, calling his captain over to discuss a possible itinerary. To Jenna's surprise, and slight horror, Captain Avery appeared at the breakfast table.

'Captain Avery!'

'G'day, missus, mister.'

'Oh, Avery, I'm not—'

'Avery can you get us a mooring at Antibes?' TG spoke over Jenna, instructing his new captain as if nothing was out of the ordinary. When they had finished sketching out an itinerary, Avery descended back to the bridge and Jenna asked TG one of umpteen questions going through her mind.

'What's Captain Avery doing here?' *And did you pinch him from Ems and Monty?*

'I offered him a job with us.'

'Us?' Jenna felt a bit silly as soon as she said that — of course by 'us' he meant *Clickbait*. Luckily, TG seemed to ignore her and carried on.

'He's the best in the business. How the Blake-Howards managed to snag him I don't know. I offered him a better package and he jumped at it.'

As easy as that . . . Jenna sipped her morning coffee and wondered if there was anyone left on the *Wavy Sloanes* who TG hadn't poached.

Moving a yacht as massive as *Clickbait* in and out of the harbour was quite a task and Captain Avery had to radio in to the harbour master to check who else was coming and going that day. In the end, an overnighter was planned — via Saint-Jean-Cap-Ferrat — the exquisite little southern French town just to the west of Monaco — then on to Antibes before heading back. 'We'll go to the Hotel du Cap, perhaps,' TG had said, referring to the gorgeous art deco masterpiece, otherwise known as Eden-Roc, built into the cliffside at the Cap d'Antibes. 'Jenna, you'll join me, won't you?'

Jenna looked up at him. The last few days had taken their toll on her and she felt wrung out. Usually the invitation to dine somewhere as beautiful as the Eden-Roc would have someone as fun-loving as Jenna as excited as a puppy at the first mention of 'walkies', but she wasn't overly enthusiastic today.

'Look, I don't want to speak out of turn here, Jenna, but all this moping . . .'

'I'm so sorry, TG.' Jenna looked up at him as he came to sit next to her in their usual work spot — on the comfortable sofas on the sun deck.

'What can I do to cheer you up?'

Heartbroken though she was, she knew that he was offering experiences far beyond her usual pay grade. In fact, just the tip needed to secure a restaurant booking at that famous hotel would usually be way more than her monthly earnings. She smiled at him. 'You mean instead of taking me to Antibes, treating me to a fabulous meal out, and generally being extraordinarily nice to me?'

'That's more like it. And hey,' he rested his hand on her leg, 'it'll get easier. I promise.'

For a fleeting second, the warmth of his touch made her believe him, before a single tear sprung up again and she gulped down air in an effort to stop herself from blubbing. It didn't work, though, and she felt the first real sobs erupt from her as TG put his arms around her and cradled her into his chest.

A few hours later, a much calmer Jenna leant against the balustrade and watched with awe as the massive yacht gently pulled out of the harbour. How something so massive could move so gracefully — albeit quite noisily — astounded her, and it reminded her of those black-and-white cine films of Southampton docks when Cunard liners set sail, but of course there were no large-hatted Edwardian ladies waving them off for a better life in the US on this dock. *Maybe TG could give her a better life in the US?*

Jenna stood bolt upright, shocked at herself and confused as to where that thought had come from. The pang of hurt in her heart reminded her that luxury wasn't everything and she glanced down at her phone, which might as well be stapled to her hand these days, to check to see if Angus had contacted her. Nothing.

The large yacht continued to pull out of the harbour and TG came to stand next to Jenna.

'Never gets dull, does it?' he said it softly, sounding in awe as he leant against the edge of the rail. Jenna turned to him and echoed his relaxed position, leaning slightly on the balustrade and looking back towards Monte Carlo and the busy marina all around them.

'I can't see how it could. It's beautiful. I feel like we're on a stately whale, gliding through the sea with inconsequential sprats teeming below us.'

'Whale song might make a more interesting fog horn, I'll ask Avery . . .'

'Very funny.' Jenna looked up at TG and saw the glint of humour in his eyes.

'Come,' he said, and indicated for her to follow him. She pulled her eyes away from the shimmering water below. The gradual motion of the yacht had created quite a distance between the quayside mooring and the boat and the sunshine bounced off the water in the most beautiful, glistening way. *If only Angus were here with me*, Jenna sighed, and followed her boss onto the sun deck.

'I can see you're still not quite yourself.'

TG hadn't quite realised, or planned for, the fact that Jenna might need more than just a few days to get over her boyfriend. Seeing her moon about, trying to fulfil the little tasks he set her, well it filled him with equal amounts of annoyance and lust. That she was loyal, and her heart ran deep was an excellent sign — and one of the things he really liked about her was her lack of pretension or, dare he say it, finesse. But climbing into some deeply unattractive pyjamas after supper each night and holing up in the cinema room took the levels of comfy casual to new heights. TG wondered if the digital suite might run out of teary rom-coms and he'd actually asked the chief stewardess to erase the file for *The Notebook* and each *Bridget Jones* film just in case they sent her over the edge. Fine, he couldn't manipulate her into falling in love with him, but he could at least stop her from moping about so much. He needed to give her more work to do.

'Sorry, TG,' she'd replied to his gentle query. 'I know I'm being a terrible employee. I think I should, well I mean, I don't want to, but I suppose I should hand my notice in.'

This was definitely not part of the plan. 'Why?'

'Well, because I'm not really doing anything.'

'Yes you are. How else would I have got my hands on the last truffle-flavoured saucisson if you hadn't hiked up to the little deli in La Colle?'

'That was bloody hard work, actually — especially when that dog started chasing me home. I mean, how was I to know he was a trained truffle hound?'

'You got home quite quickly though.'

'So would you have done with a great big spaniel chasing you down.' She smiled at him and his desire for her grew even more. To make sure she stayed he had to make sure she felt useful — he could do that.

'So, now we've agreed you're not going anywhere, let's chat about this party you're organising for me.'

'Okay, hang on . . .' he leaned back as she dutifully reached over to where she'd left her notebook earlier and watched as she opened it up, stretching the spine and running the heel of her hand over it to keep it flat. 'Right,' she continued, 'tell me your world domination plans.'

Apart from every bit of your body . . . he thought to himself, but instead vaguely sketched out a new idea for a series of smaller more intimate parties, instead of the one large one.

Jenna, like a good PA, jotted down his thoughts. He noticed her professionalism crack slightly when he mentioned some guest ideas — for some reason the mention of one stunning American model — Diane Blane — had made her blanche and reach for a gulp of water. He'd have to use his own app to find out why, but for now, he was happy that Jenna seemed to have enough work on her plate to regard her job as a 'proper' one and he decided they should both take the afternoon off and enjoy the view as *Clickbait* motored through the waters of the Riviera to its temporary home in the beautiful Cap d'Antibes.

'*Fucking* Diane Blane!'

'Language, sweetie — bump might hear you.'

'I mean, he probably is fucking Diane Blane.'

Jenna was hissing this new piece of information down the phone to Sally as she sat on the loo in her bathroom. She'd been so desperate for a chat, but also desperate for a wee, so had called her best friend as soon as her knickers were round her ankles.

'Are you on the loo?' Sally asked, the distaste evident in her tone.

'Yes, why? Does it matter? Don't you realise, I've discovered why Angus dumped me! He must be getting back with fucking Diane Blane.'

'Yes, you've said that.'

'Sals — what's wrong?' Jenna couldn't think that swearing about her ex's ex or even having a pee so remotely from her friend would be the reason for her shortness.

'I'm fine, sweetie. I just don't think Angus for one minute is fudging Diane Blane.'

'Why not?'

'Well, why yes?'

'Because it all makes sense. TG just told me she was in Monaco and wants me to invite her to one of his little soirées that I've got to go and bloody organise and *then*, to make matters even worse, bloody Bertie texted me, like, a minute later and asked me to make sure she got one of the butterfly-filled invitation boxes for her wedding.'

'Oh I see, I think in your haste to pull your trousers down and pee you forgot to mention that she was on the same continent as you.'

'Same continent? Same bloody post code. And probably being all modelly and beautiful in front of Gus as we speak.' Jenna absent-mindedly grabbed at the loo roll as she clenched her mobile between her cheek and shoulder so she could keep talking to Sally.

'Sweetie, I still don't think he'd do that to you. I think he would have been man enough to tell you if that was the case. What did his note say again?'

'I'm sorry. I love you so much, but I can't stay with you.' Jenna felt her nose fizz and her eyes start to smart as she quoted the note easily enough — the words having been seared into her heart.

'That doesn't scream to me "I'm off to shag my ex",' said Sally, matter of factly.

Jenna flushed the loo and carried on the conversation as she flumped down onto her bed. 'It just seems pretty bloody coincidental to me.'

'Perhaps that's all it is, a coincidence?'

Jenna thought about this. 'Hmm. Still, maybe I'll find out more when I get to meet her. He wants Emma and Monty, and Bertie and Max, at the same dinner party, so at least I'll have someone to hide behind if Angus gets brought as a plus one.'

'I very much doubt he will. Still, he's in my bad books, whatever happens.'

'Thanks, Sals. Anyway, what's up with you? You seem a bit crabby.'

'Nothing really. Another scan. It's all fine though. Just getting my head around parenthood.'

'You'll be ace at it, Sals, of course you will.'

'I hope so — it's just come the autumn life will never be the same again.'

'In a good way though, Sals.' *And at least you have your husband by your side*, thought Jenna, still feeling a bit sorry for herself. 'Look, I have to go. Love you.'

'You too, sweetie, take care out there.'

35

Clickbait was like a galleon in full sail, ploughing through the water away from Monte Carlo heading west, towards Cap Ferrat and Antibes and to what TG hoped would be a fun couple of days away from the memories of Monaco and give Jenna time to get over Angus. To be fair to him, he'd kept his side of the bargain and as far as TG knew he hadn't been in touch with Jenna, who was gradually starting to open up to him.

He watched her lean against the rail at the very prow of the yacht, the wind sweeping through her hair and making the cotton material of her shirt press against her body. The envy he felt for that fabric was indescribable. He pulled his eyes away from Jenna — his very own figurehead. If he'd found her online he'd have clicked through every link on his own app. And indeed he had done a certain amount of stalking, and not just about Jenna — he wanted to know what her connection was to that American model he'd mentioned. He found a reference from a tabloid online to a fashion week from some years ago when 'so hot right now Diane Blane' was linked to 'a tall Englishman our sources are out to unmask.' The gutter press and their dog-like persistence made it easy for TG to find out that the mysterious man was no other than Angus Linklater. So that's why Jenna had baulked at her being invited on board.

Jenna couldn't help but giggle as TG topped up her glass of rosé and recounted another story he'd heard from the crew. She knew that she was lucky with both of her recent employers, as it was definitely not the norm for the likes of the Blake-Howards or TG to be so easy and unguarded with staff and crew. In fact, there was one yacht owner, TG had told her over their starter of steak tartare and baby-leaf salad, who had divers suit-up and swim around his boat before he splashed into the sea, just in case there was a hint of danger in the water.

'Sharks? Around here?'

'Possibly, but most likely IEDs or surveillance planted under the yacht by paparazzi or corporate spies.'

'It's such a rarefied life, isn't it?' Jenna hoped she hadn't insulted her boss — right now her very handsome dinner companion — by pointing out what a weird world it was.

'I'm lucky. We're lucky.'

His reply was typical of him, Jenna was learning. Slightly cryptic and enigmatic.

'So you want to know what happened to these guys or not?' TG asked and Jenna found herself forgetting her heartache as he finished off the story recently gleaned from Captain Avery.

'Yes, carry on. Sorry. You'd got to the bit when they'd asked Avery to bring them here, to Antibes for a night.'

Jenna remembered Monty had mentioned that even the richest owners often 'rented' out their yachts for weeks at a time. She'd been astonished when she'd heard that the particular group he was talking about now — a gang of forty-somethings from London who all worked in the City (*quelle surprise*) had paid almost a million euros to charter a yacht for a week.

'So, they took the tenders over to the mainland and found a nightclub. Avery had told them to call him and the crew would pick them up, you know, any time of the night, whatever.' He waved his hand to emphasise the point that the crew really were on call twenty-four seven.

'And?' Jenna finished her steak and placed the cutlery together on her plate. Before TG could even start talking again her plate was whisked away from her.

'Avery was woken up by the coast guard siren. He looked through his binos and saw a huge cloud of dirty smoke coming from the nearby harbour. He just knew it — knew it was those bozos from this boat. Know what they did? Instead of calling him, they were so drunk they decided to steal a fishing boat to get back to the yacht.'

'What on earth?'

'Not only that, they chose the dirtiest, most broken old tug they could find, and the smoke was the shitty old diesel engine not enjoying being fired up after about three years of not being used!'

'What happened?' Jenna leaned back as another fine porcelain plate was placed down in front of her — this time it had an elegant spatchcocked poussin on it, accompanied by fine julienned vegetables and a fondant potato.

'Avery had to bribe the harbour master not to call the gendarmes and he managed to get them all back on board.'

'It often amazes me,' Jenna said while attacking the bird in front of her, 'how such clever men, who must have some level of acumen, can be such complete idiots!'

'That's alcohol for you. Still, it beats the guy who got so drunk that he crapped himself and Avery made him strip down and hosed him off on the quayside.'

'Oh, TG! Please, not over lunch!' They both laughed and continued chatting about the bonkers stories that swam around the Riviera like a shoal of very entertaining fish.

That afternoon Jenna took her notebook up to the sun deck, along with her two mobile phones and decided that a bit of work could go hand in hand with some sunbathing. Being nowhere near a hairdresser (although she had recently found out that one of the crew was a trained masseur — knowledge banked for a later date) she could hardly do that post-break-up thing of cutting her hair or sprucing up her wardrobe. Although with no need now to spend a fortune on Angus's birthday present she realised she really could hit Selfridges when she got back. In fact, a quick check of her bank balance showed her a rather pleasant surprise. TG had paid her her first month's salary, which at €10,000 was quite positively the largest deposit she'd ever received. She settled herself down on a sunlounger in order to soak up some rays and plan exactly which Mulberry handbag she would treat herself to once she was home.

The thought of home shook her. Where would she go once she'd finished her work here? She'd completely forgotten to think about how on earth she'd get all her stuff from their — Angus's — house when she needed it. Tears sprang back into her eyes, but she was exhausted from crying so much and refused to let herself burst into sobs again. Instead, she delved under the sunlounger for her personal phone and typed out a quick message, but hovered over the send button before deleting it all. She couldn't bring herself to text Angus, no matter what the situation — he hadn't replied to any of her other messages and she was done begging. She sent one to Sally instead, who had a spare set of keys, and felt the solemnity — and finality — of the situation as she texted her friend to start, if she could, removing her stuff.

Of course darling — and do come and crash at ours for a bit once you're home if you need to. Though you might not want to after October . . . wahwahwah

Typical Sals, thought Jenna as she texted back a thank you. Always there for me, but somehow always reminding me that I'm further away from settling down than ever. Jenna flicked open the notebook and rolled over onto her front. If haircuts and new wardrobes weren't on the getting-over-Angus agenda then she better make a note to start looking for her own place — and work on an enviable Saint-Tropez tan while she did.

36

The warm breeze gently lifted the corner of Jenna's towel and played with the tendrils of her hair as she lay on the massage table. Unlike Nikki Beach, the cabanas along the shore at the Hotel du Cap-Eden-Roc weren't merely glorified four-poster beds, these were elegant little beach huts, each one with a stunning view of the rocky coastline, a private terrace perfect for dining and enough room, as Jenna had found out to her absolute surprise and pleasure, for a massage table.

'I know what you need,' TG had said the evening before as they'd relaxed on board *Clickbait*, nursing glasses of rosé and watching the twinkling lights of the port town of Antibes across the shimmering moonlit water.

'A bloody good talking to, probably.' Jenna wasn't unaware that one's own personal heartbreak could be mightily dull for other people. Luckily for Jenna, TG had outlined quite possibly the most perfect day. Their tender would take them over to this glorious, old-fashioned but oh-so-elegant hotel where she could relax in one of the private cabanas until they moseyed down to the restaurant for lunch.

The masseur rolled her knuckles around Jenna's back and she felt the knots and tension ease away with every motion. The harder the masseur worked, the more Jenna felt released from the yoke she'd been carrying, the heavy weight of emotion that had been weighing on her shoulders. If only she could massage her heart in the same way. She closed her eyes and listened to the sounds of the world around her. Unlike Monte Carlo it was quiet here.

The constant slap, slap, slap of the waves hitting the rocks below became a mesmerising bass note, with bird song floating in above. Jenna listened to the distant chatter of hotel guests, her mind making up little stories about who was on the swimming pool terrace below. In her mind's eye they were androgynous 1930s socialites, dapper blazer-wearing gents and moustachioed waiters. She was brought very much back to the present by the sound of a deep cough. She opened her eyes and turned her head around on the massage table. TG was standing there, looking at her, smiling. She smiled back. She lazily closed her eyes again as the masseur pushed her knuckles into her shoulder blades again. She didn't mind that TG was watching, even though she was lying there, half naked, with only a towel protecting her modesty. This was the south of France, after all, and he could look in almost any direction and see a nudey sunbather if he wanted to. The masseur worked deeper, running the pressure down Jenna's spine, thumbing the small of her back causing her to arch it slightly in a cat-like response. The strong hands had absolute control over Jenna, as she responded to the kneading, pressing and rubbing. She opened her eyes again and found herself to be a little disappointed that TG wasn't standing there any more. She'd been enjoying being watched in a way: it was empowering knowing that someone so rich, so powerful was concentrating only on you.

She had wondered to herself if TG did fancy her. The thought had obviously crossed her mind — what with Ems and Bertie both suggesting he was on the lookout for more than a PA. And she had to admit that while she knew little about office admin work, one thing she did know was that being massaged in the Riviera's most exclusive hotel wasn't part of the usual daily slog.

The masseur touched a nerve and Jenna suddenly took in a deep breath. In so doing she noticed that the unmistakable cologne of TG, the warm cedar and musk, was so close to her.

'Oh!'

'Thought you might appreciate a firmer hand to work through these knots . . .'

TG's voice was soft and calm, his hands still lay on her back, their heat working like healing stones, easing the tension across her muscles. *Bloody hell!* What had she just been thinking to herself? Being massaged in the Riviera's most exclusive hotel *by your billionaire boss* — yup, definitely not your normal nine-to-five. While Jenna's muscles were soothed, her mind was in chaos, and with every stroke of his hands another thought fired off in her brain: *What would Angus think? Would he be jealous? Would I prefer it was him? This should be him. Of course . . . of course?*

After the massage, which luckily had ended before Jenna's brain went into overdrive and blew-up, TG had given her some privacy and she'd slipped her clothes back on. Meeting back outside the cabana they then wandered through the hotel grounds together and ended up on the terrace, where during a languid lunch of langoustine and more rosé they chatted about their families, their hopes, their friends . . . and throughout the whole meal Jenna could still feel the firm touch of TG's hands on her naked back and wondered if he had felt the same unmistakable tingle through his fingers as was still coursing through her body.

37

Jenna lay back on the sunlounger on *Clickbait* and closed her eyes. The afternoon breeze cooled her down as she soaked up the sun's rays — slathered in Factor 30, of course — and she took stock of the last couple of days. They'd been to Cap Ferrat and snorkelled in the crystal blue waters of Fossette beach. Then there was this morning's excursion to the cabana at the Hotel du Cap and, of course, lunch too.

Sally's words rung through her head — *if you're going to get over Angus anywhere it might as well be on a handsome billionaire's yacht* — well, she was right in a way. Although Jenna would have taken some satisfaction in knowing she was doing a good job — like she had when she worked for the Honourable Emma — she was also fully aware that she was getting away with being the world's worst PA, and getting paid a king's ransom for it.

Well, not *worst* . . . she hadn't accidentally deleted any files, insulted any clients or lost any of TG's dry-cleaning — but that was only because she didn't have any filing to do, there were no clients to speak of and the yacht's own laundry dealt with all of their washing. If she didn't feel so raw and miserable about Angus dumping her she would probably have had more of a stern word with herself about this unrealistic life she was living. She wasn't blind to the fact that it was all rather odd — the memory of TG's hands massaging her back a few hours ago was still foremost in her mind — and it didn't sit right with her usual work ethos, but she was too emotionally exhausted to question anything at the moment. She *had* managed to book a bugler for Bertie's wedding, so that was something to comfort herself with. And, from her sunbed, she had arranged a few little soirées for TG for when they were back in Monaco, and much to her chagrin, one of them included inviting Diane bloody Blane, the super-hot super model who Jenna was convinced Angus had just left her for. She'd gritted her teeth as that invitation had been sent via Diane's agent and had mouthed a little swear word or two to herself when the RSVP came back in the affirmative. Jenna was just wondering if it would be bad form to wear her new bridesmaid dress courtesy of BoBo to that party when she remembered that both Emma and Bertie would be guests that night too. Damn.

Back to the suitcase drawing board . . . or if she had some time off (who was she kidding — she had hardly anything to do on the boat) she could perhaps spend some of those, to her shame *not* very hard-earned euros, on something fabulous once they got back to port.

Jenna's musings were interrupted by TG coming up to the sun deck and sitting down next to her. Jenna suddenly felt very aware that she was only in a bikini, even though only a few hours ago TG had seen — and touched — her in substantially less . . . Still, she felt his gaze alight on her and, rather than feeling vulnerable or embarrassed as she would have done only a few days before, she felt empowered again.

'Shall I read you out the confirmed guests for the dinner party, TG?' She felt the need to break the ice.

'If you like. Shoot.'

'So, Bertie Mason-Hoare and Max Finch. He's flying in for it specially. Thanks for inviting them, nice to have some pals on board! And of course Emma and Monty Blake-Howard.' Jenna paused. 'Diane Blane is a yes, as is Roland Le Messer . . .'

'Ah yes, the fashion designer. Good. I thought he'd make a good pairing with your friend Emma and an excellent plus-one for Diane.'

Jenna didn't want TG to see how grateful she felt — to have Diane there was bad enough, if she'd been bringing Angus as a plus one Jenna's nose would have been so rubbed in it, it might have been rubbed right off. And the Voldemort look was not a good one.

'Wonderful,' Jenna squeaked out the word.

TG laughed. 'Hey, Jenna. I'm sorry. I did some research. I know Diane and Angus were a pair. But you know I wouldn't let him back on board, don't you? Not after leaving you like that?'

'Thank you, TG.' Jenna reached out and squeezed his arm and felt a rush of energy as he reached over and placed his hand on top of hers. Goosebumps spread up her arms and Jenna hoped TG didn't notice. But his hand — their hands — lingered more than she thought they might and it seemed hours until they both pulled away from each other, although it couldn't have been more than a few seconds.

'TG . . .' Jenna again felt the need to break the silence. 'Can I ask you a favour?'

'Shoot.'

'Can you spare me tomorrow morning? I need to pop to the shops as I think I might need something more elegant to wear than my jeans.'

'Sure. And hey, as it's a work thing, take this.' He reached his hand into his back pocket and brought out his wallet. Out of it he slipped a black American Express card and handed it to Jenna. 'It's on me.'

'Oh, TG, no. I mean, I really couldn't.' Jenna couldn't quite believe what TG was doing. 'You've already paid me.' Jenna pushed his card back towards him. 'Thank you though, I do appreciate it.'

'Hey, if you're sure. But it's work-related shopping . . .'

'I'm sure. Thank you.' Jenna sat upright and pulled her sarong around her and secured it around her chest. She stood up as TG was placing the smart black credit card back in his wallet. Was he smiling to himself? Jenna took a deep breath and was about to say something when she heard, and felt, the engines fire up.

'We'll be back in port in an hour or so.' TG stood up too and to Jenna's surprise, placed his hands on the tops of her bare arms. 'Sure about the AMEX?'

'Sure.' Jenna smiled at him. 'Thanks again.'

She was grateful for the offer, but even if she was the world's worst PA, she didn't need to be the world's most expensive one, too. However easily earned, she had the cash to pay her own way now, and it felt amazing.

38

What also felt amazing, at about eleven the next morning, was the raw silk of the dress in Lanvin that she was trying on, not even looking at the price tag. Its silky fabric — heck, it probably was actually silk — floated just above her knee, but the waist was cinched in and showed off her new, slightly svelter figure. Who knew so much seafood and rosé could beat Weight Watchers in securing you a belter of a belt line? Jenna did a little twirl and liked how the skirt flared out a bit and how she didn't need heels to make her legs look good in it — lucky, as shoes were *verboten* on board the yacht. In fact, it was almost a shame that she couldn't justify buying the beautiful silver high heels that the fawning sales assistant had tentatively put in front of her.

'*Combien?*' Jenna indicated the dress and the assistant took a moment to find the discreet tag that was tied to the zip at the back of the dress.

'One thousand, four hundred and ninety-nine euros and ninety-nine cents,' the assistant said in perfect English.

Jenna gulped and couldn't quite believe she heard herself saying the next bit, 'And the shoes?'

'Four hundred and ninety-nine euros, madam.'

'Gosh. They are both rather lovely though.' Jenna did another little twirl, this time with the shoes on, and liked the way the back of the dress revealed a little bit of her shoulder blades. 'I'll take them.' Jenna smiled, as much to herself in the mirror as to the waiting assistant. 'Let me just take this off.'

A few minutes and a couple of thousand euros later, Jenna left the shop feeling exhilarated. She had never, *ever* done that before, let alone done it quite so guilt-lessly. Yes, of course there was a flat deposit to save for, but at the rate that TG seemed to pay her, she'd be moving into Holland Park next to Bertie and Max in no time! She swung the smart boutique's bag by her side as she walked down the hill away from the shops and back towards the harbour. A quick check of her watch (ooh, there's another thing that could be upgraded from the simple Casio digital one, where was Cartier anyway?) and Jenna decided that she had enough time before she needed to be back for her menu-planning meeting with TG and the chef, so she walked over towards the Café de Paris on Casino Square and let the maître d' find her a little table. Wielding the Lanvin shopping bag didn't hurt when it came to being taken seriously by the staff and Jenna found herself being put on a rather good table right by the edge of the terrace with the best view of Casino Square — perfect for some people-watching. Being paid thousands of euros for her job meant that she didn't wince either when she saw the prices in the menu, and ordered herself a glass of rosé from the only-to-happy-to-please waiter. Moments later a perfectly chilled glass of wine was put in front of her along with some little crackers.

Jenna settled into her chair, pulled her sunglasses down over her eyes and decided to watch the world, or at least the wealthiest 0.1 per cent of it, go by. A succes-sion of roaring super cars paraded around the square, some pulling in outside the Hotel de Paris on the other side from where she sat, and some stopping in front of the casino only to be valet parked elsewhere or revved up and moved on with their parade. Jenna tried to count the wealth — what each one of those cars would be worth, not to mention the Monaco residents and rich tourists who walked by wearing fur (in this heat? Jenna was amazed at the lengths they'd go to show off), the children dressed to match their mothers in designer, but to Jenna's mind quite trashy-looking, clothes. The jewels that glinted sunshine back at her and then a rev as another Lambo, Bugatti or Aston Martin pulled away and throttled-down up the hill. A particularly menacing-looking black Ferrari grunted its way around the square and Jenna's eyes followed it as it thundered down towards the port.

Suddenly her heart leapt in her chest — was that . . .? No . . .? Angus? On the other side of the square? He was walking along, talking to someone. *Oh God, no.* The tall, beautiful dark-skinned woman walking next to Angus on the other side of the square was Diane Blane! Jenna sat upright in her seat to get a better view, then thought better of it and slouched down again, making sure she was disguised by her massive sunglasses and even more massive shopping bag. She squinted to try to work out more from their body language, but one thing was absolutely clear: Angus and Diane were definitely friendly. Diane was holding his arm (no wonder, those heels were something else!) and laughing at what he was saying. So, she had been right. Damn it! Damn him! Jenna downed her wine and hurriedly found a twenty-euro note to slip into the bill sleeve. She felt flustered and all the happiness she'd just gleaned from her retail therapy had disappeared as she clumsily left the table and started wiping away tears as they sprung from her eyes beneath the dark glasses. *Damn him!* There had never been a time when Jenna had hated being right quite so much.

Like a huge tinted-windowed, diesel-guzzling knight in shining armour, the Range Rover appeared from nowhere and Jenna, in a shock-induced stupor didn't care how Seb had known where to find her. She let him open the door for her and she climbed in before her legs gave way, hot tears already falling down her cheeks.

Arriving back at the yacht she didn't wait for Seb to come and open her door and she almost fell out of the large car in her hurry to get back on board. She was grateful to hear the sound of the hydraulics in motion as the massive walkway gradually lowered towards her. She leapt up onto it before it could properly touch the quayside, remembering at the last minute to take off her shoes, which meant she half hopped and half lurched up the companion way and then up the wide steps onto the main deck. No sunglasses in the world were large enough to disguise the fact that her cheeks were streaked with wetness. Jenna stumbled along, half blinded by her own tears and wanted nothing more than to throw herself onto her bed in her cabin and cry her heart out.

'Jenna.' The warm Canadian voice sounded out to her, and as little as Jenna wanted to, she felt she better stop and see what TG wanted. She turned to face him, and in a moment he had closed the gap between them and had wrapped his arms around her. 'Jenna, shush,' he said, comfortingly. 'What's wrong? What happened?'

'I saw them . . .' the rest of the sentence was muffled as she pressed her face into his chest, letting his arms take the strain of holding her up, her hands losing their grip on shoes and bag as they fell to the deck. She felt TG strengthen his hold on her and she liked it; she liked the cedar notes of his aftershave and the soft cotton of his shirt and she liked the comforting beat of his heart next to her ear as she tried to stop snuffling and raise her head to explain to him what had happened. He shushed her some more though and cradled her head with one of his hands, before starting to stroke her hair.

'It's fine, it's all fine,' he reassured her, his voice coming from somewhere so close to her ear that his lips must almost be touching her skin. Slightly reluctantly, Jenna pulled herself away from him just a little.

'I saw Angus in town. With Diane Blane. The bastard.'

'Jeez. I'm sorry, Jenna.' TG stroked her head again and then left his hand gently cradling the back of her head. She felt like she could just stay there forever, the hurt of seeing Angus with another woman dulled by the electrics that seemed to be going off inside her as she leant into him and felt him return her embrace.

'Well, we can cut her from tomorrow night's list.' TG said it matter of factly, reassuringly, and Jenna was relieved, but then another thought entered her head.

'No.' She couldn't believe she was saying this. 'Best not. She'll have no idea why and it could cause offence, plus she's friends with Bertie, I think, and probably awfully good for Emma's fashion brand.'

'Sure?' Jenna loved that TG was on her side, but she liked being the bigger person too.

'Sure.' She paused for a bit. Her arms still hung by her sides, kept there by TG's hug and she didn't know how to extricate herself, or even if she wanted to. He moved first and gradually released her.

'Still okay for the meeting with chef and Avery?'

'Uh-huh.' Jenna felt light as air as he took his arms away and wondered if a stiff breeze would be all it would take to blow her off the deck and up into the sky, free from Angus and heartbreak and the confusing feelings that had started to stir just below the surface for her incredibly handsome – and extremely caring – boss.

'Let me get myself together and I'll see you in the dining room in a mo.'

TG nodded down to her and turned and walked away, while Jenna slowly picked up her shoes and the bag containing her new dress and high heels. If nothing had prepared her for the pain of seeing Angus and Diane together, she thought to herself, then it had been even more of a shock when she realised that she definitely, probably . . . no, definitely had started to form quite an attachment to TG too.

39

The day of TG's little soirée had been busy for Jenna — so much so that she hadn't been able to dwell on her feelings for Angus as much as she ordinarily might have. She'd managed to get through the meeting with TG, Captain Avery and the chef the afternoon before without bursting into tears — although when the chef had mentioned 'steak Diane' as a possible main course choice for the dinner party, Jenna had wanted to weep into her notebook and it had taken all her resolve and mental willpower not to blub right there and then. She'd noticed TG look over to her as the chef had carried on talking about food and luckily by the time the decision had been made to start with heritage tomato tart with a goat's cheese mousse, followed by roasted guinea fowl with a truffle-infused puréed potato and finished off with tiramisu and coffee — well, luckily Jenna was thinking more of her stomach than her ex-boyfriend. With the meeting over, however, she'd made her excuses and had only made it back to her cabin before the tears were ready to spring back into action.

'I doubt she'll eat any of it anyway, if she's as thin as all that.'

Sally had answered the phone when Jenna had called, and in only the way a best friend can, had understood through the hiccups and sniffs the garbled extent of Jenna's news. 'And Bertie won't let that much saturated fat through her cake hole, we know that for sure. Gosh, what a waste. I wish I could come and hoover it all up — am craving far worse stuff at the moment!'

'At least Angus won't be there,' Jenna said in a half whisper, ignoring Sally's mention of pregnancy cravings. 'TG said he'd never let him back on board now.'

'Too right. He's been a bastard. And cowardly too, what with all that "I love you so much I have to leave you" crap.' Jenna let Sally continue as she was in full flow. 'I take it back, you were right, JJ, he may well have left you for that socialite model girl after all.'

'And I can't believe I have to be nice to her in, oh, less than twenty-four hours' time.'

'Sucks.'

'Yeah, sucks big time.'

'Could be worse though,' Sally carried on. 'You *are* on a super yacht with someone super hot. Avoiding models during nice little drinkies parties is somewhat of a hashtag first world problem.'

Jenna knew Sally was just trying to cheer her up, and yes, undoubtedly she was in the most luxurious surroundings she'd ever been in, but Sally's words didn't give her the comfort they were meant to. She ended the call with her best friend and lay back down on her bed. The sheets were soft, the mattress like a cloud, the air around her was delicately scented with posh candles. Jenna let out a long sigh. Perhaps Sally was right.

'Still sucks though,' she mumbled to herself.

The trauma of seeing Angus and Diane together, and then having to repeat the whole sorry story to both TG and Sally, had meant that Jenna slept badly and she was lucky that, although busy, she hadn't had to get up particularly early the next morning. When your commute was only a few steps from bed to sunbed you could pretty much press 'snooze' on the alarm as much as you wanted. Jenna was annoyed that her late-night sobs had left her with puffy eyes again and so donned her usual uniform of white jeans, a nice T-shirt and the largest pair of sunglasses she could find as she chased up the chef, confirmed arrival times with chauffeurs, and directed the cleaning staff around the yacht for the morning. By the afternoon she was left with the final chore: to make sure the dining table was looking fantastic.

Jenna had always loved dinner parties — usually they were cramped little affairs around someone's cautiously extended dining table, with guests squeezed into a flat far too small for the raucous games that came afterwards. Even as her friends had got older and wealthier and bought houses and larger flats, the dinners had still been quite basic — mix-and-match crockery and cutlery, last-minute calls to neighbours to borrow a kitchen chair, puddings still defrosting as hastily made canapés were passed round on plates that were then quickly washed and put on the table for the main courses. They were fun, noisy, frenetic affairs with a frisson in the air, especially when she had been single, and hoped that perhaps the promised 'I've got this lovely friend of James's coming, he's a lawyer and fearfully intelligent' would finally be The One. Usually he was just the one who bored everyone rigid with his stories that always ended, 'you had to be there, I guess'.

Jenna smiled to herself as she stood and admired her handiwork in this luxurious and vast dining room aboard *Clickbait*. How different was this to those dinner parties. There was no mismatched crockery here — the finest Wedgwood plates, each one ringed with gold leaf, sat upon golden chargers, while each place setting had different crystal glasses for white and red wine, plus dessert wine, then also water and a small glass for any liqueurs or port they might fancy. If this had been one of those London dinner parties, Jenna would have thought it either seriously pretentious or interpreted it as they were going to get shitfaced that night. But something told her that here, in these sophisticated surroundings, when the wine was of such good quality, it would be a different story.

Her finishing touch — as of course the glasses and plates, although stunning, were just the essentials — was to decorate the candelabra in the centre of the table with swags of ivy. She'd had it brought over from a florist at huge cost — who knew finding ivy in the summer in Monaco was so hard? The trails of leaves flowed around full, white blossom heads of hydrangea, the pretty multi-flowered ball-like heads each pinpricked with little lights that made them look completely otherworldly. It was a stunning look — the dark green of the ivy, the gold of the plates, the sparkling crystal and the twinkling flower heads under the dark, starlit ceiling of the dining room. Pleased with her work, and perhaps only a little sentimental for the lack of chipped mugs instead of wine glasses, she headed back to her cabin to get ready for the evening ahead.

40

Jenna dropped her phone onto her bed and sighed. No message from Angus — not even a 'so sorry tonight will be mega awkward for you with my new girlfriend there' sort of text. Although Jenna wasn't even sure if that sort of text was ever sent, but then no one else seemed to have the same sort of rubbish heap of a love life as her. She wrapped the silky bathrobe around her — she was sure it hadn't been in her cabin when she first moved in, a point driven further home by the fact it had an embroidered J on the left-hand lapel — and stepped over her discarded jeans and T-shirt into the bathroom. The mirror had de-steamed and she could see her face clearly now — tanned and blemish-free. She felt quite happy with how she looked, especially now her eyes had finally had a chance to de-puff after all the crying. This super-yacht life, heartbreak aside, was obviously working for her.

An idea suddenly occurred to her. Why not work like this all the time? Be TG's personal PA here in Monaco all year round? Why should she move back to London at the end of the summer if there wasn't an Angus-shaped birthday to get back for? And Lord knows she didn't have another job to go to. Jenna made a mental note to find TG in his study — a room in the yacht that she hadn't been into, bizarrely, given the nature of her job. Her mind wandered as she applied make-up — just a bit of highlighter and bronzer to emphasise the tan and lashings of dark mascara to complement the little black dress that she slipped on once back in the bedroom. The Lanvin tailoring looked as good now as it had in the boutique yesterday and Jenna loved the feel of the black silk against her skin as she managed to pull the zip up the back. *That was the key to being single*, she thought bitterly, *always make sure you can do your own zip up.*

TG closed the safe in his study and pulled the abstract sketch back over to hide the door. Cubism to hide a cube — he kinda liked that word play. The overhead LED lights glinted off the facets in the diamond earrings, the bright pinpoints of light a stark contrast to the black velvet of the box in which they sat. He snapped the lid shut and slipped the box into the pocket of his chinos, before turning off the light to the room and closing the door with a reassuring click behind him.

Jenna smiled as Bertie wafted up the companion way and headed to meet them on the main deck, where one of the Tweedles was waiting with a bottle of the iconic Roederer Cristal champagne, while one of the gorgeous stewardesses was positioned next to him ready with the champagne flutes.

'It's going to be a cracker of a night,' the South African said to her.

'Thanks, Seb.' Jenna prayed she had the right name and his smile confirmed it. 'Got to prove that I'm worth having around.'

'I'm sure mister thinks so.'

Jenna couldn't reply to this enigmatic comment as Bertie was now air-kissing her and then, as Jenna was enveloped in a hug by her old friend Max, she heard the most amazing thing she thought she'd ever heard Bertie say.

'You look divine, Jenna sweetie.'

'Wow, um, thanks, Bertie.'

'Def hen do applicable for next week. Celine?'

'Lanvin, actually.' Jenna couldn't quantify how good it made her feel to be able to say that — it was like every Bertie barb that had ever been uttered had now fallen, like broken arrows to the ground, and if possible, Jenna felt like Bertie was, for the first time since about 2010, treating her like an equal.

'Gorge. Love it.'

'You look stunning, Jenks,' Max reassured her as he gave her shoulder a quick squeeze before thrusting out a hand to his host, who had appeared on the main deck and now, glass in hand, was being fawned over by a particularly tactile Bertie. Jenna was just counting how many times she heard Bertie use the word 'super' when she was caught in a hug by Emma Blake-Howard. By now Jenna was used to the hugs from these angular women — when, however well intentioned, you were more likely to be left with an imprint from their massive bangles or statement necklace than a warm and fuzzy feeling.

'How are you doing, darling?' she whispered. 'Okay?'

'Ups and downs.' Jenna rubbed her arm where Emma's Cartier *Juste un Clou* bent-nail-shaped bracelet had just dug into her.

'Not surprised.'

Jenna paused for a second, before remembering what she'd been dying to quiz Emma on for the last few days. 'Ems, um, I'm so sorry about Captain Avery. I had no idea . . .'

'Oh, don't worry, sweetie. *All's fair in love and water* and all that. This new boss of yours has a way of getting what he wants.' Jenna looked confused until Emma rubbed her thumb and fingers together to indicate that some money had changed hands. 'I can't say I blame him though, dear old Avery was like a second nanny to us — he really is the best. And when you can afford the best . . .' she shrugged and gave Jenna another jangling hug before letting Monty

215

through to kiss their hostess. Just as she was helping them both to a glass of champagne from the tray, Jenna noticed a black SUV pull up on the quayside. The tinted windows and low-line suspension was meant to secure the occupant's privacy but Jenna always thought that nothing shouted 'look at me, I'm rich and famous' as much as a blacked-out people carrier — the celebrity-sized sunglasses of the automotive world.

The side door of the people carrier slid open automatically and Jenna peered over the edge of the yacht deck to get a better look at the woman who appeared to glide out. She was tall and elegant, but strong-looking too. Jenna had stalked her Instagram page earlier, scouring it for mentions or photos of Angus and had noticed the use of hashtags such as #strongnotskinny and #power. Jenna watched as she elegantly took her shoes off and treated the walkway up to the yacht like it was a New York Fashion Week catwalk. Putting on the falsest of smiles, Jenna welcomed her on board.

'You must be Diane?'

Seb poured a glass of champagne for her but Diane raised a hand to indicate that she didn't want one. *Blimey*, thought Jenna, *even Bertie drinks champagne*.

'Not for me. Do you have any sparkling *l'eau minerale*?'

Her use of fancy Franglais annoyed Jenna more than she thought possible. Through gritted teeth she indicated that Diane should follow her across the deck to meet TG. Luckily, Bertie took over the introductions, swooping in to air-kiss Diane and lavish attention on her, so Jenna could go back to her station next to Seb and the waitress and wait for the final guest, this fashion designer bloke, to arrive.

'I barely eat any products that have been touched by animals any more. It's just not morally acceptable.' Diane was explaining why she couldn't eat the carefully planned menu and Jenna was resisting the urge to ask her why she hadn't mentioned the fact that she was a vegan when she RSVP'd. Luckily, Max asked the question for her and Diane's reply had been priceless. 'Surely it should be the norm now that you assume veganism? And people should admit to eating animals and therefore being complicit in their murder when they reply. It might make them think twice.'

'But no one murdered the nice goat who just got milked for that cheese.' Jenna had been brave enough to pipe up.

Diane stared at her and Jenna wondered how much Angus had told her about his ex. 'How would you like it, Jenna, if your titties were squeezed by rough hands and forced to ejaculate milk for some other species' pleasure?'

There was a deathly silence in the room as the guests contemplated this particularly striking visual image. Diane looked smug though, and although Jenna wanted to disappear into the furnishings with embarrassment (would TG forgive her for leading the conversation like that?) she also wanted to lean across the table and rub her amazingly delicious goat's cheese tart in Diane's sanctimonious face.

Amazingly, the conversation started up again, with Bertie addressing Roland and asking about his latest collection. Emma joined in their conversation and soon Monty and TG were comparing boat engines and talking about hydro power and fuel efficiency.

Max, who was sitting next to Jenna, turned and whispered in her ear, 'Fuck me.'

'There was a time when . . .' Jenna smiled at him and he blushed slightly.

'Ha. No, I meant, bloody hell. She's a fun hoover, isn't she?'

Jenna laughed and almost choked on her steamed asparagus. When she stopped coughing she turned back to Max and asked him, 'I just can't imagine Gus with her.'

'I think she was a bit more lenient back in Singapore. More your basic veggie rather than a militant vegan.'

'Didn't you know?'

'What?'

'He's back with her now!' Jenna dropped the bombshell.

'No!' Max looked genuinely taken aback.

'I saw them together in the square yesterday.'

Max was silent. But he put his cutlery down and reached across and rested his hand on Jenna's. This little action of comfort almost made her choke up again but crying was the last thing she wanted to do tonight. Instead she squeezed Max's hand back and whispered over to him, 'I bet she keeps a packet of pork scratchings in her handbag.'

Max's laughter filled the room and from then on the dinner party conversation flowed just as it should, with only Diane looking slightly po-faced when TG swapped seats away from her to sit next to Jenna as the rich-with-dairy-cream pudding was brought to the table.

An hour or so later Jenna stood back and let the rest of the party go ahead of her to the sun deck where the crew had laid out a samovar of coffee and petits fours, along with the option of any digestif anyone could want. Max poured himself a large cognac and murmured a little 'don't mind if I do' as a short-skirted stewardess offered him a fat cigar from the humidor. TG was being an excellent host and made sure everyone had what they needed and Jenna couldn't help but get a small prick of jealousy as she saw how both Diane and Bertie seemed to be vying for his attention.

Jenna couldn't help but stare at Diane. Her skin was so smooth, so perfectly contoured and highlighted. Her hair, close cropped and naturally afro, showed off her exquisite jawline and high cheekbones. She was perfection in female form — perhaps that was what a vegan diet did for you — and Jenna's self-confidence nose-dived as she thought about Gus, her Gus, preferring this divine being to her. It didn't help when she overheard Diane talking to Bertie about her latest boyfriend. Jenna hovered by the samovar, pretending to refill what must have seemed like a bottomless cup of coffee as she listened in.

'He's newly single, which is great as I'd been eyeing him up for a while. But his last girlfriend was a nightmare, apparently.'

'Oh babes, do tell. What's he like?'

'He's a nice guy. A bit meat-eaty for my taste, but I can change that.'

'Oh, I'm totally on board with what you're saying. From now on no animal products shall touch my lips. How many likes do you get for those hashtags by the way?'

'Bertie,' Jenna heard the American accent whine, 'veganism isn't just for Instagram, you know.'

'Oh yah, obvs.'

This was hilarious, and Jenna loved hearing Bertie be put in her place, but she wanted to know more about Diane's new lover. Luckily, Bertie was shamed into going back to that conversation.

'So he's, like, British and really sweet, but damaged y'know?'

'Aren't they all, Diane sweetie? Which school screwed him up?'

Jenna almost scalded herself as she concentrated on the conversation, not the boiling water.

'Not so much the school as the last girlfriend. She was a lunatic.'

Steady on, thought Jenna.

'She'd, like, doubt everything he said, she has almost toxically low self-esteem so she'd cause arguments over nothing . . .'

As Diane continued, Jenna got more and more angry. Had Gus really described her like that? She was tempted to turn around and set the record straight about a few things when she felt a hand on her shoulder.

'Need any help with that? You've been there quite a while.'

'Ah. TG. No, it's fine.' Jenna took a deep breath and offered him a coffee. He accepted and she joined him, sadly out of earshot of Bertie and Diane and their gossiping. She kept looking over at them though and could get the gist of what Diane was saying by the way their heads were bowed low in conspiratorial discussion. Jenna knew that if Bertie could move her eyebrows, they'd be sky high by now. *Bloody Diane bloody beautiful Blane*, Jenna thought. *She's nicked my boyfriend and she has the audacity to sit there and slag me off right in front of me!*

For many reasons, when Jenna looked back on the next few minutes of her life, she wasn't proud of herself. Fired up by the bitching from Diane, not to mention the sheer annoyance of her sanctimony, she'd downed several glasses of champagne in quick succession. The party had then started to wind down — Roland had promised Emma a meeting at his hotel early the next morning so the Blake-Howards were keen to get back to their yacht and had started the goodbyes. Bertie, never one to have more than a drinkie or two anyway, was happy to go with them and so Max was shaking hands with TG and thanking him for an excellent night. Only Diane seemed intent on staying on, and even though everyone moved to the main deck to see the guests off down the wide steps to the walkway, she sat down again on one of the sofas by the pool and looked like she was resolute in not going anywhere. This had annoyed Jenna more than she could articulate — especially as, unlike Diane, she had attacked the wines that night with gusto. Bertie called over to her and asked if she wanted a lift with them in their car. Jenna rolled her eyes at the ridiculousness of getting a car a few metres around the harbour but noticed that at least this offer had got Diane up off her bum. Jenna had a thought.

'Ooh, Diane. Have your shoes gone missing?' she'd slightly slurred at her rival.

'Shit, really?' The beautiful model leaned over the edge of the boat to have a look. Jenna took her opportunity and knocked into her — expecting Diane to lose her balance and at least maybe fall down a few of the wide, wooden steps — or even head straight over the edge into the inky water below.

'Fuuuuuuck,' the coiled rope that Diane was standing next to caught Jenna by surprise, and as she was a little more unbalanced than usual she couldn't help herself as she plummeted over the side of the yacht, narrowly missing one of the huge fenders. The smack as she hit the water was enough to make anyone who witnessed the fall wince, and Jenna felt the air knocked out of her as the cold water enveloped her and dragged her under. Her beautiful silk dress snared and snagged her legs as she furiously kicked out, desperately wondering if she could right herself and find air. Salt water and the tang of fuel and rotten weed filled her nose and mouth and Jenna thought she would almost definitely die in the next minute or two, but no flashes of her life to date passed in front of her eyes; no tunnel with a heavenly light appeared before her — but luckily, and so much better than either really — her burning lungs found breath as she surfaced and her body was lifted from the water by the strong arms of who-knew-who — Jenna couldn't see as her hair was wrapped across her face — and it was all she could do not to vomit and cough in a futile attempt to get the ghastly smells and tastes of the harbour out of her system. She was heaved up onto the beach club area of the yacht, where she was bundled in a couple of towels. In possibly the most embarrassing moment of her life Jenna realised who had been the one to save it, as she vomited all over TG's lap as he cradled her head.

An hour later and Jenna was feeling the dual effects of drinking both too much booze and too much of the less delectable harbour water and although now clean and definitely more fragrant (it had taken *a lot* of showering to get the unpleasant smells off her) she felt terrible. She just wanted to curl up and cry and cry and then sleep and sleep until everything could go away — but her ruined and soaking dress, which was now a sodden lump in the bottom of the shower tray, was a stark reminder of how easily something so delicate could be ruined and she knew that an apology would be in order to TG for not only embarrassing him in front of his guests — *I mean, who else here in Monaco would have a PA who practically threw herself overboard* — but for vomming all over him too. His shorts might need urgent laundry care, but Jenna wasn't sure if there was a dry-cleaner for egos and relationships. She pulled a brush through her drying hair and checked that all her make-up had properly come off — nothing said 'likely to mess up again and again' like a nice smear of eyeliner and dripping mascara. Dragging a light cotton jumper over her still damp-from-the-shower skin and yanking her jeans up her legs Jenna wondered how the next conversation was going to go and if there had ever been a more useless employee as her in the world?

'Jenna.' TG turned towards her as she climbed up the steps to the sun deck, her hands wringing in front of her, a pained look playing across her face. 'Hey, don't worry.' He turned back towards the sofas and plumped up a cushion and indicated a spot for her to sit down. 'Need something for the shock?'

'You mean other than a stern talking to, several inoculations and a lesson in not falling overboard?'

'Ha.' TG didn't wait for another answer and walked over to the bar and poured a large brandy into a crystal balloon glass. 'Here.' He passed it over to her. Jenna wondered if it was sensible to drink more intoxicating liquor as she'd proved that downing so much in response to Diane's abstinence had already, quite literally, been her downfall.

'Want to talk about it?' His voice was so soft, so caring. Jenna didn't really want to talk about it, but he was being so absolutely lovely — *and he hadn't even mentioned the—*

'Oh, TG, I'm so, so sorry. I can't believe I—'

'Hey, no — my bad. I've got Avery looking into who left that rope there and we'll get the handrail replaced too, ASAP.'

'I was going to say "vommed all over you", but yes, sorry about breaking the handrail too.' *Those thousands of euros wouldn't last in her bank balance long if she was going to have to start shelling out for chandlery,* she thought as she wiped a little tear away, thinking of the stinkingly expensive, and now just stinking, dress that was slopped in the bottom of the shower in her room.

'Let's call it quits. I won't mention the vomming thing if you don't sue me for health and safety lapses on board.' He reached out his hand towards her, offering it to shake.

'Deal.' Jenna took one hand away from cradling her drink and slipped it into TG's. The shake was less businesslike and more tender, and his fingers curled around her hand, holding it completely for several seconds before letting go.

'Come here.' The words weren't an order, but Jenna didn't hesitate to follow them and nudged herself up closer towards him. He slipped his arm around her shoulders and Jenna tentatively rested her head on his shoulder.

'I'm so sorry I'm so useless at being a glamorous PA, TG.' Jenna almost whispered it, hoping the words wouldn't break the spell of the moment, although feeling deeply that she had to own up to being so tragically useless.

'You need to stop apologising for who you are,' TG replied, pulling his arm tighter around her shoulders. 'You aren't useless. You organised tonight, you organise me all day . . .'

'Working out when you're going swimming, when you might have a massage and when you want your supper isn't exactly board-level stuff,' Jenna teased him.

'You say that, but I am the board . . .'

'And I'm mostly overboard,' Jenna sighed and let her head rest more heavily on TG's shoulder.

At first she didn't notice when his lips had pressed slightly against the crown of her head, but gradually she felt his embrace and although she was slightly confused — as Bertie had been at pains to point out only a few days ago, it was *laughable* that a billionaire should fall for her — she had to admit that the warmth of his arms, the smell of his cedar-wood aftershave and the tenderness of his kiss was just the tonic she needed after tonight's catastrophes. Turning her head just a little was the invitation he needed to nuzzle her and drop his kisses from her forehead down her cheek to her lips.

41

Jenna woke up with a thumping headache and sense of déjà vu in that she recognised her surroundings, sort of, but couldn't quite place where she was. Then, as she blinked her eyes open again, she realised that although all the fixtures and fittings were familiar to her, they were also strangely out of place and there was more room between them than in her usual cabin. *Oh fuck*. It occurred to her in a moment of clarity where she was. And the lightly snoring man next to her confirmed it. She was wrapped up in the sheets (the thread count must have been in the thousands, it was like sleeping in whipped cream) of TG's bed and she was absolutely butt naked. A sneaky look over to where he slept, his chest gently rising and falling, showed her that he was also as naked as the day he was born, but there were some very grown up additions to his caramel-soft skin: tattoos on his upper thigh that she'd never noticed before under his swimming shorts – a clock with four hands and a symbol – Buddhist? Hindi? Jenna didn't know.

She lay back down and took stock of the situation. *Had they . . . you know?* She was pretty sure she would remember, but her memory was a little hazy after the second large balloon glass of cognac had been washed down with a fresh bottle of champagne. She remembered them kissing – lots – up on the sun deck, but instead of catching the rays up there, it was moonshine they were inspired by and they'd both laid down on the loungers and tried to block out the harbour's lights as they star-spotted and told each other stories from childhood holidays and camping adventures. TG had told her he'd always wanted to be a teacher, but had found himself drawn to tech, the mechanics of it, the beauty in the algorithms, the elegance of a piece of well-written code — for him it was like poetry or music and it gave him joy. All Jenna could think of was how convenient his initials were for his job then — TG — tech guy.

'You know, I never thought of that,' he'd chuckled as he'd reached out for her hand across the sunloungers.

'What is your name?' Jenna was appalled that she didn't know, and not for lack of stalking either — it seemed the creator of the world's number one stalking app had made his own personal information as hard to find as possible.

'Tavish. It means heaven. And then Gyandev.' He laughed to himself again.

'What does that one mean?' Jenna squeezed his hand.

'Lord of Knowledge.'

'Ha.'

Jenna seemed to remember that some rather intense staring into each other's eyes had happened and then somehow the kissing must have started again . . . she wiped the back of her hand over her brow, her head still thumping. A champagne and spirit hangover . . . the worst kind.

Not wanting to wake him from his deep sleep she rolled out of the bed and crept over to where she could see her loose cotton jumper. She slipped it over herself and quickly pulled on her jeans, before scraping around under the chair in order to find her underwear. Braced, she tiptoed towards the cabin door and gently opened it, only to find one of the Tweedles stationed outside. His presence made her jump and she almost dropped her knickers.

'No need to be startled, missus,' he whispered to her and put his finger to his lips, in what she thought was a sign that he wouldn't blab about this to his crew mates. Still, for the first time ever, as Jenna clenched her bra and pants close to her chest, she didn't correct him for calling her that.

'You did what?'

'I slept with him.'

'What?' Sally squealed down the phone.

'Not like sexy sleeping, just *sleeping* sleeping.'

'And is sexy sleeping on the cards?'

'I don't know,' Jenna whispered into her phone. 'I don't know.'

'Well, do you want it to be?'

'Arg, I don't know . . . oh, Sals, it was such a bizarre night. First Diane showed up, then she started talking about Gus, then she started going on about this ex of his, er, so like me, oh *and* she's a very vocal vegan.'

'Urg. Are you sure Angus is going out with her? He always struck me as someone who wouldn't happily tolerate a vegan?'

'I don't know. I didn't get much of a chance to find out as I got wasted.'

'Oh, JJ! Really?'

'I couldn't help it.'

'Right. Way to go to rub it into the teetotal pregnant woman. Let me guess, vintage champagne?'

'Cristal. But only the '06 not the '02.'

'I had no idea you were such a connoisseur these days, Jenks.'

'God, I am, aren't I?'

'No wonder you felt the need to fall into the arms of the billionaire.'

Jenna wondered if Sally wasn't being just the tiniest bit judgemental. 'Gus left me, you know. Not the other way around.'

'I know, chicks. I'm just frightfully jealous.'

'Of the drunkard who fell off a super yacht and almost smashed her head in, but, oh yay, instead only drank half of Port Hercule before vomiting it up all over her boss-stroke-lover? Yeah — envy be thy middle name!'

'You what? How did you not lead on this one? You fell overboard? Like Goldie Hawn?'

'Yes, and I'm not too clear how it all happened either. Let's blame it on the knock to the head, not the magnum of rosé . . . although that Garrus '15 was amazing—'

'Here we go again . . .' Sally laughed and then Jenna heard her call across the room to Hugo.

'Shhh. Don't tell him!' Jenna hissed down the phone to her friend.

'Spoilsport.'

'What if Angus finds out?' Jenna winced as the realisation hit home that her best friend was married to one of his best friends.

'What if indeed . . .' There was a pause as both friends had a think. Sally was the first to speak. 'I suppose it would make him incredibly jealous. Perhaps that's your subconscious doing the planning for you.'

'Yes, but if he's left me for hashtag-vegan-lifestyle Diane Blane then me being a drunken mess and having fun and not in any way at all "clean-eating" — I mean, the harbour water must have had at least a trillion bacteria — wouldn't attract him at all.'

'Hmm. I'm still not convinced of this relationship of his.'

'I saw them!'

'Still . . .'

'And I hate to say it, but I'm sure she was describing me as his "lunatic" ex!'

'Did she say that? Bitch. What else?'

'Something along the lines of having toxically low self-esteem and arguing over nothing.'

'Pft. Could describe absolutely any of us.'

Jenna and Sally continued to analyse as only best friends can until Jenna thought it really was only decent to get dressed properly and go and see what the world was like out there now she was a billionaire's bit of fluff.

42

Angus leant over the wall and trained the ends of his binoculars onto *Clickbait*. He scanned the decks — but the privacy glass meant he couldn't see inside the boat and could only catch a few crew members going about their morning chores. Glasses were being collected from the top deck — he moved the binoculars down a fraction and searched the lower decks and recognised one of the crew from his stay there. He'd been a guest on that yacht only recently — and five million dollars later he was *persona non grata* — but thankfully the calls from The Voice had also stopped. And Angus, though heartbroken, had at least the comfort of knowing Jenna was safe.

He lowered the binoculars and checked his watch. Time to head to the large central station and go back to Eze, the pretty hillside town where TG wanted his villa built. Angus had agreed not to contact Jenna, not to go near her — but he'd never signed anything to say he couldn't watch from afar and keep an eye on her. But with the villa plans now approved by the local government — helped by TG's generous donation to the local youth club and sports fields — Angus was needed back on site to talk through plans with the builders. He only hoped his schoolboy French would help when it came to talking about rolled-steel joists and type seven particle board membrane plastering . . .

As he turned to leave his viewing spot, he noticed a familiar face come jogging up the hill towards him. Concentration — and sweat — covered Max's face and his focus was on putting one foot in front of the other and listening to whatever was blaring through his earbuds, rather than noticing his fellow pavementeers.

'Hey, Max.' Angus stepped out in front of him, but quickly stepped back as all fourteen stone of Max almost collided with him.

'What the— oh.' Max bent over and rested his hands on his knees before yanking out his earphones and looking up towards his old friend. 'Hi, mate.'

'Sorry.'

'No worries.' Max was panting and Angus wondered if it was just his shortness of breath that had stopped Max from giving him a more friendly greeting.

'How's it going?'

'Yeah, good. Good.' Max paused again and caught his breath. He stood upright and finally properly looked Angus in the eye. 'Bertie has me exercising three times a day. I'm bloody knackered.'

'Pre-wedding?'

'Yeah. Honestly, you'd think it was me that was going to be squeezing into a couture corset the way she's lecturing me. It's less hard work actually being *at work* in London.' Angus was relieved that Max let out a quick laugh as he said it. But his dour demeanour returned in seconds. 'What are you up to?'

Angus fingered the binoculars, not sure whether he could tell Max any vestige of the truth. Hoping that perhaps Max wouldn't have noticed them, Angus casually moved the hand holding them behind his back and leant back on the parapet. 'Just one last look at Monte Carlo before I head back up to Eze for work.'

'Look, mate. I have to ask — Jenna? What the fuck?'

Angus opened his mouth and tried to find the words to answer his friend but none came. Max continued to fill the silence. 'I saw her last night. We went to TG Wilkinson's yacht — which is immense, by the way.'

'Yeah, I know. I stayed there.'

'Of course, yeah.' Max paused again but Angus could sense he was building up to something. 'Look, Gus. It's really none of my business, but as someone who's had the fallout from hurting J in the past — well, what the fuck were you thinking? And are you with Diane now?'

'What?' Angus had almost expected a dressing down for dumping Jenna — as far as anyone knew he'd done it coldly and callously with no good excuse — but to be accused of leaving her for Diane . . . 'Diane? No.'

'Jenna's convinced you left her for her.'

'I didn't. I couldn't. She's going out with some actor she's fancied for ages. Diane and I, we're just friends.'

'Pretty hot friend.' Max winked at Angus but his face clouded over again almost immediately. Angus knew Max must be divided — his natural bonhomie and playboy attitude was suppressed by the genuine love and care he felt for his friend Jenna.

'How is she?'

'Jenna? Looking hot to be fair. Scrubbed up well, thanks to the thousands of euros this TG bloke is paying her. Even Bertie approved, which is something. Didn't stop her from throwing herself head first into the soup last night though.' Max made a diving then sploshing gesture with his hands.

'Shit. Is she okay?' Angus was reminded of the time he thought about chucking himself over the edge of TG's yacht and how easy it would be to kill or injure yourself.

'Yeah, she's fine. I think ego rather than body was bruised. But Bertie reckons she fell into her own trap she'd laid for Diane — she'd wanted her love rival to be the one doused in Port Hercule grot, not her new designer dress.'

'Shit.' Angus's mind was buzzing with thoughts about how he could possibly communicate with Jenna, and tell her that he and Diane weren't a couple, but the ink was still barely dry on his and TG's contract and he knew contacting her at all would mean serious legal consequences for him.

'Why did you do it?' Max's question cut through his thoughts and Angus looked away across the harbour again. 'I thought you guys were going to be next down the aisle for the executioner's chop, I mean, vicar's blessing.'

'I had to. I can't explain it right now, but I had to.'

'Yeah — it's that sort of crappy excuse that lands us blokes a bad name. Look, mate.' Max relaxed his jaw slightly and Angus saw in his face the struggle as Max tried to work out what to say next. 'You broke her heart. She's been crying on Bertie and Emma for days. And I think part of that is she doesn't understand why you've left her.'

'I had to.'

'Fine. And fine, don't explain it me, but you could at least explain it to her.'

'I can't. She'd hate me.'

'She's not exactly your number one fan at the moment, anyway. What have you got to lose?'

'Everything.'

'Fine.' Max sighed and started fiddling with the white cord of his earphones. 'Be Mr Cryptic if you like, but just don't be Mr Shitty, okay? See you around, mate.' At that he lurched off up the hill, his head down as he rammed the earbuds into position. Angus felt deflated and ten times more terrible than he'd felt earlier, and he'd thought *that* had been as bad as a guy could feel.

He turned towards the yacht and automatically raised the binoculars to his eyes one more time. This time he saw her — his Jenna, beautiful, yawning, stretching Jenna, mug of coffee in hand, sunglasses on and casual jumper thrown over white jeans. She looked so relaxed, so at home, and when Angus saw TG come up behind her and gently wrap his arms around her waist and nuzzle his face into her neck, she looked like she truly belonged on that deck. And as Angus's heart broke again, he reminded himself of TG's last words to him when they signed the deal. *You don't own her, and I can't buy her – but she'll give herself to me, you'll see.*

Angus wiped a tear away from his eye, turned away from the port and headed to the train station.

43

Jenna was caught by surprise as the strong arms of her new lover snaked around her waist and she felt his lips place a gentle kiss on her neck.

'Morning, beautiful.'

'Morning, um, boss?' Jenna's inflexion at the end of the sentence made TG laugh and pull away from her, but she turned to face him so she could gauge just how funny he thought it. Quite funny, by the looks of his creased-up eyes.

'Look, JJ — can I call you that?'

'Of course, TG, welcome to the Initial Club . . .'

'Funny and beautiful. You see, you are the whole package, Jenna Jenkins.'

'Speaking of "whole packages", um, last night. I didn't receive your *whole package*, did I?'

'I'm not sure whether to laugh or take offence,' TG smirked though and turned around to the table to pour himself a cup of coffee from the still-steaming cafetière.

'Oh, no, I mean — of course, well . . .' Jenna stumbled over her words — *way to go to insult the billionaire boyfriend*, she thought to herself. But luckily TG just burst out laughing and held out his arms to her. Gingerly, Jenna moved forward into his embrace and rested her head against his chest, feeling his pounding heart and hearing his voice reverberate as he spoke.

'I'd never take advantage of you, Jenna. Not when it was my fault you were so, how would you Brits say it, *squiffy*?'

Jenna pulled her head back to look up at him, his dark brown eyes hidden by sunglasses but still somehow she felt them searching her soul. 'Shitfaced, more like.' She smiled at him and he burst out laughing and let her go.

'So, while you're recovering, what would you like to do today?'

'Well,' Jenna picked up her mug of coffee, took a sip, then said, 'I know we have the Red Cross Gala coming up next month and we need to confirm who will be on our table. Then I suppose I should go through your emails again re the benevolent society fund, there's heaps of admin to do for the contract for the new hospital building in Vancouver you're sponsoring and those playing fields up the road here . . .'

'Okay, okay, I get it. You're still my PA. But after that — here we are on a super yacht in Monaco. What would you really like to do today?'

Jenna squinted up at him, then gave up and pulled her sunglasses back down. She thought for two seconds then said, 'Well, if you're really asking . . . then let's go to sea, sailor.'

'Aye aye, captain. You do what you need to do and I'll go and speak to the real captain about getting this hunk of junk over to Portofino or something for a few days — I think the change of scenery could do us all good.'

'Ooh, Portofino. *Si, signor*, that sounds super-amazing.'

44

Jenna pressed send on the final email reply to one member of the charity board associated with TG's new philanthropic venture and closed the laptop. The yacht had eased itself out of port, and was now going at quite some pelt across the Mediterranean towards Italy. Portofino — even the name of it sounded so elegant and Italian. Jenna could already taste the ripeness of the tomatoes and the tang of a pepperoni pizza slice — but then chided herself for her pedestrian tastes. She quickly reopened the laptop and fired up the search engine to browse a few websites on 'real' and 'authentic' Italian cuisine. Who knew pizza was actually meant to be a Napoli thing? Jenna brushed up on pronunciations for *pesto alla Genovese* and *risotto alla Milanese* and thought that although she'd probably had *pesto alla Jenna inna bowla* heaps of times, it would not be as magnificent as the dishes served at whatever cute little trattoria TG found for them.

TG . . . she closed the laptop again and thought about her current situation. Sally's words rang true — had she really managed to get over Angus so quickly just because she'd got under someone super-hot on a super yacht? She thought back to his pounding heart as he hugged her this morning and then wondered if hers was pounding too, or just rebounding? Was she really that shallow? The sadness that crept over her reminded her that, no, she wasn't, but that the cruelty that Gus had shown her by just leaving her with barely any explanation, well, no wonder she'd sought solace so quickly. If Angus was here now, would she choose him over TG? For sure. But he wasn't, and

TG was coming towards her now, his white linen shirt loosely buttoned and even more loosely tucked into his chino shorts. He pushed his sunglasses up on top of his head and smiled at her as he joined her at the large dining table on the main deck.

'All done?' he asked as Jenna ticked off the last of her to-do list, more in a show of industriousness than anything.

'Done. The whole of East Coast society should know all about the Wilkinson Trust soon and I've been in touch with the dean's PA's vice-secretary or whatever at Harvard to sort out the lecture hall and gala dinner there for your foundation launch in the spring. I've had a quick check on Instagram too and I think there's a few celebrities who might be interested in showing their faces to help a good cause — I'll make a proper list and we can decide who to approach.'

'Great work. I'm pumped about this foundation. It's going to be so much better for the world than my stupid app.'

'TG, your app is in no way stupid. Kind of stalkerish, but in no way *stoopid*.' Jenna pronounced it 'stoopid' to try to cheer up TG, who had suddenly become rather contemplative. It worked and he smiled at her, and she liked the way his eyes crinkled slightly at the side as he broke into a broad grin.

'I'm just used to getting what I want now, I guess.' He reached out and took one of her hands in both of his. 'I need to be patient and wait until the spring I suppose to launch this thing.'

Jenna wondered how patient he would be with her — he was looking at her so hungrily right now that she wondered how long he'd wait for her to be ready to fall out of love with Gus and into his bed.

238

As *Clickbait* motored eastwards towards Italy Jenna realised that TG's patience, unlike his bank balance, may well be running low. He'd suggested they take in the view from the pool — using its infinity edge to get a fabulous look at the coastline behind them. Jenna met him out on the deck. This time she'd gone full flirt in the little black Chanel bikini, and it made her feel so good about herself to have him admire her so openly, especially after last night's disaster in the harbour. And she had to admit that the shoreline behind them wasn't the only rock-hard view she was admiring too. His hours spent in the gym on board the boat while she was working had been put to good use, and his abs caught her eye long before the geological strata in the cliffs and hillsides did. *Fuck it*, Jenna thought, letting her thin cotton sarong fall from her as she stepped across the deck to where he was about to dive into the water. She watched him as he watched her and the electricity between them was almost indecent. TG broke the circuit by slowly turning his head away from her and diving into the pool. Jenna laughed as splashes of water hit her legs — but it wasn't damp enough to put out the spark that was still fizzing away in her stomach. She looked at him as he resurfaced, and her mind flashed back to her first day on board when in this same pool she'd found it hard to take her eyes off his V-shaped muscles. Now as then, she was mesmerised by the droplets of water that traced their contours.

'Scared of the water now?' he asked as she stood on the side of the pool.

'No — just of what's in it.'

'No sharks in here.'

'I'm not so sure about that.' She dipped her toe in, and before she knew it he reached up and tugged her leg so she fell in the pool right on top of him. Spluttering to the surface she flailed about, horrible memories of the night before flashing through her mind. The same strong arms as before helped her up and into the air, supporting her around her waist as she gulped for air.

'Saved you again,' he whispered into her ear as she wiped her wet hair away from her face. Jenna wanted to biff him on the arm for surprising her like that, but her arms were wrapped up in his and he brought his face close into hers.

'Maybe it's you,' she replied, 'who keeps getting me into trouble.'

She could feel her breasts push up against his chest, their natural buoyancy keeping them high in the water. Her senses were super-heightened, the shock from the fall adding to the electricity she'd felt earlier. She let TG kiss her and softened her body into his, needing rather than enjoying the sensation of being wanted. The fizzing that had started in her stomach when she'd seen him in his swim shorts a few moments earlier had been fed by the adrenalin of the fall and she felt increasingly turned on as she ran her hands across his taut skin. He arched his neck and she kissed him there, while she reached down lower to feel his firm butt cheeks under the floating fabric of his shorts.

'You're so beautiful,' he murmured into Jenna's ear and the reassurance it gave her magnified her confidence. All the worries about money, about Angus, about life and success all fell away as he gradually pulled her bikini straps down from her shoulders and let the fabric peel away from her breasts. 'And these, these are magnificent.'

'They have names, you know . . .'

'Do tell?'

Jenna wondered if revealing the names might lower the tone, but she was feeling so saucily confident she didn't care. 'HMS *Superb*,' she indicated the right one, 'and HMS *Audacious*.'

'Wow. How, well, apt.' TG pressed his lips to them and then pulled Jenna in closer so that she was pressed right up against his body.

'. . . And it doesn't take a radar to see they're about to be torpedoed.'

Before the water could get much steamier Avery announced that they were getting close to Portofino. No one watching TG and Jenna untangle themselves from each other and rather hurriedly cover themselves up could doubt that there was a huge power in leaving someone wanting more. TG wrapped one of the large white towels around his waist, and helped Jenna into one too. Although heavy petting had definitely been allowed in this pool, it was now the slightest touch of his finger against her skin that weakened her knees and it took all of her self-control not to suggest that they just sod the Italians and their beautiful seaside towns and perhaps TG should get to know the two battleships of the British fleet currently on board his yacht a bit better . . . but TG was already towelling himself off and Jenna followed suit. They agreed to meet back on deck in a few minutes, clothed this time, but the look that TG gave Jenna after she kissed him goodbye made her nether regions fizzle again and, a few minutes later as she stood under the cleansing, hammering water of the shower in her cabin, she finished off what the allied forces had started in the international waters of *Clickbait*'s pool.

45

That evening the tender brought them back to *Clickbait* and Jenna wondered if the espresso martini had really been a sensible pudding option, bearing in mind she'd had several Aperol spritzes with the starter and a bottle of rather amazing Sassicaia red wine with the steaks they'd devoured. TG had managed to get a table at the restaurant of the Hotel Splendido, haunt of Portofino's beautiful people, but so much more relaxed than the overly showy restaurants and bistros in Monaco. Still, the aforementioned beautiful people had given Jenna cause to hover over the dessert menu before eschewing it for something less calorific but definitely more alcoholic and now she wondered if it was the tender bobbing up and down over the slightly choppy water or her own lack of balance that was making her clamber up onto the back of the yacht quite so ungainly.

'Hop-la!' TG had done that thing that Jenna always thought only embarrassing parents did of imitating the local lingo but anglicising it terribly. But she found it hilarious and replied with an exaggerated 'mamma mia!' as she finally steadied herself against the side of the beach club and stretched out a hand to help him off the unruly smaller boat too. Once upright and steadied he didn't let go of her hand and instead led her up the steps to the main deck and from there to the comfy sofas which now had a perfect view back towards the twinkling lights of the hillside town and the many yachts and smaller boats in the ancient harbour.

'Can we go back on shore tomorrow, TG?' Jenna asked, her natural curiosity piqued by what she'd seen as they'd walked around the town, their hands brushing against each other and occasionally their little fingers intertwining as they nonchalantly ignored that very fact. They'd blended in with the other well-to-do diners and promenaders with only the discreet entourage of Seb and Rob following at a few feet behind them as any indication of TG's wealth and status. Here though, with the buildings that jutted up so close to the edge of the water, the restaurants with tables that spilled out onto the quayside, well, here there was no room for the false privacy of the blacked-out SUV or wall of bodyguards like Jenna had seen in Monte Carlo and Antibes. Here the real privacy came from the fact that the locals and the other yachties all just ignored each other — no one cared who you were or what you were wearing, or doing, or being seen with — just so long as you praised their risotto and tucked into their wine with gusto. And Jenna had, especially when it had come to that espresso martini at the end. And perhaps the one she'd had just before it. And now, here she was, one leg curled up underneath her and a patient crew member making her another amazing cocktail — less of the caffeine this time, although by the look in TG's eye as he stretched his arm out across the back of the sofa behind her, he'd be having no problem keeping her awake later, even if they were in bed.

'Mister, missus.' The crew member brought the cocktails over. He wasn't one of the Tweedles, who Jenna now realised had perhaps a different role on the boat to just serving drinks, unless that came with a loaded Beretta under the tray.

'Thanks.' TG waved him away and then raised an eyebrow up at Jenna. 'Not challenging them on the title any more?'

'Oh,' Jenna blushed as she realised how cocky that must have looked. 'No, not at all. I mean, I did but then they kept insisting on it so I've rather given up.'

'They were only following orders.' He took a sip from his martini glass — no espresso this time, just a straight up vodka martini — and Jenna followed suit.

'You asked them to call me missus?'

'From the start, yes.'

'Why?' Jenna was emboldened by the alcohol. So much about TG intrigued her, some of it downright confused her, but she did really want to know.

'Because I wanted you to be here, with me, like this, from the start.'

'But you know I have a . . . had a boyfriend.'

TG placed his cocktail down and nudged himself in closer to Jenna. He moved his arm, which had been resting on the sofa edge behind her, up towards her face and he gently twirled a lock of her hair around his fingers. 'I gambled on that one.'

Jenna felt incredibly aware, all of a sudden, of the position she was in. She was being wooed — if that wasn't too old-fashioned a word for it — by a billionaire on his super yacht who'd had his eye on her from the first moment he saw her. *Wow*. If that didn't boost the old ego, then Jenna didn't know what would and in that moment as she leaned in, letting TG's hand move from her tendrils of hair to caressing the back of her head as he brought her in for the kiss, she felt pretty bloody amazing.

Jenna hadn't realised how plush the carpets were in the cabins of the yacht until she accidentally tripped over the threshold of the door to TG's stateroom and landed on her knees, hands splayed in front of her, fingers deep into the shag pile as she laughed to herself.

'This is what too many martinis do to a girl!'

'I envy those martinis then, getting you on all fours so quickly.'

'TG!' Jenna laughed and rolled over into a sitting position, raising her arms to him so she could be helped up. 'You are a naughty, naughty man.'

'Who wants to do some very naughty things with you.' He pulled her up and into his arms, and they kissed again until, as one, they fell onto the massive bed where clothes were suddenly very much not required, and they each hastily stripped themselves and each other of every thread of clothing. Jenna, who would have never usually felt so confident in front of a new lover, was on fire. She loved that TG was kissing her all over, caressing her skin, searching her body with his hands, hungrily squeezing and kneading her before lowering himself down further so that she soon couldn't concentrate on anything and the room stopped spinning to be replaced by the crashing of sexual waterfalls as he brought her to the pinnacle of pleasure before easing himself into her and bringing them both to the most explosive of orgasms.

As they lay panting, enjoying the post-coital adrenalin and endorphin rush, Jenna started to explore TG's body with her eyes, just as her hands had done moments earlier. She admired his chest, the smattering of black hairs on the caramel-coloured skin and the toned abs that led down to the slim waistline. She stopped and looked at the ornate clockface tattoo again, like a Victorian fob watch, but with those two sets of hands. Jenna sat up a little bit and looked it at more closely. TG brought his leg around closer for her to look at, obviously enjoying her curiosity.

'Why the two sets of hands?' The fob watch was tattooed in black ink, but the hands were in colours so that they could be distinguished from each other. The red pair were set at ten past four, the other, a blue pair, at quarter to seven.

'Time is money,' he murmured, and moved his leg back into a more comfy position, and enveloped Jenna into a hug. 'And I need twice as much as everyone else.'

Jenna let her head rest on TG's chest and she listened to the beat of his heart. It thumped along at a normal pace and it reminded Jenna that for all his money, his cryptic tattoos and his mind-bending algorithms, TG was just a man with a beating heart in his chest — and she was perhaps just a girl who he could hold late into the night and feel open with.

Dolls, where have you gone on that massive yacht of yours?

Need to see you URGENTLY. Probs with dress and stupid hotel people.

Jenna!! Where are you?? Hen needs organising chiefie!

Jenna read the staccato texts as she sipped on the frothy coffee which TG had brought in for her. She was still in his bed, the expensive sheets pulled up under her armpits to give her some sort of modesty, not that TG hadn't explored (and laid claim to) every inch of her body last night. She sat up against the padded headboard and decided how best to reply to Bertie, who was obviously having a hissy fit back in Monte Carlo. Jenna paused to take in the situation — the turning of the tables. She was the first to acknowledge that this was probably just a rebound fling with TG, and wasn't anywhere near the fiancé stakes, but still — she was dating someone considerably richer than Bertie and Max put together and for a fleeting moment she relished that fact. Typing her reply she felt like justice was being served for every Bertie barb that had ever been thrown at her:

Clickbait anchored off Portofino for a few days. Not sure when back. Will let you know x

There, she thought, *that should show you how un-beck-and-cally I am for you.*

'Ready to face the day, sweetheart?' TG wandered back into the room, and Jenna almost choked on her coffee as she saw he was completely naked. His nudity reminded her she was only one sheet away from being the same and she gulped down the coffee quickly and pulled the covers even further up around her armpits. However, she couldn't help but admire the chiselled and caramel-coloured contours of his abs, his muscular thighs and upper arms and, of course his, well, his joy stick.

'As ready as you are`. . .' Jenna put her mug down on the nightstand and in a rather uncharacteristic fit of confidence, the modesty and vulnerability of moments before suddenly gone, whipped the sheet off herself and got out of the bed. She felt TG look her up and down and wondered how her wobbly bits compared to the countless other women he must have had throw themselves at him since he became such a wealthy man — or indeed just when he got those abs. He crossed the room and made it very clear to her that she didn't compare too unfavourably with the kisses he lavished up her neck, over her shoulders and down her chest to her most wobbly of bits — before gently pushing her back onto the bed and continuing his kissing down her stomach to where he was able to give her the most wonderful wakeup call and let her ready herself for the day in the most orgasmic way possible.

Jenna, although now unofficially mistress of the boat, still felt the need to tiptoe back to her cabin to have a shower and find something nice to wear to go back on to dry land and mooch around Portofino. She relaxed a bit when she clicked her cabin's door shut behind her and dropped her clutch bag — these days only used for phone and lippy, not screwed-up tenners and a hope-it-doesn't-get-declined bank card. But she noticed something on her bed straight away and as she got closer to it she realised it was a little gift box — small and black, obviously from an independent jeweller. She reached down and picked it up and opened it to reveal a pair of diamond stud earrings. No note, no gift tag — nothing to help her decipher the meaning of the gift, or who it was from, but she would stake her new-found fortune on them being from TG. She tilted the box a bit and the gems caught the light and sparkled like crazy, sending off disco-ball-style glitter around the room. Jenna gently closed the box, then opened and closed it again just to check she hadn't imagined them. Ten minutes later, showered and hair up in a towel, she opened the box again and took out the earrings, putting them one by one into her lobes. Scrunching up the towel and rough drying her hair, she turned towards the main mirror in her cabin and saw herself wearing diamonds — real diamonds — for the first time in her life.

Portofino was as beautiful as it had been the evening before, and Jenna and TG browsed through shops and climbed the steps up to the renovated Chiesa di San Giorgio. The only downside was the constant buzzing in her little clutch bag, which signified Bertie's ever-growing demands and impatience at her friend's disappearance.

'She's a pain in the butt, isn't she?' TG had blurted out, after Jenna had apologetically got her phone out of her bag for the seventh time in a row.

'She's what you might call "high maintenance", yes,' sighed Jenna as she quickly read the message and then put the phone back in her bag, just as another vibration shot up her arm as another message was delivered.

'Go on . . .' TG stood back from the shop window and crossed his arms, not impatient as such, but his change in humour meant that Jenna fumbled a bit with the phone before reading the latest in the slew of messages:

We are on t-minus 3 weeks, dolls. Call me!
Am having palpitations. Honestly think might die.
Fine, am OK now. But call me!!!!!! Xxxxxx
When are you back?????
Fine. Have spoken to BHs. We're coming to you. Stay put.

'Fuck.'

Tomorrow. Stay put till tomorrow!!!! Promise me! MUST come and see PF if you lushes are having fun there.

Max saw Angus – said he's looking shit. See you tomorrow, dolls – Italia here we come!!!!! xxxx

'Ah.'

'What?'

'Um. You know how you said how nice it was to be away from the Monaco crowd, even though you'd only just met them? Well . . .' Jenna showed TG her phone and watched as his face went from one of concentration to pure horror.

'Oh jeez. Of all the people. Fine, fine.' He dragged his fingers through his hair.

'I guess we do sort of owe them . . .' Jenna looked into TG's eyes, which seemed devoid of understanding.

'What for?'

'Well, for poaching Avery from them.'

'I didn't "poach" him,' TG sounded a bit defensive.

Jenna remembered Emma's insinuation that money had changed hands. 'Did you *buy* him from them?'

'Much like, well . . .' TG paused to choose his words. 'Look, they were reimbursed, put it that way.'

'Like *what* . . .?' Jenna's question hung in the air as TG spoke over her.

'Fine, let's get them over. We better warn chef that there's going to be a party tomorrow night and you better warn Bertie not to be a pain in the ass!'

Jenna forgot her worry over TG's choice of words, her chain of thought broken by TG's quip over Bertie. She snorted a sort of laugh and put her phone away, slipped her hand into his and they continued walking through the quaint hillside town, stopping to point out things to each other, laugh and kiss under the pastel colours of the old buildings.

46

'Jenna, you have fallen on your if-they-could-be-wearing-my-cast-off-Gina-shoes-they-would feet.' Bertie seemed genuinely impressed by Jenna's new lifestyle. She'd arrived in Portofino with the Blake-Howards on the *Wavy Sloanes* the morning after texting Jenna and had wasted no time in donning her teeniest bikini and inviting herself over. 'I mean, you barely have to *work* any more do you?'

'Technically, I'm still his PA—'

'Technically-schmechnically.' Bertie waved her hand as if to dismiss the idea. 'You are mistress now of all you can see. Well, keep playing your cards right and you are, anyway.'

'That's the thing, Bertie,' Jenna wanted to say 'unlike you' but carried on without the cutting comparison. 'I haven't played anything — cards or otherwise. I don't really know how this all happened. One moment I'm barely making ends meet in London with a nice, comfortably off boyfriend in a very nice but very small and very run-down house. And the next, well, I'm here on a super yacht worth a hundred million pounds with a billionaire lover and thousands of euros in my bank account.'

'Just thousands?' Bertie almost looked unimpressed again.

'Which is plenty enough for me.' Jenna pulled her sunglasses down her nose and gave Bertie a pointed look. The pair were laying out on the sunloungers up on the sun deck of *Clickbait* while TG was giving the Blake-Howards the full tour. 'Didn't you fancy joining them, by the way?' Jenna changed the subject. 'I thought you were looking to buy one of these "margarine tubs" as well?'

'Stalled slightly on that one. Not from lack of funds, you understand?' Bertie sounded very serious. 'But Max had a work emergency and had to fly back to town and of course there's the wedding to plan — speaking of which, dolls, less of this lying around being a billionaire from you please and more action chop chop on organising my bachelorette — anyway, it's just too much, you know? I think Max and I might save the yacht shopping for after the wedding when we have some chill-out time before project pram starts.'

'Oh God, not you too?'

'What do you mean?'

'Babies . . . project pram. I don't think I can cope with all my friends sprogging at the same time.'

'Just get up the duff with TG.' Bertie waved at her friends and TG who were coming up the steps and onto the deck towards the girls. 'Sod IVF, go for la DVF . . . la dolce vita fertilisation. Nice prime billionaire baby — you'd beat the lot of us, you bitch.'

'Ha.' Jenna knew there was as much jealousy as joke in Bertie's tone so didn't push the matter further but she did take stock of the fact that yet another of her friends was about to settle down and enjoy some proper family life while she was, quite literally, still sailing on the high seas when it came to love life, home life and definitely project *bloody* pram.

'TG, darling,' Bertie mewed at him as they all enjoyed a feast of fresh Italian seafood — except for Bertie, who enjoyed one langoustine and insisted on only sipping champagne throughout the meal, while the others had moved onto a crisp white soave and bottles of the ever-present Whispering Angel rosé that seemed to be stocked everywhere on the Riviera. 'We simply must repay the favour when you are back in Monte Carlo. I was thinking of having a little shindig at the Hotel de Paris — a sort of pre-wedding party — please say you'll come. Jenna will be there, of course, won't you, dolls?'

'Of course.' Jenna took another sip of rosé, and continued. 'Hey, Bertie, here's an idea. How about we make that party your bachelorette?'

'But boys will be there?'

'I know, right — so modern and so on trend.'

'Really?'

'Yes, Ems, back me up here . . .' Jenna winked at Emma Blake-Howard who nodded her head, not really knowing what she was agreeing to as she and Monty had been in deep conversation as to whether they could afford to refurb the *Wavy Sloanes* to match the grandeur of *Clickbait*.

'I suppose hen dos are a bit sordid,' Bertie thought out loud.

'I don't think I'd like any future wife of mine to have one.' TG stated across the table.

'Why?' Jenna wondered if he was joking — she just couldn't tell.

'Leaving your fate up to others — it's not what I like doing.'

'Well, it wouldn't be you, though, would it. You could be dull and not have a stag do.' Bertie mused as she flicked a prawn shell off her plate with one of her long fingernails.

'Steady on, Berts,' Monty added his five cents to the conversation. 'Can't deny a fellow his last night of freedom.'

'Darling,' purred Emma, much to everyone's amusement, 'all you did on your last night of supposed "freedom" was to drink ten pints of ale in the local pub and try and get into that terrible nightclub in Taunton. I think the dogs helped you clear up your sick, gross as that is to think about, and you complained royally for about three days afterwards and pledged your undying love to me and my recipe for comfort-food soup.'

252

'You see,' TG leaned in and used his fork as demonstratively as possible, 'you lost control. Not something I like to do.'

'You *do* drink, TG,' Jenna reminded him.

'Never more than you, darling.'

Jenna felt a bit embarrassed by this, especially as she'd just accepted a generous top up to her wine glass, and hoped no one noticed the blush she felt spreading across her cheeks.

47

'Maxie baby, how's London?'

'Same old, same old, Berts.' If there was a strain to Max's voice, Bertie didn't hear it. 'Enjoying Monaco still?'

'I would say "same old, same old" but actually I wangled another invite onto *Clickbait* thanks to darling Jenna. She really is proving quite useful now she's shagging TG.'

'Is she? What about Gus?'

'What about him? He's snost and lost I'm afraid. Did you ever ask him about it?'

'Yeah. I need to check in on him again though. He was really cryptic when I last saw him.'

Bertie paused a little before continuing. 'I suppose I shouldn't hold you up, darling. Are you at work? Did you solve your little problemo?'

'Yeah, just working on the Imber-Roe deal.'

'Big bucks, I hope.'

'Big enough, why?'

'You know why, handsome. Weddings aren't cheap, you know.'

'Ones you plan aren't, anyway.'

'And what's that supposed to mean?' Bertie snapped at her betrothed. 'Don't you love me? Don't you want me to be happy?'

'Of course, of course. I just wonder if we need such a large spectacle. I'd marry you in a barn if that's what we had to.'

Bertie could hear the mollifying tone in her fiancé's voice but was too annoyed by what she felt was his criticism of her lifestyle choices.

'A barn? A *fucking* barn? What are we? Plebs? You'll be expecting a nice marquee on your parents' sodding lawn next with a local caterer and some hillbilly band. Max,' she shouted down the phone at him, 'we are better than that. We are alphas, darling, we set the heights to which other people aspire!'

'Fine, fine. Though a marquee and a nice band would be fine by me.'

'Oh, fuck off you. You don't understand.'

'I understand, Bertie, I do. It's just a lot of pressure, you know, to make lots of money. I'm no Wolf of Wall Street.'

'Well, maybe you should be. Try harder, darling. Or I might jump ship over to TG's super yacht.'

'Bertie . . .'

Even Bertie could tell that she'd gone too far in threatening to leave her fiancé. She didn't really mean it, she just wanted it all so much — she wanted Max to be as rich as TG, for his own sake, of course, as well as hers, but mostly for hers.

'Sorry, babe, Maxie, I just miss you.'

'Well, come home then.'

'You know I have far too much to do here now the cathedral is booked and the Metropole are under control. Plus it's easier to eat a clean diet out here than in stinky London.'

'Fine, fine. Look I have to go. Love you.'

'Love you too, Maxie, my wolfie.'

They hung up on each other and Bertie went back to flicking the file over her talon-like nails. It wasn't her fault she thought to herself, that she was the ambitious one.

Max ran his fingers through his hair. It had got longer over the summer, the short, back and sides now needed more wax to stop it from looking too scruffy for the office. In finance, as in fashion, looks were everything — the smarter and richer you looked, the more confidence you inspired in investors and backers. He earned a lot of money off the back of the fact he looked right and spoke well and was blessed by the natural confidence to walk into a boardroom, present his forecasts and projections and more often than not make the deal. Plus he was a dolphin in a world of sharks — friendly most of the time, feisty when he needed to be, but never out for blood. It frustrated him that this wasn't enough to keep his hotter-than-hot, high-maintenance fiancée happy. And he knew he could have a much easier life without Bertie nit-picking, pushing and needling him to do better and earn more, but . . . people didn't know her like he did. He wasn't blind to the side to her that was obsessed by this magazine lifestyle, the Instagram likes and being some sort of 'influencer' and how exhausting that was but what no one else saw were the times she rested her head on his shoulder after a long day, whispered 'I love you's to him as they went to sleep, made him a cup of coffee on a Sunday morning when the staff weren't there . . . these small things were why he loved her and knew she loved him too.

She'd pushed him too far the other day and he'd succumbed to his old playboy ways. He picked up his phone and scrolled through the pictures Izzy had sent him of herself after they'd shagged in a suite in the Dorchester the other night. He'd left her there with an open account. 'Treat yourself.' He'd handed her the room service menu before he left, kissing her on the forehead while tapping his phone screen to confirm his Uber home. Nice girl, but no Bertie. Remorse flooded over him and deleted the photos and then Izzy's number from his phone. Without Bertie ever knowing the reason why, he'd have to make it up to her. Perhaps adding a few more hundred thousand into the wedding — or yacht — fund wouldn't hurt. But how could he earn any more than he already was?

He looked down at his mobile again. A few swipes and taps later and his finger hovered over one of his contacts. An old friend from business school. Someone who over a drink or two might give away a few insider tips on what his company and those of the others in their class were up to — men and women who were now at quite senior levels, or at least able to eavesdrop on the board. Max knew a guy who had retired at forty after wooing a secretary who was able to tell him all about the latest stock options on the Fortune500 company she worked for. That guy had placed the right trade at the right time and made a mint. Max pressed 'call' on his phone and waited for the line to connect.

48

'One more jaunt on our way back to Monaco?' TG suggested the venture over cocktails that evening. The Blake-Howards and Bertie had come back on board, their tender bobbing alongside the beach club deck of *Clickbait* as the exclusive little party chatted up on the sun deck. The view from up there, looking over Portofino to the west with the sun setting behind the cliff-hanger of a town, was glorious. And as the sun set further and cocktails turned into fine wine and then digestifs, and the canapés were replaced by another delicious four-course feast in the dining area on the second deck, which had its glass doors fully open to catch the warm sea breezes, the friends decided on a stop-off the next morning on their way back. Both yachts would anchor just off Sanremo — another beautiful Italian town — and all the toys would be used, but mostly they could enjoy some snorkelling in the crystal blue waters around the shallows.

After dinner, the party moved over to the softer seats on the deck and with the lights on board dimmed the glittering shoreline became a beautiful sparkling back-drop to their conversation. Jenna was happy catching up with Emma and Monty — she wanted to hear all about the recce trip to India they were planning, while Bertie leaned against the handrail with TG and gently laid a hand on his arm.

'Of course this lovely beast is far too big to get a mooring in Sanremo, I suppose?' she flirted with him, making eye contact as she sipped from her champagne flute.

'Every rose and all that,' TG moved his arm slightly.

'You could probably afford to build your own dock here, if you wanted to.'

TG turned and looked at Bertie. 'I get that money is quite important to you, Bertie?'

'Well, one likes to get by. Obviously, being rich myself, I know what it's like. Gold-diggers everywhere . . .' She glanced back over to where Jenna was sitting with the Blake-Howards. TG followed her gaze, and her gist.

'Aren't you supposed to be her friend?'

'Yes. And as her friend I know how poor she is.'

'Jenna isn't a gold-digger. I can tell you that.'

'How do you know? She's settled in quite nicely here only, what, a week or whatever since the supposed love of her life dumped her? All seems quite calculating if you ask me.'

TG stared at Bertie. His knuckles were turning white as he gripped the handrail, although his face remained calm. After a few seconds more he answered her. 'There's a certain chaos to Jenna. I've seen it in coding, and it's the same in people.' He paused. 'She isn't wired to control situations.'

'God, or herself, I mean just look at the other night!' Bertie snorted and tried again to flirtily touch TG. She felt his arm tense up as she did so. 'Oh, I get it. *You* want to control *her*, don't you?'

'Control her?'

'Yah.' Bertie looked down at the white knuckles and back up to the placid face. 'Isn't that what all men want to do? Tame the wild horse? Instil order in the chaos? And someone who is in awe of you, paid by you, it's perfect.'

'No, no.' TG ran his hands through his hair and took a step back from her. 'Look, Bertie, this is some deep shit you're talking here.'

'All I'm saying is that she's looking very well and very happy. But watch out — a wild horse can't stay a show

259

pony for long. She'll bolt for the hills if you try and rope her in too much.'

'I'm not roping her into anything.'

'Just paying her to stay?'

'Whatever. Look, shall we join the others?' He gestured for her to move back towards Jenna and the Blake-Howards.

'I'm just saying,' Bertie whispered to him as they moved away from the rail, 'it might feel like it now, that you've bought a thoroughbred, I mean . . .'

'I haven't bought her.' TG was trying to smile through gritted teeth.

'Looks like it to all the world if you ask me.'

'It seems to me, Roberta, that few people ask you, yet you give your opinions quite freely.'

'Some things, darling — like *moi* and my opinions — just can't be bought.' At that Bertie dragged one of her fingernails up the front of his shirt and bopped him on the chin. Before he could reply they were back within earshot of the others and a fresh bottle of champagne was opened by one of the crew, much to the whooping delight of Jenna.

'Everyone has their price.' TG muttered to himself as he sat down next to his new girlfriend and accepted a glass of fizz from the stewardess.

The next morning as Jenna was lying in the tangled sheets of TG's bed, she wondered if it might not be easier to move her suitcase into this cabin, though something still held her back from suggesting it. Perhaps it was that, although she was being very ably distracted by TG, she still thought about Angus almost every hour of the day. She wondered what he was doing, where he was and what their first conversation would be if they were to ever run into each other again, which given their close circle of friends was likely to be about three minutes after landing back in London. She also wondered how he'd feel if he could see her now. And whenever she lay out on one of the super yacht's sunbeds or wrapped her arms around her new lover she wondered if the sight of it would pierce his heart as keenly as he had pierced hers. It didn't help that Bertie had made her promise to invite Diane to the pre-wedding party at the Hotel de Paris. Jenna felt like she might die if she saw her — especially since the last time Diane saw *her* she was arse-end up in the murky waters of Port Hercule. *No wonder Gus left clumsy old me for the elegance of a super model*, Jenna thought to herself.

She kicked off the sheets, stretched as she got out of bed and picked her nightie up from the floor — last night she'd worn something even Bertie would have been proud of, and TG certainly hinted that he preferred her to look feminine and make the most of 'her beautiful curves'. He'd bought her this sexy negligee — silky cream with pink lace edging — when they were shopping in Portofino. She'd taken the hint, even though last night she had worn it for approximately fifteen seconds before TG had slid the thin straps off her shoulders and let the silk tumble around her ankles as he kissed her naked body all over before leading her to the vast bed in the stateroom suite which she was quickly becoming rather used to.

Jenna wrapped one of the yacht's white waffle bathrobes around her for the quick walk back to her cabin. Although her negligees and naughtiest of undies now lived in TG's stateroom, she still kept the rest of her stuff to herself in her own room. She thought she'd have a quick shower and then dress ready for their little stop-off in Sanremo but when she opened the door to her cabin she spotted another gift box lying on the clean, unrumpled sheets of her own bed. The box was like the one that had contained the diamond earrings a few days ago — black leather and about the size of a pack of cards. Jenna picked it up and held her breath as she opened it. Glinting at her from the box, sparkling in the overhead LED downlighters in her room was the most beautiful sapphire and diamond pendant, which hung on a fine gold chain. The stone was the deepest blue — and cut so perfectly that the facets reflected light almost as much as the diamonds that encircled it.

'Wow . . .' Jenna exhaled and pulled on the chain. It came out of the box and she let it hang from her fingers. It was exquisite. She unclasped the chain and put it on, lifting her hair out of the way and then slipping off the bathrobe as she wandered towards the bathroom's full-length mirror so she could see how it looked against her décolletage.

TG leaned forward, getting closer to the computer screen that flicked between the streaming CCTV images from around the boat. He'd kissed Jenna on the forehead as she lay slumbering at seven this morning and crept into her room to leave the pendant on her bed, before checking how things were with the captain and heading here, into his study, to get on with some work. Jenna really was the worst PA he'd ever had and she had no idea that he worked solidly from 7 a.m. till 9 a.m., which was when she generally joined him for breakfast — by which point he'd dealt with most of the important stuff — board-related emails, enquiries from charities and follow ups from the government buyout of his Clickbait app coding. His eye had been caught by movement on the camera in the corridor and he'd followed her as she'd walked from his room back to hers. He knew it was wrong, but he pressed the button that activated the camera in her room just in time to see her open the box and admire the jewel, threading it through her fingers and holding it up to the light. The fact that she then put it on and slipped out of the robe was a bonus and he felt himself stiffen as he saw her walk naked to the bathroom, where even he couldn't have justified placing a camera.

Jenna tucked the beautiful pendant — safely in its box — into the knicker drawer in her room. Of course there was a safe, all the cabins had them, and she'd stash it in there later along with the diamond earrings TG had given her a few days ago, but for now she was still so gobsmacked by its sudden arrival she wanted to keep it touchingly, reassuringly close. For someone to buy her something quite so beautiful — well, he must have feelings for her. Perhaps this fling might be more real than rebound and she wanted time to think about how she felt about that before the manic-ness of Monaco and Bertie's wedding took over. She'd felt and heard the powerful engines start up as she was just waking up in TG's bed this morning, and they'd be on their way around the coast of Italy, past the Portofino peninsula and almost halfway back to Monaco by now. Pulling on some tailored shorts over her bikini — the little black one was becoming more of a poolside feature than the more modest swimming costume she first wore on deck — and a loose pink cotton shirt, she headed down to the beach club to see if she could help the crew prepare the 'toys'.

'What on earth is that?' she asked TG as he joined her on deck, kissed her temple and gave her a cup of coffee. Jenna had been politely asked *not* to help any more once she'd accidentally knocked one of the snorkels overboard while trying to stop her sunglasses from falling into the water.

'A jet surf.'

'A what Smurf?' the wind caught his voice and she misheard, but wondered if she was up for one of those algae drinks again.

'The jet surfs. They're like jet-powered surf boards. You can do tricks and fling yourself in the air. They're cool. Going to try one?'

'Not on your nelly.'

'Was that a no?'

'Yes. I mean, no, it was a no. And don't think you'll lure Bertie onto one either — I know in space, no one can hear you scream, but in Sanremo they'll be hearing the shrieks if so much as a nail gets chipped!'

Jenna glanced at her own nails. A manicure wouldn't go amiss — but before she could think much more about it TG had waved over to where the *Wavy Sloanes* had caught up with them and were dropping anchor close by.

'Excuse me,' he said as he squeezed her shoulder goodbye and Jenna watched as TG went over to talk to Captain Avery who had appeared on deck. She waved over to Bertie and Emma too and then wandered over to see what all the fuss was about with TG and the captain.

'What do you mean we can't get in the water?' TG wasn't shouting but his body language was expressing his irritation — his arms were folded and he stood with his feet slightly apart — a bouncer's stance.

'The sea is teeming with them. Only a madman would get in the water. Stingers, fifteen feet long some of them.'

'Won't the wet suits protect us?'

'Not your face, hands or feet . . . I can't let you in, plus the yacht only has fuel enough to get back to Monaco, not dance around these coves trying to find a clean bay.'

'Fuck.' TG's arms uncrossed but his fists were clenched. When he saw Jenna he tried to relax his pose but she could see the annoyance playing across his face. 'No point hanging around this shithole.' Suddenly Sanremo had been demoted. 'You might as well tell Bertie and the Blake-Howards that we'll see them back at Monaco.'

'Of course,' Jenna replied, then suddenly remembered the pendant. 'Oh TG, thank you.'

'What for?'

'That beautiful sapphire pendant. It's just stunning.'

He turned to look at her again and the irritation of the aborted fun and games temporarily left his face. 'My pleasure. It's not as beautiful as you.' He kissed her on the forehead and turned away, calling out behind him, 'Just call the others, yeah?'

A stark reminder that she was still his PA. She fished her mobile out of her pocket and texted Bertie.

No point staying here. Bay full of jellyfish. We're heading back to Monaco, see you there.x

The reply came back from Bertie almost immediately.

Shame. Looks like TG can't control everything! See you babes xxxxxx

Jenna popped the phone back in her pocket and wondered what Bertie meant exactly. TG didn't want to control everything, did he? It was only stupid jellyfish. Still, they had indeed scuppered their plans, but could that really be why TG seemed to have gone off in a grump?

'Another bloody present?' Sally snorted down the phone at her friend. 'Is he trying to buy you?'

If Jenna couldn't swan around in the surf, she could at least use the free time to call Sally instead.

'Why would you say that?' Jenna was indignant. Her friend's words smarted more than she realised, maybe?

'Well, every time you have sex he gives you something. It's like you're a high-class hooker!'

'At least I'm high class . . .' Jenna made the joke, but only to hide how hurt she was by her friend's insinuation. 'Anyway, they're gifts. They're not quid pro quos.'

'Whatever, sweetie.'

'Why are you in such a grump anyway, Sals?'

'Well for one, I'm feeling massively fat. And I can't sleep and my hips hurt and I pee all the time — oh and your bloody tenants keep leaving the house in such a state.'

'Gus's tenants.'

'Sorry, darling, but still, I was doing the favour for *you*, not Gus.'

Jenna sighed. 'I know, thanks, Sals. I'm sorry they're being a pain. And sorry you're not feeling too great.'

'I hope I do feel better by this bloody wedding in a few weeks. And I want to see you and the beautiful Riviera . . . it's the only thing I've got to look forward to!'

'And having a baby . . . there's that too.' Jenna knew the words sounded a bit 'woe is me' but she didn't care. Sally was always there with a humble brag and Jenna was still reeling from Bertie's announcement to start Project Pram too. She told Sally about it.

'Oh God no . . . really? She's going to multiply?'

Jenna chuckled, remembering why she loved Sally as much as she did. 'Yes . . . insider trading be damned, go buy shares in Baby Dior!'

49

'Insider trading, mate?'

'Shush.' Max shielded his mouth with his hand as he spoke to Angus. 'I'm not sure if this phone line is secure.'

'Well, I can tell you that mine probably isn't.'

Max readjusted the phone against his ear. 'What do you mean?'

'Oh,' he heard Angus sigh on the other end of the line. 'It's probably me being paranoid and it's a long story . . .'

'Believe me, I could do with the distraction.' Max was working late and coiled the phone's lead around his fingers as he sat back in his executive leather-covered chair. 'Shoot.'

'You're better than that though, mate. Really.'

'I know, I know. It's just Bertie is demanding so much for the wedding. We're having gold-plated oysters, apparently. That we then shuck and throw the bloody shells away.'

'Wow.'

'There's part of me that just wants to chuck it all in, tell her to wear something from her already bulging wardrobe and head down to Chelsea Register Office.'

'Why don't you then?'

Max sighed. 'I know how much all of the show means to her. It's just bloody exhausting.'

'And expensive?'

Angus wasn't wrong, Max thought. But also realised he'd neatly sidestepped his own turn at the story telling. 'So what's all this about you having a bugged line?'

'I'm probably being paranoid. Now at least. Look, Max, shouldn't be telling you this, so don't you dare repeat it, but I lost Jenna this summer because I had to. I had to let her go because there was a price on her head and I couldn't afford to pay it.'

'What the—?'

'The gang in Singapore, the ones who gave me this scar. They kidnapped me in Hong King and claimed I killed one of them. He died after the fight, apparently. So they demanded a life for a life but I negotiated money instead.'

'And they wanted Jenna?'

'Someone I loved, yes.'

'So you . . . sold her?'

'As good as. TG offered to pay the ransom as long as I left Jenna — I had to vanish and break her heart.'

'From what I hear you managed that bit.'

'Thanks.'

Max felt bad, but he was in a shitty mood anyway so didn't take his friend's sarcastic tone to heart.

'And then what? Jenna gets over you and falls for him and that's it?'

'I can't blame her. But I'm just saying — you have a girlfriend who loves you and wants a few fancy extras for her wedding. She's not a kidnap risk or has a bounty on her head. Appreciate it.'

'No, you're right. I'm sorry, mate. Though it sounds like you could do with a few more pennies to your name yourself.'

'Wouldn't hurt. If I could buy TG out of the contract . . .'

'Would he let you?'

'I doubt it.'

'Jenna's a free woman, though, isn't she? Why can't she just jump ship and follow her heart back to you?'

'It might be a gilded one, but she's caged. Plus in the contract I had to swear not to contact her or talk to you guys about it, hence you needing to keep schtum. So there she is, me not replying to her, her not really allowed off the boat without chaperones — you know, it's not *normal*?'

'Yeah, yeah. Look, sorry, mate. This is shit for you.'

Max held the handset to his ear while he waited for the sobs to ease off at the other end. Angus had reached breaking point and Max realised it was probably time to head back out to Monaco to sort this whole thing out.

50

Clickbait motored back into Port Hercule and, considering its tonnage, moored up as smoothly as a book sliding back into a well-polished shelf. Jenna was transfixed watching Avery and the crew effortlessly manoeuvre the massive yacht back into its mooring. The crew had been busy in other ways too and waiting for them on the quayside was a refrigerated van ready to deliver fresh groceries and special treats. Thinking of her stomach once again, Jenna kept her fingers crossed that about a ton of mozzarella and tomatoes were included, but was as equally as impressed as she saw polystyrene boxes filled with ice and oysters loaded on board.

'I should go down and help, maybe?'

TG had appeared next to her and she wanted to break the silence between them since his grumpy episode in Sanremo.

'That's not your job.' His voice was back to its usual soft but confident tone.

'Who are all the oysters for?'

'You and me,' he replied wrapping his arms around her. Then, lowering his lips to her ear, he whispered, 'And if we think they're good enough, we'll get some more for Bertie and her friends in a couple of nights' time.'

'What?' Jenna pulled away from TG and looked up at him with a slightly confused expression on her face. 'Bertie?'

'Look, I know I should have asked you first, but I saw how happy you were to have friends on board so I invited her to host her bachelorette or whatever it was on here.'

Jenna couldn't quite believe it — or TG's generosity. Staying on board *Clickbait* would save them all a fortune. 'Thank you.' She kissed him and then playfully continued. 'But I thought I was the one that was meant to be the party organiser. And if it wasn't for the fact that it's her *hen* do, or stag, or shag or whatever, I might get slightly jealous of you arranging parties with Dirty Bertie behind my back.'

TG laughed and pulled Jenna in for a kiss. She let him hold her close and knew that whatever reason he had for inviting the harpie-in-chief on board, it wasn't because he had lost interest in her. In fact, his suggestion that they go for a little afternoon siesta back in his cabin made her very much aware that he was still very much into her, and moments later it wasn't just *Clickbait* that got to lower its massive anchor into friendly waters.

Angus lowered his binoculars again. The tension that had coursed across his shoulders as he'd looked out continuously for gangsters had now gone, along with that particular problem, only to be replaced by the hollow sadness that losing Jenna to TG had carved into him. He felt like a stalker, but he couldn't help himself checking up on her. He was back in Monaco briefly to meet Max, before heading back to the UK. He'd had a stream of angry messages from Sally suggesting he could shove his spare set of house keys up his you-know-what and he knew better than to argue with Sally — especially a hormonally charged pregnant Sally.

There was something else keeping him here, lurking by the harbour, catching sight of *Clickbait* as and when he could, though. And that something was the fact that as hard as it was to see TG making his moves on Jenna, it proved to Angus that if he *did* break the rules of the contract there was pretty much nothing TG could do about it. He wouldn't get his money back from The Voice — he couldn't if he tried — and it wasn't like *he'd* want to put Jenna in danger, not now he'd obviously fallen for her too. And how watertight was that contract, legally? How would he penalise him? So many times Angus had almost sent a long message to Jenna explaining everything — why he had to stay away at least until The Voice had confirmed the money was received — but then he stopped, he deleted the words. It was too late and TG's plan had worked. He'd just seen Jenna, his Jenna, stand on the deck of the super yacht and be kissed by the billionaire bastard who had bought her. There was no point now upsetting her by coming back into her life. Or maybe, he dared not think it, she had never really loved him that much anyway. But, he loved her with all his heart and raising the binoculars again he decided he would torture himself for a few days more before heading back to London and a life without his love.

An hour later Max saw Angus across the crowded bar of the harbourside restaurant they'd picked to meet up in for lunch.

'Mate!'

'Hi!'

The hug they gave each other gave away more than each realised and the two men knew they had much to catch up on.

'Have you seen her?' they both said it at the same time, but Angus replied. 'Yes and no. Seen, not been seen.'

'A life in the shadows. Not great, eh mate?'

'You?'

'Bertie? Yes. Jenna, no, not yet — but we're due on board *Clickbait* tomorrow night for some sort of joint pre-wedding party.' Max hadn't had time to even think about a stag, or at least Hugo, his best man, hadn't. He got the impression that if Sally was having to stay teetotal while up the duff, then Hugo sure as hell wasn't going to be allowed out for a night on the razz. 'I would invite you, but I guess that's not allowed with this contract thing you've got going on?'

'I'm this close,' Angus pinched his fingers almost shut, 'to breaking it. But I don't think I can take it. I can't see Jenna upset or . . .' he flicked a stray peanut across the metal-topped table, '. . . happy.'

A waitress appeared and they ordered beers and burgers and carried on talking.

'Well, if it makes you feel any better, I've fucked up too.' Max raked his fingers through his hair.

'How?'

'Who, more like.'

'Oh mate . . . really? But you and Bertie, you're solid. I mean, you're getting married in a couple of weeks!'

'I don't know why . . . well, I do. I mean, it's been relentless. Bertie just won't stop going on about money and how much we need for the wedding, and the boat and . . . I mean, I know it means a lot to her, but I got fed up. I wanted to share the company of someone to whom I was already a success.'

'Just a randomer?'

'No, you see that's the problem. It was Izzy — remember the hot chalet girl?'

'Who got tangled up with that Jonty git as well last summer?'

'Yeah. Well, she got tangled up with me this summer. Bertie's been out here so much and I, I . . .'

'Have you told her?'

'Bertie? Fuck no.' Beers arrived and the men took much-needed swigs. 'I don't know, mate. I don't know if I should even be getting married.'

'Don't throw it away, Max. If I could get Jenna back, I would, but it's got to be true love, you know.'

'I know. And I do love Bertie, I do. I just can't take all this pushing for this fake glamorous life.'

'Did you do the insider trading?'

'No,' Max stared into his pint. 'I couldn't go through with it. My moral compass does stop somewhere you know.' He looked up and gave Angus a lopsided smile. Angus just shook his head in despair.

'Dolls, just sublime of your lovely boyfriend to let us have our little pre-wedding party here on *Clickbait*.'

Bertie had made herself at home on the sofas on the main deck looking over the pool and Jenna felt she was back to square one, notebook in hand, quickly writing down all of Bertie's ideas as she spouted them out. She flinched when Bertie said 'boyfriend' and her mind leapt back to Angus and she wondered where he was and who he was with. Her heart sank when she realised he was probably wrapped around Diane Blane and hated the fact she was on the list for the party tomorrow night. How easy would it be to just tell security not to let her on board — the embarrassment of seeing her again was enough to bring Jenna out in a bit of a sweat and she noticed Bertie look at her oddly. 'Sorry, it's just this hot weather — no breeze.' Jenna exaggeratedly shook out her blouse and tried to make light of it.

'TG is so sweet — you really have pulled way above your not insubstantial weight, you know, darling — jokesies.'

This new version of Bertie — DB Mk III, as Jenna was calling it — was a trial to get used to. The barbs were not gone, but they were disguised in falsely chummy jokes — or jokesies, as Bertie kept calling them. It took most of Jenna's reserve not to boot her off the boat altogether, but technically she was TG's guest and among the barbs there were some genuine moments of friendship — even if they came mostly at Jenna's expense.

'Could you be a dear and ask TG if he wouldn't mind getting some proper lighting on board for tomorrow night?'

'I don't think we can really change the boat's lights, Bertie. Why?'

'Oh, I just feel like if I have to constantly change my Instagram filter to Sierra I'll get RSI. So much easier to get the lighting right in the first place.'

'Honestly, Bertie, give me ideas I can work with here. Not the impossible.'

'But with TG's budget, anything is possible right?' Bertie looked genuinely perplexed.

'Maybe, Berts, but last thing I heard he was hosting your party, not paying for it all . . .'

'Fine. As it's muggins here — albeit very glamorous muggins — paying just jot down that I'd like black welcome carpet, not ghastly red — that's such a draining colour — and giant ostrich feathers in silver urns. Let's go Gatsby-style, shall we? Glitter curtains, oh pearls, yes, pearls everywhere . . . a tower of champagne glasses on a crystal table. And musicians on saxophone and double bass.'

'Ooh, a bit Jeeves and Wooster too then?' Jenna piped up hopefully, remembering her parents' old VHS tapes being brought out on Sunday nights.

'No.' Bertie sounded peeved. 'Not bloody Jeeves and bloody Wooster. God, Jenna, being a billionaire's lackey has really blown your brain cells you know.' She frowned, then added. 'Jokesies.'

'I'm not some lackey, Bertie.' Jenna stood up and tossed her notebook down on the sofa. She wanted to shout at Bertie, tell her to stop being such a bitch, but there was something to what Bertie was saying that struck a chord with her. 'Look, I don't know what I am, but at this minute I'm fed up with planning this bloody party. Get your own damn ostrich feathers.'

'It was a jokesies!' Bertie called out after Jenna, who for once didn't turn around and meekly accept the apology.

TG heard the raised voices on the deck and smiled to himself. His plan of letting Bertie and her fiancé have their pre-wedding bachelor-hen-whatever party on board his yacht was paying off. As predicted, that Bertie girl was being a right pain in Jenna's ass so although he'd get kudos for letting her have her friends on board, he'd also have her thanks when they were gone and *Clickbait* could once again be a haven away from Bertie's 'jokesies'. He had nothing against Bertie and Max per se — except that she was a piece of work and he was obviously on the make — but they were friends with Angus and he needed Jenna to cut those ties. And he needed *her* to do it, not him.

'Jenna,' he called to her as she stomped through the saloon to the main staircase.

'What?'

'Having fun with Bertie?' He smiled at her and hoped she got the fact he was joking.

Jenna sighed. 'She's impossible, TG. Just impossible.'

TG walked towards her and wrapped his arms around her. 'You know why I let her have her party here?'

'I guess . . . actually, I don't know. I guess because you're generous and amazing and . . .'

'And I wanted you to be happy and know that your friends are welcome here.' He gently pushed a tendril of hair away from her slightly furrowed brow.

'It's really nice of you. But I'm . . .'

'Not sure she's really your friend?'

Jenna let out a long breath again and nodded.

'We all change and move on,' TG counselled. 'Perhaps this wedding and all of its dramas will be the last act in your friendship with that woman? Perhaps she's not all she's cracked up to be. Don't let her use you just to get on board and climb yet more rungs of her social ladder.'

Jenna snorted in a derisory fashion. 'If you'd told me a month or so ago that Bertie would ever use me to get ahead I would have laughed at you.'

'And now?'

'Maybe you're right. Maybe she's not good for me.'

TG pulled her in closer and kissed her forehead. It was too easy. Whatever Bertie said, he could have this girl tamed and all to himself. By the time they were back in Sacramento this fall she'd have forgotten all about her London lot, especially her ex-boyfriend.

51

The day of the pre-wedding party dawned to the cacophony of workers coming on board to prepare the yacht for Bertie's *Great Gatsby* theme. Jenna rolled over and found TG had already got up. She stretched her arms out across the king-size bed and felt the luxury of the sheets. Her head throbbed a bit and a persistent banging from outside was driving her to distraction. So, although it was only 8.30 a.m., she pulled herself out of the comfort of the bed and scooped up her barely worn negligee before wrapping a bathrobe around her and heading back to her cabin.

She almost expected to find another gift box on the bed — and although she was disappointed not to, she was also a little relieved. She could prove Sally wrong by telling her that she definitely didn't get a pearl every time she opened her clamshell.

Showered and dressed in her usual white jeans and after Portofino's little shopping spree, a much smarter silk T-shirt, she headed out of her cabin to see what all the banging was about.

Bertie was directing operations as a makeshift white, wooden bridge was constructed spanning the long, narrow swimming pool on the main deck.

'What the—?'

'Morning, chicks. Better mood I assume today?'

'Morning, Bertie. And yeah . . . but what is this?'

'Well, what do you think it is? It's a bridge.'

Jenna scratched her head. 'But what's it doing on our yacht?'

'Oh.' Bertie stood even more upright and Jenna wondered if she was bristling slightly. '*Our* yacht now, is it?'

'Oh, you know what I mean, Berts.' Jenna didn't have the patience to deal with a spiky Bertie this morning, not with the slight ringing in her ears still there from the more than just a few glasses of champagne she'd had last night. TG had treated her to a fancy night out – the Range Rover had driven them all of five minutes up to dinner at the Metropole followed by drinks at the Buddha Bar overlooking the Fairmont. She'd drunk to drown out memories of Angus – the sight of the Nikki Beach Bar on the roof of the Fairmont had been enough to bring him very much back to the forefront of her mind. TG had filled and refilled her glass to the extent that Jenna wondered if maybe he preferred her drunk? To a point though . . . she remembered being ushered rather quickly into the tinted-windowed Range Rover when a group of young guys had come to join them at their table and had brought more champagne with them. It seemed it didn't matter to TG how drunk she got, as long as he was the one buying. Perhaps tonight she should stay just on the right side of tipsy.

'No!' screeched Bertie as a floundering courier dropped a cage of live doves on the wooden deck. 'Not here, not now, you imbecile!'

'Calm down, Berts.' Jenna stepped in and with throbbing head and all she gradually took over the operation, so much so that Bertie even begrudgingly paid her a sort-of compliment.

'You're so much better at this sort of stuff than me. I mean, how was I to know that doves shouldn't be brought on board more than five hours in advance. We're in France, for God's sake, I didn't think they had any animal welfare laws. I mean they eat horses. Surely they can cope with a couple of pigeons in a box for two minutes?'

'I know about the regulations, having organised the dove release at your birthday, remember?'

'Amazing job, sweets. You see, I need little people like you around to help *moi* with these things.'

'Are you getting *abso exhaust*, Berts?' Jenna borrowed the other girl's phrase.

'Oh God, yah. Totes.'

Jenna sat them both down and beckoned over a hovering stewardess. Once she'd ordered a couple of mineral waters Bertie changed her tune again.

'Getting bloody used to this, aren't you, babes?'

'What choice do I have, Berts?' Jenna only realised how desperate that sounded once she'd said it out loud.

'Choice, darling? World's your bloody oyster!'

'Is it though? I can't leave this boat without being sucked into the dark vacuum of a tinted-windowed car. When we go out, at least two Tweedles follow us around.'

'Who?'

'Oh,' Jenna waved her hand, 'it's my name for the stewards. Doesn't matter. Anyway, it's just, I don't know. I can't put my finger on it, but I'm starting to feel a little hemmed in.'

'Water, water everywhere but not a drop to drink . . .'

'Yes. Yes . . . sort of.' Jenna wondered how long Bertie would stay in this moderately normal, friendly mode.

'Sex good though?'

Jenna was a little surprised by the question, but didn't mind answering. Her life seemed so distant now from the ups and downs she'd had while in London, and she missed a bit of girly time, even if it was with Bertie. 'Yeah, the sex is hot. He's amazing. But it's all quite, I don't know . . .'

'Staged?'

'Yes.'

'Like you're acting for a camera.' Bertie's reply was very much a statement, not a question.

'Yes. Wow, Bertie, do you feel the same?'

'Sometimes.' Jenna saw a flicker of softness across Bertie's face before a steeliness crept back in, its rigid hardness more in keeping with her heavily Botoxed brow. 'But it's the game. Remember when I bedded Yuri last year? It was thrilling and he was so powerful and, oh so manly, but I was scared. I don't mind telling you that.'

'I don't blame you. After what he did to Hugo . . .' Jenna remembered the sight of Sally's then fiancé lying in the hospital bed, having been brutally beaten up by the Russian's henchmen.

'Not physically scared, silly. I was scared that I'd lose myself, me, to his whims and machinations.'

'Bertie, why didn't you tell me this before?'

'Why would I? Look, Jens, if you're going to be joining the upper-upper classes *avec moi* and Ems you need to learn to keep that bit of you locked up. You trade your soul to be part of the super-rich — and the other part of it you keep held back. Just for you.'

'But I don't want to live like this.'

'This gilded-cage nonsense doth butter no parsnips with me, sweetie.' Bertie's voice had lost its softness from a few minutes ago and she seemed back to abrupt self. 'Make your bed and lie in it, chica.'

'Is that why you love Max really?'

'What?'

Bertie's staccato reply made Jenna slightly quiver as she answered. 'Max. He's not super-rich so you can be yourself with him. That's why you love him, even though you'd like all this.' Jenna waved her hand to indicate the luxury of the yacht.

Bertie took a deep breath in and exhaled. 'Spot on, sweetie.'

*

Jenna thought about Bertie's words as the Range Rover took her up to Casino Square and dropped her off outside the shopping centre just under the Metropole Hotel. Jenna had seen advertisements for this mall in the glossy magazines delivered to the yachts and decided it might be a good place to quickly find another outfit to wear, now that her beautiful black Lanvin dress was reduced to cleaning rags. She was too embarrassed to go back to that luxury boutique — and she was worried that spending so much money on clothes might turn her into some sort of bimbo overnight — so the Metropole shopping centre it was. Not that it was a downgrade from the boutiques set up from the square — far from it. As shopping centres went it was pretty amazing. Huge great crystal chandeliers hung from the central atriums, and the galleried floors of shops were edged with marble balustrades. Glass lifts carried shoppers up and down, or there were gilded, fancy escalators too. Jenna stopped to appreciate the spectacle — then felt like a country hick as glossy shoppers barged past her, their sunglasses on (even though they were about two storeys down from the bright natural sunlight outside), hair pouffed and designer carrier bags knocking against each other.

Jenna clicked into action and scanned the shops. There were so many accessories and shoes but across the way she spied some beautiful maxi dresses hanging up in Blumarine, so headed in. Not wanting to buy anything that might be construed as being similar to Emma's designs, she found a mango-orange-coloured, one-shouldered floor-length dress, with a split that soared thigh high. It reminded her of something Bertie would wear, and Jenna wouldn't even have usually taken it off the hanger, especially when she saw the price. *Am I becoming just a bloody clothes horse?* Jenna didn't care at this minute, especially not with the party starting in a few hours. She grabbed the dress on its hanger and took it into the changing room. The colour was amazing, lifting her caramel-coloured hair and highlighting the golden tan she'd gradually built up. A bit of eye make-up and a slick of lip gloss and this dress would do all the talking for her — *maybe that's why rich women wore such stunning dresses* — so they could keep that little bit of soul to themselves and merely smile at the millionaires around them, rather than spill their secrets.

She handed over her debit card at the till. Knowing there was sufficient in her bank account (and that the credit card wasn't needed) was a satisfying feeling. But feeling the satisfaction of knowing she'd genuinely earned that money — well that was getting harder and harder.

52

The urge to go and make herself her own cup of tea had never been so strong. Jenna watched as the beautiful people of Bertie and Max's party milled around on deck — the women in sparkling dresses trying to make even more sparkling conversation with TG and the other wealthy men on board. And the younger guys too, making a play for the cougars, the older ladies dripping in diamonds who had successfully made a career from marrying well, giving them free rein now to marry as badly and naughtily as they wanted. How did Bertie know all these people? There were a few familiar faces — probably from various parties *à la domestique*, as Bertie would say.

Jenna sipped her champagne but it tasted sour in her mouth — who knew you could get bored of the stuff? She half-cocked an ear into a conversation Max and Monty Blake-Howard were having about tenders and what toys your average and above-average super yacht should have on board. Her eyes darted through the faces. Angus had not been invited, TG had put his foot down there. He'd be at the wedding, though, in a few weeks' time, no doubt with Diane on his arm. Well, at least Jenna could wear all her beautiful new jewellery — and replace the Lanvin dress for the black-tie after party. TG had paid her again and her bank account was, for the first time ever, *overfloweth* with spare cash.

'Penny for them?' Max brushed her arm with his hand and looked down at her with the sort of knowing expression only ten years or so of genuine friendship can bring.

'Oh, nothing really. Another night, another party — you know what it's like. I don't know how Bertie keeps up with all this socialising back in London.'

'She's a pro, I'll give her that. Jenna?' Max paused before asking her a question. 'Am I a bad person?'

'What? No. I mean, not really, no.'

'Huh, thanks for the ringing endorsement, mate.' He clinked her champagne glass with his.

'Well, what context are you asking it in? I mean, do you donate all your earnings to orphans?'

'Of course not!'

'So you just about slide in under Mother Teresa on the saintly scale.' Jenna looked up at Max and winked. 'But then so do I and almost every other unworthy human on this planet.'

'Ha. I mean, I don't think I'm a horrible person . . .'

'Oh Max. What have you done?'

'I slept with Izzy, the old chalet girl, again.'

'Izzy? Jonty's bit on the side Izzy?' All the memories of when Jenna was led up the garden — or in that case, château's beautiful walled garden — path last summer fizzed up inside her. Jonty Palmer-Johnston had tried to frame her for fraudulently importing wine while making her believe he loved her, and all the time he'd been having it off with young Izzy too. 'Max, how could you! What did Bertie say? Does she know?'

'No, not yet. I don't know, I can't tell her.'

'Would the wedding be off?'

'Maybe — and not because I cheated. I mean, look at her.' Max pointed his glass towards where his fiancé was standing on the deck, one arm wrapped around some paunchy Russian while the other hand traced the buttons of his shirt up to his wobbly double chin before giggling and accepting another glass of fizz from a passing stewardess.

'That's just Bertie, though.' Jenna wasn't sure why she was defending her. Maybe because flirting was one thing, fucking was another . . . And her revelations earlier that day had led Jenna to believe there really were many more layers to her than she'd assumed. Wealth was like a drug for Bertie, but Jenna knew that Max was her rehab.

'The thing is, I'll admit I cheated, she'll ask why and I'll be forced to tell her it's because I can't cope with all of this.' He waved his hand indicating the amazing deck they were on. 'I just can't keep up. I can't make the money she wants me to. I came this close to committing a crime, insider trading, before Angus told me it wasn't worth it.'

'Angus?' Jenna became more alert and stood more upright. 'What did he say? Did he mention me?'

Max sighed. 'No, Jens, well, yes, but I can't say what.'

'Oh, for fuck's sake, Max, really? What's the big conspiracy?'

'Look — I just think you should talk to him at some point, when TG lets you off this thing.'

Jenna narrowed her eyes at her old friend. She wasn't sure how to process all this information. Max had cheated on Bertie, to be expected really; Bertie had been overly demanding, also to be expected, but Angus had kept Max on the straight and narrow and he had mentioned Jenna but now Max wouldn't say what was going on? Jenna let out a big sigh and shrugged her shoulders.

'Fine, whatever. Look, you go and sort your life out with the glamazon over there and I'll see you later, Max.'

Jenna walked away from Max and the general noise of the party on the main deck. Couples and groups were sitting inside the main saloon, too, and she managed a fake smile or two, remembering she was still meant to be the genteel hostess. She was just about to mount the spiral staircase in the centre of the yacht and head up to her cabin for five minutes' respite from the crowd when she heard voices coming downstairs.

'Well, I don't blame her really,' the first voice said, and some instinct in Jenna made her hide behind the grand piano at the bottom of the spiral, and keep her ears open.

'There's a word for women like her though and it starts with *H* and ends with *ooker*,' the second voice giggled.

'I heard he bought her from her previous employer for a million bucks.'

'But she's not even that pretty?'

'And her old boyfriend was chucked off this boat — like bag overboard, security, the lot.'

'What does he see in her then?'

'Must be excellent in bed, I guess — rumour has it she was shagging the owner of her last boat too. Who knows who she'll move onto next?'

'She better save a billionaire or two for me, greedy bitch!'

Jenna held her hand over her mouth. *Were they talking about her?* She heard the voices move down the stairs and into the main saloon and only then did she dare pop up from behind the piano and try to work out who had been saying such mean things about her. She could see the backs of two very glamorous women meld back into the party — typical of Bertie's friends, raspily thin with shoulder blades you could cut yourself on. They probably survived on a diet of vitamin tablets and salacious gossip. Jenna was dumbfounded. Were all these rumours really going round about her? But they weren't true!

Not knowing what to do or where to go she stood stock still, like a doe surrounded by hunters, not sure in which direction to bolt to find shelter. Not the party, that was certain, not if everyone there thought she was a hooker with ambitions for all their husbands. And not up to the bedrooms — that would be a sure fire way to bolster their rude assumptions. Instead she quickly ran down the spiral, away from the main saloon and the cabins and down to where the cinema room was and the business suite, the gym and the staff cabins. There was one room down here she knew she'd bump into no one — *God*, she thought, *even the Tweedles probably think I'm only one more cent away from another indecent proposal* — TG's study. It was odd, she thought, that TG had never invited her down there, and she sighed as she realised that any proper PA would have been all over it and if she wasn't there to be a PA, what was she there for?

She turned the handle and the large wooden door opened smoothly, gliding across the parquet floor to reveal a large partner's desk situated in the middle of the cabin. The decor was slightly different in this room — more gentleman's club mixed with American jock than super-yacht luxury. A battered old leather armchair sat by the bookshelves, and the desk's mahogany was echoed in the dark wood flooring and shelving. A kilim, worn and frayed with age, lay on the floor in front of the desk, which had on it a large, but sleek, computer monitor and mini keyboard. Unlike the decks above, the cabins here generally didn't have large windows, but this room was completely windowless — not even a porthole. Instead, hanging on the wall behind the large desk was a set of prints that as soon as she took them in, set Jenna's heart racing. She almost staggered into the door frame in disbe-lief. The prints were the complete set of Picassos that had been stolen from Roach & Hartley, her old gallery in London.

'Shit . . .' Jenna steadied herself while catching her breath and moving into the room properly, closed the heavy door behind her. She rested her back against it as her mind churned over several possibilities. Perhaps there had been some mistake? Perhaps they were just another set, another numbered print run from the originals. She pushed herself off from the door where she'd been leaning, still needing the support from the shock, and moved around the desk to the first of the prints. Carefully, she lifted it off its hook and turned the frame around.

The rush of blood to her ears made the world around her roar as she took in the familiar printed gallery sticker on the back of the frame. Roach & Hartley, Cork Street W1. These were the prints that cost her her career. These were the prints that were stolen on her watch while she went for a pee and left the door unlocked in the gallery. These were the prints that had made Martin Roach spit feathers in anger at her as she was fired for gross misconduct . . . and here they were, in TG's study. *He wasn't such a squeaky clean, holier-than-thou, must-give-back-to-the-planet type after all*, Jenna thought, as she realised that there was no way these prints would have ever made it onto the legitimate open art market. TG must have been offered them by someone who knew he could stash them away from public view, or he had put his own feelers out to the underworld and found them via a nefarious agent.

Once Jenna had got over the shock of finding the Roach & Hartley sticker on the back of the frame she looked back up to the wall to something that had caught her eye. The print had been hiding a small safe, set into the wall and barely large enough for much except a few documents. Documents . . . perhaps this was where the sales records would be for these prints and Jenna would finally find out who had been properly behind the heist that had cost her her job.

The safe was like the ones in all the guest cabins — four digits and the hash key would lock and unlock it. If only she knew the code. She wondered what it might be . . .. TG's birthday, or just the year . . . maybe his graduation date or the amount he sold the app for.

'Gah.' Jenna felt like she was so close to unravelling something important to her — something, finally, more important than the fickle world upstairs full of fake smiles, fake tits, fake nails and fake happiness. 'Think, Jenna, think . . .' she whispered to herself as she sat down in the leather chair behind the desk and clasped the Picasso print to her. Letting out a long sigh she knew it would be useless. She could be here all night guessing the code and soon she would be missed, by TG or Bertie or just by someone thinking she might be off blowing some other billionaire tonight. She lay the print down on her thighs to look at it again and the thought suddenly occurred to her. 'Time is money. The safe . . .. is money. Time is . . .' everything was fitting into place now, 'time is the hands on a clock. The tattoo!'

She put the print down on the desk and squared up to the safe. *Think, Jenna* . . . She pressed her fingers to her temples and tried to recall the elaborate clock tattoo on TG's thigh. The hands pointed to, what was it . . . 10 past four and quarter to seven! She tapped in 2, 4, 7, 9 and pressed the hash key. The bolt catch released and the door opened a little on its spring. 'Bloody hell!' Jenna was quite impressed at herself and was caught slightly not really knowing what to do. But her inner sleuth took over and she pulled out a bunch of papers that had been filed in there. One manila envelope caught her eye. Her name was on the front, written up in the top left corner, so not addressed to her, but definitely relating to her . . .

She opened the unsealed envelope and slid out the papers inside. A contract . . . interesting. *Must be my employment one*, she thought to herself, before remembering that she had never signed anything — *God, what a fool*, she thought as the words she heard from those gossips stung her afresh. She was about to slide it back into the envelope and go and show a brave face at the party again when she noticed another name on the front of the contract. Angus Linklater. She looked closer. The words began to blur as tears sprung to her eyes — angry tears as she read the contract and saw that Angus had sold her, *sold her*, to TG for five million dollars. Her heart broke all over again and she read and reread the contract, trying to understand what had happened. She knew Angus had spent all his money buying the house, but surely he wasn't that badly off? And he had never been one to be impressed by money, perhaps because he always knew he'd inherit enough to live comfortably on. Jenna wiped a tear before it splashed down onto the paperwork. She read through various clauses — financial penalties if Angus contacted Jenna; minimum distances to be maintained at social events; sub-clauses on using friends to pass on messages with the penalties for each person outlined — $10,000 for passing on a message verbally, $20,000 for passing on a letter, email or text — *no wonder Max had stayed schtum just now*. Then, on the last page there was a paragraph she'd missed before. Monies to be made payable to a holding company, Chung Plc in Hong Kong. Angus didn't have a holding company, did he? Her assumptions started to crumble. Why wouldn't it go into Angus's account — why bother with this part in a contract? There was a line underneath it — 'Chung Plc to issue receipt on monies received and confirmation that they will cease and desist from the monitoring, following and eventual execution of Ms Jenna Jenkins.'

'Execution!' she blurted out loud, wiping another tear from her damp cheek and checking the wording again. 'What the . . .?' There it was, in black and white — she had had a bounty on her head. 'Fucking hell . . .'

Thoughts, like jigsaw pieces, fitted together in her mind. Angus's hasty return to Europe after only a few weeks in Hong Kong, his jitteriness, his sudden departure . . . TG bought him off, but not because Angus wanted to get rid of her. No, it was the very opposite — Angus needed to save her life!

She dropped the paperwork down on the desk and rubbed her temples again. This whole situation was absurd. Why on earth would a Chinese corporation put a bounty on her head? She needed answers and she needed to know what TG knew. She slid the contract back into the envelope and popped it back into the safe. She paused — tempting as it was to rifle through the other papers in there to work out who he bought the Picassos from — she better get back to the party. Reaching up to place the print back on its hook concealing the safe she accidentally nudged the desk with her hip, the motion of which woke up the computer monitor. The screen flickered from black to full colour and as she turned round Jenna saw a grid of nine boxes on the screen — three rows of three — obviously CCTV cameras around the boat. She glanced over them and saw the party still in full swing on the decks — guests spread around the yacht on the sun deck, the main deck, the saloon, the beach club . . . a couple of screens had no one in them and Jenna froze again. One of the cameras was trained directly onto her bed.

53

Jenna ran up the spiral staircase to her cabin — her beautiful, luxurious, sumptuous, wretched cabin. Knowing the camera was focused on the bed she darted into the bathroom, grabbing her phone from the dressing table on the way in. Slamming the door behind her she put the seat of the loo down and sat on it. Her fingers swiped and tapped and in only a few seconds she had sent a message to Angus.

If you're still in Monaco, come to Clickbait NOW. I'll meet you on the quayside. I know about the contract.

She hoped the message would be enough to convince Angus that it wasn't just another plea of hers, like the beseeching messages she'd sent just after he'd left her. She needed to see him this time, not to ask why he left her, she knew that now, but to find out how this fucking price had been put on her head.

On my way . . . I'm so sorry. I love you so much.

His reply hit her right in the solar plexus and Jenna, who had stood up to check her make-up in the mirror, had to grab the edge of the marble basin and brace herself. Of course . . . his note. *I love you so much, but I can't stay with you . . .* He had never wanted to leave her. He was forced to by whoever this gangster was, and by TG, who paid the ransom . . . but at a price. Taking a deep breath, Jenna picked up her phone again and opened the bathroom door. As nonchalantly as possible she crossed her bedroom and opened the door, hoping that no one was patrolling the corridors between here and the main deck.

*

'Hey, Jenna,' TG called over to her as she emerged up the spiral staircase. She knew she'd risk seeing partygoers on her way out, but it was bad luck that the one she did bump into was TG. She wasn't sure she could bear to look at him right now.

'What?' she snapped back at him, realising she couldn't ignore him altogether.

'Hey, okay, what's up with you? Where are you off to?'

'It's a free country, isn't it? I'm not trapped here, am I?' *Keep calm*, she tried to tell herself, *keep calm*.

'Yeah, I was just asking. Bertie wants to make a speech.'

'Shit.'

'Look, Jenna, what's wrong?'

Jenna took a deep breath. Should she spill it all out to him now? Call him out on his shitty scheme to not only buy her, but to buy the stolen prints too. No . . . actually, the less she apparently knew about those the better – she didn't want him to pay someone else to kill her off for revealing what she knew there.

'Jenna,' his voice had become darker, losing its usual softness. 'I think you should come back to the party.'

She looked through the saloon to the party on the main deck. Beyond was the quayside and hopefully Angus. When she turned to face him again she barely recognised the expression. Not anger so much as frustration. She wasn't doing as she was told and it was infuriating him. He held out a hand to her and she took it, wondering if it was the last time she would ever touch him.

TG led Jenna to where the majority of guests were watching Bertie standing on the fairy-light clad mini bridge. His hand held hers so firmly it was uncomfortable. Jenna felt less like a human and more like a chattel and for the first time since coming aboard *Clickbait* she realised that she was just another object in TG's life, just another purchase. Bertie was just finishing off saying some words that had had the thinner women of the crowd sniggering — no doubt she'd made some joke about water displacement in the harbour or something — and then turned to TG and Jenna with a beatific smile, which was hard, bearing in mind the amount of Botox she'd recently had injected pre-wedding, and thanked them.

'TG,' she mewed, 'you are such a sweetheart, thank you for letting us celebrate our love on your gorgeous yacht. Love is fragile, we all know this, so to be able to support and bolster our love with champagne and caviar here on *Clickbait*, well — you've got us hooked, sugar.'

Bertie winked at TG and Jenna saw what she thought was Max cringing, disguising his discomfort in a fake smile. *Love is fragile* . . . what did that mean? Jenna desperately tried to free her hand but TG held it clamped in his while he accepted the thanks from various guests who were there for the free fizz and kudos. She looked up at the man that only this morning she had thought she could so easily fall for — her saviour from heartbreak, her chivalrous knight. Did he suspect now that she knew, or was this show of power and dominance just him revealing his true colours?

Finally, it was Bertie who came to her aid to separate them as even TG couldn't refuse her insistence that she needed just a few moments with her 'chiefie' for wedding-planning purposes. Jenna felt his eyes follow her and she was relieved when Bertie led her to a rather secluded part of the deck, away from TG's gaze.

'Oh, Bertie.' Jenna flung her arms around her and didn't even care that Bertie stayed as rigid as a mannequin. 'What you said earlier about selling your soul. You're right. I've been such a fool!'

'Um, whatevs, babes.' Bertie peeled her friend off her and held her at arm's length. 'God, what is wrong with you? Nice dress, by the way. Gucci?'

'Blumarine, actually.' Jenna didn't get the same sense of satisfaction that she had when she'd shown off about the Lanvin dress. 'Anyway, it's TG. Bertie, I'm sorry, but can we talk?'

'Gossip about Monaco's hottest billionaire . . . fill me in, sweet cheeks.'

'It's not gossip Bertie, it's . . . gangsters!'

Jenna told her about finding the contract between Angus and TG and how she had asked Angus to come to the boat now. 'I can't say anything to TG, though, because you'll never guess what else was in his study?'

'Pray tell?'

'The stolen Picassos from Roach & Hartley. That I lost my job over! I don't know, Bertie, maybe they were stolen to order? Maybe TG wanted them so much . . .'

'Hang on, dolls, why wouldn't he just buy them if he wanted them so much?'

'Hmm, good point.' Jenna paused to think. 'Oh, I don't know, Bertie — maybe he bought them from the person who stole them. No questions asked. The thing is . . .'

'The thing is, *sweetie*,' Bertie clenched Jenna's arms with her spindly but strong fingers, 'you do not need to think about this. You are here in this amazing place, with that hot billionaire, living the dream. Just enjoy it, sweetie, and stop bloody complaining. If you piss him off or walk out, you'll be replaced like *that*.' She clicked her thumb and middle finger together, with the force of the click jingling her gold bangles that hung loosely around her thin wrist.

'But, Bertie, I don't want to be here if I was bought. If I was traded like some pig at the market place.'

'Unflattering simile, but sort of apt.'

'Oh, fuck off, Bertie.'

'I would but I like this yacht too much.' Bertie paused and Jenna saw her expression change just slightly — whether that was due to her shallow emotions or her

Botox, Jenna couldn't be sure. 'Look, sugar, I'm just mega jealous of this little racket you seem to have going on here. Do you know how many girls out there would kill to be in your position — by which I mean, under TG most nights — me included.'

'Bertie! You love Max! We spoke about this . . . you know how fake this world is. How this cage is gilded but, buttered parsnips aside, it's still a cage. These trappings of luxury which are nothing but a . . . a trap!'

'God, steady on — you're getting a bit archbishoppy about this, aren't you? Preaching to the very much unconverted here, I'm afraid.'

'Look, I think you should go and find Max. I've got to go, Angus should be here soon.'

Jenna scurried away from Bertie, hoping to miss bumping into TG a second time too and headed back to the beach club and the quayside.

54

Angus strode along the harbour. His hands clenched and unclenched as he made his way to where *Clickbait* was moored. Financial penalties be damned, if Jenna knew about the contract, surely it was now null and void. He heard the party going on long before he got to the boat, and the sight of Jenna lurking by the walkway inspired him to speed up, his loping strides closing up the space between them as he charged along the quayside.

'Missus, the mister is looking for you.' Tweedle-Dee placed a firm hand on Jenna's shoulder as she stood, her arms wrapped around her, peering down the harbour, trying to catch sight of Angus. She was about to shrug off the hand, but its firmness suggested that that wouldn't be possible — plus she remembered the concealed firearm that he'd carried when they were out in Portofino. Probably best not to mess with this one. *God though*, what had she got herself into when it had come to this?

'He doesn't own me.' She blurted out, as much to herself as to the bodyguard-cum-steward.

'He just wants you back at the party, missus.' The soft South African tone belied the strength she could feel as he guided her back up the steps of the beach club to the main deck, his hand now firmly pressed against her back. 'For your own safety.'

'Sebastien!' The Australian accent of Captain Avery cut through the air and Jenna felt the pressure on her back lessen. 'You're needed on the sun deck.'

As the Tweedle left her side, Jenna exhaled and looked

up to where Captain Avery was standing on the wide steps of the beach club. She mouthed a 'thank you' to him and he nodded, before disappearing into the yacht.

Jenna quickly had to morph back into hostess mode and managed to smile as some of the guests passed her on the steps, saying their thank yous and air-kissing her. As the girlfriend to one of the wealthiest men in Monaco, she could expect this sort of fawning over her from people she didn't know. The two bitchy models gave her the briefest of 'mwah mwah's as they flounced down the steps, one barely looking up from her phone as she summoned the black people carrier stationed down the harbour to come and pick them up, ready to head off to the next glamorous party.

Angus lost Jenna in his sights. He was still a couple of hundred metres away — but he was sure he'd seen her — her honey-blonde hair, her familiar stance — he knew it had been her. But now, as he slowed to a trot, he was finding it hard to pinpoint her in the crowd of partygoers and cars that were crowding around the walkway onto the boat. He craned his neck and caught a glance of her again, being frogmarched it looked like up the steps at the back of the boat. He stopped and wondered if he'd get on board without her to invite him on, but then started trotting again as he realised that the commotion out on the harbour — SUVs and mini-vans blocking each other in as the wealthy and beautiful guests were crowded around the yacht and ushered into their awaiting vehicles — could provide him with adequate cover to sneak aboard.

TG was saying goodbye to the last of the guests and only Bertie and Max were left, also air-kissing and shaking hands with their friends and acquaintances. Jenna looked across to her friends — wondering if they could see the plea in her eyes, hoping they could psychically work out that she was desperate for them to create a reason for her to leave the boat. But they seemed lacking in sixth sense — although Bertie did seem to be slightly less flirty with TG than before. She reached over and grabbed Jenna by the arm, pulling her over to stand by the sofas and whispered into her ear while TG and Max were talking to each other.

'I've been thinking about what you said.'

'Really?' Jenna smiled up at Bertie, who even without vertiginous heels was still a good few inches taller than her.

'I need to talk to Max, you're right. We've been beastly to each other this summer. I don't think there's an opportunity either of us have missed to piss the other one off.'

'Oh Bertie, but the wedding . . .'

'Oh it's still on. I think.' Bertie, for the first time since Jenna had known her, looked contrite, and just a little bit sad. 'We've just had a chat.'

'Berts, did he tell you about—'

'Shagging Izzy? Yes. And then the rest of it. The insider trading, or almost. I realise I've pushed him too far.' Bertie dragged Jenna down to sit next to her as she carried on. 'I have been a brute demanding so much from him, but it was only seeing you so desperately unhappy here, of all places, that made me realise . . .'

'It's not all it's cracked up to be. Go on?'

'Well, I realise it's better to be merely millionaires, but happy, than billionaires, but bloody unhappy.'

'You see! Yes. It's what I was saying earlier. But, Berts, what can I do? TG *bought* me!'

Bertie looked taken aback. 'Oh my God, woman! Grow a spine! If I can admit that I love Max more than money, then you can bloody stand up to the old white slaver over there.'

At that moment Jenna sensed a movement behind where TG and Max were standing. The men turned and TG suddenly called out to his security team.

'Seb!' The Tweedle appeared from the other side of the deck.

'No!' Jenna leapt off the sofa but couldn't get to Angus before Seb had him in a painful-looking hold. Bertie laid a cautionary hand on Jenna's shoulder. Annoyed as she was, she knew words were her best weapons in this fight. 'TG,' she took a deep breath and let it out. 'I found the contract.'

'What contract?' Max chipped in.

'The one TG made Angus sign to dump me, so that he could . . . I don't know, "have" me.'

'I did it to save your life, Jenna.' TG's eyes, those chocolate brown mesmerisers, widened as he spread out his arms to emphasise his point.

'I know. And I'm obviously more grateful than you could know. But I can't be bought, TG. I'm not a—'

'Pig at the market place?' Bertie interrupted, but quickly shut up as everyone glared at her.

'Look, I thought it made sense. And don't say you didn't start to fall for me.' TG stared hard at Jenna, defying her to say anything to the contrary.

'Of course. But there's a huge difference between real and proper love,' Jenna locked eyes with Angus, 'the kind of love that doesn't need super-fancy super yachts or sunshine every day, the sort of love that copes with the jellyfish life throws at it.' Tears sprang to her eyes and she wiped them away while defiantly looking back at TG. 'You can't buy love.'

There was a silence for a few moments before Angus broke away from the restraining arm of Seb and burst past TG to wrap Jenna up in his arms. Jenna had no idea, as she lost herself into the familiar scent of Angus's chest, that Bertie raised one perfectly manicured finger to the corner of her eye and complained about a moth or something flying into it.

'Fine,' TG said, 'fine. Pay me back the five million and we'll call it quits. Breach of contract is something my lawyers are particularly hot at.'

'But, TG . . .' Jenna, still in Angus's embrace, turned to look at him. 'We don't have that kind of money.'

'Pocket change, you called it.' Angus reminded him of the phrase he used only a few weeks before.

TG looked at Jenna, who suddenly felt awkward in Angus's arms. He opened his mouth as if to say something but thought better of it. Then he spoke, all the time looking at Jenna, his eyes boring into hers, 'Couldn't you learn to love me? I can give you everything you want. Everything you need. We could see the world from this yacht, or my plane, or the space ship I'm funding.'

'Cool. Oh sorry.' Max shut up when he received a sharp elbow from Bertie, who was still dabbing at her eyes every now and again and muttering about moths, bugs and bright lights.

'No, TG. I love Angus. You saw how heartbroken I was when he left. How can you pretend to love me, when you were willing to see me so hurt?'

'It was better than seeing you dead.' Angus shocked Jenna by defending TG. 'Look, I was desperate. You know I would never, ever "sell" you just for money, don't you? The gang who beat me up in Singapore, who gave me this,' he pointed to his scar, 'well, they kidnapped me in Hong Kong and said they'd kill you — an honour killing, eye-for-an-eye sort of thing.'

Jenna pulled away from Angus and looked up at him, the concern on her face fleetingly changed to fear and she wondered if she was still in danger.

'I bargained with them to save you. I'm so sorry, Jenna, I failed you so much. I put you in so much danger. I know

I don't deserve your forgiveness but at least I knew you were safe here, with TG, on this floating fortress.'

'Why didn't you tell me? We could have found the money together?'

'And risk you hating me for putting you in that position? Never. And what could you have done? You don't have a bean.'

'Look, this little reunion is all very touching,' TG's voice had become hard again, and Jenna wondered if the whole scene, the chaos of it, was making him uncomfortable. He couldn't control what was going on and control . . . yes, control was what made him tick.

'TG. We can't pay you back the money you paid to save me. But I can promise you something in exchange.'

'Jenna?' Angus's voice wavered.

'No, not *that*.' Jenna shook her head in despair at Angus, a familiar little action that bolstered her into going ahead with her play. 'TG, you know I know about the *you know whats* on the wall of your study.' She winked at him.

'Sorry?'

'What?'

There was general confusion between Bertie, Max and Angus. Jenna continued. 'You made your fortune creating an app that can pull up almost any information you need to know about someone, so don't tell me you didn't realise that I worked in a certain place where the *you know whats* are from — last year. When they were, well, you know . . .'

TG sighed while the others all looked more and more confused. Jenna was bargaining on the fact that TG would do anything not to have his squeaky clean image tarnished by the fact that he was a fence or recipient of stolen goods — high-value stolen goods at that. Naming it out loud would shame him too much and anger him, but standing there now and calling him out on owning those

Picassos in a sort of disguised way — well she hoped it would be the leverage she needed to break the bonds of the contract — no lawyers necessary.

'Jeez. Fine. Go. All of you, just go. I'll send your things later, Jenna. Just go.'

55

The hand that held Jenna's was as firm as TG's of only an hour or so before, but the difference was *she* was gripping it just as hard, too. Bertie and Max had been shown the exit just as surely as Jenna and Angus had — and now Jenna could hear her bickering with Max behind them as all four of them walked along the quayside. Happy bickering though; normal service resumed.

Jenna walked along, still barefoot from the party. Angus let her hand go, only to put his arm around her and pull her in close to him, and she felt his lips touch the top of her head as they walked along. Jenna couldn't put into words, or describe the relief she felt to be off the boat — to be away from the glamour and artificial happiness that everyone pretended was the norm. She giggled to herself — bin bags and cardboard boxes that had held tinned foie gras were dumped in piles awaiting the recycling lorry, a kid on a bike whipped past them and they had to move to avoid a blacked-out SUV that was heading down towards one of the larger boats — the rich occupants no doubt hermetically sealed in from the world around them, just as she had been. She was a second-class citizen again and nothing gave her more happiness, except that she had her favourite other second-class citizen by her side.

'Mwah, darling, mwah.' Bertie air-kissed them goodbye. 'I'm too impossibly tired to chastise you for losing us our place in the yachtirati, sweetie, but at least you had the good grace to save your melt down until after the guests had gone.'

'Yeah, thanks, JJ — I can now notch being thrown off a super yacht onto my bedpost of experiences.' Max winked at her and hugged her goodbye.

'That's twice for me . . .' mused Angus as Bertie air-kissed him.

'Honestly though, dolls,' Bertie turned her attention back to Jenna. 'Hark what I said earlier this summer. *À la domestique* is the only way to go — it's all this gadding about that gets you into this mess. Now, come on, Maxie, we've got a wedding to sort out.'

'Wish me luck.' He raised his eyebrows at his old friends and followed Bertie back onto the Blake-Howards' yacht where they were staying.

'Drink?' Angus said to Jenna as he stopped waving.

'God yes.'

'I still don't know why you couldn't tell me,' Jenna said to Angus as they sat in a bar up in the old part of Monaco, as far away from the yachts in the harbour as possible. A waiter busied himself around them clearing away plates of pizza crusts, the restaurant side of the bar packing up for the night. The barman slowly cleaned thick-rimmed tumblers with an old tea-towel, not especially interested in the pair sitting close together at the bar, she in a floor-length, mango-orange gown, he in his jeans and jumper, their knees touching, hands clasped over their laps, only detangling from each other to take another sip from their wine glasses.

'I thought you'd hate me,' Angus replied, raising his hand to his cheek, feeling the scar. 'It's hard enough living with this reminder of what happened, but when this guy told me I'd killed someone — his nephew — I could barely look at myself in disgust, so how could I expect you to?'

'Do you think you did? Kill him, I mean.' Jenna looked Angus straight in the eye.

'No. I don't know. I don't think so. I don't know.'

'He died later in hospital?'

'Of his injuries, they said.'

'Hmm.'

'What?'

'Just an idea.' She reached down to her clutch bag which was hanging off the back of the high bar chair and fished out her mobile phone. For the first time ever she downloaded the app that had made TG so rich.

'What are you doing?'

'You don't become a billionaire selling an app to various governments for it not to be pretty good at tracking down information about people. There . . .' the app had down-loaded in a matter of seconds. 'What was his name?'

'Um . . . hang on.' Angus looked up to the ceiling, accessing his memory. 'Ah — yes! Ho-Yin.'

'Ho-Yin what?'

'Fuck, I don't know. It's his nephew so it could be anything. I think his name was Chung though. Can you search with other parameters? Like Emerald Dragons, try that? That was the rival gang.'

'Okay, hang on.' Jenna tapped some information into the app and set the search engine going. She reached over for her glass of wine as the spinning wheel worked its magic.

'I can't believe we're using TG's app . . .' Angus filled the silence.

'Another twenty-five cents in his back pocket, I guess.' Jenna snorted. 'To think, with all that money and the one thing he wanted to buy was me!'

Angus smiled at her and leaned over and kissed her. 'Even if I could afford you, I wouldn't buy you, JJ.'

'Oh.' Not sure whether to take this as a compliment or not Jenna frowned, but then realised she would be hugely hypocritical to complain — she had spent the last few hours ranting about how she couldn't be bought.

Angus chipped in quickly. 'Not because I wouldn't want to, but I've already won you in the Loose Change Lottery . . .'

'Oh, you . . .' Jenna biffed him on the arm and smiled back. 'Ah, look, here. It's worked.' She skipped down a few articles translated from Mandarin about various court cases surrounding the Emerald Dragons. 'Damn. There's not much of any use here.'

She kept scrolling. Ho-Yin seemed a pretty popular name, but when she tried searching for 'Singapore' and 'hospital' something of interest caught her eye.

'Look, Gus . . . from a few years ago.' She started to read aloud from the online article. 'Ho-Yin Chung, nephew of the notorious Hong Kong crime boss Kim-Su Chung, was released yesterday from the private Gleneagles Hospital in Singapore. He was admitted along with several other associates of the Red Cockerels crime syndicate, some of whom were more seriously harmed and died on the operating table. He had suffered superficial wounds to his face and chest, believed to be defensive strikes from a weapon improvised by one of the unarmed businessmen the gang ambushed, who was released from the scene without charge. Chung was taken into the custody of the Singapore police department and will stand trial in October.'

Angus looked puzzled. 'That definitely sounds like him. The situation, the timing . . . it all fits.'

'But he seems very much alive. Hang on.' Jenna came out of the document and scrolled down some more. 'Here!' She read out loud again. 'Report from the Changi Prison Complex. Riot in the east wing was quashed by the valiant efforts of our staff. Three injured wardens, seven injured inmates and one fatality. The riot was believed to be started as a cover for an assassination, that of the one fatality. Ho-Yin Chung of the Red Cockerels was found dead in his cell, puncture wound to the throat. He was taken to Knoo Teck Puat Hospital but declared dead on arrival.'

'Shit.'

Angus and Jenna just looked at each other in disbelief. 'You didn't kill him, Gus. It wasn't your fault.' Jenna could see the relief on Angus's face, his whole body lifted and the twinkle behind his eyes, that she hadn't seen for a month or so, flamed back into place.

'The fricking bastard. I bet it was done on Chung's orders too. But to cover up the fact that he ordered a hit on his own nephew, he had to frame me.'

'But the crime families would have known he was in jail, not dead.'

'Yes, but they wouldn't know how he was killed. I mean, I *or you* would be dead to compensate for me killing him, but although Chung made *me* believe that it had been a result of the fight, he could have spun the story to his family that I had been operating as an Emerald Dragon and organised the hit on his nephew. Timing isn't the issue — deflecting from *him* is.' Angus was getting more animated now and Jenna could see the life flowing back into him; he was becoming the Angus she remembered and loved so much. What had been missing over the last few weeks — even before he left her that note and disappeared — was back.

'I'm not sure I should be the first to mention this . . .' Jenna smiled at him. 'But do you realise you were basically done over by a big red cock?'

Their laughter filled the night as relief swept over them both, the realisation that no gangster now lurked in the shadows, no controlling billionaire was ordering them around. They were free.

*

'You know, I went to the casino to try and win the money to pay Chung,' Angus confided in Jenna as they walked down the hill from the old town in the early hours of the morning. Jenna was wearing Angus's jumper over her dress, and walked while trying to keep the thigh slit more or less together. The sun was still a while away from rising and Monaco, for once, was quiet and still. The daylight hours and their noise would come upon them soon enough but for now, as two lovers walking the moonlit streets they could whisper their hearts to each other and make up for all the duplicity of the last couple of months.

'You idiot, Gus, you know the house always wins.'

'Well, they did and they didn't. I won enough to—'

'Please don't say buy a yacht . . .'

'Ha. No. But enough to treat to you to, oh I don't know, maybe a cheeky Nandos when we get home.'

'I can think of nothing better.' She squeezed his hand and they walked on, the steep downward slope of the road helping their tired legs go on. The lights of Monte Carlo and the harbour were almost bleached out by the brightness of the moonlight that night, its reflection highlighting the water, making it shine like mercury glass smashed into a thousand pieces. The yachts lined up like cows in a milking parlour, rows of them along the harbour wall, each one representing wealth and privilege that Jenna had been part of oh-so briefly. And indeed they were milked, in a way; by the city around them, the industry that knew thousands of euros could be squeezed out of them for cars, parties, food, wine, experiences, drugs, women . . . She searched along the nearside of the harbour where the largest boats lay like beached whales, their white flanks glowing in the full moon. There was a gap along the quayside. *Clickbait* had gone.

56

Emma and Monty had been kind enough to invite Jenna
and Angus to stay on board the *Wavy Sloanes* 'for as long
as you need to, darlings. We're off to India after Bertie's
wedding, so do stay on if you fancy it.'

Right now, though, the pair crept back on board, realising that noisily boarding a yacht in the early hours
may push the realms of charitable hostessing. The text
message inviting them on had told them which cabin to
head to, and as Jenna knew her way around they were
able to slip into their guest cabin relatively sneakily. The
only loud noise they made was when Jenna yelped in
exclamation at the sight of all her luggage – her handbag,
the second-hand Hermès Birkin from Bertie, her suitcase
plus the shopping bags from Portofino. There was even
a dry-cleaning bag containing the good-as-new silk dress
from Lanvin, plus the beautiful silver shoes she'd bought
to go with them.

'Wow, that was quick.' Angus sounded impressed more
than anything else.

'Amazingly so. And . . .' Jenna knelt down and opened
up the suitcase and saw that all her clothes were perfectly
folded; her knickers too and amongst them a manila
envelope and the two black leather jewel boxes that had
contained her gifts from TG. '. . . Oh gosh.' She opened
up the larger of the two boxes. The sapphire pendant
sparkled back at her. She showed it to Angus.

'Blimey . . .'

'Well,' she said, matter of factly. 'It's a start.'

'To what?' Angus asked her.

'Helping pay you back for the mortgage!' Jenna smiled at her boyfriend then remembered the large envelope she'd seen in her suitcase too. She reached over for it and sat down on the bed to open it. Inside there was a scrawled note and a couple of documents. Jenna was silent as she took it all in.

'What is it?' Angus asked.

'I think it's the answer to what's been bugging me since last year . . . here.' She gave the documents to Angus and read the note out loud to him. 'Jenna — saw this envelope had your name on it. Avery.'

'These are sales documents.' Angus stated.

'From Roach & Hartley to TG Wilkinson. I know, I just saw. I'm not sure I totally understand though.'

'It means that those Picasso prints were never *stolen*, not by a real thief at any rate. An inside job by Clive and Martin to claim insurance *and* get the sale value.'

'Do you think?' Jenna tried to get her head around it.

'I reckon they gambled on the fact that TG would keep them far away from the public view. Maybe he'd mentioned wanting them for his yacht. I mean, who would be better than someone with a floating fortress, a study that even his PA barely ever went in?'

Jenna rolled her eyes at Angus. 'But obviously his captain does . . . I bet TG got those prints at a steal too. Clive and Martin know enough people in the art world to send out feelers as to who might like to do a deal. Billionaires love bargains.'

'What are you going to do?'

'It's obvious, isn't it?' Jenna looked triumphant, clearly exceptionally pleased with the thought that had just crossed her mind. 'These,' she took the documents back from Angus, 'are better than any CV. They're my interview, probation period and first-year bonus all rolled into one. I'm going to get my old job back!'

57

Dawn rose over the slumbering harbour and Jenna woke up to the hum of traffic, the clanking of a construction site just up the hill, and the usual shouts and cries of life above and below deck. Moored at the Quai des État-Unis, the *Wavy Sloanes* was in the middle of the harbour's action — closer to the casinos and shops than other yachts — but also deep in the hustle and grind of Monégasque life.

Jenna gently moved her shoulders and began a stretch. She rolled over and wrapped her arm around Angus, who lay gently snoring next to her. She focused her eyes on his face, tanned from a summer out here too, though she wondered if the stress he'd been under had taken its toll. His scar looked whiter against the deeper tan of his cheek and she traced it with her eyes from almost his ear lobe all the way down his jaw. She gave into the urge to touch it, this manifestation of the brutality and lies he'd had to put up with this summer. She'd have done anything to help him, and knowing that he was willing to sacrifice everything to save her filled her heart with so much love for him. Her rock, her anchor.

'Morning, Jenksy.' He stretched as well and sleepily nuzzled her neck, rolling over to cuddle her.

'Morning, you.' Jenna held him tight, loving hearing the familiar name he used for her. It wasn't like the last couple of months hadn't happened, of course it wasn't, but something about the summer had strengthened them. *I guess surviving a death threat or two will do that to a couple*, she thought to herself as Angus's hands realised they were awake too and seemed to be independently getting to know her body again, as his head lay innocently on her chest.

The cacophony of the outside world grew stronger as delivery vans chugged along the quayside, cranes clanked into action on nearby building sites and traffic thrummed along the Avenue J. F. Kennedy. No one then, either on the yacht or outside it, would have heard the squeals of pure delight from Jenna as Angus woke himself up fully and made her morning the most orgasmically happy one she'd had in a while.

'I missed you so much, Gus,' she whispered in his ear as they lay panting, their bodies exhausted but exhilarated; refreshed by sleep and sexercise, but knackered too from the late night and emotional toil of the last few weeks.

'I missed you so much, too.'

'Where did you go, when you left me?'

'Didn't TG say?'

'No . . .'

Angus propped himself up on his elbow and met Jenna's enquiring gaze. 'He sent me up to Eze to work on his villa.'

'Bloody cheek!' Jenna, who was still lying flat in the bed, tucked the duvet up round her armpits and crossed her arms over it. 'He never said at all. He made it sound like you'd buggered off and that you'd never be welcome back on his boat, so I sort of assumed that meant his whole property.'

'I wish I could have told you everything.' Angus rolled back onto his back and looked up to the ceiling.

'I know you couldn't. I don't blame you, Gus, not for wanting to protect me.'

Angus rolled up onto his elbow again. 'I did get my own back a little bit.'

'How?'

'His villa.'

314

'What did you do?' Jenna's curiosity was definitely piqued.

'Let's just say there might be some head scratching from the builders when they try to follow the plans.'

'Did you write them in double Dutch?'

'No, I just "forgot" to put a staircase in.'

'What?'

'I know, it's juvenile. But there are two teams working on the build, and each one will think the other is responsible for the side of the house that should have this massive staircase in.'

Jenna burst out laughing. 'Oh well, he's a billionaire, he can just use all those spare rungs on society's ladder to get upstairs.'

'Ha, very good.' Angus nudged Jenna and soon they were wrapped up in each other's arms again, with kisses turning more passionate as they explored each other's bodies afresh, and not without certain rewards.

58

'Jenna!' The screech could be heard across the beautiful square outside the cathedral, or the Cathédrale Notre-Dame-Immaculée to give it its full name, which Jenna had had to on countless invitations that had been sent out in a hurry. Far from planning the wedding to end all weddings, in the end, after a night of heart-to-hearts, Bertie and Max had decided to have a lower-key bash. The Metropole was cancelled — much to Bertie's displeasure — but when Max had seen the quote for the full gala-style ball for six hundred guests he'd turned a particularly ill sort of colour and put his foot down. Losing the deposit was unfortunate, but Bertie promised Max she'd make it up to him. The wedding had officially been cancelled, and only about 10 per cent of the original guest list had received hurriedly handwritten notes informing them of the time and place of the nuptials.

'I'm here, I'm here!' Jenna grabbed her floaty skirt — the dress from Emma Blake-Howard's BoBo collection had been sent back to her along with her other belongings from *Clickbait*.

She mounted the steps outside the cathedral and took her place beside Emma, the two of them dressed almost identically in the designer's beautiful gowns. Bertie stood in front of them, in her dress, which had been flown over in a private jet from the couturier on Bond Street. And Jenna had to begrudgingly admit that it was pretty amazing. The brief of Grace Kelly v Kate Middleton with a dash of Meghan Markle had been fulfilled rather well — the dress was tailored into an A-line skirt that emphasised Bertie's tiny waist, which was cinched further by a diamond and pearl-studded belt. The bodice had a boat neckline and was made of such delicate lace, layered over the satin of the gown, that Jenna was scared to get too close in case one of her more imperfectly manicured nails snagged it. The whole dress, though, cathedral-length train included, was so stunning that for a fleeting second Jenna actually felt a bit bad for Bertie that she had been denied her massive wedding in front of hundreds of people. Some of the original guests hadn't received the message about the 'cancellation' and had turned up anyway, which in a way was a good thing as the cathedral would look bloody empty with only sixty or so guests inside.

The organ sounded the opening notes of the processional voluntary and Jenna and Emma floofed out the long veil one last time before walking up the last few steps of the cathedral, following the bride into the dark interior of the large nave. Their eyes had to adjust somewhat from the bright sunshine outside but once they had blinked and smiled and nodded and processed their way towards the altar they were acclimatised and Jenna could take in the magnificence of the building. Yes, the stone work was mostly grey, but Bertie had insisted on grey morning coats for the gentleman guests so that they all complemented the church; and in-between the columns, filling each internal archway of the nave, a wall of white and soft pink flowers seemed to fall from the top of each arch, hiding from view the side aisles and their rather dour religious paintings and tombs. For the guests sitting in the nave, their experience must have been like that of sitting in the middle of Covent Garden flower market, so close were they to the thousands of white and pink blooms. Jenna remembered Max muttering something about 'the money saved on the Metropole had gone to the florists' but still, Jenna thought that it was all worth it. Her own bouquet was something in its own right, long and teardrop-shaped with countless small buds and blooms among gossamer light greenery, perfectly designed to match the etherealness of her dress.

Max stood waiting for his bride and Jenna was gladdened, even with all their history, to see him look genuinely awestruck when he saw Bertie walk towards him. The eagerness on his face was like that of a small boy allowed to climb into a fire engine for the first time. Standing beside him was Angus — and beside him Hugo — both serving as best men to the groom. Jenna smiled at Angus, who grinned back at her.

The service itself was beautiful — simple and relatively quick as weddings are if they're not stretched out by hymns and readings. Due to the location, the couple had decided against any of the more traditional hymns — perhaps singing about England's green and pleasant land wasn't so apt out here in the heat of the Med. Vowing to your country . . . ditto. But Jenna had helped Bertie choose a couple of the more romantically minded classics and the opening chords of 'Love Divine' from the organ were soon joined by the chorus of voices from the congregation. The volume was enough to disguise the slight buzzing sound made by the state-of-the-art drone that hovered high up in the clerestory — again, Bertie's compromise if she wasn't allowed a whole camera crew following her from vestibule to vows.

White Rolls-Royces lined up outside the steps of the cathedral ready to carry the bridal party up into the hills for more photographs before heading down to the harbour, where the Blake-Howards had generously donated their boat for the wedding breakfast and reception. After the cars had left, a catering-style truck pulled up and started dismantling the flowers, ready to whisk them down to the harbour to decorate the yacht before the bridal party turned up.

'Bloody hell, it's a good thing I don't have hay fever along with distended hips, gestational diabetes and high blood pressure.' Sally declared as they finally crossed the walkway onto the *Wavy Sloanes*.

'You don't half make pregnancy sound alluring, Sals . . .' joked Jenna, as she navigated them both to some seats up on the main deck so her slightly panting friend could sit down.

'It's bloody not. And I've still got three months to go.' She gratefully found a seat and lowered herself down.

'I hope you don't mind me saying this, Sals, but you look massive for only six months pregnant.'

'Ah, well, you might as well know . . . actually, it's twins.'

'What?' Jenna sat down next to her best friend and held her hands in hers. 'Why didn't you say so?'

'It's silly, I know, but I didn't want to rub your nose in it. We only found out at the second scan, can you believe, and by then you were all weepy over Gus so I didn't want to shove the news down your throat.'

'Sals!' Jenna was shocked at her friend's level of sensitivity. 'But that's amazing, honey. I mean, wow. Twins.'

'Double trouble.' The two friends giggled but stayed clenching hands until Hugo bundled up to them and Jenna leapt to hug him.

'What ho, Jenks!'

'Oh, Hugs, congratulations!'

'Ah, she's broken the news then?'

'Yes! It's so exciting!'

'Girls too!' Hugo beamed at her.

'What? Oh, guys!' Jenna was brimming with genuine excitement for her friends. Now Sally and Hugo were here with her, she only felt happiness for them, not envy or jealousy – especially not over the nappy-changing – and she wanted to squeeze them both tight and tell them how lucky they were, but how lucky she felt too, to have such amazing friends and finally, after a summer of ups and some serious downs, her perfect boyfriend back, too.

That 'perfect boyfriend' joined in the group standing around the seated Sally and soon he was clinking his glass with Hugo too.

'Girls, eh?'

'I'm still planning on taking them to Twickenham throughout the season,' Hugo said, matter of factly.

'And ballet at the weekends please, too!' Sally called up from her seat.

'Any thoughts on names?' Angus chipped in.

'Horatio had to go out the window, but Horatia is strong, don't you think?' Hugo was silenced after that as Sally pulled him down next to her and muttered something about him being an idiot.

'Let's leave them to it,' Angus whispered to Jenna and they mouthed quick goodbyes to their friends and walked through the wedding guests, past where Bertie was holding court (Jenna rolled her eyes as she recognised the bitchy pair from the *Clickbait* party), past Ems and Monty chatting about India to someone who looked like another potential investor, and to the prow of the boat, where it was calmer.

Jenna stood looking out across the marina at all the yachts.

'Nice to see a few old proper sailing yachts among all these tubs,' Angus stated as he stood next to her and handed her a glass of champagne he'd picked up from a passing waiter.

'This whole world is a trade off between heart and soul — like those sailing yachts, still with the passionate sailors on board.'

'Albeit very rich ones.'

'Well, yes, and the super yachts — no heart or soul any more, just luxury and control.'

'Soul or control — a tough choice indeed.' Angus leaned over the handrail.

'Not for me.' Jenna looked at him. 'These guys,' she indicated the harbour and its denizens. 'They think their wealth alone allows them to do what they want, if they can buy it, they can have it.'

'Including you.'

'Ha. Yeah.' She paused. 'But not any more.'

Angus turned to face her and then slowly took the glass of champagne out of her hand. He placed it, along with his, on one of the little coffee tables a few metres away on the deck. He came back to join her by the handrail and placed both his hands on her upper arms.

'Jenna, I love that you can see through all this luxury to what really matters. And although it broke my heart to leave you this summer, I'm grateful beyond belief that not a hair on your beautiful head was hurt — physically, at least.' He took a deep breath. 'I can't imagine ever being without you again and I don't know how else to let you know how I feel about you, how I want you by my side forever: no more secrets, no more schemes.'

Jenna started to tremble slightly as Angus got down on one knee.

'Jenna Jenkins, I love you and I would be so honoured if you would agree to be my wife.'

A tear rolled down Jenna's cheek, but unlike the tears of hurt and confusion from this summer, it was a tear of pure joy. She wiped it aside and half pulled Angus up, half collapsed into him as she blubbed out her 'yeses' again and again.

Epilogue

'Hurry up, Jenna, the taxi's waiting!'

'Coming!'

Gus stood holding the door of the black cab open as Jenna hastily locked the front door of their little house. Around her on the pavement were pink gift bags, spilling out tissue paper, each one containing a little present for the babies and new parents. Angus left his position by the taxi door and helped his fiancée into the cab with all the bags.

'Sorry. Right, let's go. Lindo Wing, St Mary's please!' Jenna didn't need to say any more to the knowledgeable London cabbie. She sat back in the seat and clasped Angus's hand in hers as the cab manoeuvred its way through the streets of London. Of course, Sally and Hugo had chosen London's most famous maternity hospital to have the twins in, but Jenna couldn't blame poor Sals. Ever since she'd got back from Monaco after Bertie's wedding she'd been having such a bad time of it — she'd even spent the last few weeks on strict bed rest. Jenna had been on entertainment duty, but it hadn't been hard, she still had so many stories she'd picked up from her time on the Riviera that she could spin them out and elaborate on them, so that in the end both girls could be in giggle fits at the mere mention of a blue-eyed captain or over-the-top yacht owner.

Emma and Monty had been true to their word and after Angus's proposal at Bertie's wedding, they'd let them stay on board the *Wavy Sloanes* for a week while they jetted off to India to recce fairtrade fabric factories. Jenna and Angus had wandered the streets, especially up in the old town, in a romantic haze, and on one of their walkabouts they'd found an antique jewellery shop. It was a far cry from the ultra-high-end shops in the newer part of town, although it was full of beautiful old classic pieces of jewellery. Jenna had possibly the most fun hour of her life, and had finally walked out with a sparkling three-stone diamond ring on her left hand. 'It feels real now,' she'd whispered to Angus as she walked back to the harbour, her hand stuck out in front of her so she could see the stones glint and glisten in the sun. 'I don't think my left hand has ever been worth so much!'

They'd flown back to London, having treated themselves to the helicopter transfer from the harbour to Nice airport. After a summer spent on super yachts Jenna thought the bus would have been a bit of an anti-climax for them both. But London was dear old London when they got back and things returned to normal, bar the onset of wedding planning, which Jenna relished sharing with her mum and best friends. Sally, especially, had started about ten Pinterest boards on Jenna's behalf, claiming she could do little else with herself while she was waiting for her babies to be born.

And so here they were, a little early as twins tend to be, and Jenna and Angus were invited to the private wing of the hospital to meet the two little bundles before they went home to Putney.

'JJ!'

'Oh, Sals, congratulations, my love!'

Jenna swooped down on her friend, who was still bed bound, though looking very elegant in a little pink bed jacket.

'You look amazing — how do you do it?' Jenna stood back and looked at Sals, as Angus pumped Hugo's hand

and slapped him on the back.

'They have a hairdresser here and everything . . .' Sally whispered conspiratorially. 'But here, let me introduce you . . .'

At that moment a nurse walked in with a tiny baby in each arm. Hugo met her at the door and took one of the little pink bundles from her arms, letting the nurse then carry the other one over to Sally.

'Oh, let me see.' Jenna peered over the little girl in Sally's arms. 'She's definitely got your nose.'

'And this one seems to have inherited my arse.' Hugo wrinkled his nose as he smelt his daughter's bottom.

'Don't be silly, Hugs,' Sally gently reprimanded him. 'They can't produce anything smelly yet. You just wait though.' She winked at Jenna as Hugo pulled a face. His pride in his two little girls was palpable though, and Jenna looked lovingly at Angus as he too seemed captivated by the little scrunched-up faces in the pink baby blankets.

'So,' Jenna tried to look more serious, 'did Horatia make the cut?'

'No.' Sally had her usual school-marmy voice back. 'Hugo agreed that after seeing what I went through to produce these two little pickles I could choose the names.'

'So?'

'So over there is Emily Frances, and this, this is Charlotte Jenna.'

'Oh, Sals!' Tears welled up in Jenna's eyes as she looked at her little namesake.

'Thought we better name her after her godmother . . .'

A look passed between the two old friends, and in that moment Jenna thought that mortgage payments could take a backseat and she knew exactly what the little girl's christening gift would be.

'I hope she likes sapphires . . .'

Acknowledgements

My thanks as always to my agent Emily Sweet for her constant support and encouragement and Clare Hey and the team at Orion for getting this book out there for you all to hopefully enjoy!

Thanks also to my friend Tet Staveley, who chatted through plot ideas with me on a beach in beautiful Norfolk — TG is your creation as much as mine! And our co-conspirator Kat Watters, who snuck onto yachts to send me pictures of blue-eyed captains — thank you, too, for all your help.

Special thanks to those who shall stay anonymous for obvious reasons — your insights into the world of the super yachts and the super rich were invaluable and I appreciate them so much. You'll recognise your stories on these pages — fact oftentimes being much more hilarious and shocking than fiction!

Without my family's support I would be useless, so thank you to you all and especially to my husband Rupert who is my rock. The cat is less helpful, but an absolute legend too, so thank you Toby for keeping my feet warm while I type.

Lastly, thank you to you, dear reader, for getting this far and if you feel like the book made you laugh, think, shed a little tear, or chuckle then please leave me a review on the platform from which you bought it.

Head for the slopes for a glamorous week of fondue and festive fun . . .

Join Jenna and her university chums as they jet off to the French Alps for a week of festive fun. On the agenda: flirting, drinking, dancing — and a bit of skiing along the way.
But once they arrive, they are soon waylaid by secret passions, chairlift shenanigans, sexy ski-instructors and the sort of social climbing that requires more effort and planning than a solo ascent of Mont Blanc!
Will it all snowball into disaster or will there be someone waiting under the mistletoe this Christmas?

Clip on your skis, dig out your salopettes, and get ready for some fun on the slopes...

Escape to the south of France for sizzling sun and fizzing flirtation . . .

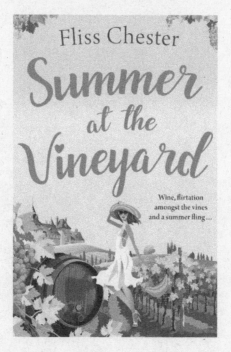

Fliss Chester

Summer at the Vineyard

Wine, flirtation amongst the vines and a summer fling . . .

Jenna Jenkins needs to get away. She's been unceremoniously sacked from her job and it's make or break time with her boyfriend Angus, so a summer job at the beautiful Château Montmorency in the south of France seems like the perfect solution.

Planning the party of the century, dining out with suave Frenchmen, and giving in to a little temptation among the vines are all in a day's work . . . but is there a secret lurking in the chateau cellars?

Caught in a trap she can't talk — or drink — herself out of, Jenna is well and truly corkscrewed. Things are really hotting up under the sun when a mysterious benefactor helps her out of her jam. But why does he seem so familiar...?